continued . . .

WITCH FIRE

"Deliciously sexy and intriguingly original."
—Angela Knight, *New York Times* bestselling author

"A sensual feast sure to sate even the most finicky of palates. Richly drawn, dynamic characters dictate the direction of this fascinating story. You can't miss with Anya."　　　　　—*A Romance Review*

"Fast-paced, edgy suspense . . . The paranormal elements are fresh and original. This reader was immediately drawn into the story from the opening abduction, and obsessively read straight through to the dramatic final altercation. Bravo, Ms. Bast; *Witch Fire* is sure to be a fan favorite."　　　　　—*Paranormal Romance Writers*

"A fabulously written ultimate romance. Anya Bast tells a really passionate story and leaves you wanting more. . . . The elemental witch series will be a fantastic read."　　　—*The Romance Readers Connection*

"A terrific romantic fantasy starring two volatile lead characters . . . The relationship between fire and air makes the tale a blast to read."
—*The Best Reviews*

MORE PRAISE FOR ANYA BAST AND HER NOVELS

"Had me sitting on the edge of my seat from page one."
—*The Road to Romance*

"The characters were so alive that they leapt off the pages."
—*Fallen Angel Reviews*

"A lovely erotic tale . . . This unique and passionate story is filled with humor, fire, and heartwarming emotion."　　　—*Romance Reviews Today*

"Anya Bast pulled another winner out of her pocket."
—*Night Owl Romance Reviews*

"An entertaining erotic romantic suspense tale."
—*Midwest Book Review*

Jeweled

ANYA BAST

HEAT
NEW YORK

THE BERKLEY PUBLISHING GROUP
Published by the Penguin Group
Penguin Group (USA) Inc.
375 Hudson Street, New York, New York 10014, USA
Penguin Group (Canada), 90 Eglinton Avenue East, Suite 700, Toronto, Ontario M4P 2Y3, Canada
(a division of Pearson Penguin Canada Inc.)
Penguin Books Ltd., 80 Strand, London WC2R 0RL, England
Penguin Group Ireland, 25 St. Stephen's Green, Dublin 2, Ireland (a division of Penguin Books Ltd.)
Penguin Group (Australia), 250 Camberwell Road, Camberwell, Victoria 3124, Australia
(a division of Pearson Australia Group Pty. Ltd.)
Penguin Books India Pvt. Ltd., 11 Community Centre, Panchsheel Park, New Delhi—110 017, India
Penguin Group (NZ), 67 Apollo Drive, Rosedale, North Shore 0632, New Zealand
(a division of Pearson New Zealand Ltd.)
Penguin Books (South Africa) (Pty.) Ltd., 24 Sturdee Avenue, Rosebank, Johannesburg 2196,
South Africa

Penguin Books Ltd., Registered Offices: 80 Strand, London WC2R 0RL, England

This book is an original publication of The Berkley Publishing Group.

This is a work of fiction. Names, characters, places, and incidents either are the product of the author's imagination or are used fictitiously, and any resemblance to actual persons, living or dead, business establishments, events, or locales is entirely coincidental. The publisher does not have any control over and does not assume any responsibility for author or third-party websites or their content.

PRINTING HISTORY
Heat trade paperback edition / November 2010

Library of Congress Cataloging-in-Publication Data

Bast, Anya.
    Jeweled / Anya Bast.
    p.   cm.
    ISBN 978-0-425-23686-4
    I. Title.
    PS3602.A8493J49 2010
    813'.6—dc22   2010017218

PRINTED IN THE UNITED STATES OF AMERICA

10   9   8   7   6   5   4   3   2   1

ACKNOWLEDGMENTS

Thank you to my husband for supporting me through my writing career and enduring me during my most angst-ridden times. When I see the world as a dark place, you give me light. When I think the worst, you give me the best.

Thank you to Brenda for being my sister from another mother. You are much more to me than a BFF.

Thanks to Brent K., Jamie S., Marcia B., Lauren Dane, and Jody Wallace for giving me feedback on this plot idea when it was just a wee seed planted in my brain.

One

Enchantress. *Manipulator. Magick-twister.*

Evangeline was called all these things and more, but she'd never understood why. In truth she was a thief, tapping into a person's emotional currents, stealing them, and redistributing them. She was a master at it—a master thief.

This day, of all days, she held on to the truth that she was a *master* even as her hands trembled with nervousness. In order to make the Court believe it, *she* had to believe it. Normally she felt almost no emotion at all, but she'd spent her life building up to this day. A thin strand of anxiousness had broken through her walls and wreaked havoc.

If *she* was experiencing uncertainty and fear, she couldn't imagine what the other adepts must be feeling. She wasn't going to taste their emotions to find out either; her concentration needed to be on her upcoming performance.

A sphere from the current performance floated toward her and spun. Sunlight streaming in through the stained glass window shot cerulean, scarlet, and emerald through the crystal orb. She glanced at Anatol, the adept of light and illusion who wielded the sphere. His sculpted lips were pursed, midnight blue eyes narrowed in fierce concentration. Small, barely noticeable lines creased the smooth skin between his eyebrows. His hands were clasped neatly and held almost completely within the voluminous sleeves of his white robe, though the tense lines of his body revealed the effort necessary to control the orb.

Anatol Nicolison was a powerhouse of magick.

The Edaeii and their Court murmured in a delighted hush as the orb darted in front of them, down then up, as though sentient. The sound of the spectators rippled around her like a live thing, but she hardly felt it. The magick cast in the room brushed over her skin like velvet, overwhelming all other sensation. Sometimes the magick of the other adepts prickled, rubbed, occasionally even stung, but this power was a pure, clear note of brilliance dancing through Evangeline's body. It was a testament to Anatol's power and the reason she both respected and despised him. His magick seem to come effortlessly and he seemed to pay no price for it, unlike her.

A tinkling rang through the air, drawing her gaze back to the mental confection just in time to see the sphere dissolve into fat crystal teardrops that rained down from the center of the glittering theater to the delight of all gathered. The Edaeii and the Court nobles laughed and clapped.

Evangeline studied Anatol a moment longer as he graciously accepted the delighted response with a slight smile and half bow. That was practically effusiveness for him. He'd never been good at playing a crowd, though the strength and skill of his magick allowed him the luxury of reserve.

With an annoyed jerk of her head, she ripped her gaze away. Surely Anatol would be Jeweled this day. Surely *his* future as J'Edaeii was now assured. There weren't many who could sculpt light and awareness to such amusing levels of deception. Not even the newest mechanical wonders of their age, the rolling steam transport or the helium float, were a match for what he could do.

He was beautiful, too. By far the most gorgeous of all the men at court. Tall, broad through the shoulders, and narrow at the waist. He had the muscled body of one of the guards—lean and strong—but the mind of a scholar. And his magick . . . even she had to admit it was amazing.

Anatol was the full package with such dark blue, soulful eyes, and that silky dark hair that made a woman wonder what it would feel like brushing over her skin. He had a body that made women fantasize, period. Even she had wondered and she didn't often think about sex for pleasure. Sex as a tool, yes. Fucking as a necessary evil, definitely. Not sex for pleasure. That was just a dream for some-one like her.

A man who looked like Anatol could have anyone at Court, male or female—a few of each at a time if he wanted. He could have anything he desired if he was willing to use sex to get it, yet he never did. She couldn't think of one liaison that Anatol had ever been in. He was either very noble or very stupid. Evangeline didn't know which.

Maybe he was just frigid. A pity. It was a waste.

A muscle working in her jaw, she glanced around—anywhere but at Anatol, who now received fervent accolades from Czz'ar Ondriiko himself. Ondriiko sat on his jeweled throne, surrounded by fifteen descending stepped tiers. Upon each sat members of the Edaeii family. Roane, the dark-haired, dark-eyed second in line sat on the tier just below the Czz'ar. Tadui—a charming Edaeii who often sought her company because he wanted to fuck her—sat lower down.

On the gold and silver inlaid floor of the theater gathered

the rest of the Court—those born high enough or who were rich enough to have finagled an invitation to reside at Belai for an allotted amount of time. It was an enviable position that afforded one the ability to gain favor with the Edaeii family, maybe even the Czz'ar, which could get one all manner of niceties—wealth, power, control.

Though Czz'ar Ondriiko, himself, was not the all-powerful, virile man that a foreigner might expect of the ruler of Rylisk. Far from it. Pallid of skin and pale of hair, he cut a fragile-looking figure on his throne. Right now his bright black eyes gleamed in his delicately boned face, revealing his love for all things magickal. Indeed, he was obsessed with it for its own sake, never mind the value of it to his family line. All in all, he gave the impression of gentle ineffectualness. Far too good-natured to rule a vast country like Rylisk competently. But what could you do when power was handed down through families? The family tree was bound to produce a little weak fruit here and there.

Czz'arina Prademia sat to Ondriiko's left. One would think she'd take an active interest in the proceedings, since she had been J'Edaeii before Ondriiko had taken her to wife. Instead she surveyed the theater with a bored look on her horse face. No, Prademia was not beautiful, but the strength of her magick far outweighed her personal appearance in terms of her overall value to the Edaeii. And she was a strong woman—likely the brawn behind Ondriiko. It was nice to know there was some.

Gold and silver laced the walls of the theater in a fetching pattern that incorporated the Edaeii coat of arms—a sword crossed with a magick-wielding rod that the Edaeii were said to have used long ago, before the magick was all but exhausted from their bloodline. The vaulted ceiling with its silver leafed pattern flowed into an entire wall of windows that gave an exceptional view of Belai Square and the city of Milzyr. The guards kept the square fairly clear of commoner riffraff most of the time, allowing for an uncluttered view of the cobblestone area and the tall buildings flanking it.

There had been much unrest in Milzyr recently, a fact of which Evangeline was only vaguely aware. She could not be bothered with the common-blood squabbles occurring in the city. The turbulence had not reached Belai and never would. The Royal Guard would put the rabble-rousers down and keep them there.

Out of the corner of her eye, she saw Anatol—finally—take his seat. They did not make formal announcements so as not to interrupt the enjoyment of the Edaeii. So, she, along with all the other adepts yet to perform, searched for Borco, the director of the ceremony and majordomo of Belai. The short and squat black-haired man hovered self-importantly on the fringes of the crowd. He looked at her meaningfully. Her turn.

She took a moment to compose herself. She'd come to Belai, the national palace, when she'd been four years old. Her entire life she'd trained alongside the other adepts to get to this point, this day.

Failure was not a possibility.

Unlike some of the adepts, her family had never had enough money to finance a trainer. In fact, according to Kisa, the sour-countenanced housemother to the female adepts, her family had opposed the Edaeii's desire to foster and train her for the J'Edaeii. As was the policy with recalcitrant and unwilling families, Evangeline had been forcibly removed from her family home and denied access to them.

According to Kisa, she'd cried a lot the first year she'd been here, though Evangeline didn't remember that. Eventually she'd grown beyond such sentiment. How her family must have hated her to try and deny her this opportunity! She only had one memory of her mother. It was hazy and muted. Maybe it wasn't even real. Still, there was warmth in that memory. When she'd been a child the warmth of that memory had contented her.

Then she'd grown up.

Borco jerked his head impatiently and she realized she'd been so nervous that she'd been rooted in place. What a horrible thing this anxiousness was. She couldn't wait to be rid of it. She drew a breath, gathered her confidence, and walked to the center of the chamber. Halfway across the floor she reached up and pulled the binding from her hair. Her tresses cascaded, thick and glossy—silver blond and curling softly to the small of her back. With a practiced—yet seemingly haphazard—shake of her head that accentuated her hair's glory, she allowed it to fall in becoming waves around her shoulders. Her hair was the primary tool of her seduction—and this was every bit a seduction as a test of magickal ability.

Everything was a seduction, in the end.

Evangeline stood in the center of the chamber and relished the rapt attention of the spectators. She would make them wait for her. With a slow sweep of her gaze, she took them all in. Multicolored brocade swathed figures, jewels shining at throats, wrists, and ears. The highest born in the realm were here to watch her dance. She, the daughter of a swine farmer. She, who'd come all the way from Cherkhasii Province. The name of that place never passed their lips unless it was accompanied by a sneer.

She struck her pose—the classic reverence—heel of her right foot touching the instep of the opposite. Right leg slightly bent, arms loose at her sides, shoulders thrust back proudly, yet her head drooping just a little, as though tragically bowed from the weight heaped upon her fragile shoulders.

Her hair, parted in the middle, hung like two curtains of light across her face. The dancing dress she wore was of a sheer, pale pink fabric. Despite the chill in the palace, the design left her arms bare and pulled tight over her breasts, which were generous for her slender frame, and outlined her nipples. It draped taut yet flexible over her waist. The skirt hung long, to her ankles, though several long splits in the fabric allowed her freedom of movement. The slits went all the way to her upper thigh and revealed her legs when she moved.

The dress was alluring, but it was of little consequence. Lust was desirable and highly useful, but this day she was not endeavoring to elicit it in her observers. She was going for a far more memorable response. Her magick was of a subtle nature, and therein lay the danger. What if it didn't impress enough? What if it didn't astonish as Anatol's illusions could? She had to ensure she made a powerful impact so she had the proper amount of emotion to work with.

Goose bumps pebbled her flesh, perhaps more from her fear than the temperature. Though she was cold all of the time. Apparently, that was one of the prices of her gifts, or maybe it was merely a physical reflection of her inner self.

Cold without to match the cold within? Cold, unfeeling, calculating, and frigid. These were the prices of her gift. Usually no other emotion reached her to cause anything else.

She used the moments before the music commenced to focus, to open up and pull in what she would spin out as she danced. Movement was not required to perform her particular brand of magick, but dance made an impressive presentation. Her body was made for dancing, so she did.

She drew emotion in from those around her, like a spider drawing different threads, all the while protecting herself against the power of her own magick. Weaving, grasping, coiling, she let them find their respective places within her body. It always tingled, this preparation, and made her vaguely ill. It was as if all those emotions compressed her very being into a tiny fraction of her body. It was uncomfortable, that sensation of being squeezed out of herself. She was always relieved when she could start to move and channel the emotion out.

A thread of boredom here. A snippet of joy over there. Anticipation. Lust. Anger. Jealousy.

She continued to fill herself up with it all until there was barely room for herself. Just a sliver, pushed to the side and out of the way, even as she built up the walls to contain the threads and keep them safely away from that remaining slice that was Evangeline.

The music began and her heart started to pound. In her nervousness, just for a fraction of a moment, she nearly lost control of her threads. She gripped them tightly and drew a careful breath.

All those years came down to this . . . one fateful dance.

She'd selected a flute piece, simple yet sophisticated. Her body was lean and her muscles honed from day after day of strenuous practice and training. Releasing a deep breath drawn seemingly from the center of her soul, she began to move her arms. The sounds of the spectators faded away, and she heard the music as if it were miles off. Now things were at their very simplest. Nothing but her body. Her magick. Evangeline moved her feet in the way she'd practiced so many times. She didn't have to think about it. She just danced—simple and involuntary as breathing.

Her left arm swept out and up. She rotated on the ball of her foot, following through the motion with the rest of her body. With a mental sigh she gave in to it—the long stretch of her spine, the bend of her knee, the arch of her slender neck. She took one turn around the performance area in front of the Edaeii and then began to unravel the threads.

No one tracery of the magick she'd lifted returned to its original owner. Evangeline sent each to the person who currently experienced its opposite in order to induce the most dramatic response.

Even such a small amount of magick-imbued feeling could turn the tide within each individual so that the enthusiastic became apathetic, the uninterested became engaged, and the anxious became unconcerned. But to the Czz'ar she sent a special concoction, woven using a little slivers of the emotion she'd drawn in. Bit by careful bit, she manufactured his response. After all, he had the final word on whether or not she would be Jeweled. He required an exceptional reaction to her dance.

When most of her threads had been spun out, she gave in to the fluid physical joy of the dance. She arched, leapt, twirled, and spun until the last note of the song sounded. Then she came to her place before the Czz'ar and curtsied low.

Silence.

Panic scrabbled at the edge of her confidence. She stayed in place; etiquette dictated she must. Her breath came short and fast from her physical exertion and from her concern. The great expenditure of magick made her light-headed and nauseous. She gritted her teeth and forced herself to remain standing. If she had the luxury, she would sleep well into the afternoon tomorrow.

"Rise."

She stood as gracefully as she could, considering her nausea, and brought her gaze up to meet the Czz'ar. Tears streamed down his face and she breathed a sigh of relief. She'd succeeded.

"Beautiful," he gasped through his carefully constructed sorrowful euphoria. The Edaeii and the Court broke into fervent applause.

He'd uttered one word only but she knew with certainty that she'd soon count herself among the Jeweled.

The rest of the afternoon went by in a blur of magickal performances. Mihail breathed temporary life into a heavy oaken chair, making it do a jig in the center of the room. Ellyn created fire in one palm and water in the other that she used to douse it. In an especially pathetic display, Siador altered his own voice and cast it across the room, pretending to be Borco. But then, it had always been clear Siador would never be J'Edaeii.

The jeweling ceremony came at the end of the afternoon, when the performances were finished. All the adepts stood to the side while Borco read a list of names. When Evangeline was called she walked to the area before the Czz'ar and the Edaeii and knelt.

They asked her to remove the top of her dress and she made a slow show of it, making sure Roane caught a definite flash of her full breasts and their rosy, erect nipples. Men loved her breasts. Along with her hair, they were her best feature. She dropped the top of her dress to her waist and demurely covered herself with her hands while the jeweling master inset the sapphire with a jeweling gun at the base of her spine. It stung terribly. She bit her lower lip until it bled so she wouldn't cry out and disgrace herself—or worse, ruin the work she'd done to attract Roane.

As she rose she raked her gaze across Roane, the most eligible and sought after of the Edaeii males. He watched her covetously, his dark eyes full of unmistakable lust.

Hiding a smile, she backed away. She wasn't the only one he'd looked at that way; he'd had his eye on many of the adepts, but she intended to be the first in line. Roane's sexual appetite was large and included both sexes. Today was the first day he was allowed to indulge, since the adepts were off-limits to Edaeii. The Jeweled were not.

In fact, the J'Edaeii were looked upon as a pool of marriageable individuals. The Edaeii constantly sought to breathe new life into their nearly depleted magickal bloodline and wished to distance as much as possible the unpalatable truth that many of the Jeweled—like herself—came from humble beginnings. Hence the title and the jewel to set them apart. It washed away the commonness and made them fit for royalty.

The last of the adepts were Jeweled and welcomed into the hearts and arms of the J'Edaeii. Anatol was included in that group, though men received a much smaller jewel, inset on the back of their necks, under their hair.

The failures, the inept and inferior magick wielders—if they even deserved the title—were sent, weeping in most cases, from Belai. After that, the Czz'ar announced that the customary dinner and ball in honor of the new J'Edaeii would be held that evening.

A prayer was said for the newly Jeweled, a supplication to Blessed Joshui that the magick within them might flourish. Evangeline knelt piously on the ornate floor and shuddered at the thought. If her magick flourished any more, it might overwhelm her. There would be nothing left of herself inside her, only ragged hanks of other people's stolen emotions. There was barely any of herself left as it was—though perhaps it was better that way.

After they were dismissed, Evangeline filed from the theater with the rest of the new J'Edaeii and back to their quarters.

She entered the small sitting room that connected four of the bedrooms in the House of the Adepts. It wasn't actually a house, per se, but a wing of Belai. One floor—a block of thirty-six rooms— was dedicated to the female adepts. Another floor with a block of around thirty-two rooms was for the male adepts. There tended to be a higher number of magick wielding females born in Rylisk. The sleeping chambers were cordoned off into little clusters of four rooms apiece. The two other floors of the wing were comprised of chambers for the trainers that lived within the House, and, of course, there were many rooms for practice.

There was no place for education of the non-magickal kind. She'd been taught to read and not much more than that. Magick was the priority here. Though she pilfered books when she could. She'd slept once with a trainer who had a whole collection just to get several history books. Now she had a small library of cherished tomes.

Katya and Melasann, two of the adepts in her quad, were too young to perform this day. Performance Day was reserved for adepts of twenty and older. Pauliane, the fourth resident, had failed in her performance and had not been Jeweled. Evangeline hovered in the sitting room and listened to her weep as she packed her bags.

Pauliane's magick was incredible when she performed well. She could shape-shift items. An apple into an orange that would truly taste like an orange, for example. However her abilities were uncontrolled and unpredictable. She'd attempted to shift a raven into a dove this afternoon, but had instead ended up with a dead raven. Evangeline had almost felt sorry for her, standing there in the center of the theater with a dead raven in her hands. It had been written on her face; she'd known they would not choose her for the J'Edaeii.

Evangeline entered her bedroom, sat down on the bed, and closed her eyes, finally giving in to her fatigue. She had to muster enough strength for the ball that evening.

Depending on what kind of family the adept had been born to, the rooms could be sumptuous or austere. Her bedchamber was definitely austere. The small area was furnished with a narrow bed with a threadworn blanket covering its thin mattress, a cupboard filled with clothing, and a dressing table upon which sat a pitcher and bowl, her cosmetics, and her jewelry, and her one shelf with all her beloved books.

She hardly spent much time in her room anyway. All her spare moments were spent training. Her stipend money went to practical things like adornments for her body. She might come from a poor family, and her accommodations might reflect that, but her person would not. She'd made that vow to herself long ago when she first started to understand just how much worth lay in her appearance.

She was beautiful and had a gorgeous body—and she could use it like currency. To do that, it had to be embellished properly.

Evangeline opened her eyes, slid off the mattress, and pulled the linen-wrapped gown from beneath her bed. She'd saved a little of each stipend payment every year until she'd had enough to have the gown commissioned from Madame Huey to wear to the J'Edaeii dinner and ball.

Beyond her doorway, Pauliane went out sobbing into the sitting room where Katya and Melasann consoled her in low, compassionate voices. Evangeline brushed her hand over the gown and flirted—briefly—with the possibility of going to her quadmate. Instead she stood and laid the gown on her bed. It wasn't as if Pauliane were her friend. She wasn't *friends* with any of them. In any case, she doubted Pauliane would welcome her condolences. She was J'Edaeii now, after all, and could hardly identify with Pauliane's failure.

She'd had a close friend once. Her name had been Annetka. They'd tittered and gossiped their way through adolescence together. Annetka had shared Evangeline's talent for drawing—the only other thing she could do besides magick. As children they'd drawn pictures and passed them back and forth. Evangeline still had them tucked away in a box under her bed. When Annetka had died of an unidentified wasting disease, Evangeline had cried for months.

But she had time neither for such memories, nor to indulge in maudlin behavior now.

Soon it was too late to go and say anything to Pauliane. A personal assistant arrived to help Evangeline get ready for the ball. Sorna was a small brunette whose wide, dark eyes darted about as though she were nervous. Perhaps she feared magick? Many of the commoners did.

But Evangeline quickly learned that Sorna's tiny hands could cajole and seduce her hair into a plethora of beautiful configurations. Sorna created four lovely styles that Evangeline would've kept on any other occasion, but tonight she was particularly picky. Evangeline finally declared satisfaction when Sorna piled her tresses atop her head in a cluster of small, smooth knots. One long, lustrous section trailed down from the back and over her shoulder to lie like a precious ribbon of light against her collarbone.

Before Sorna had dressed her hair, she'd assisted Evangeline into her gown. Now Evangeline admired herself in the looking glass. The gown had been hand-sewn by the best designer in all Milzyr. It was white tulle and appliqué embroidered with a design of curling silver branches, with small blossoms accented with gold interspersed within the careful tangle. The gown left her arms bare and possessed a low décolleté, as was the fashion. It had a bell-formed skirt with a small train of sheer white material. The highlight of the gown was that her entire back—down to the very base of her spine—was revealed. She turned and looked over her shoulder. It displayed her jewel to glittering sapphire perfection. She smiled.

"Are you pleased, then, miss?" asked Sorna.

"What? Oh, yes. I believe I am."

"You're quite lovely, miss. I'm sure you'll be earning notice and quite a bit of it."

Evangeline barely heard her. Instead she curtsied before her reflection, rose, and did a little twirl. Her skirts shimmered and rippled like the surface of a pond on a breezy summer's day.

"While you're at the ball, myself and a couple other servants will see that your belongings get to your new suite in the J'Edaeii wing. You'll have to find Borco when you want to go to bed so he can get someone to take you there. I'll be in the antechamber if you need me during the night."

Evangeline would have completely missed everything Sorna had said if the words *your new suite in the J'Edaeii wing* had not received her undivided attention. "Very well. You're dismissed."

Sorna bobbed in a deep curtsy. "Thank you. Enjoy yourself at the ball, miss."

When Evangeline left her room, her quadmates were nowhere

to be seen. It was just as well. She hurried down the corridor in her white silk slippers. She'd allowed Sorna to fuss with her tresses a little too long. She reached the staircase leading down to the main part of Belai, and to the grand ballroom, at the same time Anatol did.

Two

He inclined his head and swept his arm to encompass the staircase. "After you."

She started down the stairs in a rush and the unfamiliar silk of her slipper made her slip on the polished marble. Evangeline would've toppled headfirst and broken her neck, or at the very least disgraced herself beyond redemption, but Anatol caught her elbow to steady her.

"Careful." He released her when she was balanced once more.

She touched her bare skin where he'd grasped her. The few times he'd made contact with her skin-to-skin, the result had been the same. Sexual awareness skittered through her, made her think of sweaty, entangled limbs and twisted sheets.

This strange attraction she had to him was incredibly bothersome. He was her equal; there was no gain in sleeping with him.

She frowned and fidgeted. She supposed she should thank him for catching her. It was odd she was so discomfited by Anatol. Ordinarily she had no problem dealing with people. Perhaps it was his eyes. They were deep and straightforward. The man was a mystery to her in the way he didn't play Court games, but his eyes were honest and clear. Really, they seemed to look straight into a person's soul. How . . . *nice*.

It was almost naïve, really.

At Belai it was far more expedient to play your cards close to your chest. "Congratulations," she said instead of *thank you*, "on becoming J'Edaeii. I knew you would pass before today, but after I saw what you did with that sphere, well, then I knew for certain."

Not waiting for an answer, she carefully made her way down the stairs, grasping the heavy gilt balustrade.

Anatol descended next to her. "Ah, yes." He sighed. "The J'Edaeii. I guess I should thank you for your congratulations."

She gave him a sharp look. "Why wouldn't you?"

He gave a terse laugh. "I don't look forward to spending my life doing parlor tricks for the wealthy. We're like permanent court jesters. In fact, the rest of the country regards us as little more than the lapdogs of the upper class."

"Why should we care what the rest of the country thinks of us? The only people that matter are here in the palace."

"Do you really think that?" He inclined his head and gave it a slow shake. "I suppose we are all products of our environments. I simply believe our magick could be used in more effective ways, Evangeline," he finished.

She hadn't ever considered the possibility. After all, no one . . . *no one* turned down the chance to be J'Edaeii. It just wasn't done unless, perhaps, one was touched in the mind. What else could you do with magick other than become J'Edaeii? The entire concept dumbfounded her for a moment. The notion completely dowsed her anger over his ridiculous inference that living at Belai was somehow a *bad* thing.

They reached the end of the stairs and she turned and gave him a disbelieving stare. "Then why didn't you simply throw today's performance? You could even now be on your way back to"—she tossed her hand in a careless gesture—"wherever it is you come from."

Clouds passed through his eyes. "It's far more complicated than that."

"Well." She frowned and fidgeted again, unsure of what to do. Strains of music, emanating from the grand ballroom, met her ears. She would rather be there than here, talking with this man. Anatol had always been different and she didn't care to know the inner workings of his mind. He could stay at Belai for his "complicated reasons," or be gone tomorrow. None of it had any bearing whatsoever on her life.

He was intriguing, however. Anatol stood there, staring into her soul, and she felt laid bare before him. She blinked and looked away. "Are you going in?" she asked, finally.

"No. Once the champagne begins to flow they won't miss my presence. I'm headed off to play a game of strategia with a friend. Enjoy yourself, Evangeline." His gaze swept down her body, lingering on her cleavage and making her nipples go erect. "You look beautiful. I'm sure you will interest the particular Edaeii male"—he raised an eyebrow—"or female for whom you are eager."

How rude!

It took every ounce of her willpower to smile tightly and murmur her good-bye in a civil manner. She didn't know what enraged her more, the fact he'd mentioned aloud her intentions or that he'd noticed them to begin with. Were her ambitions so obvious? And if they were obvious, must he point them out? The man had no ability to dissemble at all.

A quartet of silver and gold-attired servants stood outside the grand ballroom doors. One of them took her name and delivered it to the usher, who announced with much fanfare, "Miss Evangeline Viktoranka J'Edaeii." She smiled in pleasure to hear *J'Edaeii* in the place of her former commonblood last name of *Bansdaughter*.

She carefully composed an expression of mostly boredom tinged with slight interest—she wanted no one to think her new and naïve, nor did she wish to offend any of the Edaeii—and stepped through the double doors. Evangeline had been in the grand ballroom before, but never during a grand ball. Her jaw went slack and she quickly corrected it, though she couldn't seem to keep her gaze from darting wildly over the large room, much as Sorna's had roved her chamber.

The entire room was awash in gold, accented by many burning lights. Large chandeliers hung periodically through the chamber, reflecting brightly in the mirrors that hung along one wall. They gave the impression that the already enormous room was even larger. Courtiers, Edaeii, and J'Edaeii flitted around the chamber like oversized butterflies in silks, brocades, tulles, and glittering jewels.

Various scents assaulted her nostrils, making her nose twitch. Perfumes, colognes, and pipe smoke competed for dominance. At the far end of the chamber a large band of musicians tried to play over the bustling swell of conversation, laughter, and the swish of the gowns on the finely clad ladies.

Oh, she was glad she'd had her gown commissioned! Even with the lack of expensive jewelry glittering at her ears, throat, and wrists, she was fit to stand among this crowd. She'd done well. Besides, she had one very special jewel and that was the only jewel that mattered.

For a fleeting moment she wished Annetka had been able to see this. How her wide blue eyes would have shone!

Czz'ar Ondriiko and Czz'arina Prademia sat on a silver swathed dais to the left of the chamber. In contrast to that afternoon, Ondriiko looked bored and Prademia appeared lively and alert.

Presentations to the Czz'ar and Czz'arina had occurred at the jeweling ceremony that afternoon and so were not again performed at the dinner and ball. Well, dinner, such as it was. Several long tables lined one wall, filled with stuffed cana wraps, salmon, quail, and a wide array of sumptuous desserts—cakes, petit fours, and bite-sized chocolates. She'd arrived late, and the hungry ball-goers had already ravaged the tables. Servants bustled to and fro, trying to right the wrongs.

Evangeline's stomach fluttered. She planned to avoid the food anyway, though the peach champagne punch definitely held appeal.

It didn't take long for those around her to begin to notice her— deep, appraising notice. The men regarded her with gallingly apparent interest. The women gave her chilled looks and talked amongst themselves behind their colorful fans. Criticizing her clothing? Her hair? Perhaps they were all simply miffed that their husbands, or the men they sought, were taking notice of her?

Well, it hardly mattered. She wasn't here to make female friends. This was a world ruled by men. The way a woman got by was through manipulation.

She noted Tadui Edaeii, second cousin to the Czz'ar, a small distance away with a female companion Evangeline did not recognize. Tadui was tall and lithe, with a hook nose centered in a not-completely-unpleasant face. Now he stared openly at her. Evangeline smiled at him and looked away, searching the crowd—albeit with bored affectation—for Roane. Finally, she located him. He was surrounded by, unsurprisingly, a bevy of female admirers. They laughed and hung on his every word, practically elbowing one another out of the way in an effort to win his favor.

Entirely the wrong way to go about it. *Really,* she sniffed. *How pedestrian.*

Not only was Roane first in line to the throne and still unmarried, he was handsome beyond all reckoning, with a muscular build, strong chin, and dark hair and eyes. Although not as physically appealing as the useless-to-her Anatol, if she were to be truthful.

Roane was a complete and utter contrast to his brother, the Czz'ar, and made one wonder what was going in the family's lineage.

Roane made far more the dashing and virile character one would expect a Czz'ar to be, and, indeed, many had often said that Roane truly should've been the one to take the ruler's scepter. True to form, Ondriiko seemed, at least outwardly, to show no consideration of these sometimes open concerns, or unease at the relative proximity of his brother to his throne.

Perhaps he was oblivious to the danger.

After Evangeline had taken a turn around the ballroom, she took up a position near Roane. Those she knew stopped and conversed with her and moved on. She kept her conversation light and her smile constant.

Several courtiers asked her for dances, all of which she—seemingly, anyway—reluctantly agreed to. It would be important for her to seem to be sought after by many men, yet she could not encourage any single one of them too much. The last thing she needed tonight was her time monopolized. She crafted her body language and comments to engage her admirers at first, and then gently nudged them away.

Charlotta Edaeii, cousin thrice-removed from Czz'ar Ondriiko, brought her a glass of fine red wine. When Charlotta gave the glass to her, her fingertips deliberately brushed the back of Evangeline's hand. Ah, she was interested. That was a surprise.

Evangeline lowered her eyes in a feigned gesture of demureness, then looked up and gave the woman a coy smile. Charlotta was a beautiful woman with many connections. Allowing herself to be seduced by her would be neither foolhardy nor a chore.

The wine slid down her throat with velvety richness as she watched Charlotta walk away in her fine, shimmering gold gown and wondered how she'd be in bed. She took another sip of the wine and closed her eyes for moment, thanking Joshui for her magick. Without it, she'd be tending pigs in Cherkhasii right now.

Tadui approached her and gave her a deep bow. "The lovely Evangeline, as beautiful as her personality is cool. I welcome you to our extended family."

As he straightened she offered her hand, which he kissed. She gave him a genuine smile, the first of the evening. He was a pleasant man. "Tadui. I wondered when you'd venture over to say hello. You're as silver-tongued as ever."

"And you are as sly. Don't think I can't tell what you're doing." He put his hands at the small of his back, widened his stance, and affected a serious frown. "Tell me, miss, did you know you have positioned yourself in the line of sight of my illustrious second cousin?" He glanced at Roane.

She laughed. "Oh, Tadui, I didn't do that on purpose," she lied. "Why, look, he hasn't even noticed I'm here."

"Believe me, miss, he has noticed. I know my cousin too well. He doesn't fail to detect any attractive females in the room."

Oh, she hoped he was right.

She swatted his arm playfully. "Please, sir, I'm too plain to interest Roane. Look at all the beautiful women that surround him!"

Also vapid and without strategy, no doubt. Silly chits.

"Now you're fishing for compliments." He shook his head. "You're breathtakingly gorgeous and you know it. With your grace and beauty and the strength of your magick, you shall soon command fashion here at Court. All the women will wish for a slender body with plump, kissable breasts, for hair that's long and light, and dove-gray eyes, not to mention a countenance as cool and detached as your own."

"You flatterer! And what's all this about coolness? You've mentioned it twice now."

His expression turned serious. "I only flatter so I may procure a dance with you this evening, Evangeline."

More like a place in her bed tonight.

"Tadui, you're evading my question."

"If I answer may I have a dance?"

She gave him a wide smile. "You, Tadui, may have a dance regardless." He had a hot rivalry with Roane, so dancing with him was only to her advantage. It did not hurt that she truly did enjoy his company. It was unfortunate he was not closer to the throne.

"Very well, but I'm sure you've already heard the theory."

"Theory?"

"They say that magick wielders often experience a countereffect of their talents. For example, one who can change the shape of objects is often far less malleable within his own character. One who can sculpt illusion from light can see the truth in people. And you, my dear, who can channel emotion and affect it within others so easily . . . well, you must see where I'm going with this."

Evangeline stared at him for a moment, and then gave a light laugh. "My, what an imagination you have!" She knew, of course, it was true. It was the cost she paid and she was well aware of it.

"Ah, but it's true! I have observed it borne out in many of the J'Edaeii. It can be quite vexing at times, but the value of the J'Edaeii, of course, is beyond compare. Especially one like you, Evangeline, who possesses such a rare talent."

She took a sip of her wine, then rolled her eyes. "Ah, but, no. We are the lapdogs of the upper class and have no value," she said, recalling Anatol's comments. "We live to sit up and beg at the whim of the Edaeii and hope they throw us a bone."

She'd angled for laughter, but instead Tadui became grave. "The commoners have been exposed to some dangerous ideas of late. Their thoughts grow too loose, too easy. We managed to politically neutralize the author, but all it did was martyr him. In recent years this man, this *Gregorio Vikhin* has breathed life back into the text and added texts of his own." Tadui shook his head. "The situation becomes more explosive by the day."

Evangeline understood what he talked of, even though politics and the social conditions of the proletariat held little interest to her. Years back Kozma Nizli had written a book called *A Future without Royals* that had sparked a tiresome controversy that seemingly had no end. The book had spoken of freedom and equality to all social classes within a democratically elected government.

It had called the rule of the Edaeii dispassionate and irresponsible. Self-serving and reckless. It called for the lower classes to take control of their future and overthrow their government in favor of democratic rule.

Nizli had been caught and executed—beheaded—by the Royal Guard for disloyalty to the crown, a fate that Evangeline had found far too extreme. But who was she to judge these things?

All the copies of the book that could be found had been publicly burned, but illegal hand-copied tomes still circulated. Even after the burning the country had seemed to simmer, or so some said when she'd been unfortunate enough to be caught in conversations about the subject.

And then this Gregorio Vikhin had popped up. A self-educated commoner who'd risen to take up the cause put forth in Nizli's book, he published his own inflammatory texts and distributed them under the nose of the Royal Guard. He gave impassioned speeches and encouraged the people to rise up and seize the government for themselves.

How ridiculous. And boring.

Just then, Roane looked in her direction. She caught his gaze briefly and held it for a heartbeat before looking earnestly into Tadui's face. She affected a look of deep interest and batted her eyelashes. "Has there been unrest of late?"

He gave her look of blank disbelief. "Don't you know about the riot in Belai Square led by Gregorio Vikhin just last week?"

She didn't have to feign attentiveness now. She straightened and

frowned. "Truly? No. I—I must have been so immersed in my prep-
arations for Performance Day, I didn't hear about it." Plus, Belai
Square was on the opposite end of the palace from the House of
the Adepts, and Belai was a very large place.

He harrumphed. "Borco and his staff do keep the adepts well
isolated from such unpleasantries. And Ondriiko has a tendency to
want to discount these little uprisings, which is the height of hubris
and it's hazardous to boot. Vikhin is a cagey one and the Royal
Guard has not located him. His town house has been empty for
months." He smiled reassuringly. "But don't concern yourself. We'll
find him before he rouses the people to anything truly dangerous."

"Truly dangerous? Was anyone hurt in last week's occurrence?"

"Some commoners were shot by the Royal Guard, yes, but none
of our soldiers were harmed. The killings did seem to inflame the
rabble, however." He stuck out his elbow. "Come, this conversation
is far too dreary for this evening of celebration. Let's dance."

Uneasily, she took his elbow and allowed him to lead her toward the dance floor. She knew little of the character known as
Gregorio Vikhin. He cut a charismatic—and perhaps dangerous—
figure in her mind, but she'd never given him much thought until
now. He was responsible for spilled blood directly outside the place
where she lived.

A faint shiver of unease skittered up her spine. None of this
boded well. Violence, so close to the palace . . .

"May I cut in?"

Roane appeared before her, chasing all concern about the uprising in the square away.

"We haven't even begun to dance yet," Tadui growled.

"Ah, good, then I'm not interrupting." Roane whisked her away
from Tadui and into his arms without even asking what she wanted.

She masked her annoyance with a smile. "My lord Roane."

He yanked her flush up against his body and dipped his head

toward her throat. His breath smelled of alcohol and his teeth nipped her skin. "My lovely lady Evangeline." He whirled around with the music and ground his hard cock against her stomach. There was no question in her mind that Roane was attracted to her now. The man had all the subtlety of a hammer—a very valuable hammer. Apparently her game had worked. All thoughts of the uprising left her mind.

His hand slid from her waist over the curve of her rear to the small of her back. He fingered her new jewel. It was still sore and she winced from the contact, but tried desperately not to let him know he was hurting her. He circled it with his index finger. "I can tattoo around it if you would like. I'd use a pattern as beautiful as you are."

Her breath caught. To be tattooed by Roane was more than she ever could have hoped for. It was commonly known that for a J'Edaeii to bear his mark meant Roane had claimed them as a favorite. To be called upon for sex at any moment of the day or night.

And she hadn't even shown him how good she was in bed yet!

He danced her back toward a corner of the ballroom and pinned her up against a wall. His hand slipped down the back of her dress and he cupped her rear. "Come to my room tomorrow evening and I will tattoo you." He leaned down and nipped her lower lip. "Then I will fuck you so hard you won't be able to walk the next day."

She parted her thighs to allow him the access he sought and he pushed two fingers deep inside her cunt. Slowly, he thrust in and out. It did not excite her at all, but she let out a low moan anyway.

His eyes flicked possessively down her body. "Don't wear the dress. It's ugly."

Then he turned and walked away.

Three

The door opened to reveal Roane, framed by the decadent lushness of his royal apartment. He wore a purple silk robe and nothing else. Ordinarily that would have offended her. Far too presumptuous. But this was *Roane Edaeii*. He ushered her in and gave her about thirty seconds to note the sitting area with its high-backed chairs, the massive fireplace along one wall, and the equally massive four-poster bed opposite it before he set his lips to her shoulder and moved up.

She closed her eyes and faked a moan. His lips were dry and she wasn't in the mood for sex right now, but there was no way she could muck up this opportunity. This was everything she'd dreamed of since she'd been old enough to have such mature dreams—it was more.

Roane would be how she would survive. In this palace, he was her lifeline. She was lucky to have one, no matter what she'd have to give up to secure it.

His hands slipped her gown off her shoulders, down to her

waist, and pushed it so it puddled on the floor at her feet. Beneath the gown she wore only a silky pair of underwear. She had a dancer's body, but her breasts were above average large. Too large to go without a brassiere, really.

His broad hand was strong on her back, almost cruel. It made her shiver, but not with desire. Desire was something she'd felt remotely from others, but never experienced herself. This was business. A performance. Survival. Just like everything else. She steeled herself as he skated his fingers down the arch of her back to her still-sore jewel. He pushed at the skin surrounding it and she fought a swift intake of breath from the pain.

"Yes, I can make a nice, simple design around this jewel," he murmured. His hand slipped down lower and his mouth neared her ear. "After that you can pay the fee for my kindness."

She gave a light, trilling laugh, the one she'd practiced so many times with so many different people at Court. "A price I'm more than willing to pay."

Steadying herself, she turned, giving him a full view of her bare breasts. Fluttering her eyelashes, she purred, "Where is the tattoo gun?"

First things first. She wanted that valuable mark before she sacrificed her body.

His gaze had settled unswervingly on her breasts and nipples, which, luckily, had pebbled in the cool air of the room. He licked his lips. "Perhaps we should—"

She leaned back, out of his way and smiled. "Oh, I think it's better to wait a bit. Don't you? Get business out of the way, and then get to the pleasure."

Anger crossed his face for a moment and then was gone. She'd taken a risk there. One did not deny the heir to the throne anything he wanted *when* he wanted it. Yet she sensed her show of will would excite him a little—give him something to punish her for later.

His eyes went heavy and half hooded. He made a low, sweeping bow, the front of his robe falling open to reveal a nice chest, the chest of a man used to swordplay. "Whatever my lady wishes, so long as my lady understands the cost has just gone up."

Of course it had. She was happy to pay it.

He sought a small silver tattoo gun from a drawer and guided her to a small table near the bed. Then he dropped his gaze to her panties. "Off. Lean forward. Hands on table."

She hesitated, foolishly wanting to hold on to that last piece of covering. Then she did as he requested, rear facing him, slightly bent over.

Silence.

"Roane?" She turned to look behind her.

"Just admiring the view." The whirring, buzzing sound of the tattoo gun began. "Hold still. If you move I can't be held accountable for the result."

He held a hand to her waist and set the thin, cold nozzle of the tattoo gun to her back. She braced herself, fingers gripping the smooth lip of the table. The needle bit into her skin like a thousand stinging bees. She bit into her lower lip until she tasted blood, and closed her eyes. She didn't even care what sort of pattern he marked her with. It only mattered that he was marking her.

Two minutes passed like two years and the tattoo took far longer than a paltry two minutes, but finally he was done. "Stay there," he commanded her after he'd turned the tattoo gun off and set it on the table beside her.

Her back aching, she eyed the small silver device. The gun was powered by elusian crystal, the mined mineral that also gave energy to the lights in Belai. Elusian crystal was not cheap and Roane had just burned through a lot of it on her behalf. Clearly she was doing something right.

He returned with a small black mirror in his hand and then led her to a floor-to-ceiling mirror not far away that stood by a small table holding a vase of lilies. She took the small mirror from him and angled it so she could see the reflection of her lower back. Her eyebrows rose. For such an artless lout Roane was actually quite an impressive artist. Beautiful multicolored swoops and swirls lined either side of her sapphire jewel. She'd been worried he'd mar her body for life with some tactless scrawling brand, but this was beautiful.

"I love it." She smiled as she handed the mirror back to him.

He took the mirror with his gaze centered on her breasts and tossed it to the side. It hit the marble floor with a crash and shattered. With a lascivious grin, he yanked her toward him and squeezed one of her breasts until she winced. Sweet Joshui, how could anyone stand to lie with this manhandler?

He turned her to face the mirror and she forced a small smile to her lips. Her reflection quickly showed the expression on her face that he would want to see—soft, desirous, hardly able to wait for his hands on her.

For a moment she considered reaching out and stealing emotion from someone else nearby, maybe a little calmness or happiness, *anything* to curb the edge of lust in his eyes just a little. But she stopped herself. If Roane figured out she was manipulating his emotions, she'd be done for.

His hands came up and cupped her breasts, squeezing again. Did he really think women liked that? Poor man probably never had a woman in his bed with enough courage to set him straight. She certainly wasn't going to be the one to do it.

"Pretty." His gaze skated down her body and then back up. "I've always thought so."

"As I have always thought you handsome." She tried to turn

toward him, but he caught her almost cruelly and forced her to stand still.

"I have wanted to fuck you for years now." One of his hands landed between her legs, fingers seeking her clit, which was safely buried deep inside her golden curls, not at all aroused. He poked at it, sending jolts of pain through her, and she bit her lip to keep from crying out.

"Now you have your chance."

He stared at her blond thatch of curls as though seeing heaven for the first time. Well, she was glad she could impress him. He certainly didn't impress her, but she supposed he was in a position to not have to care about that. Enviable.

He pushed her roughly facedown onto the table, sending the vase of lilies crashing to the floor. She stared at the broken clay of the vase and the slowly spreading pool of water on the marble while he fumbled to get his cock free.

With his knee he spread her thighs wide, exposing her. Then he pushed his hand down on the back of her neck, making her go onto her tiptoes and involuntarily lift her hips. Clearly he intended to take her like she was some farm animal in the mud. She closed her eyes and let him fumble with the head of his cock at her dry entrance. This would hurt, but hopefully it would be over quickly. He found her entrance and pushed the crown of his shaft inside, ready to ram the entire length into her.

She bore down, prepared to endure when a clamor came from the hallway. Shouting. Fighting. All of it growing louder and louder.

Roane backed away from her. "What the bloody hell is that racket?"

She rolled her eyes at the interruption. Now this would take longer. Sweet Joshui damn it all!

He was pulling on his robe and striding toward the door as she straightened and turned. Flinging open the door, she could see people running and screaming down the corridor. What was going on? Roane strode into the melee without a backward glance.

"Bloody hell," she echoed, retrieving her dress and shoes. More agitated and put out than alarmed, she dressed as she walked to the open door.

Her eyes widened as she registered the oddness of the scene. There were peasants in the palace. Peasants! And they were wielding weapons . . . attacking the nobles. *Blessed Joshui!* They were killing the nobles! They were overrunning the palace!

An uprising.

Revolt.

Revolution?

It couldn't be. Her eyes couldn't accept what she was seeing.

A man swung a scythe at her head and she yelped, closing the door quickly and locking it. The scythe hit the door frame on the outside with a chunk and immediately several peasants began turning the doorknob and banging to be let in. The heavy door held firm on its gold hinges, but she wasn't going to wait until they figured out a way in. They wanted her head!

She stared at the shaking door, the angry cries of the men and women on the other side ringing in her ears. They hated her. They wanted to kill her.

Why? What had she done to them?

She ran for the recesses of Roane's chamber, grabbing a heavy elusian crystal candlestick from his bed that she could use as a weapon. At the back of his bedroom, she found another door, this one leading into the servants' hallway.

Opening it a crack and finding few people beyond, she slipped out and began to hurry down the corridor. She had no idea where she was going, but surely the Imperial Guard would put this horrid rabble down soon. Really! The nerve of these unwashed farmers daring to darken the hallowed halls of Belai! Attacking the Royal

Family? The J'Edaeii? The nobles? They would be properly pun-
ished, she had no doubt.

"Evangeline." Someone grabbed her elbow and whipped her
around.

She found herself staring at Anatol. His hair was bound in the
back, throwing his angular face into sharp relief.

His gaze shifted to the candlestick still gripped in her hand. "We
have to get out of Belai now."

Yanking her elbow away from his grip, she yelled over the din.
"Don't be ridiculous. The Imperial Guard will have this put down
in no time."

He gripped her again, shook her. "No. They've lost control.
It's over." He gestured to the ornate hallway. "*This* is done with.
Haven't you been keeping up with the news?" Someone screamed
at the end of the corridor and a cluster of rabble started toward
them. He yanked her down the corridor. "We need to get out of
here. They're rounding up all the royal family, nobles, and J'Edaeii
they can catch, even the adepts."

She dragged her feet. "For what?"

"Nothing good."

Some sort of iron weapon flew over her head, almost removing
it from her shoulders, and she stopped dragging her feet. Maybe
she could follow Anatol for the time being. Surely he was wrong
about the state of Belai in the long term, but the short term looked
a little ominous.

Gripping Anatol's hand, she fled down the twisting halls and
narrow staircases of the palace. Foul smelling, badly dressed rabble
attacked the nobles at every turn. A balding woman with bad teeth
grabbed her arm and she yanked it away and pushed her, making
the hag fall back. A hulking man with an axe tried to block their
path, but she whacked him over the head with her candlestick and
he fell to the floor, head bleeding. Another man grabbed her arm,

but one of the guards—a few of them still fighting futilely for control of the place—put a sword through his stomach.

They burst out of the palace and into the winter cold gardens. The sunlight blinded her. Even here there was chaos, bloodshed, and violence. It seemed so at odds with the manicured foliage and neat pebbled pathways. All she wanted was to get away.

Now running blindly, her impractical shoes long gone, she plunged through a hedge behind Anatol. She had no idea where she was—visiting the palace gardens had never been high on her list of things to do—so she followed Anatol, who seemed more than passingly familiar with the natural environment outside Belai's walls.

They finally lurched and stumbled past the gates of Belai and onto the backstreets of Milzyr. The rabble was busy rioting in the streets.

Lady Alyssa's beautiful ebony and silver carriage had been tipped over on the cobblestone, the horses gone. Blood made a dark brown smear on the street leading away from the door.

The rioters threw rocks at the storefronts of the high quality dress shops and hatmakers, making off with the items within. A man was pulling off the gown of a noblewoman half a block away, cackling loudly while she screamed.

Evangeline had long ago made sure all her emotional walls were firmly up. She wanted no part of what had to be emotional chaos—not even in the detached, diluted way she sensed other people's feelings. Even so, this was complete anarchy and it nearly cut through all the numbness that had shielded her since childhood.

For the first time in a long time, she felt the faint stirring of fear trying to push its way through to her. *Her own fear*. Thick. Cold. Cloying.

"Come on," Anatol growled.

She glanced at him, realizing she'd stilled in the street, staring at

the cut leather of the reins that had been used to control the four
gorgeous bays of Lady Alyssa's carriage.

His hands closed over her arm and pulled. "I swear I'll knock
you out and throw you over my shoulder if you don't move. You're
going to get us caught."

She looked up to see a burly, redheaded farmer take note of them,
gesture to a gaggle of blood-smeared men, and then point. Acutely
aware of her fine dress, healthy fall of sunlight-colored hair, and
creamy, unblemished skin—all of it marked her as "enemy"—she
moved, running with Anatol into the shadows of the alley.

"We need to change our clothing," Anatol said, running down
the cobblestone beside her. "We need to try and blend in with people if we're going to survive."

"You mean, act and dress like a commoner?" She couldn't keep
the note of distaste out of her voice.

He shook his head and muttered under his breath. "You're more
trouble than you're worth. Do you know that, Evangeline?"

She would have answered, but at that moment the mouth of the
alley they were traveling down was blocked by a group of peasants, all of them men and all of them holding weapons.

They came to a halt and both turned at once, only to see the
other end similarly blocked. Her heart pounded. She couldn't remember being forced to feel this much of her own emotion for a
very long time—maybe not since she'd been a tiny child and had
first come to Belai. It was distasteful and brought back bad memories she could only just catch the tails of.

Anatol began looking around for a way into one of the buildings and she helped him. A staircase, a doorway, anything.

Nothing.

No escape.

She cast a glance at Anatol, who didn't look back. His hands fisted at his sides, he was staring down the pack of men approaching them as if he could defeat them with his thoughts alone. Which, if he used illusion, he could.

She reached in and pulled a thread of her power, tasted the emotional currents that flowed around them. Anger. Hatred. Killing rage. Fear. There was nothing here for her to work with. Nothing to sample and redistribute to positively affect the situation. Just negativity. Only ugliness. The backwash of it stung the rear of her throat and caught behind her teeth. It made her want to spit.

And then they were there in front of them, the brutes.

She lifted her chin at the leader, a hulking, sweaty man with blood smeared across his cheek and a mass of messy red hair. Behind her the other group had come to a halt. She didn't look, but she could feel them, smell them, hear them. Their body heat warmed her.

No way would she demean herself in their presence. She would not cower, would never beg. She was better than they were. She was—

The redhead punched her and she fell backward into darkness.

Four

E vangeline?"

Anatol cupped Evangeline's head in his hands and shook her lightly. She'd have a whopper of a headache when she woke. Probably a black eye, too. The men who'd spotted them had taken one look at the haughty expression on her face, had declared her trouble, and knocked her out first thing.

They were right. Evangeline was trouble. He, of all people, knew that.

He still wasn't sure why he'd helped her get out of the palace. He stared down at her closed eyes, the thin veins purple. A bruise had begun to bloom violently on her upper cheek. She looked so fragile, so innocent this way. Vulnerable. Not soft, not weak—but misused. She was a survivor.

And that was the truth of Evangeline.

No matter the act she might put on for others, she was injured, defenseless, and broken on the inside.

Who was he kidding? He knew why he'd helped her. He loved

her. He had for a long time. She was hopeless, lost in a tangle of her magick and the cruel environment she'd grown up in. Yet there was vulnerability beneath the mask she wore, and it was that part he was drawn to. Maybe he thought he could help her—fix what was broken.

He was an idiot.

She roused, her eyelids fluttering open. She immediately winced, her hand coming up to touch her injured cheek. "That man punched me!"

"Yes, he did."

"Where am I?"

"Safe." He paused and looked around at the alley. "In a manner of speaking."

She looked around, shakily sitting up. He'd found a space between a couple of buildings, the opening hidden by some large, discarded boxes. Stars shone down from above. Even at night, hours after the initial siege of Belai, the city seemed to seethe with anger. Shouting, screaming, crying, and the sound of things breaking could still be heard in the distance.

Her lip curling as she took in her surroundings, she noticed what she was dressed in—little more than rags. While she'd been unconscious, he'd snatched more appropriate attire for them and thrown away the costly garments that marked them as fresh from the palace. She probably had never seen herself dressed this way, though if she'd grown up with her birth family in Cherkhasii Province she would've worn clothes like this all the time. As a trade-off, she would've had love, but Evangeline didn't know that love was better than nice clothing.

He'd dressed her, too, though Evangeline wasn't the type to care if someone she barely knew had seen her naked. It would be low on her list of concerns, but it had affected him. Despite the circumstances, despite the danger, touching the bare body of the woman he'd wanted for so long had made him tremble with need.

She touched her head again, apparently deciding her head hurt too much to become overly offended by the clothes. "What happened with all those men?"

He settled down beside her and sighed. "I used magick." He kept his voice low. "I created an illusion of the Imperial Guard and sent them running. It will be the last time I can do that. You should try to avoid using your magick, too."

"Why? It's our right to use our abilities." Her voice, as ever, held unbreakable pride.

"It may be our right, but it will also be our death. They're rounding up the J'Edaeii, all the nobles, especially the royalty." He paused. "They've already started killing them."

"What? Where is the Imperial Guard? The Royal Army?"

He snorted and hung his head. "You really are a beautiful, clueless little bit of fluff, aren't you?"

Except, he knew different. The good part of her was just buried under all that magickal backlash. His gift went both ways, just like hers. He could cast illusion, but he could also see through it. She could sense other people's emotions, but could too easily block her own—which is what she'd been doing since she was a young child. For good reason.

He understood the truth of Evangeline, but that didn't make her any less of a pain.

She bristled. "Listen—"

He held up a hand. "I'll tell you what you should already know. The army is made up of commoners. Most of them have laid down arms and taken up with the people. Those who didn't join the rest are now dead or imprisoned. The Imperial Guard was defeated right off, overwhelmed by the number of peasants who stormed the palace. Our time is over with, Evangeline. The rich are reaping what they sowed with the poor. Taxing them into starvation. Confiscating their goods and the fruits of their labor. Suppressing inventions to deny the rise of the lower and middle classes and keep power in the hands of the royals. Dancing and feasting while they died in the streets from neglect and hunger. It's no wonder they hate us."

"I had no idea."

"Because you weren't paying attention. Because you are self-centered and oblivious. This has been going on for a long time now. Everyone but you and the royals saw it coming."

Her jaw locked. "No."

"Yes."

She surged to her feet. "No! This isn't possible. None of it!"

He hissed through his teeth, grabbed her arm, and yanked her down. "Stop it. You'll get us both killed. Now calm down and settle in. We can't move from this spot until morning. It's not safe."

She sat back down next to him with a thump. "I'm hungry." There was more than just a note of petulance in her voice. She probably couldn't remember a day in her whole life when her stomach had rumbled and she hadn't been able to put something in it.

"So am I, but we'll stay here anyway. Turn over and raise your shirt."

"Excuse me?"

"When I dressed you, I noticed the skin around your jewel and the tattoo Roane gave you is looking red and irritated. You run the risk of it being infected. I need to look at it again."

She scowled at him for a moment, but turned. Efficiently, he assessed the area. The skin around her sapphire looked like it probably hurt, but maybe her mind was on other matters at the moment. He couldn't blame her for that. The tattoo was a fine swirl of color to either side of the jewel—a brand that marked Roane's "ownership" of her.

"It's too soon to tell."

Shivering, she pulled the rough shirt back down. "I'll be fine."

"So you say. We'll keep an eye on it. Now settle down and try to sleep."

"How can we sleep at a time like this?"

He sighed. "I don't know." The truth was that he wouldn't sleep at all. He hooked an arm around her and pulled her close for warmth. She stiffened. "Hush, princess, we need to share body heat."

"What will we do now?"

"We wait. Rest as much as we can, sleep if possible. In the morning we'll see where the city stands. We'll have immediate concerns— food, shelter, water."

She pursed her lips. "Thank you, Anatol. You have your head much more right than I do at the moment."

Shock vibrated through him. *Had she just thanked him?*

"I've been expecting this." He paused. "Not quite like this, but I've thought about the possibility."

"And I'm just a little bit of pretty fluff that never saw this coming."

"You see it now."

She looked down into her lap. "I see much more clearly than normal."

There was a note of something in her voice—emotion. He frowned. It was probably the first time ever he'd heard such from her. First it had been a note of panic, then chagrin at her own short-sightedness. But this last bit was regret, sadness.

Perhaps this experience was breaking down the barriers that kept her magick of empathy so carefully away from her. Did that mean the walls were about to break? That could happen if something traumatic happened to her, he supposed. After all, it had been the separation from her family at the age of four that had built the walls in the first place. If so, she was about to become a mess of major proportions.

Evangeline hadn't allowed herself to feel emotion since she was a child. At least, not enough of it to be of consequence—only enough to help her survive her life in the palace. Little bits of feeling here and there, driving her actions in a way that would keep her fed and with a roof over her head. He knew; he been watching her closely for her entire life.

It wasn't that her feeling emotion would be a bad thing. Anatol thought it might be the best thing for her, but it would complicate matters out here while they were trying to survive. Having her break down emotionally would not help them in the coming days.

He glanced over at her. She'd leaned her head back against the wall and her long lashes shadowed her cheeks.

"Evangeline? Are you still awake?"

"Yes."

"Do you remember your family?"

She opened her eyes and looked at him for a long moment before speaking. He thought for a moment he'd overstepped and she was angry, but then Evangeline would need to actually be in touch with her anger for that. He had a pragmatic reason for asking. It might be time now for both of them to seek their families.

"Not really," she answered, diverting her gaze downward. "Just brief flashes."

"But you know your last name and the province they live in."

"What are you saying? That I should go back to being a pig farmer's daughter?"

"We're going to have to explore all our options."

She blinked at him slowly and looked away with her chin raised. "I don't think being a pig farmer is an option."

He composed himself before answering. "You might have been very happy being one."

She gave him a look of complete scorn and closed her eyes again. "Who were your parents before the royals tracked your magick?"

He gave a quick grin. "Hatmakers. They lived—live, I guess—in Ameranzi Province. I don't know much about them. They're not dirt-poor, more middle class, but I haven't seen them since I was a child. Belai strongly discourages visits, but I remember them trying to see me."

"Mine never tried." There was no note of sadness in this sentence. It was a statement of fact.

"You don't know that. They may have tried many times and were turned away without your knowledge."

For a moment, he thought he saw pain cross her face. But then she settled back against the wall and said, "I'm going to try and rest now."

"Yes. You should. Tomorrow will be eventful."

He suspected what would happen. Gregorio Vikhin had gotten exactly what he wanted, exactly the result he'd sown for so many years, but it had come with a brutal twist. Anatol could hear the voices in the street, the jubilance, the drunkenness. The people had what they wanted and now they were elated, power hungry . . . and frightened. They were excising hundreds of years of life under an unfair yoke.

There would be bloodshed and it would be legion.

Tomorrow the steps of Belai would run red with the murders of the royals, the nobles, and the J'Edaeii alike. There would be no mercy. The people would wrap themselves in the wise words of Gregorio Vikhin, but those words would be viewed through a haze of hatred and revenge.

Anatol saw the truth of things. He knew it would come to pass.

And where was Gregorio Vikhin tonight? Undoubtedly, he was mortified to see his dreams running so out of control. Anatol just hoped the great man could find a way to stem this tide, bring the people back to their senses and get some real work done. But that wouldn't happen tomorrow.

Tomorrow would be day one of the nightmare. This illness would need to run its course, work itself out. Until then they would just have to find a way to survive.

He pulled Evangeline closer to him.

Gregorio Vikhin stood looking out the window of his town house at the bonfire made of expensive furniture in the street below. The houses and storefronts on either side glowed with the reflected red light while the drunken, celebrating citizens of Milzyr danced around it like devils. They were so drunk on alcohol and their new-found power that they even burned the fine things they'd wrested from the dead or soon-to-be-dead nobles, things they could have kept or sold for food.

He let the curtain fall back and stepped away from the window. They wouldn't come into his town house. They wouldn't steal his furniture, or drag him off to the steps of Belai to be executed. No, they gave him respect. Respect he didn't deserve.

This was his fault.

He pressed the heel of his hand to his eye socket and sank into a nearby wingback chair. His ideas. His words. His fervor that he'd whipped from one end of Rylisk to the other. But not like this. He'd never meant for it to happen like this.

He wondered what Kozma Nizli would make of this.

But maybe this was the only way. Clearly, the royals and their cronies hadn't been listening to anything they had to say before now. Perhaps bloodshed and chaos were the only way to get change in Rylisk.

After all, it wasn't like the royals were ever going to give the people a say in their governance without violence. Blessed Joshui, the royals had been deaf and blind! Lost in a fantasy of their own making, heedless to the danger they created for themselves with every tax hike.

Most would say they were getting what they deserved.

Yet, there would be innocents who would be hurt in this mess. The J'Edaeii, for example. Most of them were already victims, having been forcibly taken from their families at a young age. Brainwashed into thinking they weren't prisoners. Used as a breeding pool to infuse the royal bloodline with the magick their pride had lost through inbreeding. Though they came from common peasant stock, they would be swept up in the bloodshed along with the guilty.

Magick would leave their world because of him. His words. His ideas.

Yet he couldn't help but feel proud as well. After all, now the people would have a say in their lives. There could be a new order. Fairness for all. Democracy in governance. They would set up a new system of government, hold elections, have debate. The people would no longer starve as they had in the past. They would no longer be used as mules, whipped by their "betters" until they were bloody.

He had done that. *His words. His ideas.* But, yes, there would be a price to pay. Innocents would pay it. He would feel every one of their deaths to the center of him. Their shed blood would weigh him down forever.

That would be the price he paid.

"This cannot be." Evangeline's fingers gripped the iron bars in front of Belai and watched the pool of blood at the top of the steps grow larger. Beside her Anatol seemed bereft of words, even of breath.

Emotions pierced and prodded and tangled her gut. And they weren't the removed, watered-down emotions of the crowd she felt, these were *her* emotions. If she allowed herself to taste the feelings of the people around her it wouldn't be horror, revulsion, fear, and disbelief she would sense. It would be jubilance, victory, and pride. Their emotions would match the expressions and actions of those around her—the smiling faces and pumping fists. No, these were *her* emotions coursing through her in a flood right now, so hot and so hard that no wall she could build could stop them. Like a tidal wave of feeling, it crashed over her head, stole her breath, squeezed her heart. All the defenses she'd built up around her for so many years were just gone.

Gone.

She couldn't remember the last time she'd felt so much. She was reminded of why she'd undertaken the task never to do so. *Feeling.* There was nothing but pain in emotion.

"Anatol," she whispered.

"I see."

But she was sure he wished he couldn't. Just as she did. Deafness and blindness would be welcome right now. Heads were rolling on the steps of Belai, and they were heads she and Anatol both knew. Aleksander Edaeii had gone first. He'd hung low and precariously on the Edaeii family tree, but he'd been a royal.

They were killing the royals. The idea of it was so alien to her, so unbelievable, that she kept thinking—hoping—this was a nightmare. However, the roar and jostling of the crowd assured her it was not. The happy cries of the observers grew louder as they saw the blood getting bluer.

Her hand flew to her mouth as they brought out the next people slated for the guillotine, and she turned her face into Anatol's chest. Annabelle Bellama, a noble, and Sorcha J' Edaeii, a magicked woman who was only a year older than Evangeline.

Anatol thrust her away. "Look amused or we die. They're already suspicious of us."

"Look amused?" She glanced around the reveling crush around them. Indeed, a few were casting long looks their way. Anatol looked grim and resigned, and she was sure she appeared pale and shaken. "Let's get out of here, then."

He gave a pointed glance around him and raised his eyebrows. "Impossible."

He was right. The crowd had them pinned against the gate. They had front row seats for the show and if they left now it would only make them look more suspicious. Her knees were weak, bile burned the back of her throat. Wooziness nearly overcame her for a moment and she wished it would—anything to escape this—but Anatol held her up and she remained horrifyingly conscious.

Her gaze fixed on the next victims being led out from the palace dungeons. Oh, Blessed Joshui, *no*.

Tadui walked down the stairs followed by Borco, both flanked by peasants turned executioners. Heads held high, the men stood with hands tied behind their backs and their toes just touching the large bloodstain on the pavement made from those who'd gone before them. A wagon filled with headless bodies was parked nearby, yet neither man batted an eyelash, or showed a moment of fear. Tadui stared out into the crowd, his proud, accusatory gaze settling on individuals of his choice. The Edaeii line had more courage than she'd presumed.

One of the big farmers muscled Borco up to the slab. Borco looked impassively over the heads of the crowd as if he were about to be served tea, not have his head severed from his neck. Evangeline was too afraid to probe with her magick and taste Borco's emotions. She was too much of a coward. There was resignation in his eyes, however, and defeat.

The executioner forced Borco to kneel and place the side of his face down on the cold slab. Then, almost as if the executioner were bored, as if he worked in a factory and this were only his next-in-line, a simple job, he stood and pulled the mechanism that dropped the blade.

Evangeline jerked in Anatol's arms at the juicy thumping sound that could be heard prior to the explosion of cheers from the crowd. She turned away at the last moment to avoid seeing the cut, then turned back.

Borco's head rolled across the concrete at the base of the steps.

"Oh, Blessed Joshui," she breathed.

Tadui had taken a step backward. Now she saw reaction in the royal's eyes. Tadui, such a harmless, *nice* man. A man who had been as close to a friend as she'd ever had in Belai, save Annetka. *Oh, Tadui.*

The executioner grabbed him roughly by his bound arms and forced him down on his knees. Evangeline's body tightened, grief clogging her throat and pricking at her eyes. And anger! Hot anger poured through her, made her want to scale the iron fence she was pressed up against and charge the stairs, free him from this fate.

But she could do nothing. Helplessly, she watched the executioner force Tadui's head down to the chopping block. Tadui's eyes searched the throng desperately—looking for a friendly face?—found her and locked his gaze with hers as his head came to a rest on the platform that was sticky with the majordomo's blood. His gaze was vacant, confused—shocked—yet he recognized her. She read that clearly in his gaze.

Unable to stop herself, wanting to try and share his pain if she could—she tasted his emotion. Cold terror slammed into her. Fear of what would happen to him after his head rolled. *Was this it? Was this the end forever? What would happen after he died? How could this be happening?* Questions and confusion roiled through Tadui during these last moments of his life. Her face was a comfort to him, his only one.

Knowing she was taking a risk, she cast out into the crowd,

swimming through the nausea-inducing elation and excitement, searching for . . . calm. Finding it in some faceless person at the back of the throng, she drew a thread and exchanged it for Tadui's horror. Immediately, Tadui's face slackened with peace.

The stained brown blade hoisted high, the small clean part gleaming in the bright sunshine. Evangeline drew a shaky breath, vowed not to turn away, but to hold Tadui's gaze until it was over. She owed him that much.

The blade dropped. Wet chunking noise.

Tadui's head rolled and then came to a stop. His gaze still held hers, but now it was dead.

Her gorge rose.

She turned, hand to her mouth and pushed her way violently through the crowd, forcing people to move. People made way for her, not wanting to wear her breakfast—little of it she'd had—on their persons. At the perimeter, she bent over and retched into the gutter. Someone touched her back. Anatol.

Closing her eyes against the sting in her throat, she wiped the back of her hand across her mouth and forced herself to stand. A distance away, some of the peasants were watching them a little too intently. "I'm sorry. I just couldn't."

He took her by the upper arm and guided her away, calling out behind him with a smile, "Too much celebrating last night. Girl can't take all the excitement." His accent was dead-on perfect to pass for a low-born.

They walked down the street, leaving the press of the crowd and their gruesome festivity behind them. The fragrance from a vendor selling smoked turkey legs made her stomach rumble and her gorge rise in quick succession, and Anatol turned, leading her down a narrow alley instead.

"You used magick, didn't you?" His voice was a low, angry whisper. He shook her by her upper arm as they walked. "Didn't you?"

Mute, overcome with heavy grief, she could only nod.

"Hey, hey you!"

Anatol squeezed her arm until pain shot up it. "Keep moving," he growled.

"Hey, stop, you two!"

Footsteps running toward them. Men's voices. This was the second time in twenty-four hours they were being pursued by a gang of men. They weren't doing so well on the streets so far.

Anatol cursed loudly, dropped her arm, and turned. Evangeline stopped and turned as well.

There were three men in front of them, all of them working class. Two brunettes, one blond—all of them dressed in ratty clothes and hats with holes in them. She would give any amount of money to never see a working-class lout again in her life and here she was surrounded by them.

The blond smiled, revealing rotting teeth. "Where do you think you're going with such a sweet little thing like that? Even with that black eye she's pretty. How much does she cost?"

Evangeline opened her mouth in indignation. He thought she was a whore! She may have had sex with individuals to obtain something material in the past—all right, that was the only reason she'd ever had sex—but that didn't mean she'd do some ill-mannered, ugly lout in an alley for a few crowns.

"She's not a prostitute, she's my sister." Anatol used that same perfect accent, stepping forward. "And if you keep calling her one, I'll have to take offense."

The man held up his hands. "Sorry, my mistake." He narrowed his eyes and leered at her. "You don't look much alike, though." He poked Anatol in the chest.

"Listen, you imbecile," Evangeline said, stepping beyond Anatol. "You're dreaming if you think I'd ever lay hands on you, not for all the money in the world." She gave him a sneer and a once-over designed to find him lacking. She'd perfected that look at court. "I wouldn't touch you for anything."

The man bristled and his friends swelled with manly indignation. The energy of the alley tensed with violence. Evangeline could feel the emotion of the men imploding. They wanted to teach her a lesson for being a female with a smart tongue and they were going to do it by pounding her flesh.

"You ain't his sister," the blond man spat.

"You calling me a liar?" Anatol pounced on the blond before the man could take further action. His fist connected with the blond's cheek and he went flying backward. Pivoting to the side, Anatol caught the second in the gut, turned and kicked the other in the side of the head. It was over so fast, Evangeline could only stare.

"Where . . . where did you learn to fight like that?" she stammered, watching the three men scramble back away from him and then turn to limp down the alley.

"That was not a fight. They didn't have the will. They didn't really want it. They were just men out sowing their oats. It was easy to discourage them."

She blinked, frowning. What he called discouragement, she called lots of blood.

Anatol rounded on her, cradling his hand. "Listen, princess. You need to take off your tiara right now. That attitude will only get you killed on these streets. I will only be able to protect you for so long. That's twice now. Three times if you count Belai." He turned and kept walking, shaking his hand once like it hurt and swearing.

She stopped and stared at Anatol's back. Rage coursed through her veins at his reprimand, but she knew he was right. These were not the treacherous, back-biting halls of Belai. These streets were a different kind of vicious, the sort she was not groomed for. She needed to find a new set of armor, new weapons, but she was at a loss as to how to construct those things. She knew how to survive palace life. That was all.

She had no idea how to survive on these streets.

Her rage turned to cold fear and she marveled at the change in her emotion. How long had it been since she'd felt actual emotion—her own, not someone else's? It was strong. It was horrific. She didn't want it.

"Evangeline?"

She blinked and looked up, seeing that he'd backtracked to find her staring at a puddle in the alley, lost somewhere in her head. "You're right."

"What?"

"You're right. I'm not prepared for this. I don't know"—she motioned at the alley—"this. Oh, Blessed Joshui, I'm afraid." She swallowed hard and pulled the frayed cuffs of her ugly dress over her hands. "I'm filled with grief and terror in equal turns. So much emotion. I can't remember the last time I felt anything and now I'm feeling everything." She drew a ragged breath. "I hate it. I *hate* it." She shook her head, closing her eyes for a moment. "I can't remember the last time I had enough emotion of my own to hate so much."

He stood there, looking stunned.

"Anatol, don't look at me like I just grew another head."

He blinked. "You did."

She swallowed hard. "I'll be fine." *Lie*. Nothing would ever be fine again. Her stomach roiled.

Anatol only kept staring at her.

Scowling, she reached out and took his hand, looking at the already-blooming bruise and split skin on the back on his hand where he'd punched the man on her behalf.

"It's all right."

"It's not." She frowned. "It needs to be washed and disinfected."

He glanced around them. "Not much chance of that."

She held on to his hand, warm, broad, and strong in hers. "It will give us a goal. We need something to concentrate on other than what's going on in front of Belai."

He drew his hand from hers. "We have another goal—finding food and shelter."

"Yes, there is that." Her stomach still wasn't sure if it wanted food or not yet, but give it a couple hours and she'd be starving.

"You can feel now," said Anatol with wonder in his voice.

"It was the beheadings." She glanced to the side and pressed her hand to her stomach. "Or, I don't know, it's all this. I used to have beautiful strong walls up all around me. Now they're gone. Now I can feel."

Anatol smiled. "I'm happy for you."

She licked dry lips, her breath puffing white in the cold. "I'm not. It's a curse."

"It's a gift. It just might take you some time to see it that way."

She shook her head. "No, Anatol. You don't understand. I don't remember much from my childhood, but I remember emotion. I remember feeling." She paused, catching the tail end of a memory and then losing it before she could close her mental fingers around it securely. "Emotion almost killed me as a child. Grief. Loss. Rejection. The walls I built saved my life and now they're gone."

Anatol took her hands, making her flinch. "You'll adapt. Eventually you'll see this for the advantage it is."

She met his gaze and held it for a long moment. She didn't believe what he was saying, but she couldn't find the words to reply to him. Using just the thinnest threads of her power, she reached out to touch his emotions. Hope had bloomed in him. He liked her. Blessed Joshui, Anatol was *fond* of her.

Footsteps on gravel drew their heads to the mouth of the alley. Evangeline's blood chilled at the sound, expecting more trouble, but it was a finely dressed woman who stood there instead of a group of men. She wasn't a noblewoman, that much was clear. Someone from the middle class, Evangeline assumed. The middle class had mostly been left alone by the mob. Evangeline shivered, jealous of the woman's expensive coat.

The dark-haired woman blinked once, slowly, her jaw locking as she took them both in. Then a smile spread over her lush, red lips. "Who do you two think you're fooling?"

Five

Excuse me?" The chill had returned to Evangeline's blood. She'd give anything to have the walls back up around her emotions. Numbness was far more comfortable. Like a newborn babe, she felt ready to cry at anything and everything right now.

The woman studied them with dark eyes too keen by half, then took a couple sauntering steps toward them. "You're both too beautiful to come from anywhere but the aristocracy." She encompassed them head to toe with a sweep of her gloved hand. "Oh, sure, your clothes are worn and tattered, and you're bruised and dirty, but look at your healthy hair, perfect skin, straight white teeth. You have no glow of the sun on you from outdoor work. You, beautiful dark-haired man, you have a far more muscular build than would be expected of a well-heeled court fop, yet you can still tell you're no low-born. And you," the woman motioned at Evangeline, "there's no question you came from Belai. Where are your reddened, calloused hands? The stoop in your back from bending over a washboard? Where's the hungry, defeated look in your eyes. I gaze into your eyes and I see icy pride."

Beside her, Anatol stiffened.

The woman held up a gloved hand. "I won't turn you over to the mob. You can trust me. My name is Lilya."

"We can't afford to trust anyone." Anatol put an arm around Evangeline's waist in an almost protective gesture. "What do you want, Lilya?"

Evangeline took her in—from her classy, expensive heeled boots to her fur-lined coat to her perfectly coiffed hair. Her makeup was minimal, her accent educated. Her glossy dark hair hung in voluptuous, artful curls around her shoulders. This was a courtesan from the Temple of Dreams. It was the only way a woman dressed so richly could travel these streets right now, middle class or not.

The woman smiled and dropped her hand. "That's smart. I wouldn't say my intentions are completely innocent, so maybe you shouldn't trust me. All the same, you're hungry, aren't you? Cold? You look like you could use a warm fire about now. In need of shelter?"

Neither of them replied.

"I'll take that as a yes." Lilya turned and walked toward the street. "Come with me if you'd like to eat and maybe I can find you somewhere safe to lay your head tonight. All I desire is a few moments of your time, during which I can provide you both with options." She glanced over her shoulder and offered an annoyingly confident smile. "You could both use some options right now, couldn't you?"

Evangeline turned to look at Anatol. He stared at the back of the retreating woman, his jaw locked and his blue eyes intense. "Anatol? What do you think?"

He glanced at her. "We go with her, but not too far. We need to be careful. Keep your eyes open and stay aware."

She agreed.

They followed the woman to a nearby cook shop, where the scent of fresh baked bread and meat pies made Evangeline's stomach forget its earlier revulsion and remember it hadn't been filled by anything of consequence in over a day.

Lilya guided them to a table near the kitchen and gestured for them to sit down. Evangeline couldn't see the harm, so she sat, soaking up the heat from the fire in the hearth and letting it sink into her frigid limbs.

Anatol hesitated a moment longer, eyeing Lilya with a glittering and suspicious gaze. Lilya peeled her gloves off, set them on the table, and stared up at him with a challenge in her eyes. "You remind me of me many years ago, after I'd lost everything. Sit."

He sat.

The waiter came to the table, dislike of the two poorly dressed patrons clear on his face. He eyed them. "I don't think—"

Lilya held up a hand, cutting off his sentence. "These are friends of mine." Her voice was steel.

"Very well." The server's shoulders slumped in defeat.

Lilya ordered. "A baked chicken, boiled potatoes, whatever vegetables you have in season, and a bowl of steamed rice, please. Enough for two. Oh, and three glasses of wine." The server retreated to the kitchen.

"You're doing this to make us grateful to you," leveled Anatol from his seat across from Lilya. "Why?"

"How do you know I'm not simply a helpful person, giving aid to those who need it?"

"You're from the Temple of Dreams," Evangeline countered.

Lilya's face went from surprise to slyness. "I see I'm not the only one with the power of keen observation."

"Your position is secure," Evangeline continued. "Why would you care about us? We're perfect strangers and have no power. We can do nothing for you."

Lilya's face took on an expression of pity. "Do you really think the only reason to help another is for personal gain?"

Evangeline's shoulders straightened. "It's how the world works."

Lilya shook her head. "Not my world. Tell me your names."

Anatol seemed to relax a little even as Evangeline's anxiety racheted upward. He leaned back in his chair. "My name is Anatol and this is Evangeline. I don't need to tell you where we came from or what our circumstances are because you've already figured all that out."

Lilya leaned toward him and whispered, "You're nobles hiding out from the raid on the palace."

Anatol hesitated. "No, we're J'Edaeii."

Evangeline leaned forward and gave an alarmed whisper. "Anatol!"

Lilya leaned back in her chair with a small smile playing around her mouth. "How intriguing."

"Now why are you interested in us, Lilya?" Anatol asked. "And stop with the altruistic intentions, they're not ringing true."

Lilya pouted. "I think I'm offended."

"Just tell us."

The waiter brought the wine and Evangeline drank deeply, closing her eyes and enjoying the sip of the half-rate vintage as it slid down her throat. She was so thirsty that she didn't even care about the common quality. The alcohol warmed her blood, too. Maybe a glass or two more and she could dull the emotion that battered her so much. Or at least trade her fear and anxiety for silly giddiness. She'd never felt silly or giddy in her life. She'd only ever had weakened sips of such feelings secondhand.

Lilya took a far more measured drink of her wine. "You're both very pretty and at a bit of a loose end—"

"And you're recruiting for the Temple of Dreams?" Anatol asked.

Shock rippled through Evangeline. The possibility that Lilya was attempting to lure them for the temple had not occurred to her.

Lilya nodded. "I'm not saying the temple would even accept you, but you're both good candidates—educated, cultured, and nice to look at. It would be an option for you. It's nice life, a good life."

Evangeline set her empty glass down, feeling the first effects of the wine on an empty stomach. She shouldn't have drained it so fast. "You want us to be prostitutes?"

Lilya made a moue with her lush red lips. "That's an ugly word. I like courtesan much better."

"Semantics," Anatol growled.

The food arrived, breaking the sudden tension. The scent of the warm baked chicken nearly made Evangeline swoon. Both Anatol and Evangeline tore into the food, eating and not speaking for about five minutes while they wallowed in the sensation of full mouths and stomachs.

"The life of a courtesan is not for everyone." Lilya sipped her wine and watched them eat. "You must enjoy sex while not attaching emotional tethers to it, loving it for the pure acts of ecstasy and the giving and receiving of pleasure. You must enjoy having sex with many partners and be open to all the various kinks and fetishes of those you sleep with. You cannot be predisposed to falling in love—"

"We're not interested," said Anatol. He set his fork down. "We appreciate the meal and your interest, but we're not looking to become . . . courtesans."

"You speak for Evangeline? Why?" Lilya pursed her lips and then smiled. "Ah, you're together. You're in love, is that it?" A sneer accompanied the words *in love*.

"No," said Evangeline. "We're not in love and Anatol cannot speak for me."

Anatol gave her a sharp look. "I guess it's true you already were a prostitute at Belai, weren't you, Evangeline?"

Evangeline leveled the coldest look she could manage.

He took a slow drink of his wine. After he swallowed, he continued, "You have the tattoo on the small of your back to show for it. You allowed yourself to be marked as the property of a single man, no less. A man who didn't care about you at all. Who left you, in fact, when the palace was overrun. Ring any bells?"

"I did what I had to do to survive. I will continue to do so."

Anatol leaned toward her. "But did you enjoy it? According to Lilya, that's a requirement. She wants men and women who enjoy sex to join the Temple of Dreams. I would say that rules you out. You've used sex as a tool to gain things since the moment you realized it was possible. But it's only a tool for you, wielded cold and dispassionately."

Evangeline sputtered for a moment. "You don't know anything about me! How dare you make such judgments?"

Anatol narrowed his eyes and smiled. "I know everything about you. Everything. Now that you can feel, Evangeline, sex will be different. Right now you're basically a virgin, though your hymen was broken long ago. Now you won't be able to stand the touch of any person unless you care about them. The force of the emotion you feel now will not allow it. There's no way you could ever be a courtesan."

She stared at him for a long moment before pushing away from the table, rising, and backing away. "Anatol, thank you for all you've done for me up until now. Lilya, thank you for your kindness." And she left without a backward glance at Anatol.

She didn't need him. She'd never needed anyone. All she had to do was remember to keep her mouth shut in the presence of those questioning her origins, never draw attention to herself, and she'd be fine. She'd survived at Belai; she could survive this.

Once out on the street, she headed in the opposite direction of the palace, down the road past shops and street vendors. The chill bit into her unprotected flesh and she drew her arms over her chest. She wasn't going to think about the fact that she didn't want to be alone. As much as Anatol rubbed her the wrong way, she would miss his presence, the low, soft way he spoke with her, and she would especially miss the heat of him at night.

Damn it, she would miss him.

But her pride couldn't allow her to stand there and take his abuse. He didn't know her. He didn't! He could not presume to know her heart—now that she had one. He couldn't tell her what she could or could not be, or determine the shape of her future.

Anyway, she could travel faster on her own—not that she knew what direction she was going. But being alone was something she knew. Being paired with someone else was complicated and messy. Fraught with risks she didn't want to take. Too much emotion. Too much danger. If she aligned with one person she might come to care for him. Eventually he might reject her; surely at some point he would. A cold ball fisted itself in her stomach as the ghost of a memory reared its head.

No. She wouldn't be able to bear that.

"Evangeline, wait!"

Anatol.

Her feet came to a shuffling stop on the cobblestone street, but she didn't turn. All she did was wrap her arms even more tightly around herself and stare at the tattered shoes he'd managed to find for her.

"I'm sorry I said that back there."

She closed her eyes for a moment and drew a breath before speaking. "Don't be sorry. You were right."

"Even if I was right, it wasn't fair of me to throw it in your face. You did what you had to do to stay alive and worked with the reality you were given. You're a survivor, Evangeline."

She looked up at him. "I never said I regretted anything I did. I never said I was ashamed. I never said I wanted to hear your opinion of me. I just said you were right."

His face shuttered.

Rage bubbled through her veins. "Don't ever talk that way to me again, Anatol." She pushed past him. "You have no right to assume you know me so well. It's irritating."

He caught up to her. "Does that mean you don't want to go your separate way?"

They'd come to the end of the street, to an area that began to make way for a lower-class residential neighborhood. Fewer people passed them here and the cobblestone was slowly turning to packed down dirt. If one traveled farther, one would end up at the steam transport station. There you could take a transport to anywhere in Rylisk, even rural Cherkhasii Province.

She turned to face him. "I'm used to being on my own. It's easier that way."

Anatol looked up at the sky, where heavy white clouds had begun to roll in. "Snow's coming. Warmer with two."

Perfectly rational. Rational stood no chance against strong emotion, especially when that emotion was fear. Her eyelid twitched. Still, she was determined. "I do fine alone."

He shrugged, dropped his gaze to hers, and held it. "All right, good luck, Evangeline." He turned and walked away.

"Anatol?"

He half turned toward her.

"How did you know all that, back there? We grew up together, but we were never close."

He turned to fully face her, stared a moment, and then walked toward her. "I watched you, Evangeline. Watched your every move, every decision."

Her eyes widened. "Why?"

He came up so close to her that she took a step back. Blue eyes intense, jaw locked, he walked her back even farther, until the wall of a knitting shop was flush against her back. "I had my reasons."

"That's not an answer." Irritation had her narrowing her eyes and practically hissing at him. The man was more infuriating than she'd ever imagined.

"Maybe I'm not ready to give the real one."

"I've never slept with you. How do you know I never enjoyed sex? No one knows that. Not even the men and women I've shared a bed with. You're not the only one who can cast an illusion."

"Because to enjoy sex you have to feel emotion. You never did." His gaze bored into hers. "That's how I know."

"I feel emotion now." Her voice even shook with it. All the careful walls she'd built over her life had been stripped away by the events of the last day, washed away in the flood of feeling brought on by seeing those she'd cared for—in her own way—beheaded in front of the palace.

Her old life was gone and she was like an infant in the new one, dangerously vulnerable and helpless. She hated it, hated it so much it burned in the back of her throat, shot rage through her bloodstream with every pound of her heart.

"I know." He paused for long moment, his gaze dropping to her mouth and his face drifting closer to hers. "Maybe it's time you learned what you've been missing."

Her breath caught, her eyes widening.

"I despise the emotion I feel now." Venom coursed out of her with the words. "If I could stop feeling it, I would. If I could, I would return to the way I was before—unfeeling, uncaring for anyone but myself. Life is a lot easier that way."

"Being a real person hurts." His voice was a low murmur now, his lips almost touching hers. "But there are benefits. There's sweetness with the sorrow, pleasure with the pain."

"I haven't felt any sweetness yet, definitely not any pleasure."

"Let me show you."

The heat of him warmed her in more ways than one, making her heart rate ratchet upward and her body tense with something a lot like anticipation. All of it was strange to her. She wanted it to go away. Fisting her hands at her side, she readied herself to tell Anatol off.

"Anatol, Evangeline."

Anatol stilled at the sound of Lilya's voice, his lips almost touching Evangeline's. His gaze caught on hers for a moment before he backed away from her, turned, and looked at the courtesan.

Evangeline cleared her throat and turned on shaky legs to face her as well.

Lilya smiled, watching them in silence for several long moments. "I see now quite clearly that neither of you are suited for life at the Temple of Dreams. I would still like to help, however, if you'll let me."

Anatol tipped his head a little to one side. "Why would you want to help us? We're no one special to you."

"Oh, but you are. You provide me with a way to pay back a kindness that was once extended to me. Once I had nothing, was left for dead, and someone helped me. He gave me my life back. I want to help you and I hope you'll let me." She paused. "I also want to do it because Evangeline needs to be shown that sometimes people will lend a helping hand even if there's nothing in it for them but the satisfaction of knowing they've done the right thing." She took her gloves from her pocket and drew them on. "Come with me. I know someone with a room to rent. I'll pay your rent for a fortnight, just until you can get on your feet."

Anatol shook his head and opened his mouth, but Lilya interrupted him. "I will not take no for an answer." Glancing skyward she added, "There's heavy weather on the way. You don't want to spend it on the streets. Believe me, I know."

The room was nothing like what Evangeline—or Anatol, she was sure—was used to. Anatol seemed far less disappointed by the sparse room, but she stood in the middle of it with a hole of despair opening up inside her.

"It's clean and it's warm. Vermin free." Anatol took a turn around the room and surveyed the one highly elevated, rickety bed with a thin mattress, the cracked full-length mirror, the slanted night table, and the pock-holed dresser—the only furniture in the room. "And the landlord said there's even a bathroom down the hall with running water. Mostly cold water, but we could be worse off."

She could debate that the room was warm, and she was certain she'd seen a mouse on the way up the stairwell. Still, he sounded pleased. She stifled a small choking sound.

"Evangeline? Does it suit you?" asked Lilya.

She forced her vocal cords into action, knowing she needed to readjust her expectations in her new reality. "It's better than an alley," was all she could manage. It wasn't exactly a gracious response. She was going to have to work on those.

But it *was* better than an alley. Especially since snow had begun to come down outside. It was falling faster, harder, and heavier, turning into a serious storm. She was at least grateful they weren't shivering in an alley somewhere, without decent clothing or food in their belly, about to become frozen corpses in a snowdrift.

"Thank you again," Evangeline added with a forced smile.

"It's yours for the next two weeks at least." Lilya walked toward the door. "Twenty crowns every week thereafter, so you'll need to find a way to make some money. Now I'd better get back to the temple while I can still see my way. Good luck to you both. I'm certain I'll see you again. And, of course, you always know where to find me. Consider me a friend."

Anatol said his good-byes and Evangeline followed Lilya out, poking her head past the door frame as Lilya walked down the corridor toward the stairs. "Why did you change your mind? Why don't you think we're suited for the temple?" she asked Lilya's retreating back.

Lilya paused, and then turned. "Because you're in love with each other. That's clear as day." With a small smile, she continued down the corridor and descended the stairs, leaving Evangeline staring after her with a knitted brow.

Frowning, Evangeline shut the door. In love with each other? How ridiculous. Apparently she'd misconstrued that rather heated moment she'd witnessed back on the street in front of the sewing shop. Anatol might feel some lust for her, most men did, but that's where it ended.

The man in question stood looking out the second story window at the deepening snow. "We need food, enough so that we can settle in for a while and wait out this weather," he said without turning. His voice was low, serious.

"And how do you propose we get that with no money?"

He turned. "I'll find a way. I have to. I have to do it soon, too." He started for the door.

Evangeline had a ridiculous urge to ask him not to leave her alone, to tell him to be careful and not take any chances. The thought that he was going to leave her and perhaps be captured made her stomach go cold and empty. Maybe he would never come back. Maybe now that she'd decided to stay with him, invested her emotion in him, he would leave her alone.

And this was what aligning her life with another person's brought. Nothing but confusion and pain.

She bit her lip against everything she wanted to say and turned away. "All right."

His hand touched her cold arm. "I'll be back soon. I promise."

She swallowed hard, tamping down the thought—*I hope so.*

To distract herself after Anatol left, she walked down to the

closet-sized bathroom that all the tenants on the floor shared and
bathed with the inferior soap that was provided. It made her skin
dry and her hair feel like straw, but she was clean—if chilled to the
bone. Using the soap, she also washed her disgusting peasant clothes,
which were sooty and stank of wood smoke.

Once she'd hung up her wet clothes to dry—something that
would take a while in the chilly room—she clambered up into the
high bed, curled up nude in the center of the mattress under the
thin blankets, and wished with all her might for a fire. Her new
tattoo and jewel ached and her hands and feet wouldn't warm. Still,
exhaustion stole over her and sank her deep into sleep not long
after her head hit the lumpy pillow. She barely even thought about
bedbugs.

Sometime after dusk the bed creaked and the weight of another
person getting into it woke her from her deep sleep. Her eyelids
cracked open to find the room dimly lighted by a kerosene lamp.
She rolled over. "Anatol?"

"Are you hungry?"

She sat up, the blanket falling to her waist and the chill air kissing her bare breasts. Shivering, she covered herself. "I guess that
depends on how much food we have."

He gave her a part of a loaf of bread.

"Thank you." She took it and bit into it. Chewing, she looked
around the room, seeing his clothes hanging near hers. Then his
state of dress registered. He wore a pair of underwear, tight ones
that defined his rear and the shape of his cock in front, but that was
all. She couldn't help the sweep of her gaze over his body. She had
always known that Anatol was a good-looking man in the face, but
his body was good-looking, too. Muscle rippled and flexed over his
chest, stomach, and down his strong-looking legs. She wondered
how he'd come to be so in shape, since he'd lived in the palace his
whole life and his magick was cerebral in nature.

Of course, there were many mysteries to Anatol. How was it he seemed to know his way around the streets? Why was he so much more at ease with their situation than she was? Why had he never played the palace political games like everyone else? Anatol remained an enigma to her on many levels.

She swallowed her bit of bread, her body reacting in a wholly new—and completely unwanted—way. "I found food for at least a couple of days if we ration it." He jerked his head toward the top of the dresser, where a burlap bag lay.

"How did you get it?"

His face darkened. "I took risks."

Her stomach dropped out as images from the beheading flooded her mind. "Don't do that."

He flashed a cocky smile at her. "I didn't know you cared."

She stared at the rest of the bread in her hand and forced her voice to be flat as she answered, "I only care because you're linked to me. My care for you is only selfish."

"Of course, Evangeline. Are you cold?"

"A little."

He took the rest of the bread from her hand, wrapped it in a bit of cloth, and set it on the night table. "Move over and I'll warm you."

She turned over and settled down on her side. Anatol blew out the lamp and tucked in beside her, his strong chest flush against her back and his legs against the backs of hers. His arm curled over her waist and his hand lay on the mattress snuggled just near her stomach.

Her modesty had left her sometime while she'd been growing up and she'd stopped caring about showing her nude body to others, but there was something different about this, something unsettling. Something intimate. It made her stomach roll and flutter.

"Relax," Anatol sighed against her ear, raising gooseflesh all along her arms. "As beautiful as you are, I'm in no condition to take advantage of the situation. Sleep."

The state of his lower body gave lie to his words, his cock poking into the flesh of her rear, but she closed her eyes anyway, too tired to care very much about it. Men had hard-ons for women. They lusted and wanted to fuck anything that moved. It was no big surprise that Anatol would want to fuck her. He was a man and she was a woman. Those were the rules.

Six

Anatol finally fell asleep sometime during the night despite the fact he had Evangeline naked in his arms. In the morning he woke up before she did and sat on the edge of the bed watching her sleep. The morning light eased through the window, bright as it reflected off the deep, fresh snow that had fallen all night long. They were very lucky they'd managed to find shelter. She'd tucked the blankets up tight under her chin, concealing the rest of her body. He'd had an eyeful of her bare breasts the night before when she'd sat up, groggy from sleep, and the feel of her soft, bare skin all night had tormented him.

He was no virgin. Anatol had been with plenty of women, though he was sure his number of sexual conquests couldn't touch Evangeline's. That was because he needed to care about the women he bedded. He'd learned that early, after a series of empty affairs in the palace had left him ravenous for more sex—something to fill the hole that his life there seemed to produce in him. That was when he'd begun to sneak out at night, sometimes during the day, leading a dangerous double life that could have gotten him killed.

Whereas Evangeline had learned to reject relationships and emotions, Anatol had embraced them. That had been his survival mechanism. It was also how he understood the harder path Evangeline had taken.

She shifted and sighed, turning over. He wanted to ease the blankets down and stroke her body until she responded, until she woke panting for him, slick between her thighs and needing him to fuck her. He wanted to touch her breasts, explore every hill and valley of her nipples. He wanted to go lower, pet her pretty cunt and suck on her clit until she screamed his name.

His hands clenched. He could do it. He knew he could seduce her, make her enjoy sex for the first time in her life.

But it was too soon.

He wanted Evangeline, but he wanted the whole of her—he wanted her to care for him before he took her, though there was a dark part of his mind that whispered maybe the way to her heart was through her body. Through sex, pleasure. Maybe if he gave her enough orgasms, he could touch her heart. He was certain she'd never climaxed during sex before. He wanted to be the one to make her do it for the first time.

He pushed up from the bed and stalked to the window. The street was silent and still, save for a few tracks from the intrepid or the desperate.

The rustling of blankets drew his attention. Evangeline rose and, shivering, made her way across the room to see if her clothes were dry. He knew they were still damp because he'd checked them already.

He let his gaze drop from her narrow shoulders to her small waist to the flare of her heart-shaped rear. She was lithe, like a dancer, slender as a reed. Her breasts were topped with luscious red nipples he could suck on for hours. Her long blond hair brushed the small of her back and the same color of light hair covered her mound. The area around her tattoo and jewel were still red. He scowled, examining them from afar. He didn't like the looks of that at all.

"I know what you want, Anatol," she said without turning around. She sounded bored. "I can feel you watching me." She turned and spread her arms. "So take me, I don't care."

I don't care.

He wanted her to *care*.

"I was looking at your jewel and tattoo," he grumbled. *Partly.* "It's cold. Get back into bed." His voice came out gravelly in frustration.

She retreated under the covers, nibbling on the rest of the bread from the night before. "You should come back to bed, too. I promise I won't bite."

Yes, but *he* might. And he might do a whole lot more than just bite her. He might give in to the strong urge he had to fuck her so well and so hard that he would emblazon himself on her body and in her mind so that forevermore she would remember him.

"I'm coming back to bed just as soon as I make a disinfectant for your lower back."

"How are you going to do that?"

"I took a little salt from a cookshop the other day in case it looked like your jewel needed to be cleaned."

He sought the small paper-wrapped amount of salt, found a suitable container in the items they'd gathered from the street, and headed into the bathroom. When he came back he had the best disinfectant he could manage under the circumstances.

"Turn over." Grabbing a scrap of material, he walked to the bed and sat down on the mattress to examine the skin around the jewel. It was red and infected-looking. "This is going to hurt a little."

She sighed and turned her face toward him. "Go ahead."

He dribbled the salt water onto her jewel, using the scrap to catch the dribbles before they hit the mattress. She jerked and her breath hissed out of her. "Stay still." He poured the rest over the jewel slowly, using it all up. Then he put the container and material aside and blew gently over the wound to dry the water.

He straightened and pulled the blankets over her. "That's the best I can do right now. We'll do it again tomorrow if it looks like it needs it."

"Thank you." She settled down on her side and looked up at him.

His gaze searched her lovely face—her pretty eyes that seemed to be weighing him every time they lighted on him, the curve of her full mouth, the slant of her cheekbones, the fall of her hair that his fingers itched to stroke.

She smiled as if she knew what he was thinking. Maybe his expression gave him away. "I offered you my body and I know you want me. Why not take me? We're stuck here all day with nothing to do."

"And you think that's an excuse to have sex? It's just something to kill time?"

She shrugged. "Why not?"

He ground his teeth together. Clearly, although she could now feel, not all of the old Evangeline had washed away.

Sighing, she flopped onto her back. "Tell me about yourself, Anatol, why are you so odd?"

"Odd?"

"You've never been like the others at Belai. You've always held yourself apart, disappearing at strange times, not attending many of the social functions."

"I think one could make the argument you never attended *any* of the social functions, Evangeline. Not really. Your emotions have been absent, leaving you an empty shell. An automaton."

She stared up at him. "Don't be cruel."

"I wasn't trying to be cruel. I'm just trying to make you see the truth."

She looked away. "Well, don't. Anyway, no one cared where my emotions were."

"If you say so." He'd always cared.

"They cared if I would sleep with them or not, or whether I could do something that would move them upward in our social circles. No one ever cared about *me*."

That was true, though he'd cared for her. Likely he'd been the only one.

She made a sound of frustration. "You changed the subject. Tell me why you're odd."

"Odd." He gave a small, cold-sounding chuckle. "I was often absent because I escaped Belai whenever I could. At least, the building itself. I practiced swordplay with the Imperial Guard—"

"That explains it."

"Explains what?"

She shook her head. "Never mind."

"I practiced swordplay with them, helped them train."

"So that's how you fought those three men in the alley."

He nodded. "Like I said, I trained with the guard when they'd let me. They were usually eager for sparring partners. I also tended horses in the stable and walked the city streets whenever I could. Borrowed books from the depository and read them in the park."

She propped herself up on an elbow and the blanket fell down, exposing her breasts with their tight red nipples. He looked away. "Why?" She sounded mystified.

"I wanted more from life than what being J'Edaeii offered me. I was searching for that *more*."

"Did you ever find it?"

He looked down at her. "Yes, but I found it back where I started.

Unfortunately, by the time I found her, she was already too damaged to see me clearly."

"Who?"

"You." He couldn't believe he'd said it out loud, yet there it was.

"Me?" She laughed and looked away from him. "You're insane. Are you saying you've been . . . what? . . . admiring me from a distance for years? That's completely—"

He had her pinned beneath him in a heartbeat, his gaze boring into hers. Her breath caught as she stared up at him with surprise and fear on her face. "True. It's true, Evangeline."

Her words and breath seemed to leave her.

He rolled away from her, sitting on the edge of the bed. Damn it, it was too soon for admissions like that. What was he thinking? He'd scare her away.

"Anatol?"

He said nothing.

"Anatol, you're playing with me. Why?"

"I'm not playing." To his own ears, he sounded miserable. That's because he was.

She laid a small, warm hand on his shoulder, her touch making him stiffen. "I don't know what to say."

Yes, he didn't either. That wasn't something he'd never intended to say to her. Now he was afraid to open his mouth lest something even worse came out.

She slid out from the blankets and came around to face him. He wasn't sure what he'd been expecting, but it wasn't what she did. Pushing his hands to the side, she straddled him, her cunt coming flush against his cock with only the thin material of his underwear separating them. His cock noticed the heat of her sex so close, the press of her breasts against him, and went to hard, almost painful attention.

"What are you doing?" He gritted his teeth. If she continued this, he would pin her to the bed, part her thighs, and thrust his cock root-deep inside her. It was too soon for that.

"I don't know," she answered in a whisper, her voice trembling.

He looked up at her and saw her eyes were glistening. Not in the twenty years he'd known her had he ever seen her cry. Not when she'd slipped and fallen down the stairs at the age of ten and broken her arm. Not when she'd failed her quarterly magick test in front of everyone at the age of fourteen. He'd thought she wasn't capable of it.

Lifting her slightly, he rolled her onto the mattress and came down over her. Dipping his head to hers, he slowly rubbed his lips across her mouth. She shuddered beneath him and his cock pulsed in response.

Shivers that had nothing to do with the cold made goose bumps rise on her arms and legs. Anatol pressed his lips to hers and rubbed slowly, deliberately, like she was a luscious treat he was savoring. Her body responded to his kiss in a way it never had before, her nipples going hard and the area between her thighs becoming warm and aching in a pleasurable way. Her breathing coming faster, she gripped his shoulders and pressed her mouth more firmly to his, wanting more of the sensation.

He gave it to her, sliding his mouth more firmly over hers and forcing his tongue between her lips. It brushed up against hers with a jolt of eroticism that registered in parts of her body much farther south.

Hiking his knee up between her thighs, she rubbed against him like a cat wanting to be petted. For the first time in her sexual life, she wanted *more* from a man. She wanted to be touched, kissed, to be given pleasure and to give it in return. To experience a sexual climax.

Oh, she knew what orgasms were. She'd even achieved a couple stuttering and unfulfilling ones in the black of night with her sheets in a twist, her hand plunged between her thighs and her eyes squeezed shut. She'd wanted to know what they were and she'd been less than impressed.

But now, with her emotions running through her body as hard and as hot as her blood, she wondered if there could be more than what she'd forced her body to experience those few times. She wondered if maybe Anatol was the man to show her.

He nipped her bottom lip and slid his tongue back into her mouth. Experimentally, she explored his shoulders and upper arms, enjoying the flex and bulge of the build of a man who used his muscles on a regular basis. Ropy strength coiled in his body in a way that made her feel deliciously vulnerable and feminine. It wasn't often that she was with a man who had a body like Anatol's. Mostly they'd been Belai born and raised, pampered from birth, with soft limbs and even softer hands.

One of Anatol's rough hands, calloused from swordplay, no doubt, covered her breast. She arched against him, pushing her hardened nipple into his palm. He shuddered against her and nipped her lip again, as he worked her nipple with his thumb and forefinger until she moaned deep in her throat.

"I want you, Anatol," she breathed. "Please, don't stop."

"How many men have you been with?" he murmured against her lips.

She breathed out sharply, trying to form the ability to answer his question. "I don't know. Too many to count."

"Women?"

"Yes, I've been with women, too. Many."

He eased his hand between her thighs and found her clit. Stroking it back and forth with just the right pressure, he growled into her ear. "I'm going to make you forget them all."

Her breath caught in her throat as he pushed first one broad finger deep into her and then a second. Thrusting in and out, he rocked her back and forth on the bed. Pleasure rose up in her, a drowning rhythm that kept time with his hand.

"Does it feel good?" he murmured.

"Yes," she breathed.

He thumbed her clit, working his fingers a little harder and faster. "Do you want my cock inside you?"

"Yes." Her fingers found the bedclothes and fisted, holding on against the onslaught of sensation.

He shifted downward and covered her clit with his mouth, sucking it into his mouth and tonguing it as he thrust his fingers in and out of her in a rhythm that made her moan. The pleasure that had been welling up in her body crested, overflowed, crashed down in a wave over her. She cried out, her toes curling, her finger gripping the blankets and the muscles of her sex milking his pistoning fingers. It went on and on. She couldn't think; she could only feel the sensation of her climax sapping all the worry and tension from her body. Her brain stopped and her body ruled. It was glorious and overwhelming.

"Anatol," she breathed when it finally ebbed.

He remained between her thighs, licking her all over. His fingers explored every fold of her, petted her sensitive clit until she shivered and shuddered. "You are beautiful," he breathed against her inner thigh. "When you come . . ." he trailed off, his voice shaking.

"Come up here. Take me if you think so. I want you."

He only shook his head and laved her slit, pushing his tongue deep inside her. The sight of his dark head between her pale thighs ignited something deep inside her again. He caressed her climax-sensitive clit with the pad of his finger and her back arched as she moaned. She was shameless in her desire for more, like a sponge long dried up and now thrown into the ocean. Again he pushed her into orgasm. When it was spent, all she could do was lay limp and exhausted on the bed.

He came down beside her and she rolled to her side, facing away from him. Inexplicable emotion welled in her, tears pricking her eyes until they hurt. She wouldn't let them fall. She'd never cried in her whole life that she could remember. It had always been a point of pride for her. She made a dry sobbing sound, pushing the tears away. They wouldn't go away. *Damn it, they wouldn't go away.*

"What's wrong?"

She shook her head. "I don't know." She couldn't name the feelings she had now and didn't know where they came from. They just assaulted her and she had no way to control them or beat them into submission. "I hate this. I hate it."

"Just let it go, Evangeline. Cry. Scream. Do what you need to do with the emotion you have bottled up inside you. Go ahead. It's all right."

The tears came like a flood, breaking down the last of the walls she'd built up over so many years, washing away the bitterness and sadness that had forced her to build them in the first place. Her body shook as she sobbed in Anatol's arms, letting it all go.

Anatol didn't say anything. He was only a warm presence at her back, holding her tight as she cried, until all her tears were spent and she fell into a deep, dreamless sleep.

Evangeline picked her way down the icy street with a basket of three-day-old bread clutched in one freezing hand. At least it wasn't four-day-old bread. If it was soaked in a little water, it would be edible.

The wind whipped at her thin cloak and kissed her skin mercilessly. Hunger had become a constant companion. She dreamed of rivers of beef stew navigated by boats made from loaves of fresh, warm, flaky bread. No amount of this old stuff, which was all they could afford, ever seemed to fill her.

She remembered all those meals she used to pass up at Belai, afraid she'd ruin her dancer's figure. She couldn't believe she'd ever refused food—she never would again. In fact, she would never take anything for granted again—not food, not a warm bed or a cozy, soft coat. Certainly not safety.

It was amazing how a few weeks of hardship made one see so much clearer. All the petty, stupid things she used to care about— the proper dress to wear to a party, whom to sit next to at dinner for the greatest social advantage—all of it was crushed to dust. It had all disappeared during that first week when she'd seen heads roll, worried for her own head, and all her walls had come tumbling down.

She no longer lusted for spacious, cold apartments in Belai. Now all she wanted was a warm room, a full belly, and someone she trusted to share it with. That sounded like a fine life to her now, whereas a month ago she would have considered it squalor.

Was Anatol that person she could trust? Should they aspire to a cozy, warm rented apartment in a poor part of town? Rent cheap enough that they could afford firewood and fresh bread? Food in their cupboards? Warm water from the taps?

Sounded like heaven to her.

Trudging past a narrow alley, she heard a low sobbing. Stopping, she went back, straining to hear the soft sound. It was coming from a ways down, near a pile of rubbish at the back of a cook- shop's rear door.

Normally she would have lingered a moment, waiting to make sure it was safe to step into the concealed area. The alleys of the city of Milzyr were no longer anything anyone could call safe. However she had her magick and her magick could feel the despair coming from the sobbing individual—genuine grief and hopelessness. This was no trap.

So she secured her grip on her bread basket and stepped into snow that went as high as her calf. Wincing from the cold, she made her way to the huddled shape. It was small, and the sobbing childish.

Kneeling down, she set her basket on the snow. "Are you all right?" she asked the dirty bundle of fabric.

The material shifted and a small, feminine face came into view. The girl was perhaps seven or eight. "My parents are dead. I don't know what to do or where to go." Her eyes were hollow and haunted. Her speech was educated. A nobleman's daughter, perhaps. Many of them had been orphaned as a result of the beheadings. The rabble was happy to kill off the parents, but they didn't know what to do with the offspring. Oftentimes they were turned out into the streets to find their own way.

Evangeline sighed, glancing away and licking her lips. Sweet Joshui, what could she do for this child? She and Anatol couldn't even take care of themselves. The girl gazed longingly at the bread basket. Well, at least she could offer that much.

Evangeline held the basket out to her. "Go ahead."

The girl snatched up a piece of bread and tried to stuff the whole thing in her mouth, but it was very hard, of course, and she ended up having to suck on the end of it, then gnaw on it when it was soft enough to bite.

Evangeline let her eat for a while, though her feet were growing numb in the snow. "How many nights have you spent on your own?"

"I don't know. Many. I can't remember now." The girl spoke between bites. "My parents were taken by some of the rioters. I hid under the bed when they came. Once the men were gone, I snuck out."

"That was smart. The men probably went back to ransack your house. They would have found you there." And there was no telling what would have happened to the child then. Not all the young girls were fortunate enough to simply be turned out as penniless orphans into the street. Not when ransacking men found them. Females always seemed to have to endure the most violence.

Of course, there was no telling what would happen to her now, either. Nothing good, if she stayed out here on the streets. She couldn't leave her. Evangeline could only think of one place to take the girl, though it was hardly ideal.

She stood. "Come with me. I know a place where you can get warm and have a meal that's much better than that old bread."

The girl stared up at her with dark mistrust in her eyes. Ah, they learned so quickly. That was good—it was a credit to the child. In this brave new world mistrust would serve her well.

Evangeline smiled and tasted the air for an emotion that wasn't suspicion. "What's your name?"

The child blinked. "Marta."

Evangeline found a thread of calm from a patron of a local cook-shop and traded a little bit of it for the girl's mistrust. The patron would be confused for a moment, but he would live. It was important the girl trust her enough to come with her. The manipulation was for her own good. "Marta, I promise I won't hurt you. You're lost and I know what it is to be lost. I only want to help." She stretched her hand out.

Marta hesitated a moment, then, clutching the bread in one hand, she took Evangeline's hand and stood. "I trust you."

"Good. Now come with me. It's a long walk to where we need to go."

Seven

They trudged through the treacherous streets, dodging mounds of snow and trying not to slip on the slick parts. Finally they reached the Temple of Dreams and she showed Marta inside. The interior was warm and smelled of spice. Immediately both she and Marta relaxed, taking deep breaths of air and allowing the comfort to seep past their clothes and into their bones. They stood shivering in the foyer and looking very out of place. Soft music played from one of the inner rooms. The large living room spread before them was thankfully empty of people.

Evangeline took in the furnishings with the eye of someone who had once known quality. The divans, chairs, tables, and fainting couches all smacked of money and good taste. She could not have decorated the room better herself.

A tall, thin woman with long, unbound black hair passed them, did a double take, and then approached. "This is no place for a child," the woman chided Evangeline.

"Yes, I know that, but the streets are worse. Is Lilya here?"

The black-haired woman gave Evangeline a look up and down, taking in her dirty, threadbare clothes and the food basket. "Lilya is busy right now."

The woman wore pride just as well as her lovely silk gown, but Evangeline wore her pride even better. Her jaw locked, she stepped forward and stared in challenge at the woman. "Get me Lilya. *Now*."

The woman took a step backward, doubt flashing through her amber eyes.

Just then Lilya passed through the entryway on the far side of the richly decorated room. "Dora, it's all right. I know her."

Dora gave Evangeline a puzzled look and drifted away.

Lilya approached with a smile on her face and warmly embraced her. Evangeline had a moment of wistfulness so strong her knees almost buckled. The material of Lilya's dress was a sturdy, expensive gray brocade. The heavy, full skirts fell to high-buttoned black boots, just the kind of boots that Evangeline had lusted over in a store window only a month ago. Sweet Joshui, had it only been a month? It felt like two years. The perfume Lilya wore enveloped her in a lingering cloud of luxury and Lilya's skin was soft, as soft as hers had once been before the cold and the grime and the hardship.

For a moment it made Evangeline want to run away to the Temple of Dreams, but that would mean leaving Anatol and she couldn't do that. She wasn't sure why, but she couldn't. They'd been through too much together, she guessed. He'd done too much for her. She felt like she owed him some loyalty, gratitude, something like that. Surely that had to be the reason why.

It was odd how her feelings for him had overtaken her desire for fine things. That was definitely a first in her life. Never had the intangible, the *emotional*, held sway over the tangible.

Evangeline cleared her throat of a sudden clog of wistfulness. Gods, stupid stuff. It always got in the way and made everything so much less clear. "Lilya, please meet Marta. She's had a rough couple of days." She fell silent for a moment. "You helped us once and I thought perhaps you might be able to help her, too. Help where I am unable."

Lilya knelt and smiled into the frightened child's face. "Hello, Marta. I bet you're cold and hungry."

Marta nodded and sniffled loudly.

Lilya held out her hand. "We have a kitchen here. I'm sure I can find you something to eat."

Marta flew into Lilya's arms as if she'd suddenly been reunited with a long-lost relative. Lilya's surprise filtered up to Evangeline, followed closely by a rush of pleasure. Lilya hugged the child, and then stood, holding on to her hand.

"Can you help her find safety?" Evangeline asked.

"She can't stay here, obviously, but I think I may know someone who can house her. A good friend of mine who lives uptown."

Evangeline let out a breath of relief. If Lilya had refused to help Marta, she hadn't been sure at all of what she'd be able to manage for the girl.

Lilya glanced down at the basket of bread. "You look like you could use a meal, too. Would you like to stay?"

She couldn't turn down food. Not now. In fact, she was salivating at the very idea of something other than hard bread filling her stomach. But Anatol. How could she enjoy good food while he starved? No matter how badly hunger gnawed at her, she couldn't do that. She looked at the door. "I—"

Lilya smiled as if she knew exactly what she was thinking. "We can make up a package to send back to Anatol."

Evangeline relaxed and smiled. "Then, yes."

The place seemed empty of patrons, unless the Temple of Dreams got a fair amount of well-dressed females. Though she knew there were men employed here, too. Apparently it was too early in the day for much clientele. She and Marta followed Lilya down narrow corridors decorated with thick runner rugs, accent tables with vases of flowers, and mirrors, through numerous sitting rooms where expensively clad women reclined, talking and laughing together.

"This is one of the few women-owned and -operated businesses in Milzyr. Ellabeth, the owner, is a good manager with excellent sense," said Lilya. "She's one of the most powerful citizens in the city." The words went unspoken, but hung between them—*now that the royals and noble people are gone.*

Evangeline said nothing. She only followed behind Marta, who had a death grip on Lilya's hand. She supposed that Lilya seemed far more like her mother than she had, since she was dressed in rags.

The kitchen was a huge affair with a modern heated cooking surface and a cold chest all powered by elusian crystal. The delicious smell hit her immediately. The women had eaten porridge with cinnamon for breakfast and it immediately made Evangeline's stomach clench with ravenousness.

Lilya sat Marta and Evangeline down at the table at the far end of the room and served them both steaming bowls of porridge topped with butter and sprinkled with cinnamon. Marta fell to it like a starving animal and Evangeline wanted to do the same, but she forced herself to eat with some decorum. All the same, not a word was spoken until both their bowls were empty and Lilya had served them seconds. Evangeline had never really liked porridge all that much when she'd lived at Belai, but now it tasted like the food Joshui likely ate in paradise.

When they worked on their second bowls, Lilya got out thick slices of brown bread, a hunk of cheese, and thin slices of meat. Slathering the pieces of bread with fresh butter, she made several sandwiches and wrapped them in thin cloth. After she'd finished, she turned toward them. "For Anatol."

Evangeline finally set her spoon down. "Thank you for the meal and sandwiches."

Marta pushed her bowl away and also thanked her. Leaning back in her chair, the girl smiled and all the worry and distrust disappeared from her face. Evangeline revised her age downward a little.

Just then a young woman with auburn hair entered the kitchen. "I heard we have guests."

"Yes," Lilya answered. "This is Evangeline and Marta, Lissan. I think Marta might be going to stay with Annalise, if she's amenable to it. She has recently lost her family."

Marta's eyes welled up with tears suddenly and she leaned forward, covering her face with her hands as though she was embarrassed to be showing her emotion.

"Oh." Lissan's smile fell. "I'm very sorry to hear that." She walked over and touched Marta's shoulder. The girl looked up into Lissan's kind face. "I lost my parents when I was about your age, too."

"You did?" asked the child in a quavering voice.

Lissan nodded solemnly. "It was a house fire. I was the only one who got out." She pressed her lips together for a moment. "Would you like to come with me into the sitting room? We can talk." She looked up at Lilya. "Is that all right?"

"Of course. I think Marta could use someone to talk to. I will pay a visit to Annalise with her later this morning."

Marta surprised Evangeline by giving her a hug and a kiss on the cheek. "Thank you," she whispered. Then she slipped down from the chair and followed Lissan out of the room.

Lilya watched them go and then turned to Evangeline. "You did a wonderful thing by bringing her here. These days, most people would have just passed her by. There are so many orphans on the street."

"I wasn't sure if you could do anything to help her. I just hope she'll be all right."

"Oh, I think it will be a good long while until she's all right, but I do think that Annalise will take her in. Annalise used to work here a long time ago. She's married now, to a wonderful, kind man."

"And he won't mind letting a child stay with them?"

"I would be very surprised if he did. I don't think you'll have to worry about Marta any longer. She'll be well cared for."

Evangeline smiled and looked down at the cuffs of her woolen pull where they lay on the table. Seeing how dirty and frayed they were, she quickly put them in her lap, away from Lilya's view.

"And how are you doing, Evangeline?" Lilya asked softly.

She glanced up at her. "Better than the dead bodies on the palace steps. Not as good as others. But we're not starving. We have a roof over our heads. Running water."

"It will get better."

"Maybe. One day." She glanced around the kitchen. "I see no men here. Only women. Don't men serve here at the temple, too?"

"We do have some men, but mostly we're women."

"Because your patronage is mostly male."

"Yes."

"But there must be fewer clients now. I mean, I'm sure many of the people who came before were royals or nobles."

"There has been a slight decrease in our patronage. However I think that as the social condition for the lower classes increases it won't last long."

Evangeline tried not to look or sound sour, but it was hard. "So you were in favor of the revolution."

"Of the revolution, yes, no doubt. Not of the aftermath, however. Not of the bloodshed and the new influx of orphans it has brought. Not many are in favor of all that."

Evangeline looked into her lap, her lips twisting. "Could have fooled me. Have you ever attended a beheading? Seems lots of people are in favor of it. Revel in it, in fact." She felt a heavy gaze on her—one that wasn't Lilya's. She looked up to see the shadowed form of a man in the doorway of the kitchen. He seemed to be staring at her. Evangeline stared straight back until the figure moved away.

"Yes, well." Lilya sighed. "We don't live in a perfect world."

That was the understatement of the century. Evangeline bit her lip until she tasted blood. This was not a good topic of conversation. She liked Lilya; she'd done so much to help them. If she wanted to keep liking her, they needed to change the topic of conversation.

"So do you get many odd requests?" She couldn't keep the note of curiosity out of her voice. Then Evangeline's eyes bulged as she realized the impoliteness of the question she'd just blurted. "I mean—"

Lilya laughed. "It's all right. I don't mind talking about what I do. I suppose if I did mind talking about it I should probably stop doing it, yes?"

"Some people are prudish about these things. No one in the palace that I ever met, of course, but others."

"Are you calling me prudish?" Lilya laughed.

Evangeline laughed with her. It felt good. It was the first time she'd felt any sort of levity in a while. "No, I'm not. Not you. I apologize." Talking with Lilya reminded her of how she used to talk with Annetka so long ago. Could it be she was developing a friendship with Lilya? That would be nice.

"To answer your question, most requests are relatively tame, but our job is to provide a way for people to find pleasure without judgment or repercussion. So occasionally we have requests that go beyond the ordinary, people who want to be tied up or to tie us up, people who want two women at once or two men. Some people crave pain with their pleasure, or like to give pain with pleasure. As long as the acts are consensual and as long as no one is hurt who doesn't desire it, anything the patron wants is delivered."

"How did you come into this profession?"

Lilya paused, pressing her lips together. "Well, that's a long story. Do you want some tea?"

Evangeline nodded and Lilya poured them both cups of steaming chamomile, then she sat down opposite her. "My background was poor and filled with hardship. I came from a destitute family and my father died when I was young. I had no other family, so I was forced to live on the streets."

"I'm sorry."

"I survived." She went into detail, telling Evangeline how she'd made it, the places she'd slept, and how she'd fed herself. "I never turned to common prostitution. In fact, I managed to keep my virginity until I was over eighteen years old. That's when I met Ivan." She looked into her cup.

After a moment of silence, Evangeline prompted her. "Ivan?"

"A bastard I thought I loved. We'll just skip that part of the story and say I almost died. If it hadn't been for a special and unexpected friend of mine, I would've."

"The mysterious man to whom you're indebted. The reason you helped me and Anatol."

She smiled. "The very one."

Evangeline played with the delicate handle of the teacup. "You've had a very hard life, but you don't sound like you came from a background like that. Your speech is educated."

Lilya's full red lips twisted. "Ah, yes, that's where Annalise comes in. After I'd recovered from my ordeal, she befriended me. She asked me to come here and consider this as a lifestyle. I declined at first, but eventually I decided to come and stay for a while. To watch and consider. After I understood the philosophy of this place, the reason behind what we do here, then I fell in love with the Temple of Dreams. I agreed to work here. I've been here ever since."

"The philosophy?"

"Love by choice. Every courtesan runs her practice as she sees fit. I hand select each of my clients after careful interviews. Typically I take men who are ineffectual in their personal lives, the lonely, the hopelessly shy or awkward. I don't have many clients and my work isn't all about sex. I'm a paid companion, essentially."

"And you thought Anatol and I might fit here," Evangeline ventured, "then erroneously interpreted our behavior for love and decided you'd made a mistake."

Lilya threw her head back and laughed. "Not erroneously, Evangeline. Not erroneously. You just haven't seen it yet."

Evangeline shook her head and stared into her tea. It was best she left that alone. In any case, her emotions for Anatol were too tangled to know what they were. And *love*. Well, she didn't know love. She'd never known it and had no idea what it felt like.

"You and Anatol will find your way," Lilya finished.

"So you can't be in love to work here?"

She shook her head. "No, once you fall in love, if it's pure and deep, you can't have sex with anyone else. Makes working here a bit ineffective."

"So you've never been in love, not since you came to work here?"

Lilya gave a small smile. "No, and I never will. Annalise fell in love and then she had to leave. I truly adore it here, so maybe it's for the best." She fell silent for several moments, smiling wistfully. "Or maybe falling in love would be even better, the true kind of love with a man who would treat you like a princess and never raise a hand against you. Maybe one day you can tell me, Evangeline."

A little while later, Evangeline trudged her way back through the treacherous streets to the boardinghouse.

"Where have you been?" Anatol fairly accosted her as soon as she crossed the threshold. "It's been hours!"

Unwinding her makeshift scarf, she felt how chilly it was in the room and wound it back around. She handed over the sack of sandwiches wrapped in material. "This is from Lilya."

"Lilya? You went to the Temple of Dreams?" He looked suspicious. "Why?"

"Are you afraid I'll leave you to go to work over there, Anatol?" She shook her head. "Oddly enough, even though that life might give me some semblance of what I used to have, I won't. I went there for another reason." She told him about Marta and taking the child to the temple.

He opened one of the sandwiches as she talked and bit into it. Closing his eyes, he groaned as if in ecstasy. It was a strangely sexual sound and she noticed it in every part of her body. He polished it off in record time and started in on a second after offering her the sandwich, which she declined.

Once he'd finished, he set the remnants of the material aside and stared at her so intently that she winced. "You used your magick, didn't you? On the little girl?"

Sweet Joshui, how could he know that? How did he see the truth of things so annoyingly clearly? Or maybe he was just presuming. "Yes, I had to. She didn't trust me in a situation where she should, a situation in which she *needed* to trust me. I had to manufacture her emotional response to me for her own good."

He nodded. "You're just lucky that no one noticed."

"I won't do it again."

"Using magick is second nature to us. Of course you will. Just be careful." He paused and gave her a suspicious look. "Now explain that bit about not going to work at the Temple of Dreams, would you?"

She swallowed hard, sorry she'd said anything at all about it.

Wandering over to the window, she gazed down onto the street. It was close to twilight and all the factory workers were returning home from their shift. Steam and smoke belched from the tower of the metal working factory behind Belai, spoiling the cold winter blue sky. She'd be lucky to find a job there. At the thought, she closed her eyes. *Oh, sweet Joshui.*

"You saved me, Anatol." She opened her eyes. "If it wasn't for you finding me in the palace and getting me out, my head would have rolled with all the others. I don't intend to abandon you anytime soon."

She could feel his body heat behind her. He leaned on the windowsill, a hand on either side of her, pinning her there. Her body tightened, although being trapped there by Anatol wasn't exactly an unpleasant thing. His heat warmed her and he smelled good—like the soap he used to bathe with that morning.

"Are you sure there's not something more to it?" he murmured.

"Don't get too confident, Anatol." Scowling, she pushed away from him. "I'm just saying I feel loyal to you, nothing more."

His eyelids had lowered a little and his pupils had darkened. Men were always the same. They always thought with their dicks. "Maybe one day you'll feel more. I *want* you to feel more for me, Evangeline."

She blinked. Though few men thought of any emotion that went past lust, especially not love, fewer talked of such things openly. "Don't waste your time on me, Anatol. I'm too damaged. Even if you could heal me, I wouldn't be worth it."

"I don't believe that."

She snorted and turned away. "Then you're a fool."

He gripped her upper arm and whirled her to face him. "Don't say that. Remember that I can see into the true heart of you. I have since the moment I took notice of you over a decade ago." He cupped her chin gently in his strong fingers, forcing her to look at him. "I know you better than you know yourself. I know the value that is in you. Don't discount yourself that way within my earshot, all right?"

He actually sounded angry. "That's a pretty arrogant thing to say."

"Maybe, but it's the truth. I'll never give up on you."

"Because you love me," she whispered.

He released her chin and her upper arm. "Yes, Evangeline." He stared into her eyes. "Because I love you."

She blinked again, not knowing how to react to that. Not even knowing if she could continue to look him in the eye. She turned away, but he caught her by the arm. This time when he turned her to face him, his hot mouth came down on hers, his lips firm and demanding. She stiffened in his arms, surprised. His arms snaked around her waist and pulled her flush against him as his tongue eased into her mouth and brushed up against hers.

She relaxed against him in spite of herself, her body molding to his. He moved her back toward the bed a few inches, then stopped. His mouth parted from hers and he looked down at her as if fighting with himself. Then he swore under her breath and turned away from her.

"Anatol?" she asked as he walked away from her. "What's wrong?"

He grabbed his coat and went toward the door. Pausing in the threshold, he half turned toward her. "When we make love for the first time, I want it to be *making love*, Evangeline. For both of us."

Then he was gone.

That night the weather was bad. The next day the roads and streets were packed with heavy snow, but the city's inhabitants made ruts to walk in the drifts in order to keep the city running. Needing to get away from Anatol and the way he stared at her so intently, the words he had to say to her—*the things he expected of her*—and to get away from the sight of his strong hands, which made ripples of want go through her whenever he touched anything in the room,

Evangeline took the few coins they possessed and offered to go out to buy some supplies.

When she'd asked Anatol where the money had come from, he'd looked away from her and mumbled something about helping in the stables for pay. But she couldn't remember him ever smelling of horse. Of course, he always bathed before he came to bed.

The thought of the bed had been what had finally driven her out of the room, down the stairs, and into the street, where the frigidness of the air stole her breath.

The first thing she'd done, heedless of the snow chilling her feet and legs, was walk past the steps of Belai. It was empty, the executions suspended due to the weather. Fingers curling around the cold bars in front, she breathed in clean air and closed her eyes, imagining that the snow covering the bloodstains, making everything look so fresh and clean, had also turned back time. Ignoring the sight of the guillotine that not even the pretty white snow could banish, she imagined all was as it had been before the revolt.

But of course, once she opened her eyes the illusion was shattered. Emotion tightened her throat and her face twisted as she tried to thrust it away like a bit of rotten fruit. The more she fought, the more it sank its claws into her. There was no getting rid of the grief and sorrow that seemed ever-present. It was only momentarily eclipsed by the confusion and lust that Anatol made her feel.

Turning away from the palace gates, she headed slowly and clumsily back into the city center, needing to find food for herself and Anatol before she returned to the room. After buying half a loaf of two-day-old bread—they were going to be eating a lot of bread in the coming days—she headed back to the boardinghouse. She'd wrapped her feet and legs as best she could with what was available, but cold had long since bitten into her flesh. Her nose was frozen and her thighs had gone numb.

Noticing that the alleys were clearer of snow because they were sheltered by the buildings, she headed down one to take a short-cut. She was so preoccupied by the cold that she didn't notice the flicker of emotion in the alley that would've alerted her to another presence.

Not a good presence. Not positive emotion.

Something moved out of the corner of her eye and she turned her head to see a dark form unfold itself from the ground and stand like some great black monster. She came to a stop in the middle of the alley, thinking about retreating back the way she'd come. It was probably too late for that.

"Well, well, what do we have here?" The man's dirty, bearded face spilt into a grotesque smile.

She glared at him, more angered than afraid, and tried to hasten past him.

He caught her by the upper arm before she got far. The bread fell from her hands and lodged in a small snowdrift. She wrenched away from him. "Leave me alone."

He pushed her up against the wall of the building behind her, his forearm pinning her throat. "Do you hear that?" He said nothing for a moment to emphasize the silence. "That's the sound of no one to help you. Seems you took the wrong alley, girl."

This man was not like the three louts in the alley who'd thought she was a whore. Her magick tasted him on a deeper level. This man was a different animal than she'd ever encountered.

Evil. Evil through and through. There was something wrong with him. He didn't see her as a person, he saw her as a *thing*. And he wanted to make that thing hurt.

He pulled at her clothing with his free hands, exposing too much skin to the cold air. Now she was afraid. She kicked out with all her strength, catching the man in the stomach. He flew backward, holding his gut, and she stood up, ready to fight him, though he was easily twice her size.

Realization slammed into her. Blessed Joshui, there was no way she could defeat this man. Her throat closed and her hands trembled. *Panic.*

Barely aware she was doing it, she reached out a thread of her power and felt his emotions. Thick, heavy—cloying—they wrapped a cloak of hate around her until her body seemed poisoned with it. The man would kill her, but first he'd rape her. She was nothing to him—an object to make scream and cry. Hurting her would make him happy for a little while. She'd wandered into a nightmare complete with a real monster.

The man stood up, swung a hand free to show her that he wasn't injured, and smiled.

For the first time since her ordeal had started, Evangeline was absolutely and perfectly terrified. She cemented her numb feet on the icy cobblestone and prepared to fight. She wouldn't go down without taking her pound of flesh from this beast.

Then a flicker of another emotional stream came to her from near the mouth of the alley. The person was troubled, worried, a bit regretful. Overall, however, this person was calm. She leapt on the opportunity, snatching the emotion from the monster in front of her and the unsuspecting individual walking down the street and exchanging it. She didn't just take a little, she gouged into them both and traded every drop she could plunder.

It was her only hope and she was taking a huge risk. She'd just transferred all that anger and hatred into another vessel. The person could be just as bad—she couldn't imagine anyone being worse—than the man in front of her. She might have just exchanged one problem for two.

The monster shook his head and took a step backward, touching his temple. He looked up at her with confusion on his face.

She bolted for the street, leaving her bread behind. Fabric-wrapped feet slipping on the ice, she reached the mouth of the alley, where she was immediately blocked by the person she'd transferred the anger and hatred into.

Staggering backward, she started to slip. A strong hand snaked out and grabbed her by the upper arm, steadying her. The man was big, his dark brows drawn together with the rage she'd placed in him. He was a just a little older than her. Dark brown eyes. Full mouth. This was the kind of man she'd avoid in an alley and she'd practically called him to her. *Bad choice, Evangeline.*

Eight

His gaze flicked behind her, caught on the monster. His frown deepened, the air of violence already clinging to him became thicker. He'd taken one look at her, then at the monster, and seemingly understood the situation.

Moving her to the side, he stalked past her and grabbed the monster by the shoulders. She should have run. She should have turned tail, forgotten the food she'd left behind, and run back to the boardinghouse. But her feet wouldn't move. Instead she watched with fascination as the two men fought.

The stranger drew back a meaty fist and punched the monster in the face. The monster fell back, swearing, and then leapt on the other man. The two toppled to the snow, punching and kicking. She inched to the mouth of the alley, ready to run if the monster was victorious. Even though she knew she should escape while she had the chance, she felt responsible for the man who'd jumped into this situation. She'd never meant for him to ride to her rescue and put his own safety in harm's way. If the monster killed him, his blood would be on her hands.

She needn't have feared. The stranger quickly got the upper hand in the fight and she watched with horror as he bashed the monster's head against the wall over and over with a bone-chilling brutality. The monster crumpled to the snow, blood leaking from his head.

That one would not be raping and murdering any other women. Not ever again.

The man turned and pointed at her. Inanely, Evangeline noticed he had blood on his hands. He stalked to her. "*You*. You did that to me, didn't you? Somehow you made me insane with rage and called me to you."

"No." She held up a hand to ward him off. "I didn't. Not all of it, anyway. I never called to you. I never meant for you to come charging into the fight. I was just trying to get away."

He cocked his head to the side. "So you admit you manipulated my emotion. You've got some kind of magick, don't you? You're Jeweled." He grabbed her and turned her around, yanking her shirt up to reveal the jewel embedded at the small of her back. He held her firm, despite her squirming.

"Let me go," she yelled at him.

He let her go and she stumbled forward. She turned, casting him a look of rage and groped for the bread in the snowdrift. "I suppose you'll turn me in. Have my head cut off on the palace steps. Would that make you happy? Would that give you justice? It's not my fault, you know. You don't deserve to die for having brown eyes, do you? Well, I don't deserve to die for having magick. Do you want to see my blood run just because I happen to have been born with a specific talent?"

The man hung his head, suddenly looking weary. "No. I don't want that."

She stilled, holding her half loaf close to her chest. The regret she'd felt from him initially had returned. "Who are you?" Her guess was that he was some animal who'd done horrible things during the riots and now felt guilty. There was something familiar about him, as if she'd seen him somewhere before.

"I'm—" He shook his head. "No. Just go on. Get out of here." He waved at the mouth of the alley with a bloody hand.

"You're letting me . . . go?"

"Of course." He looked up at her sharply. His face was brutal, not quite handsome, though it was compelling. His eyes were keen—intelligent. "What did you think I was—" Understanding overcame his face. "Go. Get out here. I have no quarrel with you."

Heaviness laced his words. It made her study him a second longer, wonder about him.

"Go!" he barked.

She went.

"Why are you all wet?" Anatol scolded her as soon as she opened the door. "Did you fall in the snow? Get those clothes off. You need a bath. There's a little warm water today."

She shook her head, her teeth chattering. "We already used our water allotment."

He pushed a hand through his hair in an expression of frustration. "Yes. All right, take off those clothes and get into the bed. Cover up and get warm."

She handed over the food and started doing exactly what he'd said. "There are stores open now. People are out, but not in hordes yet." She paused. "The beheadings have been suspended because of the weather, of course."

He caught her by the upper arms and forced her to look up at him. "What happened to you out there today? *Damn it*, I knew I should have gone with you."

She looked down at his feet and licked her lips. She didn't want to tell him about what had happened because she didn't want to relive it, but he needed to know. "Let me finish undressing and I'll tell you."

He released her and soon she was snuggled deep into the bed, finding all the warmth she possibly could. She sighed, resting her head on the pillow, and ignored the gnawing in her stomach as she told him about cutting through the alley, meeting the rapist, using her magick, and calling that strange man to her.

Anatol listened to it all in silence, stroking his fingers through her hair. "It was risky to use your magick, but I see you had no choice. You were lucky."

"I just wonder who that man was," she murmured, nuzzling into the pillow. The worst of her shakes seemed to have passed.

"Can't know for sure." He paused. "But it sounds like it could have been Gregorio Vikhin."

"What?" She raised her head from the pillow. "No, he wasn't Vikhin. That man was not an intellectual. He looked more like a street fighter."

"Looks can be deceiving. In fact, Gregorio Vikhin is often described as looking like a knuckle dragger. Big, brutish. Make no mistake, his mind is as sharp as they come."

"Why do you think it was him?"

Anatol threaded her hair through his fingers and watched it drop to the pillow. "You described him as regretful over your circumstances, as though he'd caused it. I've heard that Gregorio is happy for sparking the revolution but not so happy about the execution." Anatol paused and winced. "That was not a pun I meant to make."

"So, you think he's walking the streets in the snow, grieving the fate of the nobility?"

"Maybe not the nobles, per say. More like grieving the loss of his people's nobility. The ravening mob has turned something that could have been beautiful into a chaotic bloodbath."

Anger sparked. She bolted upright. "Beautiful? How could you think any of this could be beautiful, Anatol?"

"It's a *beautiful* thing to put the fate of the people into their hands, to create a government of the people and for the people. This is a point on which I hope one day we agree. The time of the aristocracy is over."

She knew her eyes were flashing with rage. "Yes, it's just the *execution* that's lacking."

He winced again.

"I will never see eye to eye with you on this point, Anatol. If I could go back to the way things were before the revolt, I would."

"I'm hoping that as time passes you might begin to see life in another way, Evangeline. In a larger way. I know you're capable of it."

"Don't condescend to me, Anatol."

He stared at her for a long moment, then rose from the bed. "Are you warm now?"

She nodded.

"You should try and take more care with yourself. There's no physician to treat you if you fall ill. This isn't Belai."

"It wasn't my idea to have my clothes half torn off in an attempted rape and murder."

"I know. I'm just saying that if you get sick, it could be the end of you." He looked at her. "I don't want that."

"I bet not as much as *I* don't want that."

"Turn over and let me see your jewel and tattoo."

She gave him a coy look. "Oh, come on, Anatol, just admit you want to see my bare ass again."

His jaw locked and she had a moment to feel pleased with herself. She liked throwing him off. "Your bare ass is always a pleasant sight, but I'm more concerned with the infection around the jewel setting."

She rolled onto her stomach, giving a sexy, heavy-lidded look, and shimmied the sheet and blanket down to just below her butt. He watched her with interest he tried to hide, but failed. It was there in a spark of his eyes and the way he swallowed hard. She knew she was provoking him. She was *trying* to provoke him.

Another woman might shy from sex after the ordeal she'd had, but she craved Anatol's touch right now. His hands stroked her with caring. He endeavored to please her. She was not just a *thing* to him. She was Evangeline and he *saw her*, all of her—even the bad parts. He alone could banish the taint of the monster in the alley and the dark intentions he'd had that still clung to her already battered emotions. She needed them scoured clean in a wash of the erotic bliss she knew he could give her.

But her teasing didn't work. His fingers were businesslike as they explored the flesh around her jewel. He pulled the covers over her body and paced to the window. She rolled onto her back to watch him. "So, doctor, what's your verdict."

"You're healing fine."

"Good." She couldn't help but be relieved.

He gazed out onto the street. "The snow is starting to melt. By tomorrow the town will be getting on its feet again. I need to find steady work."

She sat up. "What about me? Shouldn't I try to find work?"

He didn't look at her. "Eventually, yes, you will have to. What do you think you can do?"

"The only thing I know is magick."

"Yes, that's a problem. I have a strong back and arms, good for building things or loading ships at the dock. We'll have to think about possible professions for you, however."

"I know . . . fashion." It sounded so dumb that she wished she could call back the words. She shrank back into the pillows, waiting for him to make some scornful remark.

He looked at her, nodding. "That's something. Maybe you could get a job in a dress shop."

She relaxed at the approval in his voice and then hated herself for her reaction.

Working in a dress shop didn't sound incredibly exciting to her. Shopping in them had really always been more her thing. But times were changing, and even though she didn't like it, she knew her survival depended on her changing with them. It would be better than working in a factory. "I can look into it."

"What about sewing? Have you ever done that?"

"Yes, I've sewn a bit, when I didn't have the money for a dressmaker and needed clothing fit for the palace."

"Maybe you could build on the skill. You know fashion and you're also very creative. I remember that you can draw."

She looked up at him sharply. "You remember that?"

He nodded. "You used to trade drawings back and forth with Annetka. You showed incredible promise as an artist. I was always amazed by it, since you'd had no training."

She blinked, at a loss for words. He'd been aware of her since childhood.

"Maybe it's possible you could combine the two things," he finished.

"You're saying that I should become a dressmaker?"

"Yes, with your own designs. It's a possibility. It's a thing you might eventually find fulfillment in doing." He pushed a hand through his hair, turning away from her. "I don't know what the future holds for us. I think that the new government of Rylisk, whatever form it will take, would be foolish to discount the magicked. We are a valuable resource to this country. But last time I checked, they weren't asking my opinion. I do think, perhaps, that when the smoke clears and the call for noble blood has waned, the Jeweled may be able to walk the streets freely again. So perhaps eventually we'll both be able to carve livelihoods that involve our magick. That's what I hope will happen, anyway."

Her cheeks flushed. "What, exactly, is it you think we could do with our magick in this new world, Anatol? Will you set up a curiosities shop and throw illusions for a few coins? What can I do with my skill? Be a politician's pet and help him manipulate the emotions of voters? No one wants their emotions tampered with. In fact, I think you and I still run the risk of having our heads separated from our bodies. People with differences like ours tend to be frightening."

"Of course." He paused. "Don't forget the Revolutionaries."

"Yes, exactly." The self-proclaimed "Revolutionaries" were a group of men and women who had taken it upon themselves to hunt down all the nobles and magicked who had escaped Belai during the siege. "They would really like to see us dead."

"This morning I heard they found two J'Edaeii."

"What? Who?"

"They've taken Irena and Aleksi."

She put her hand to her mouth. They were both older, well-respected. They'd married into the Edaeii family the way she'd wanted to.

"Just be careful, Evangeline."

She lowered her hand. "Believe me, I'm not going around displaying my magick." Her head drooped as she remembered Irena and Aleksi. "You see, Anatol? We'll never be able to be out in the open. There will always be someone or something to fear."

"I don't know, Evangeline." He spread his hands. "The future is not known to any of us. Maybe we'll always have to be underground. Maybe we'll be hunted down like dogs. That's why I'm saying you should pursue a career you can accomplish without magick and we'll see."

"All I've ever had in my life to use was my looks and my willingness to have sex." She swallowed hard. "Honestly, Anatol, I should go to the Temple of Dreams. It's all I'm really suited for."

His jaw locked and something dangerous flashed in his eyes. "We've had this conversation before."

"Why are you so against the idea of it, Anatol? We could *both* go there to work. I know you say you're in love with me, but that's just silly—"

He rounded on her, arresting the end of the sentence in her throat. Fire jumped in his eyes. "Not silly, Evangeline, *true*. I don't want to make love to any woman but you. I couldn't do it. So you go, if you think that's what you want." He turned away. "I won't stop you."

She chewed her lower lip and let emotion rise up to swamp her for a moment in punishment. She deserved it; she'd hurt him. Wrapping the blanket around herself, she stood and walked to him. "I don't want to leave you," she murmured at his back.

He turned and pulled her into his arms. "Good. That's a good thing to hear, Evangeline, because I don't want you to leave me."

She wrapped her arms around him, letting the blanket fall to the floor and his body heat warm her. Nuzzling her nose into his chest, she inhaled the scent of him. "I want you to . . . make love to me, Anatol. I want to know what it feels like." The words came out as a whisper, like she was afraid to say them too loudly. She wasn't sure why.

His body tensed against hers. "Don't tempt me."

She gave a soft laugh. "Haven't you noticed that's exactly what I've been trying to do?"

"Yes, I've noticed." He made a tortured sound in his throat. "The scent of you tempts me. The sound of your breath tempts me. You tempt me even when you're not trying." He turned her and she saw that the cracked head-to-toe mirror was directly in front of them. "Look at yourself, Evangeline. You're beautiful."

She smiled. "Like I said, it's been my currency in life."

He moved her closer to the mirror. "I don't just mean your face, hair, and body. Look into your eyes, hold your own gaze in the reflection."

She met her eyes, blinked, and looked away. Staring into her own eyes was uncomfortable.

He gripped her shoulders. "No, *look*, Evangeline. See what I see."

Her face flushing, she raised her gaze to her eyes again. They were gray, the color of metal. That's what she noticed first. But if she went deeper, which felt a little like diving into her own soul, she saw . . . vulnerability. Honesty. *Emotion.* Joshui, so much of it. Her eyes seemed to swim with it. She saw strength, too.

Anatol dropped his mouth near her ear. "Your eyes have always been this way, even when you were at your worst. There was always beauty in you, complexity, empathy, caring, and I always saw that beauty. Always. No matter what you did or what you said to me, it was there."

Her lips parted as she stared into her own reflection in a way she'd never done before. Anatol was helping her see herself in a way she never had.

His hands rested on her hips as he took a slow sweep of her body. "You are, of course, also beautiful in the more traditional sense."

"Touch me," she murmured, meeting his gaze in the reflection.

His eyes went dark with lust. He brought his hands up her abdomen, thick fingers splaying over her delicate, pale skin, bringing them up to cup her breasts. Her breath caught as he rolled her hard nipples back and forth between his fingers until they were bright red against the milk white globes of her breasts. He pinched them a little as he rolled them, making her breath hiss between her teeth and pleasure course through her body, drawing moisture between her thighs.

He drew her back a step and sat down on the edge of the bed with her in his lap, still well within viewing distance of the mirror. His hands slid slowly up her outer thighs.

Her reflection in the mirror almost didn't seem like her own. Her eyes were larger and darker than she ever remembered seeing them, her face more gaunt. But it wasn't the weight loss that made the woman in the mirror seem like a stranger, it was the look of amazing passion on her face. Had she ever before looked this way when with a man? Lips parted, eyes heavy-lidded, yearning for more of the touch that he was doling out in little drips and drabs? No, of course not. That only came with Anatol. Only him.

"Part your thighs," he whispered.

At his instruction, she spread her legs. Her sex pouted in the mirror's reflection—pink, slick, swollen with arousal and begging to be touched. Anatol licked his finger and brought his hand down slowly between her thighs. Finding her clit nestled in her soft curls, he found the blooming little bud and stroked it. Pleasure blossomed through her body, making her nipples go harder. She sank her teeth into her lower lip, watching him pet her into incoherency. He knew exactly how to touch her, not too hard and not too fast.

He caressed her clit until it was huge, once in a while dipping down to find lubrication to make the pad of his finger slick over it easily. Her head fell back and she moaned as he skated her up to the edge of a climax and held there, suspended in pleasure and with the promise of even more pleasure dangling just out of reach.

"Watch, Evangeline," he murmured.

Wickedly, before she came, he slid a finger deep inside her cunt, then added another, stretching her inner muscles until she moaned. Rapt, eyes wide and lips parted, she watched his big hand between her slim, very feminine thighs. He thrust in and out exactly the way she wanted his cock. The fact he was denying her what she truly wanted made this even more agonizingly erotic.

His other hand came up to cup her breast, thumb moving over the nipple, keeping time with the thrusts of his broad fingers into her sex. Her body tensed and her gaze went to Anatol's eyes in the mirror's reflection. He was watching her face, looking like a wolf ready to devour a savory snack. He ground his hand against her clit as he fucked her with his fingers, the movement causing a friction that immediately put her on the edge of an explosive orgasm.

"Come for me," he murmured.

Her back arched and she came. His name spilled from her lips as he rode her through it, the muscles of her sex milking his fingers. Pleasure slammed over her again and again, stealing her thoughts and her breath along with it.

He rolled her to the bed, roughly pushing her thighs apart with one hand as he desperately worked the button and zipper of his pants with the other. She yanked at his shirt, pulling it off so she could enjoy his beautiful chest. Finally his pants were off and his gorgeous cock was free. She reached out and took the long, wide length in her hand, stroking it from base to tip. His head fell back on a groan.

He yanked her so her ass was just on the edge of the bed and roughly spread her legs. Standing on the floor, he guided the head of his cock to the entrance of her slick sex and pushed the crown inside.

She gasped at the sensation, her mouth open and her eyes wide in the reflection of the mirror. His buttocks flexed and he leveraged his body against her, driving his cock into her another inch, and then another, until he was seated to the base deep within her.

They stayed that way for a moment. The mirror's reflection showed her thighs spread as wide as they would go, his cock thrust into her body deeply. He had his arms around her, muscles flexing in his minute movements, his sun-kissed skin looking so dark against her thin, pale body. Anatol was breathing hard into the curve of her neck and trembling just a little.

"Anatol," she pleaded. Her body shook and she closed her eyes. The sight of them so entwined was going to make her come again without him even making one movement.

He pulled out of her body and pushed back in so slowly she could feel every single ridge, valley, and vein of his shaft.

Evangeline bucked against him, gasping. His cock was wide and long, filling up every part of her. Over and over, slowly and methodically, he pulled out and thrust back in. She watched every movement in the mirror, every flex of his beautiful ass and thighs, until she was incoherent with lust.

He took her slow for a while, and then began to gather pace and force. The bed was high, just the perfect level for him to stand at the side, pull her rear flush up to the edge and fuck her hard and fast. He slammed in and out of her, thumb finding and stroking her extra-sensitive clit. Another orgasm caught hold almost immediately and she stuffed her fist in her mouth to keep from crying out. Pleasure poured through her, stealing everything but her moans, which she couldn't stifle.

His cock jumped deep within her, he groaned her name, and he slumped over her. "Evangeline," he kept saying over and over.

Her body trembled and shivered from the force of her climaxes. He was still buried deep inside her. She wrapped her legs around his waist and kissed his temple, not wanting him to leave her.

His hands fisted in her hair. "I love you," he whispered.

Her body tensed and her breath arrested in her throat. Those were words she couldn't return. She cared deeply for Anatol, but was it love she felt? She had no idea. What did love feel like?

"It's all right," he breathed against the curve of her shoulder. "For now, this is enough."

Her body melted against his. He found her mouth as his hands began to once again restlessly explore her. Soon everything that didn't concern the slide of his body against hers was forgotten.

Nine

A week passed and hunger gnawed at them. Anatol went out every day trying to find work and came up empty. Evangeline also went out, though now she kept her head down and her eyes carefully away from other people's, mostly because she felt she couldn't risk another encounter with someone who might wish to harm her and force her into using her magick again.

Her magick burned inside her now like a foreign thing, eating at her. She sensed all emotion around her, as well as felt her own. It made her sick to her stomach to be near crowds, but try as she might to find some barriers to protect herself, it was like forming walls from water.

Here and there, they picked up odd jobs. It was the only thing that sustained them. Anatol loaded shelves at nearby stores sometimes for a few crowns. Evangeline picked up a little work at a local bakery that garnered them some of the leftover stock as her payment.

Then one day Anatol landed a more permanent job—down

at the docks of the Tibrian Port. It offered him steady pay, if not much. It was enough to pay the rent on the room and to buy food, at least.

He came into the room one afternoon, after a morning of work, and threw a heap of tangled material on the end of the bed where Evangeline sat, looking out the window.

"I thought you could do something with it, maybe make some clothes." He gestured at the pile of fabric. "I know you only sew a little, but Martha, the daughter of the hotel's owner, said she could give you some instruction. I thought it would be a good thing to occupy your time."

He was apologizing for dumping work in her lap, but she would be happy to have something to do. She picked up a coarse length of blue material. "This is a good thing, Anatol." She smiled. "Thank you."

Over the next week, with Martha's help and with quite a few errors that she learned from, she transformed the heap of scrap into a new wardrobe for them. Apparently she had some aptitude for something other than magick. *Amazing.* She made two new shirts for Anatol and a pair of pants.

She even made a new dress for herself. The style wasn't anything like what she was used to, and the material chafed her skin instead of kissed it, as she was accustomed, but *she'd* created it and somehow that made it the most valuable piece of clothing she'd ever owned.

She turned in front of the mirror, admiring the way she'd bunched the material just under her breasts to push them to overflowing a little at the bodice. The sleeves were flared and the waist hugged her waist perfectly. Turning to view the side, she frowned, thinking about different ways she could improve the design the next time.

A warm sensation filled her chest, an emotion she recognized as contentment. It made a smile play around her mouth. There was an advantage to feeling emotion. Happiness and contentment were nice. Lust was pretty good, too. Anatol made her feel that on a nightly basis.

Overall, things were looking up for them. She gazed at herself in the mirror. Funny she should think that. Her cheeks were hollow, dark smudges marred the skin under her eyes and her hair seemed thinner than it had when she'd lived at Belai. And yet . . . she could say she wasn't unhappy. At least, not all of the time.

"That looks incredible on you," Anatol said from the doorway.

She turned, smiling. "Thank you. I just finished it this morning."

He walked toward her. Sunlight streaming in from the window seemed to catch on him. He was dressed in a pair of worn trousers that fit him just right and a heavy, dark brown sweater and work boots. His job loading boats down at the docks left enough for sewing supplies and even the occasional extra hot water.

Evangeline never would've imagined she'd be so happy to have so little.

"The dress does look incredible," Anatol murmured as he approached her, pulling her up against him. He fitted his mouth to hers—a place she liked it often these days—and whispered, "But you'd look even better if you were out of it."

She smiled against his mouth. "You have to go to work."

He kissed her lower lip slowly, dragging it gently between his teeth, making her knees go weak. "I still have some time before I leave."

He drew her back toward the bed and pushed her gently down onto it, coming after her to pin her wrists to the mattress. He stared into her eyes in that way that made her heart beat faster and moisture pool between her thighs. That intense look said, *you're mine. Nothing in the world will keep me from having you.* It spoke to the part of her that wanted to be claimed by him, even as the idea of it scared her nearly witless.

They'd made love daily since the first time they'd come together.

It didn't matter the time of day or how tired he was—he wanted her. Sometimes he woke her in the middle of the night, slid between her thighs, and brought her to a sweet, shattering release while she was still drowsy from sleep. Sometimes it was the afternoon, up against a wall, or while he pinned her facedown on the bed. It was like he had to touch her to survive, as though he lived to give her pleasure. These days she knew his body as well as her own, where best to touch him and how.

She'd been forced to find birth control after their first encounter. Luckily, it wasn't difficult. Palace life had taught her how to prevent pregnancy with a certain combination of herbs, a concoction she'd been taking since she'd first lost her virginity.

He reached down and slowly undid the buttons on the bodice of her dress one by one, revealing more and more of her skin as he went. Her breath came faster as he reached her waist, and his gaze ate up the sight of her breasts only barely covered by the material of the dress, her nipples hard as diamonds under the thin fabric. He pushed one half of the bodice away, the scrape of the material erotic against her nipple and the cool air of the room making it tighten even further. Then he pushed the other half away and lowered his hot mouth to her breast, letting his tongue explore every hill and valley of her nipple while she watched. He covered her other breast with his hand and toyed with her nipple, pinching and rolling it until she tossed her head and moaned.

She reached up and pulled at the hem of his sweater until he dragged it up and over his head, tossing it to the bed. Her palms ran over the muscled expanse of his chest and arms, down his back to the waistband of his trousers and pushed past it to cup his gorgeous rear.

Reaching down, he bunched her skirt up higher and higher until he could slide his hand between her thighs. He found her hot, wet, and bare. Pausing for a moment, he raised an eyebrow.

She laughed. "I was trying on the dress, not waiting for this." Which wasn't perhaps completely true.

"Whatever the reason, I like it." He pushed two fingers inside her at once and she gasped, her spine arching. His thumb found her clit and petted it, making her moan his name and close her eyes.

"Anatol," she breathed, licking her lips and swallowing hard. "It's getting late. You'll have to go. You can't risk . . . losing your job." She could barely think, let alone speak with his hand working its magick between her legs. If he touched any more like this she'd go completely incoherent.

"I only plan to make you come, Evangeline. I know you're close."

Her eyes flew open. She reached out and cupped his rock-hard cock through his pants. "No. You can't do that. You'll be miserable all day."

"How are you going to stop me?" He stroked her clit a little harder and a little faster, rotating in a devilish circular motion that nearly made her come.

With a shimmy of her hips, she pulled up and away, going on her hands and knees on the bed and throwing her skirts up over her waist. She spread her thighs and raised her hips, showing him her pink, slick, swollen sex—just waiting for him—and twitched her rear. She looked over her shoulder at Anatol—he looked stricken . . . and hungry. "That's how."

His hand went immediately to the button and zipper of his trousers and she hid a smile. The bed squeaked under his weight and then he was there behind her, hands to her hips as he pulled her back against him and fitted the head of his cock to her entrance. He pushed inside and Evangeline threw back her head and cried out in pleasure. He rocked in another inch and then another.

Soon he was riding her fast and hard, the sound of their bodies coming together and their labored breathing the only sound in the room. They'd made love like this several times before, sometimes in front of the mirror. Evangeline could remember the sight of his thick, long cock pushing in between the pink lips of her entrance, disappearing deep inside her over and over. He filled up every inch of her, stretching her muscles so far that it rode the sweet edge of pain, yet managed to be only pure, complete pleasure.

Every outward thrust seemed to drag the crown of his cock over a place deep inside her where it felt extra good. Bunching her skirts in his hand, he brought his hand down between her thighs from the front and stroked her clit with strong, slow fingers, rotating and releasing, rotating and releasing, until delicious ecstasy broke over her body.

Her groans of pleasure were nearly animalistic when she came, her inner muscles pulsing and releasing as she orgasmed long and hard. Anatol cried her name and she felt his cock jump deep inside her and spill as he came, too.

They collapsed to the mattress in a tangle, breathing hard. After a moment, Anatol reached out and pushed her tangled hair away from her face. She laughed, a post-coital reaction she had often these days.

"You're beautiful," he murmured. "I love it when you come. You're so uninhibited."

She felt her face color and smiled. "Well, I love it when you make me come. You're the only one who has ever been able to do that, you know."

He studied her for a long moment and then kissed her tenderly. "I know you can't get pregnant now, Evangeline, but one day . . . one day . . . I want children with you."

Her breath arrested in her throat and her smile faded. Children? She'd never even considered the possibility of ever having them. She wasn't sure . . . children? Did she want them?

Anatol's smile faded. "I'm sorry. I shouldn't have said that. I'm pushing too hard." He sat up and stood, searching for his clothes.

She grabbed his wrist before he disappeared into the bathroom. "It's all right, Anatol." She sat up, holding the bodice of her unbuttoned dress to her bare breasts. "It's just that this is all really new to me. I'm not sure what I want." She looked up at him. "But I know I want you."

He blinked, looking surprised she'd said that. Then he sat on the bed beside her and pulled her to him. His arms wrapped her tight, fingers tangling in her hair. He nuzzled her throat and inhaled, as though trying to breathe her into him to keep forever.

"You're going to run away from me," he breathed against her skin.

"What? Anatol—"

His grip tightened. "I can see truth, remember? I'm not everything you need."

"Anatol . . ." she trailed off, not knowing what to say. Her feelings for him scared her to death, it was true, yet she knew what he was saying was *not* the truth. *Of course* he was everything she needed. "I'm not going to run away."

"Yes." He pulled away from her, looking deeply into her eyes. "You will run eventually. But I'm going to do all I can to stop that from happening. I won't let you go." He paused, then added fiercely, "*Not ever.*"

She stared at him, lips parted and eyes wide, at a loss for words.

After a moment, he rose, dressed, and went into the bathroom to get cleaned up. After he'd kissed her and left for work, Evangeline sat on the edge of the bed, her body still tingling where he'd touched her. Brushing off the disturbing bit of conversation they'd just had, she buttoned her bodice and adjusted her skirts.

No matter what Anatol thought she might do in the future, she knew better. It was very possible she was falling in love with him.

She wasn't exactly sure what love felt like, but whatever emotion filled her when she thought of him was good. Warm. Soft.

All-consuming. It was the kind of emotion that, if given the option, she would choose to feel all the time.

She missed him when he was gone and cherished the moments when they were together. She loved to hold his clothes to her nose when he was absent, just to catch the stray scent of him. She loved to sit up into the early morning hours talking to him. She loved his mind; she loved his heart. She loved his compassion and the way he saw into her so clearly, uncovering facets of her personality she'd never known were there. In his eyes she felt valued, and he was helping her to feel valued in her own eyes as well. His addition into her life had improved her in ways she never would have imagined when she'd been at Belai. She didn't know what she would do if she ever lost him. In fact, that was a thought she couldn't hold in her mind. She couldn't even think about it.

Was all of that love?

She wished she had someone to ask. Her mother, maybe. Her mother would be the right person to talk of these things with, wouldn't she? Or maybe a good girlfriend? She had neither. There was Lilya, of course.

She looked toward the window. There was snow on the ground and it was still very cold, but the sun was bright today. Perhaps she would take a trip to the Temple of Dreams and see if Lilya would talk with her about this.

It would be nice to know if she could call what she felt for Anatol *love*. It would be nice to tell him she loved him and know she wasn't lying or deluding herself. At any rate, she was happy. In fact, she could go the rest of her life living here in this room, if only Anatol were here with her.

But that was only a stray thought in one moment. After that came the next one.

Shouting in the street beyond the window drew her attention. She ran over, her hand going to her throat as she glimpsed Anatol in the middle of the icy street, corralled by five commoner thugs she recognized from the beheadings on the steps of Belai. They had him on the ground and were kicking and hitting him.

Forgetting even so much as a coat, she raced barefoot out of the room, down the stairs, and onto the street. She ran over, barely noticing how cold it was, pushing through the gathering crowd, but was caught immediately by a fine-gloved hand on her upper arm. "Don't say a word, little rash one, or they'll have you, too."

She turned wild eyes to find Lilya gripping her. "But they're taking him!" She couldn't say the rest. They had to be taking him to Belai. Somehow, they'd discovered he was J'Edaeii.

"Yes, he's been recognized."

The men tied Anatol's wrists at the small of his back and lifted him. Anatol's gaze went first to the window of their room and, not finding her there, searched the crowd. Their gazes collided and his bruised and bloodied expression beseeched her to stay quiet.

They dragged him down the street toward the palace, his boots making furrows in the snow.

Evangeline's knees went weak and she almost sank onto the street. Lilya steadied her. Her eyes swept her. "You're nearly naked, girl." Her voice was a harsh whisper. "Come with me, we'll go back to the Temple of Dreams and have a chat, you and I. A nice cup of tea?"

A nice cup of tea? Lilya wanted a nice cup of tea when Anatol was being dragged to his death for the crime of being who he was?

"No." She shook her head and tried to pull away from Lilya, but the courtesan was stronger than she appeared. "I need to do something."

"You need to do *nothing*," Lilya whispered into her ear. "You are about to lose your head, Evangeline. Don't you understand? Anatol has been outed and it's only a matter of time before someone remembers the woman he shared a room with. You are in grave danger. Not only from the mob, but from the Revolutionaries who are cleaning up the magicked the rabble misses. You cannot go back to that room. You must come with me."

Oh, it didn't matter anymore. Anatol was captured and as good as dead. Nothing mattered now.

"Tea. Now." Lilya's voice and grip were firm as she guided her through the dispersing crowd.

She let her lead her through the frigid afternoon to the Temple of Dreams. It was a tall, ornate building that took up a corner of a busy intersection of the city. It was a place Evangeline had passed many times on her way to the nearby upscale neighborhood of Rhimes, where all the best stores and cafes were located. She wondered how that part of town fared now that all the people who had supported those businesses were dead. It was an inane thought coming from her shocked mind. Who cared how the area was doing now that Anatol was going to die? Who cared about anything?

Once inside the building, she caught the stares of everyone in the sitting room. Her teeth were chattering, she noticed vaguely, and her feet and calves were completely numb.

"Misa!" Lilya gave a sharp yell.

A young woman in a servant's outfit appeared in a moment, her eyes wide as she took in Evangeline's appearance.

Lilya was all business. "This is a friend of mine. Help get her into a warm bath and take some clothes from my closet. They should fit her." She gripped Evangeline's arm when she staggered. "She's a bit in shock, I'm afraid, so be gentle. I'll have some hot food waiting in the kitchen when you're done."

Evangeline barely heard the words. Images of bloody, rolling heads were dancing through her head and all of them wore Anatol's face. She wanted to tell Lilya that she wasn't hungry and would never be hungry again in her life, but she couldn't make her vocal cords work. She turned to Lilya and opened her mouth, but nothing came out.

Lilya's face went soft and she smiled sadly. "Go, Evangeline," she said. "You're blue with cold. Go warm up in the water, then come to the kitchen. We'll work this out." She rubbed her arm. "Please, take care of yourself."

A hand reached out and snagged hers. Evangeline looked up to see Misa smiling at her. "Come on," said Misa with the rolling accent of a person from the rural Arkian Province. "Come with me now."

She went.

The bath drove the numbness from her body, but not so much her mind. She sat in the waist-deep water, staring, trying to process the unprocessable. After she'd soaked in the warm, scented water long enough to drive the cold from her body, Misa urged her out, dressed her in a soft pink gown, and gave her a pair of doeskin slippers. Then she brushed her hair out, pinned it up, and led her down to the kitchen, where Lilya waited for her.

Lilya was sipping a cup of tea at the large table. She looked up when Evangeline entered. "Do you feel better?" Her face fell when Evangeline didn't answer. "I guess that's a stupid question."

"They took him. They're going to kill him."

"We don't know that yet."

Finally, her shocked numbness gave way. She blinked and took a step forward. "Don't know? Lilya, haven't you been seeing the executions?"

Lilya stood. "Life is not so predictable. Come and have some tea. It's an herbal brew that will help to calm you."

She hugged herself. "I don't want tea."

"It will help you to think clearer, Evangeline. Drink it for Anatol."

She hesitated for a moment, then walked over and let Lilya pour her a cup. It was hard to believe that she'd only an hour ago been thinking of coming over here to talk of love.

She held the cup in hands that didn't feel like they'd ever warm up, staring down into the dark swirl without taking a sip. "I'm getting him out." She stood and set the cup down on the table, sloshing tea over the side. "I'll go and offer myself in his place."

"Don't be stupid. They'll just capture you and behead you along with him."

"I can't let this happen. I can't allow Anatol to be killed. He's a good man." She paced the room, shaking her head. "He even believes the revolution was a positive thing. Can you imagine the irony? He thinks the people should have a chance to govern themselves. As if they could ever do such a thing on their own." She made a frustrated sound. "If I ever meet Gregorio Vikhin I'm going to scoop his eyeballs out with my bare fingers."

"I offer you the chance to try," came a deep voice from behind her. Evangeline stilled, recognizing the deep timbre from the alley. "Some days I'd be happy to let you."

Lilya's chair scraped the floor as she stood. "Evangeline, meet Gregorio. Gregorio, Evangeline."

Evangeline whirled to face the brute who'd killed the rapist in the alley two weeks ago.

"Actually, we've already met." Gregorio's dark eyes met hers. "Haven't we?"

"What are you doing here?" Evangeline narrowed her eyes, her hands fisting at her sides. She tried to drudge up some gratitude for what he'd done for her in the alley, but it was drowned out by the knowledge of his identity. "Need a quick fuck during the break in the executions at the palace?"

Gregorio winced as sure as she'd slapped him. "I want you to know that this was not what I'd planned. This was nothing like what I'd hoped for when the lower classes rose up and took their fates into their own hands. I'm deeply shamed that the executions going on at Belai are being done in my name." He paused, seemingly at a loss for words. Then he spread his hands. "I was too much of an idealist."

Evangeline stalked toward him. "I don't care how you feel, sir. I don't care what you would have wanted, or if you were too much of an idealist." She sneered the last. "The only thing I care about is that an exceptional man is in the claws of your rabble-rousers and is soon to lose his life for the mere crime of being who he is. Anatol's blood is on your hands, Mr. Vikhin. This is *your* fault!"

He said nothing in response, but he didn't need to speak to let her know what he was thinking. Nor did she need to taste his emotions to know how he felt. Thick, dark hair shadowed eyes heavy with guilt. He shifted, looking away from her. "You're right."

"I *am* right. I'm right about something else, too." She gripped his sleeves and forced the huge man to look at her. "You started this madness, and that means you're the only one who can end it. *You* are the only one who can save Anatol now."

The woman's gray eyes should have seemed cold given their coloring, but instead they were hot, full of passion and emotion. A faint hint of hopefulness sat in her expression and even in the lilt of her voice. She thought he had the power to save her lover. Gregorio's belly tightened with that familiar sense of helplessness, the one he'd had ever since he'd gotten his fondest wish and the nightmare it had sparked.

Gregorio had tried to stop the madness. Oh, he had. Over and over. He'd tried the impassioned speeches that had worked to call the lower classes to arms. He'd tried coercing them. He'd appealed to their sense of right and wrong and asked them to have mercy.

But the bloodletting never stopped.

The lower classes were drunk on the carnage, lost in the joy of their newfound freedom. It was an outcome he'd considered but had never actually thought would come to pass.

Some gifted intellectual he'd turned out to be.

And now here was this beautiful J'Edaeii female before him, pleading with her eyes for the life of the man she loved. A J'Edaeii who had a gift, a *wondrous gift* bestowed upon her, one she couldn't help possessing but would be killed for if the mob discovered it.

Like in the alley, a powerful sense of protectiveness rose up in him, only this time it was natural and genuine, not the result of this woman's magick. He would protect her from harm with his dying breath. He would protect her lover, too . . . somehow.

Maybe he clung to this woman and her lover as a way to find redemption. Or perhaps he'd fallen into her expressive, soulful eyes and found some sort of connection with her. Maybe he'd even fallen in love with her a little back in that alley, after she'd emptied him of his emotions and then filled him back up as easily as a serving woman managed her wine carafes. Gregorio didn't know what drove him to do it, but he did it anyway.

He reached out, cupped her cheek in his hand, and said, "*I will.*"

But it was wrong to make promises he might not be able to keep.

Ten

Pain blossomed through Anatol every time he moved. Blood crusted the left side of his face and streaked his arm. The only thing that made the wounds of his beating bearable was the cold of the cell they'd thrown him into. It numbed his body and dulled the aches and pains they'd inflicted on him in the street outside the boardinghouse.

It had been the second week of his new life working the docks and he'd been recognized. Sold out. One of the J'Edaeii who'd also been working there had slipped and showed his hand, used magick to lift a heavy crate. *Stupid*. Anatol had used illusion to cover the gaffe. Instead of making a show of solidarity, the man he'd helped had thrown Anatol to the wolves for the reward, and the wolves had been only too eager to tear into his flesh.

No good deed ever went unpunished.

They'd taken his jewel, scooped with a rusty spoon from the flesh at the back of his neck. They'd taken a clump of his hair along with it.

He moved his hand, fingers dragging across the gritty floor of the cell. He touched straw and the scent of it filled his nose—moldy and sharp with the smell of other people's unwashed bodies. His head ached and his throat burned for lack of water. Pushing himself over on his back, he groaned. His chest burned with pain, as though on fire.

"I know you," came a broken voice somewhere near his left. A man. Cultured tones. A nobleman, maybe.

It took a minute for Anatol to move his head around far enough to peer into the shadowed corner where the voice had come from. It looked like a heap of rags sitting there, face cloaked by grime, a beard, and shadows.

The heap shifted a little. "I know you. The hair and eyes. Black and blue. Striking. I recognize you. They took your jewel. Your neck is bleeding."

His neck was bleeding, but since pretty much everywhere else on his body was also bleeding, he hadn't paid it much mind.

"So, you recognize me." Anatol gave a tired groan. "So what." He closed his eyes. Saw an image of Evangeline. The only thing he could be thankful for now was that she was safe. He didn't know how things would turn out for her, but she had a chance. His heart squeezed at the thought of never touching her again, not being able to watch the beautiful transformation she was beginning to undergo. If she made it through, Evangeline would be a sight to see—crystal and steel and the softest velvet.

Loss opened in him like a chasm, darkness sucking him down into a spiral of despair.

"You're Jeweled. I was with one in my room when the palace was stormed. Lithe little light-haired one, cold bitch with a hot body just asking to be fucked. I can't remember her name. She's probably dead now."

No, this was not a nobleman. This was royalty. Anatol's eyes opened. "You're Roane."

Nothing.

Anatol closed his eyes again.

Roane's voice came from the shadows. "I'm dead."

Sometime near dawn Anatol was awoken by the sound of the iron door whining open on rusty hinges. It clanged and Anatol roused, looking down the length of his body to two men coming toward him. They grabbed his arms and legs and dragged him toward the door, grunting under his weight.

Anatol twisted around, grunting at the agony in his chest, and peered into the shadow of the cell to search for Roane. It was empty. There was no trace that anyone had ever been there. He wasn't sure if he'd hallucinated the encounter the night before or if they'd come and taken the royal out while he'd been sleeping.

"Off to the Lady for you." One of the men carrying him spat on the floor as they entered the corridor. "Morning crowd needs a bit of amusement. May Joshui have mercy on your soul."

Anatol had already figured that's where they were taking him. He watched the ceiling of Belai's dungeon pass by, rusted and water-spotted. The heels of his boots dragged on the stone floor of the corridor. To either side of him were cells filled with moaning, desperate people, their grimy fingers reaching past the bars.

The cold air of early morning rushed through him and the sounds of the crowd filled his ears—the shuffling, sighing anticipation of another day of seeing what they believed was the fruition of their dreams—the exultation of the people over power.

They were so deluded.

His body sagged as they deposited him on the icy ground. Cold water seeped into his clothing, numbing his skin. Above him rose the wood and steel contraption that would bite his head off.

He closed his eyes. *Evangeline.*

Blessed Joshui, he hoped she wasn't watching. God, he just hoped she wasn't going to see him die. He hoped she was far from here, fled back to Cherkhasii Province to find her family. Or perhaps gone to seek shelter at the Temple of Dreams. He hoped she was anywhere but here.

He wished her well.

Wished her the best.

He wished he'd had more time to love her. He wished he'd been able to show her she was capable of loving back with a full and open heart, without fear of loss. It was in her and someone would be lucky enough to bring it out of her. Someone would be honored to show her that she was worthy of adoration.

But it wouldn't be him.

That truth was worse than the hands that pulled him upward and set him on the slab of wood frozen with the dark brown blood of those who had come before. It was worse than the kiss of the cold blade as they set it to his neck, making sure he was positioned correctly so that it would sever his neck and not stick into his shoulders or head. Worse than the tacky blood of the recently dead against his cheek, or the sight of the decapitated heads resting on the badly cleared snow of the steps below him.

Anatol closed his eyes and called his magick.

It rose up from his depths, blowing away the grief and fear that clung to him. It bubbled out of him like a fountain turning into a gusher. His back arched, his chest screaming in pain, and he yelled out—a hoarse, guttural sound that grated the frigid air.

He wove a spell around them all.

A forest, dark and deep, tangled with vines and tree limbs. Shadows slipping and churning in the ground beneath their feet. Low growls of savage animals echoing through the foliage. His power filled the air all around the perimeter of Belai, immersing all the viewers in the illusory depiction of the wild tangle of emotion that clawed at his heart and mind.

The people gasped and screamed. Some ran, only to bump into one another or collide with the iron fence that separated them from the palace courtyard. They jostled one another. Fights broke out. The guards surrounding Anatol backed away into vines that coiled down from tree limbs, grabbing at arms and legs and pulling them screaming into darkness.

Straining, body on fire from the pain of his wounds, magick hammering out from every pore of his body and burning him up, Anatol contracted his stomach muscles and rolled off the blood-soaked slab of wood. He hit the cold ground with a hard thump, shoulder and chest exploding with pain and making him grimace. His magick never flickered. Chaos reigned.

Above him the guillotine came down with a silvery *thwack*, blade embedding where his tender throat had just rested.

"Enough!" roared a man from about ten feet away. "Be calm!"

The man's voice broke through Anatol's magick, made him lose his grip. It was the voice of command—heavy and low. The people stilled, watching the man—awarding him with respect. The bustling about him stilled. The shouting and murmuring quieted.

Anatol's magick slipped from his lax metaphysical fingers— spent. He rested his head against the ground and breathed out a long breath, and then closed his eyes.

"It ends now!" the man roared.

Silence.

Stillness.

Boots crunched on the ice and snow-crusted pavement. The man— Gregorio Vikhin, Anatol had no doubt—walked up and down in front of the gate like a schoolteacher reprimanding his class. If only it were so innocuous.

"You have had your victory." Each word was loud, punctuated

in the chilly air. "You have prevailed over your masters and thrown off their yoke." He threw an arm up to encompass Belai. "You now rule the ruins of their short-sightedness and ineptitude. You now have the power."

A cry went up, but died back down after a few moments.

Anatol forced his eyelids open, feeling the faintest stirring of magick affecting him. It roused in him a sense of respect and hopefulness, pride, and the desire to do the best, most noble thing he could. Emotional magick. *Evangeline's magick.*

"Now it is time to harness that power. It is time to take this new world in hand and make something new, something better, something different, something that *honors you.*" Vikhin swept his arm down to show Anatol lying on his side. "To take the broken and make it whole. It is time to leave the bloodshed behind, my friends, the brutality and the violence. It is time to take the higher path, to create a state that honors us and is worthy of us all!"

A ripping roar of approval that hurt Anatol's ears rang out through the air.

"No more bloodshed! Time for positive action!" Gregorio pumped his fist into the air. "No more bloodshed! Time for positive action! No more bloodshed! Time for positive action!"

The crowd took up the chant and Gregorio ran in front of the gate, fist pumping, driving the energy of the people higher—in a new direction.

Several of the guards, impassioned by Gregorio's speech and Evangeline's magick, took axes to the guillotine. Wood rained down on Anatol, hitting his head. The men who had brought him out to the steps came toward him, intending, perhaps, to throw him back into the dungeon. It appeared his neck had been saved from the blade for the moment, but Anatol was sure a darker, quieter death awaited him back between the walls of the prison.

Gregorio caught sight of him and walked over, holding up a

hand. "No, no. This one comes with me. He's shown an exceptional amount of spirit and I want to talk to him."

The men hesitated, hands gripping Anatol's arms and legs.

Gregorio Vikhin straightened and locked his jaw.

The men dropped Anatol and moved away.

Watching him closely, Anatol noticed Gregorio release a pent-up breath. Then he leaned down and helped Anatol to his feet. "Can you walk?"

Anatol grunted and mumbled through his swollen lips, "Just get me out of here."

Anatol wasn't a small man by any measure—but Gregorio was even bigger. He half carried him and Anatol half dragged himself to an opening at the back of the palace courtyard. There Lilya and Evangeline waited for him.

Evangeline had her hand over her mouth, her eyes a riot of emotion like he'd never seen in them before. She ran over to him and braced his other side. Suddenly every hurt in his body ebbed away to warmth. That was the power of her touch. "Blessed Joshui," she breathed into the crook of his neck.

"Get him to the Temple of Dreams. I've got work to do here." Gregorio strode away.

Evangeline stood in the doorway of the bedroom where Anatol lay. She and Lilya had managed—with much hardship—to get Anatol back to the Temple of Dreams. There she and Lilya had stripped him of his fouled clothes, cleaned him up, and had a doctor attend him.

He had three broken ribs, multiple deep lacerations from a whipping, two black eyes, a split lip, and a concussion. No broken limbs. That was a miracle. Now he was bandaged and had been giving a sleeping draught. He needed rest to heal.

She pressed her hand to her mouth, hating the way her insides heaved every time she looked at him and thought about how close she'd been to seeing that blade come down on his neck. Watching it almost happen had killed a part of her; she couldn't imagine what it would have been like if it had truly occurred.

The feelings she had for Anatol were deep and terrifying. She couldn't remember the last time that had happened. Not since she'd been a child. She actually cared if he lived or died, and if he died . . . she couldn't even think about the possibility. The idea dredged up the remnants of thick, sludgelike grief from the bottom of her soul. It was from her childhood, locked away in a part of her mind she couldn't open.

She'd felt like a child as well, watching Anatol almost die as she clung to the gate in front of the palace, stomach heaving with emotion. Her magick had taken in the swell of the crowd. She would have used her ability to turn things in Anatol's favor, but there hadn't been enough of any opposite emotion to feed back into them and turn their sentiment in another direction. There had only been anger and bloodthirsty vengeance. When Anatol had cast his illusions there had only been fear and confusion—not usable. There'd been no positive feelings at all.

At least, not until Gregorio had begun to speak.

Then pride and elation—hope—had begun to filter into her awareness in drips and drabs from the people. Knowing she was taking a risk, but unable to stop herself, she'd siphoned off as much of that positive feeling as she could and fed it back to them—spawning more and more—until the emotional tide of the crowd had turned in Gregorio's favor.

And Anatol had been saved.

Footsteps sounded behind her and a warm, strong presence pressed at her side. "Thank you," she whispered, her gaze still on Anatol's form in the bed.

"I think I should be the one to thank you. I know what you did this morning with your magick. You risked your life."

She looked at him. Gregorio would never be called a handsome man, but there was something so very compelling in his brutal face. His eyes were fathomless, full of such intelligence and depth. His gaze rested on Anatol.

She looked back at the bed. "I did it for him."

"I know you did, but that doesn't change the fact that what you did . . . *worked*. Helped me and that helped Anatol. You did a good thing today. You may have aided me in gaining the foothold in the people's psyche that I needed."

"Your words." She swallowed hard. "Your ideas. That's what they need. That's what they'll follow. My magick is just a parlor trick, like Anatol's illusion. It fades fast and leaves nothing of substance behind."

He shook his head. "The emotion you engineered in them will fade, but people remember an event that's been paired with such a great emotional response. I need you."

She looked up at him. "What?"

He pushed a hand through his hair. "I need you both. I need your perspective and maybe your magick."

Frowning, she shook her head. Ambivalence came off Gregorio in waves. "What are you saying? I wouldn't feel right about manipulating people's emotions." She paused, thinking about what she'd just done at Belai and about the rapist in the alley. "At least I wouldn't feel right about it in most situations."

"I don't mean that I want you to stand in the back of the room and throw magick whenever I speak. That wouldn't be right." He paused for a moment as if he couldn't think of what to say. "Come to stay with me. You're in danger on your own and I can protect you. In return you can help me, consult with me on the path I now have to walk."

She bit her lower lip, contemplating the irony of the situation. This man, Gregorio Vikhin, was the one responsible for all their current woes. They were supposed to help him? Everything about this felt wrong. Frightening.

She pushed past him to leave, shaking her head. "No, we don't owe you anything."

"Yes, but I owe you something."

"No. You saved Anatol's life today. Let's call it even. We're done with you now." She walked toward the door.

"Evangeline." Anatol's broken voice stopped her a step away from the threshold.

She turned and went to his side. He stared up at her through an eye that was half swollen shut. Gregorio went to the other side of the bed. "Swallow your pride. We need to take him up on his offer." His words came haltingly.

"Why?"

Anatol swallowed hard. "Revolutionaries know my face. We need to hide. Need protection."

"But—"

"Evangeline, please. For once . . . don't fight me."

Evangeline looked up at Gregorio, who regarded her with a guarded expression. "I'll agree if that's what you want, Anatol." She paused. "At least, for now."

Anatol grimaced a little, closed his eyes, and appeared to relax.

She glared at Gregorio and stormed out of the room. He caught her with one of his massive hands before she could leave and she shot him a look that could kill.

"I'm not the enemy," he growled into her face.

She shook him off. "Yes, you are."

Eleven

Gregorio lived on the edge of Milzyr in a tall, middle-class town house. It was not a palace, but it was a far cry from the boardinghouse.

A confirmed bachelor far too consumed with his writing and his work to take care of things himself, Gregorio kept a housekeeper and a cook. The furniture of the house was serviceable and comfortable, but had an air of neglect. Gregorio lived inside his head most of the time, Evangeline was sure, and so didn't pay a lot of attention to his surroundings, and he had no woman to give the house a feminine touch.

Once Anatol had been stable enough to move, he'd been relocated from the Temple of Dreams to Gregorio's town house, where he was installed in a spacious bedroom at the back of the residence. Evangeline stayed there with him.

It was easy to avoid Gregorio for the next six weeks while Anatol recovered from his injuries. Gregorio was gone most of the day, coming home for lunch occasionally, but always leaving after a scant half an hour. He wandered in late at night looking exhausted, with his tie and the top buttons of his dress shirt undone.

The episode in front of Belai where she had helped to drive the emotion of the people to a more positive place was paying off. A council of citizens had been organized to discuss their next form of government. Gregorio was leading it and, therefore, was spending most of his time in meetings.

The council had decided to appoint a representative from each of the provinces of Rylisk in order to allow the rural areas their say. Gregorio worked with them from first light to star shine every single day of the week.

He hadn't asked for any more of Evangeline's help, leaving both her and Anatol to themselves in the big house. Perhaps out of a sense of guilt over their circumstances, he was very generous with them both, having the cook make them meals three times a day and sending clothes makers to them. Evangeline was well dressed, clean, and had a full stomach every day. She'd gained back some of the weight she'd lost, her hair had regained its thickness and luster, and the skin around her jewel had finally completely healed.

She didn't feel guilty about accepting Gregorio's generosity at all. After all, he was the one responsible for their being destitute in the first place.

On the second day Evangeline had stumbled upon Gregorio's huge library. It was a well-used room, filled with all kinds of tomes, both fiction and nonfiction. All of Gregorio's books were housed there, too, as well as a clearly loved copy of Kozma Nizli's, *A Future without Royals*. Wanting to entertain Anatol while he was prone in bed, she'd picked some of the fiction up, eschewing the Nizli book and everything penned by Gregorio.

Finding the library in the house had been like discovering treasure. Books had always been her guilty secret, something that seemed so frivolous in the context of palace life. Reading had always been a way to escape, even if she hadn't realized it back then. After the revolution, it had been the loss of her book collection that had grieved her the most—not the gowns or the small amount of jewelry she'd been able to amass.

So she spent her afternoons sitting at Anatol's bedside and reading him books about sea captains, warriors from distant lands, explorers who fell off the edge of the world, and tales of valiant princes who waged war against angry tyrants.

Even as the weeks passed, she avoided Gregorio's political tracts at all costs.

Gregorio apparently enjoyed strategia, a strategic board game wherein pieces had to be moved around on a board. Anatol asked her to bring the board to his room, and they played a fair amount of that, too, after he'd taught her the game. She got good at it. Soon Anatol was losing to her almost every time.

After Anatol was able to move around again they often went to the porch on the back lawn that was enclosed by a high fence, separating them from the bustle of the city streets and alleys. As the weather warmed, going from winter to early spring, they drank tea there and talked about everything and nothing, sharing more in those weeks of healing than they'd ever shared in their years of being together at Belai.

Anatol reached over and caught her hand in his. His eyes held a heat that hadn't been there in the weeks he'd spent bed-bound. Apparently, he was feeling better.

She smiled and pushed a tendril of hair out of her face, suddenly feeling shy with him for some reason. It was funny how emotion seemed to change everything—made things richer and so much more complicated at the same time.

He tugged on her hand. "Come over here."

She rose and walked to his chair. They were alone on the porch on this exceptionally warm day. The cook and the housekeeper had both gone to the market. Steaming cups of tea sat side by side on the table between their chairs, but from the timbre of Anatol's voice, she had a suspicion they'd soon be cold and forgotten.

At his urging, she sat down, straddling his lap. When she leaned over, setting her forehead to his, her long, loose hair made a curtain around their faces. "Is it wrong to say that I've been enjoying our time together, considering the reason we've had that time to spend?"

He reached up and cupped her cheek. "So have I. Although, it's true, I would have rather have been well." His other hand slipped to the small of her back. "I'm feeling better today, though."

She grinned. "Are you, really?"

He grinned back at her and something light and free fluttered through her chest. Joy? "You know what that means." His hand moved up and down on her thigh suggestively, the heat from his palm warming her skin through the material of her skirt.

She went breathless for a moment. "I can guess," she murmured, dropping her mouth to his.

She kissed him slowly, first his lower lip and then his top, running her tongue along the seam of his mouth until he groaned and opened for her. His hand caught and held at the back of her neck, forcing her face down to his so he could spear his tongue into the depths of her mouth.

Heat caught and flared to life in her belly. She moaned against his mouth, feeling the jut of his cock against her softness where she straddled him. "Are you sure you're well enough for this?" she whispered against his lips, breathless.

"I need to feel you, Evangeline. That will mend me better than anything."

His fingers loosened the buttons of her dress bodice, exposing her bare breasts. He palmed them and then brought each rosy nipple to his mouth. With the tip of his tongue, he explored every ridge and valley thoroughly, making her hot and damp between her thighs.

Her back arched and her sex swelled with anticipation, her body readying itself for him.

He slid a hand under her skirt and roughly pushed the panel of her panties aside to swipe his fingers over her slick folds. She shuddered against his hand as he speared inside her, her muscles clamping down and milking him. Her breath caught in her throat and came out as a little sob. It had been a long time since she'd felt him inside her and she wanted him so much.

He speared his fingers in and out of her, dragging a ragged groan from her throat as she rolled her head, eyes closed. When she looked down at him, he was gazing up at her with a raw expression of carnal hunger on his face.

She fumbled for the button and zipper on his trousers even as he yanked her skirts up and her panties down. One clumsy, impatient adjustment of clothes had her panties off and his cock free. She sank down onto his shaft, working herself over the crown and down his thick length inch by wonderful inch. When they were finally completely joined, their lingering sighs and groans emanated out into the air of the porch. She stayed that way a long moment, with his cock seated deep inside her, filling every part of her. Then she rose up and down slowly, making them both moan.

Mouths working, she rode him faster, his thick and wide cock tunneling deep into the heart of her and rubbing that place inside where it felt especially good on every downward thrust. His hands found her hips and gripped, guiding her movements. They fell into a perfect rhythm, bodies and mouths fusing into one animal.

"Anatol," she whispered against his mouth as he stroked her clit with his thumb. "Ah, I've missed the feel of you inside me."

From inside the doorway off the kitchen, Gregorio clenched a mug of coffee in his hand hard enough to shatter. He'd come home in the middle of the day, something he didn't do very often these days, and had happened upon Evangeline and Anatol on the porch.

She was magnificent. Her gently bouncing breasts were unbound from her dress's bodice, kissed and covered by Anatol's hands and mouth. Her well-worshiped nipples were ruby red and rock hard, glistening with saliva. Her hair hung down her back and her eyes were closed as her hips moved up and down on Anatol's shaft, slowly milking the length of him.

Gregorio wanted to be the man inside her. He wanted to touch and suck on her breasts. He wanted his cock stretching the velvety soft muscles of her pussy, and he wanted to feel her body pulse and explode in orgasm while he stroked her clit and made her come.

It had started in the alley, maybe even before that—maybe it had begun the day he'd seen her at the Temple of Dreams when she'd brought the orphaned child to Lilya. He'd stood in the doorway of the kitchen and listened to her curse the revolution and all the damage it had wrought. He'd thought she was so beautiful.

He was not only fascinated by Evangeline; he was becoming obsessed with her.

The cup cracked in his hand and hot coffee dribbled down his hand. He set the cup down on the counter and turned away, gripping the edge of the table and closing his eyes. There was no reason for him to feel this way about her, but reason and logic didn't seem to play any sort of role in his emotions.

Many nights after his day was done at Belai, which had been taken over for the People's New Republic, he headed to the Temple of Dreams and sought out the women there who looked most like her. The ones with long, blond hair and large, soulful gray eyes. The ones with lithe dancers' bodies that he could lift up against walls and fuck hard and fast, pretending they were Evangeline. It kept his hunger for her at bay, took the barest edge of it off—but it wasn't enough.

The scent of her hair and skin permeated his house now, taunting him at every corner. The sight of her bare ankle as she turned a corner or the sound of her voice made his cock hard in an instant. Listening to her come apart in Anatol's arms on the porch right now was driving him insane, yet he couldn't make himself do the decent thing and move away. This might be as close as he ever got to intimate contact with her. This might be the only time he ever heard the beautiful sound of Evangeline in orgasm.

He remained there, feeling guilty for listening in on the lovers' tryst. *Blessed Joshui*, he was jealous of Anatol. He closed his eyes, listening to their soft coital aftermath, their low murmurings and kisses, the rustle of clothing being put to rights. Finally, all was silent.

He tore himself away from the counter and fled.

"Gregorio?"

He froze in the doorway of the kitchen, then slowly turned to see Evangeline standing just inside the kitchen.

She tilted her head to the side a little. "Are you all right?"

Could she sense the emotional turmoil inside him? He tried to answer her, but no words came out.

Her gaze went to the coffee cup and then to his face. Her clothes were once again arranged and all that showed of her encounter with Anatol was a slight flush to her face and her mussed hair. She looked beautiful. "Gregorio—"

He cleared his throat, straightening. "I just came home for a break. I'm headed back to the palace now."

"Oh." She fidgeted, looked at the coffee cup again. "We never see you, it seems. It feels wrong to stay here when you're never in residence. I feel like we've taken over your home."

"Things are busy right now, but you're more than welcome to stay here. Just make yourself at home." Which, clearly, they were. Jealousy shot through his gut once again. Just once, if he could touch her the way Anatol did . . .

"Perhaps you could make it home for dinner tonight? I mean, you have to eat, don't you? You might as well do it in your own home. It's time you took a break, anyway. You look exhausted."

He hesitated, pushed a hand through his hair. This behavior from her was odd. He thought she hated him, blamed him for the revolution and the beheadings. She'd called him the enemy. He assumed she was only staying here because Anatol had asked her to stay, and perhaps to fleece him a bit—make him pay for what he'd done. His guilt was such that he was happy to let her.

"I'll try," he said at last. "Things are finally stabilizing a bit in the new government. It should be fine if I leave a little early." Of course, that would mean no stop at the Temple of Dreams tonight, and he badly needed it after walking in on that encounter on the porch.

She smiled and he melted. "Good."

He started to turn away, but stopped. "Evangeline, please tell Anatol that the group of vigilantes who are hunting down escaped nobles and magicked have been more active lately. I know you're both careful, but please just continue to stay that way. Allow the cook to do the shopping and stay indoors."

"But they wouldn't dare touch anyone *you've* taken under your wing, would they?" There was a definite note of sarcasm in her voice.

He nodded. "As long as you reside with me, you're safe. Still, you never know. This group is unstable."

"Of course. Thank you for the warning. We'll look forward to seeing you tonight."

Evangeline watched Gregorio walk out of the kitchen, wondering just what, exactly, had come over her. Why had she been so kind to him?

He'd looked so harried and disturbed standing there. So . . .

lonely. When she'd probed his emotions, she'd found jealousy, lust, confusion. She had no idea where all that strong sentiment came from, but it was clear the man was miserable.

Despite the ill feelings she still harbored for the man, she couldn't say he hadn't done them a good turn. Sensing how unhappy he was, she'd needed to reach out to him. After all, it was clear he genuinely regretted the aftermath of the revolution. She wanted to keep punishing him for it, but she knew it wasn't fair.

For as powerful and intelligent as Gregorio was, he had the air of a lost puppy sometimes. That attracted her to him—and attraction was something she did *not* want to feel.

He disappeared into the shadows of the hallway and she went back out onto the porch. Anatol studied her with his keen dark blue eyes. "Was that Gregorio I heard?"

She nodded. "I tried to get him to come home for dinner tonight."

"Really? I thought you disliked him so much. Why did you do that?"

Shrugging, she gave a little laugh. "I'm not really sure. I'm still trying to figure it out."

Twelve

Gregorio came home for dinner.

Anatol watched Evangeline take a sip of her wine and cast a cold glance at Gregorio when the man wasn't looking. It was clear that her burst of good feeling toward him had long since faded. Gregorio cast looks at Evangeline when she wasn't looking, too—though his were not cold, not by anyone's measure.

Gregorio coveted Evangeline; that would be obvious to anyone, even someone who didn't have the insight into people that he did. He wondered why Evangeline couldn't feel it, but maybe she could—maybe that was part of why she seemed to detest him so much.

Although Anatol suspected that abhorrence didn't go very deep. Every exchange between Gregorio and Evangeline seemed heated with an underlying current that had nothing to do with anger.

"More asparagus?" Gregorio offered the plate to Evangeline.

"No, thank you. I've had enough," she responded in an icy tone without looking up from her food.

"You've hardly eaten anything." Gregorio put the plate back down on the table. "And you seem displeased. I came home tonight for dinner as you asked. Should I have stayed away?"

"Of course not. This is your home. We're only guests here."

"Then why the change in your attitude toward me? This afternoon you seemed to want me here and now you don't."

Anatol put his fork down and watched Evangeline carefully. She raised her head and looked at Gregorio. "I'm trying to be a good guest, Gregorio. You're putting a roof over our heads and I'm grateful for that."

Gregorio blinked slowly. "But?"

Evangeline sighed and put her napkin on the table.

"You can't get past who I am and what I began." Gregorio spoke the words that Evangeline didn't want to voice. "You think I'm responsible for the deaths of your friends."

"You *are* responsible for their deaths."

"He's not, Evangeline," Anatol broke in. "He was the tool that set the people free, but it wasn't his hand who lopped off heads. You know this."

Evangeline looked down at her plate and shook her head. "When an animal keeper lets loose a pack of ravening hyenas that mindlessly rips the throats from a bevy of swans, do you blame the hyenas or the keeper?"

"That's not a fair analogy, Evangeline. You can't compare—" Anatol stopped speaking when Gregorio raised his hand.

After a tense moment, Gregorio laid his napkin to the side of his plate, rose, and went down on his knee next to Evangeline's chair. "Please believe me. I never intended the bloodshed, though I should have known it would happen." He paused, bowing his head. "*I should have known.*"

She remained still, staring at her plate.

"But, Evangeline," Gregorio continued, "you must see that even though I was the tool that broke the floodgates, the floodgates would eventually have broken without me. The Edaeii family could never have held power when their people were so dissatisfied, starving, *dying* the way they were. When that happens, the people rise up, they throw off their oppressors." He paused. "It was inevitable."

Finally, she shifted in her chair to look at him. "You destroyed our way of life, Gregorio. How do you expect me to feel about that?"

"Yes, I did, and I'm glad!" Gregorio made a frustrated sound and stood. "Don't you see that your way of life impinged on the rights of most everyone around you, Evangeline? How can you defend setting your table with feasts every night while the rest of the people in the country starved? How can you think it was right to clothe yourself in finery stolen from the backs of children who went cold in the winter?" He shook his head. "I know you're not cruel, so you can't possibly think the former way of running this country was the right way. You don't have that in you."

She fidgeted and then stood. "I don't like being told what I should think and feel."

"Admit you think your former life was unfair to everyone but you."

"Gregorio—"

"Admit it."

She opened her mouth, closed it, and her jaw locked. "I will admit that equality is not a bad thing and that perhaps there might be a better way." Her eyes flashed. "But how it was done was brutal and merciless and came from the depths of hell. There was a better way to do *that*, as well."

Inclining his head, he slid back into his chair. "Maybe."

"These people need to be told what to do, Gregorio. You'll see. You'll have chaos on your hands with the will of the commoners leading the way."

Gregorio raised his head, his eyes glittering with challenge. "Do you really think so?"

"Yes. People are sheep. They need a strong shepherd and you, *you* want to let them vote! It's insanity!"

Gregorio's lips curled in a mirthless smile. "I guess we'll see just how insane it is together, Evangeline."

"You're infuriating!"

"I've been told."

She made a frustrated sound, and then nodded at Gregorio. "Thank you so much for the dinner. Thank you so much for . . . well, everything."

"Don't thank me. I like having you both here."

"I can't imagine why."

He swirled the drink in his glass and leaned back in his chair. "I'm lonely, if you must know the truth."

"Thousands of people look up to you." She walked to the doorway.

"Thousands of people make me feel alone."

She studied him for a long moment, her face softening a little. "You're not alone now." Then she disappeared into the hallway.

Anatol had spent the conversation watching Gregorio watch her. It had been easy since suddenly neither of them had seemed to remember he was in the room. Gregorio's eyes had been focused, sharp, and deep, soaking in every little movement she made. Once she'd left the room, the light had left his eyes. Now he was gazing down at his wreck of a dinner plate.

Anatol spoke. "You want her, don't you?"

"*What?*" Gregorio's gaze snapped to his.

"It's in the way you watch Evangeline. You covet her."

Gregorio looked away, wiping his mouth with his napkin. "I'm a man and she's a beautiful woman, of course I want her. Don't worry, I know she's yours." The words came out with a trace of bitterness.

But that was just it, Evangeline wasn't his. Not completely. Anatol was no fool. Evangeline had only recently begun to feel emotion again. She wasn't ready to lock herself into a relationship with only one man, no matter how much Anatol might wish it. If she did, he would lose her.

As much as it pained him, he needed to leave her free to explore her emotions as they arose and to give her the ability to act on them. Anything else would drive her away.

"She's not mine." The words hurt to say, but they were the truth. "I'm not her keeper. We have sex, that's all."

Gregorio gave a decidedly unamused laugh and turned his face away. "You love her. I can see it on your face. *We have sex, that's all.* For someone who can purportedly see truth, that's a pretty big lie."

"I *do* love her. I love her more than I've ever loved anyone else, and I suspect she loves me though I don't know for certain. I understand her, too, probably better than anyone in the world, much better than she understands herself. Her magick is a gift, like you say, but it's also been her curse. My gift is illusion, but it has a flip side. It means I can see into the truth of things and people. Her gift is giving other people emotion, and that gift robbed her of her own for nearly her whole life. She's only just started to feel again, and she barely knows what love is yet."

Gregorio rose from the table and crossed the room to the fireplace. He leaned heavily against the mantel, one hand clutching the edge. "That's all fascinating, but what does it have to do with me wanting to fuck her?"

"It means that Evangeline is free to do as she wishes and she might wish to sleep with you." Anatol rose from the table. "You might get to fuck her, Gregorio, but never expect her heart. She's not ready." He strode from the room.

*   *   *

Anatol slipped into bed beside Evangeline and pulled her close to him. She sighed in her sleep and cuddled against his chest. Her hair, damp and fragrant from her evening bath, brushed his nose. Her warm, soft body fit perfectly to his, as though they'd been made for each other.

Her hand strayed to his cock and it went hard against her palm. Groaning, he nuzzled the back of her head and found her breast under her nightgown. Her nipple went hard against his palm and she let out a little sigh that went straight to his blood like the finest liquor.

After seeing that flash of attraction between her and Gregorio, he needed to claim her. He would free her emotional will, but also put his mark on her body. If she strayed to another man, he would always be here waiting for her to come back.

He would never give up on her.

She shimmied the hem of the gown up and thrust her sweet backside against him, wanting his shaft. A ragged breath escaped him. He could never resist when she did that and she knew it, the minx. He freed his cock and gave it to her, slipping the head into her entrance and pushing deep. They both sighed into the cool darkness of the room as they moved together, their bodies straining gently toward climax in the dark.

He cupped her breast, rolling her nipple between his thumb and forefinger as he thrust slowly in and out of her. "I care very much about you, Evangeline," he whispered near her ear, then dragged the lobe through his teeth. He didn't use the word *love*, knowing it might drive her away. "I also know that you are not mine to command."

Her movements faltered. "What are you saying?"

He slipped his hand between her thighs and found her clit, pressing and rotating until he heard her breath catch. "You are free to do what you wish with whomever you wish."

"Anatol, I don't know what you're talking about."

"I can see what you can't yet." But soon, she would see. She would recognize that her animosity for Gregorio was, in fact, attraction.

She opened her mouth to reply and he thrust his hips forward slowly, impaling her deeply on his cock and making her moan. He moved over her, dragging her beneath his body, parting her thighs and sliding deep inside her so he could look down at her face. He searched her beautiful eyes.

She reached up and pushed his hair behind his ear. "I can see just fine, and I see *you*, Anatol. *Only you*."

He knew those words were true.

For now.

Evangeline watched Gregorio's blunt fingers move pieces across the strategia board. Every evening for the last week Gregorio had been home in time for dinner and not returned to work afterward, instead choosing to play the game with herself and Anatol at night before bed. Tonight Anatol had gone to sleep early, complaining of lingering fatigue from his injuries, leaving her alone with Gregorio.

She tried—and was mostly successful—to keep her emotions under control and her tongue civil when in Gregorio's presence. She'd seen firsthand the misery the beheadings had caused him. The tension sat in his shoulders and deepened the lines of his face. She also was well aware—and grateful—that he'd saved Anatol from the kiss of the executioner's blade.

So they avoided the subject of the revolution completely. Instead they talked of history, literature, and art. All the things that Evangeline had neglected to learn at the palace because she'd been too busy scheming to get ahead and then sleeping with her tutors so they would give her a passing mark for doing nothing in her studies.

Gregorio had a way of teaching her that made it interesting, too. He did it in a conversational way, through stories, avoiding the high-handed, superior, pompous way of teaching that she was far more familiar with.

"Have you seen the steam transport that is taking passengers from Milzyr to the provinces?" he asked as he capped her empress.

She suppressed a sigh of resignation at the move. He had this round of the game sewn up. "Oh, yes, the nobles were enraptured with it. I took several sightseeing tours out to the station to watch it pull in, though I never rode on it." She tapped her index finger on her lower lip, contemplating her next move. "I figured it stopped working once the rev—" She looked up at him, realizing she'd almost broken their unspoken law. "Now that everything is different."

"It was out of commission for a while, for a lack of travelers. They've lowered the fares they charge and now many can afford to travel by rail."

"Have you ridden on it?" She moved her iron soldier, hoping to block his gold horseman.

He nodded idly. "I have. Several times. It's a much more efficient way to travel than by carriage or even by balloon."

She looked up at him, game forgotten. "Balloon? You've traveled by balloon?"

He smiled. "Many times. It's incredible. You can see everything from up there. Incredible, but slow."

"Slow." She snorted and looked down at the board. "You're always moving. Don't you ever slow down and just enjoy the view?"

"Sometimes I do," he murmured.

She looked up and he was rolling a game piece between his fingers, staring at her with heavy-lidded eyes. Something in her stomach fluttered and rolled. It was not unpleasant. If she tasted his emotions right now she was certain of what she would find. *Desire.*

Suddenly flustered, she studied the game board for a moment, then stood. "You've got this won, I think. There's no sense in continuing. If you'll excuse me—"

"Do you bear me even the slightest bit of attraction, Evangeline?" Her eyes flew to his. "What do you mean?"

"You know what I mean. Surely you've felt mine for you."

"I'm with Anatol." She'd gone for a scandalized tone of voice, but it had come out thick and heavy because a part of her did crave this man.

He nodded. "Yet Anatol tells me you two are not in a committed relationship. He tells me you're free to live, and love, as you will."

Swallowing hard, she looked away from him. Why had Anatol and Gregorio had that conversation?

And why had Anatol said such a thing?

"What Anatol said has no bearing on our relationship. It's true Anatol and I have no formal understanding of commitment"—and clearly he didn't want one— "and I'm free to *love* as I choose. I'm sorry, but I don't choose you."

Gregorio looked for a moment like she'd physically slapped him and, just for a heartbeat, she felt bad about it. Then she turned and went for the door—safety. Fleeing her suddenly hard-beating heart and her body that was reacting in an unwelcome way toward the prospect of having Gregorio touch her.

But he came after her, not letting her run away. He whirled her around to face him and her body tensed. If he touched her, she might lose her resolve, if—

He handed her a book.

It was thick and leather bound. She looked at the spine, *A History of Inventions.* "Why are you giving me this?"

"You seem interested in such things, like the steam transport and the helium float. You'd be amazed at all the things the Edaeii family suppressed during their reign in order to keep the people under their thumb. All the inventions were put back into production as soon as the mob hit the gates of Belai. Read it. I think you'll enjoy it."

Flustered, and a bit uncomfortable, she hugged the book to herself. "I'll give it a try," she said slowly. Then her anger snapped. "But don't expect me to finish it if it bores me."

He smiled at her, but there was something hungry, almost predatory, in his eyes. "Of course not."

"Good night." She nodded at him and turned to leave the room.

"Sleep well, Evangeline."

As she turned, his words swept over her, laden with innuendo. They seemed to stroke her bare skin like a hand in a soft leather glove.

Thirteen

She hated to admit it, but the book was interesting.

For two days she'd refused to pick it up. She'd set it on the dresser in her room and ignored it. This afternoon, as Anatol was on his way out the door for the afternoon, he'd put it in her hands. "Try it," he'd urged her. "I read it while I was at Belai even though it was a forbidden book."

"Forbidden?" she'd asked.

"Illicitly published, like Gregorio's tracts. The whole story is in there." He'd tapped the cover and left the house.

She'd watched him leave the house, bound for she didn't know where. She didn't like that he was leaving. The Revolutionaries were still out there, yet they could hardly be expected to stay inside Gregorio's town house for months on end.

The day had been beautiful. Unusually warm for so early in the spring, so she'd taken a glass of wine out onto the porch and settled in to at least look at the book, which had been carefully copied by hand and was probably quite valuable. Soon she'd been leafing through pages as fast as she could read.

Apparently there had been all sorts of inventions in recent years, but the royals had forced the shutdown of most of them, save the ones that benefited them in some way or had improved their lives—like artificial light and heating, for example. The rest of the inventions had been gathered up, placed in a large storage facility, and locked up. The royals, the book posited, feared the inventions would take power from their hands and place it in the hands of the merchants and manufacturers, changing the face of Milzyr's economy forever.

Evangeline wasn't sure she believed any of it, but that wasn't the most interesting part of the book for her anyway. She loved reading about the various inventions, both those in progress and those already created. She wanted to go see and touch them for herself. Things like a small steam-powered transport that would replace the carriage, though she couldn't see why that was necessary. Or a contraption that would actually stitch material, a thing that sounded wonderful and unbelievable to her. She couldn't imagine how it might be accomplished.

"Like the book?"

Evangeline squealed in surprise and jerked, almost tossing the book to the ground. She looked up to find Gregorio in the doorway with an apple in one hand. "Do you have to sneak up on people that way?"

"I made lots of noise in the kitchen. I figured you knew I was here."

"No." She pinched her face a little, unwilling to give him an inch. "I've been engrossed in my reading."

He grinned at her and then took a snapping bite out of the apple. Just looking at him that way, leaning up against the door frame, his thick hair mussed and his top shirt buttons undone, made her stomach do a little flip. An unwanted flip.

Making sure he saw she was curling her lip at him, she gave her attention to the book once more and hoped he'd go away.

Instead, he sat down in the chair next to her. The man could not take a hint.

She lifted her gaze from the page to find him staring.

"Where did Pearl go?" Pearl was the cook.

"She went to the market. She's getting ingredients for dinner. Giana is cleaning the upstairs as we speak."

"And where's Anatol?"

She frowned, glancing down at her book and adjusting her position in the chair. "Out. He wouldn't tell me where he was going." She didn't want to admit it bothered her that Anatol would keep a secret from her.

He didn't say anything else, so she attempted to finish the paragraph she'd already started twice.

Gregorio took another bite of his apple. "Beautiful day."

With a sigh, she gave up and closed the book. "Why aren't you at Belai?"

"I decided to take the rest of the day off."

Her eyebrows rose. "Really? I thought I'd never hear you say something like that."

"I decided that for everyone's well-being, I need to relax a little. Things get tense with so many opinions vying for attention." He took another bite of apple and chewed. "The representatives from the provinces have arrived and it's mass confusion. Everyone speaks at the same time and over everyone else. Most of them want the same things, but are saying it all differently and none of them will listen long enough to realize it."

Smugness washed over her. "I could have told you that would

happen. Not *everyone* can have a say in government. Not *every-one's* ideas can be realized. Not *everyone* can be right."

"I agree with you, Evangeline. That's why majority rules. There are votes, wherein everyone gets to register their opinion, but, in the end, it's the numbers that make the decision. The most votes wins."

"I predict discord."

He laughed. "Oh, I do, too, Evangeline. Beautiful, tumultuous discord during which everyone gets their voice heard, if not all of their dreams realized."

Sniffing, she glanced away from him. "Better than what was before."

"Much. In this system of government the people will be healthy enough to make their will known. There's a loaf of bread for every peasant table these days now that the royals are gone."

"Dead, you mean."

His face shuttered. "Some survived. Many J'Edaeii as well. They're free now, though they've been stripped of their wealth. Now they must make it on their own merit."

Yes, and she was still deciding what she was going to do in this brave new world where her magick was a hindrance instead of an honor.

"Speaking of which, I would like to offer you some sewing lessons. I know you were taking them before Anatol was captured. I was hoping you'd want to continue down that path. Anatol tells me you're very talented, and clothing design could be a way for you to stand on your own financially."

She looked down at the cover of the book, tracing the title with her fingertip. "I can't accept your generosity, Gregorio. You've already done so much for us as it is. Anatol is healed now. We should be leaving your house, not making ourselves more beholden to you."

"You are not and will never be beholden to me for anything, Evangeline. And you're most certainly welcome to stay as long as you wish. In fact, I hope that you both *do* stay. It's been much less lonely in my house with you and Anatol here, and Anatol has been helping me understand the perspective of the noble people, who, after all, are part of the governance themselves now. They also have a say."

Yes, but it was dangerous for her to stay here. Dangerous because of her attraction to Gregorio. She wanted Gregorio, that was true—but she didn't want messy emotional complications. She'd barely managed to learn to control her newfound empathy; adding Gregorio into the mix now would throw her into chaos again.

She needed *less* emotion, not more. Anatol, she was sure, would disagree with her. He would tell her she needed to explore all her newfound feelings, not look for ways to suppress them.

She studied Gregorio. This man ignited all sorts of new feelings in her.

"You never answered my question."

She looked up from the cover of the book and realized she'd been lost in thought. "It's true I will need to find some sort of livelihood for myself and I enjoy designing clothes."

"Good. It's settled then. I'll have Emily come over first thing tomorrow morning. The upside is," he looked pointedly at the book, "she'll be showing you how to sew on a stitching machine."

Excitement made her face light up. "Really? Like the one described in this book?"

He nodded. "It's one of only five in existence. Soon they'll fill every dressmaker's shop and be the way all clothing is produced. You'll be among the first to learn how to do it."

"That's—" She swallowed a laugh, again not interested in encouraging him. Yet she was pleased and very excited. "That's wonderful. Now I'll have something to do with my days again. I've been feeling very idle."

"What were your days at the palace like?"

"Full from morning until night. Every day I practiced with my magick, getting ready for the day I would audition to become J'Edaeii. Anatol, too. We had classes as well, though education always came second to the training of our magick."

"Do you want to go back to using your magick on a daily basis?"

"I don't see any possibilities for that. Most people don't like to have their emotions manipulated. Anatol's skill with illusion is perhaps viable since it's amusing, but my magick is intrusive. It could get me beheaded, even now in this new, glorious, blood-free world." She couldn't quite keep the sarcasm out of her voice toward the end. She laughed. "I suppose I could be a performance artist, dancing and weaving emotion on a street corner for a few coins."

"So you think it will never again be possible for you to use your magick."

"Not openly."

"Not . . . openly?"

She smiled and tilted her head to the side. "Gregorio, I use my magick every day. I'm very empathic."

He swallowed, his Adam's apple working.

"That's right. I pretty much always know what you're feeling."

He hesitated a moment and then leaned forward. "So what am I feeling right now, Evangeline?"

"Lust," she answered right away. She blinked slowly. "It's what you're usually feeling, along with some other flavorings to blend."

"Any ideas as to why I feel lust so often when I'm around you?"

She looked back at him, holding his gaze coolly. "I have a couple. Maybe just one."

"There's only one for me."

She raised an eyebrow. "Not according to Lilya. She says you're a regular."

"Does that bother you, Evangeline?"

"Of course it doesn't bother me, *Gregorio*," she snapped. "I'm simply pointing out your lie."

He leaned back in his chair and rubbed his hand over his tired face. The half-eaten apple hung in one limp hand draped over the armrest. "I haven't been to the Temple of Dreams in weeks."

"Why?"

Gregorio caught and held her gaze. His pupils seemed to grow larger and darker. "Because no woman can compare to the one I want."

"That's the real reason you want me and Anatol to stay, isn't it? Because you think you'll eventually get to sleep with me."

"And you, Evangeline, what do *you* want?"

Anatol. Gregorio. Both of them. Her body wanted them both, but her mind knew it was a bad idea.

She glanced away from him, afraid her eyes might reveal her desire for him. "I want to not be in this situation."

Anatol appeared on her right, startling her for the second time that afternoon. "What are you two talking about?"

She made a frustrated noise, held her book to her chest, and stood. "Ask Gregorio. I'm going to my room."

As she left she could hear their exchange. "What's wrong with her?" Anatol asked.

"Me," Gregorio answered.

That was true enough.

Emily came the next morning. She was a thin woman with thick chestnut hair and an easy smile. About her own age, Evangeline found herself warming to her right away. Emily brought several bolts of fabric with her and a container filled with various supplies, some that Evangeline recognized and others she didn't.

She also brought a heavy iron contraption with her that Anatol helped her to carry and set up before he faded away to do whatever mysterious thing he was doing every day. The stitching machine had a needle set into a small metal piece that moved up and down, presumably into the fabric. Instead of being powered with elusian crystal, there were small pedals that hooked up to the machine to work it.

Evangeline stared at it, trying to figure out how it operated while Emily bustled around, setting things up. Finally Emily stood back. "All right. Ready for your first lesson?"

She smiled. "I can't wait." Finally, something to throw herself into that didn't involve either of the men. Something that would be hers and *only hers*. She hesitated and then added shyly, "I have some designs."

"Excellent! That will be a great place to begin."

They spent the day with her designs and the stitching machine. Evangeline ate up every lesson that Emily had to teach and wanted more. She hadn't been this interested in anything since training for her audition to become J'Edaeii. By the end of the day, Evangeline had made her first stitches on the new machine, beaming the whole time she did it.

Anatol came home in the late afternoon and Evangeline forgot to be grumpy with him for the secret he was keeping. Gregorio came home not long after and they settled in to a dinner of roasted lamb with a rosemary dressing that the cook had prepared.

"Emily tells me your designs show promise." Gregorio raised a forkful to his mouth.

She suppressed a flush of optimism at the praise. "Yes, but she also told me I would need to change the fabrics I use. They're too rich for the market I'm aiming to reach."

"That's an easy change."

She frowned. "Not really. The type of fabric determines the cut, the way the dress drapes, all sorts of things."

"You're intelligent and resourceful, not to mention determined. I have no doubt that you'll find a way to make it work. If you need to buy fabric to experiment with, feel free. Money is no object."

She set her fork down with a displeased sounding clink on the table.

"Don't you like your dinner?" Gregorio asked.

"The *dinner* is wonderful."

Gregorio set his glass down and gave her his full attention. "Have I said something to upset you?"

"This is not the Temple of Dreams, Gregorio. There is no price on my body."

Gregorio frowned. "I didn't mean—"

"Really? Because that's how it sounded." She sighed and removed her napkin from her lap, placing it alongside her plate. "You've done too much for us as it is. Maybe it's time we leave, Anatol."

Up until now Anatol had been seemingly ignoring the exchange, calmly chewing his food and sipping his wine. "I don't think that making you a whore is what Gregorio intends." He looked over at Gregorio. "It might be time we reveal our surprise."

Gregorio watched her with wary eyes. "She might take it the wrong way."

She glanced between the two men. "What . . . surprise?"

Gregorio set his napkin alongside his plate and pushed away from the table. "First, I want to make it clear that I didn't do this to buy your affections. I have other reasons for spending my money on you, chief of which are feelings of guilt. I owe you a new livelihood." He paused. "Anatol, do you want to tell her?"

"Gregorio and I want to help set you up in your own shop. Gregorio organized the instruction you need and I was busy locating and renting the shop. We didn't tell you because—" He broke off, pushing a hand through his hair. "It was meant to be a *happy* surprise."

"A shop of my own?"

"Yes."

She swallowed hard, looking down at the table. "I'm very touched that you two would go to such great lengths for me." Now she felt foolish for overreacting to Gregorio's comment. Managing this on-slaught of emotion was still not her strongest ability.

"Does that mean you want it?" Gregorio asked.

She considered the issue for a moment and then met his gaze, then Anatol's. "What you have done is truly wonderful, but I want to build this business on my own. I want it to be *mine*. I need the lessons to get me started, but the rest of it—finding and renting the shop—*I* want to do that part. I need something outside of myself to focus on. Most of all, I need a challenge like the one I had at Belai, a goal. Otherwise I'm going to shrivel up."

When she'd finished speaking, both the men were watching her intently. Anatol appeared confused, but Gregorio's eyes shone with respect.

Gregorio nodded. "You're strong, intelligent, and determined. I think you *can* do it on your own."

"Thank you. What you two did . . . it's the nicest thing anyone has ever done for me." Emotion clogged her throat and she swal-lowed hard, cursing it. How did people cope with so many feelings bombarding them at once? Thankful sorrow on the heels of angry indignation. It was like being caught in a storm.

"I should have seen that you'd want to build the business on your own," said Anatol. "You're a different woman than the one who lived at Belai." He meant that a scant couple of months ago she would have expected everything be handed to her. Now she understood the look of confusion on his face. "I'll make the ar-rangements to halt the rental of the shop tomorrow morning."

"I'm glad you understand."

"I'm only sorry the possibility didn't occur to me sooner."

"Once I learn the stitching machine better and come up with a few solid designs I think I can sell, I'll look into building a business. I'll start out slow because I'll want to use my own money. That means locating clients without a storefront at first."

"It sounds like you've already thought about this." Gregorio rose and began clearing the table. After preparing the meal, the cook had left for the evening.

She and Anatol rose and began to help him. "It may be the only thing I'm capable of doing in this new magick-free world."

"I hope it's not magick-free forever," Gregorio growled. "The magicked are Rylisk's most valuable resource."

"I thought elusian crystal was our most important resource," Evangeline quipped lightly.

Gregorio halted in the doorway with plates in his hands. "Are you still planning to leave, Evangeline?"

She paused, glancing between the two men. She and Anatol *should* leave. Danger still lurked in Milzyr for the magicked, but they couldn't hide in Gregorio's town house forever. They needed to stand on their own.

And then there was Gregorio, himself. The man left a confused tangle in her stomach that she couldn't parse. Part of her wanted to run away from him and the other part wanted to dash straight into his arms.

Fidgeting, she looked at Anatol. "The time is nearing, don't you think?"

"Nearing, yes, but it hasn't arrived." Anatol's eyes held hers. "I want to keep you as safe as I can and *safe* is here."

"Good," answered Gregorio with a happy smile, "then it's settled. You stay where it's safe and I can keep the loneliness at bay a little longer. The arrangement works for all of us."

They finished clearing the table and Anatol headed up to bed. "Are you coming?" he asked Evangeline as he stood at the bottom of the stairs.

She walked to him. "Not yet. I want to apologize to Gregorio for overreacting earlier."

He cupped her cheek in his hand. "He's a good man."

"I know he is."

He searched her eyes. "I love you, Evangeline."

She studied his face, wanting to tell him she loved him back, but the words just wouldn't come. Her feelings for him ran so deep, but she wasn't totally sure what it was she felt. Was it love? And if it was love, to admit it . . . A shadow of grief stole her body heat for a moment. To admit she loved him would be opening herself to unimaginable pain if—*when*—he rejected her.

Surely at some point Anatol would see she was still more trouble than she was worth, changes in her since Belai or not.

He leaned in and kissed her lips softly. "It's all right. You don't have to say it back." Then he turned and went up the stairs.

When she returned to the dining room, Gregorio had just walked back in holding a dish towel, a look of mild surprise on his face.

Hugging herself and wanting to run up the stairs after Anatol, she said, "I wanted to apologize for earlier. It was wrong of me to assume the worst about you."

"It's all right." He threw the towel onto the table. "Game of strategia before bed?"

She opened her mouth to say no, but it was time she stopped punishing Gregorio. Still, the prospect of spending time with him alone always curled something in her gut—a mix of anticipation and reluctance. She tried to smile, but failed. "Sounds like fun."

"You don't sound all that excited about it."

"No, I want to play. Really." She managed a halfhearted smile.

They headed into the study and Gregorio set up the board while she wandered over to the fire. "So, aside from the chaos, has the shiny new political system of Rylisk been taking shape?"

He looked up from the board. "It has. We've been making progress, though it's messy at times. Democracy is a cacophony of conflicting voices."

"I have to say that I'm impressed you haven't asked me to come in and help to calm and influence their emotions."

He finished setting up the last pieces and then motioned to the chair opposite him. She sat. "Well, if I did that I would be infringing on their free will and basic rights. The new government has a goal of honoring those." He shook his head. "I'll never ask you to use your magick in that way, Evangeline. Not you and not Anatol."

She pressed her lips together and looked down at the board, impressed by his answer. "Would you like to move first? I'm prepared to give you a head start." She lifted an eyebrow and smiled saucily.

He laughed. "Do you think you can beat me tonight, Evangeline?"

"There's a first time for everything. I beat Anatol nearly every time I play him."

"Ah, well, we will see." He made his first move.

"You and Anatol grew up together at Belai?" he commented after a few minutes spent in silent strategy.

"We did." She placed her tongue at the corner of her mouth and frowned at the board. Then she made her move, taking his ebony archer. "Aha!" She clapped.

"Nicely done."

"Thank you." She inclined her head and waited for him to make his next move. "We lived together at Belai and we knew each other, but we were never close. It wasn't until the siege and its aftermath that we became friends."

"Why not?"

She shrugged her shoulders. "I wasn't close to anyone at Belai, not really. Well, there was one person whom I called a good friend."

"Tell me."

She related the story about Annetka. This time when she talked about her, she felt light instead of heavy, remembering the good times they'd had together. "But she was the only one who really knew me there."

"Why?"

She frowned at the board. "I don't remember when or why, but at some point the backlash of my gift presented itself. I suspect I triggered it myself after I was taken from my family. I remember feeling grief like nothing I've endured since I was first brought to Belai. Annetka was the only one who made it through the barriers, probably because she was such a special little girl. In any case, I ceased to feel most of my own emotions in order to shield myself from feeling everyone else's. That made me incapable of forming any meaningful relationships."

"That must have been hard for you."

"Not really. I didn't know any different."

"And now?"

"Now . . ." She considered her answer while he finally made his move. "Now there are times I miss those walls that protected me so very well, but there are other times—the good times—that make me regret they ever went up at all. As I grew up, I missed a lot by not interacting with my peers. In a way, it feels as though I were never a child. I grieve for that woman I was."

"Do you ever wonder what your childhood would have been like if you'd stayed with your family?"

She made her move on the board and then sat back in her chair. "Sometimes I wish I'd been left with them. The housemother at Belai told me my father fought the royals when they took me. She told me his leg was badly injured as a result."

Gregorio fell silent, studying the board fiercely. "Don't you want to find them?"

She didn't reply, concentrating on the game for a long time before replying. "I don't know. There is a dark fear deep inside me that makes me afraid to seek them out."

"You have time to think about it."

She nodded.

They fell into a companionable silence, once in a while discussing books that Evangeline had read from Gregorio's library. By the end of the game she'd forgotten she was supposed to feel animosity toward the man and instead purely enjoyed his company.

Gregorio and Anatol were different in that Anatol touched her heart and Gregorio touched her mind. She was attracted to both of them, but in many ways they were the flip side of the same coin. Anatol was emotional fire and not always logical. He was sensitive and understood people. Gregorio, while also passionate, was as rational and intelligent as a man could be. She could see what each of them could offer her.

But she wondered what it was that *she* offered these men. Why, exactly, they were both so attracted to *her*? In this new world of constant emotion, she had bouts of severe self-confidence. The old Evangeline would never have asked such a question.

Finally they were down to their last few moves. Evangeline made her final move and captured Gregorio's green goddess, winning her the game. She threw her arms up and laughed with the piece in her hand.

Gregorio leaned back in his chair and smiled at her. "You're getting way too good at this game, Evangeline."

She lowered her arms and looked at him suspiciously. "You didn't let me win, did you?"

He leaned forward. "I'm very serious about strategia. I would never let any opponent win, not even one as beautiful as you. You're just an excellent player."

Her smile broadened even as she flushed from the compliment—both of them. "Good."

She set the piece back onto the ravaged game board and looked at the tall clock ticking away in the room. They'd spent a long time on the game and it was now into the early morning. "That was fun, but I need to go to bed. Emily is coming in the morning to give me more lessons."

She stood and he did as well. Smiling a little, she inclined her head. "Good night, Gregorio." Then she moved toward the door.

"Evangeline?"

She turned back to him.

"Do you like me even a little?"

Her smile faded. The problem was that she liked him a lot. She wasn't sure, exactly, why that was a problem for her, since Anatol didn't seem to think it was one. "I do like you, Gregorio."

"Do you still blame me for the deaths of your friends?"

She studied him for a long moment. "No. You were easy to blame in the beginning, but the matter is far more complicated. I see that now."

"I'm glad."

She turned to leave again, but he caught her gently by the arm and turned her toward him again. He had a hard, hungry expression on his face and it made her stomach do a warm flip. She knew that expression.

Reaching out with her magick, she tasted his emotions and found undeniable desire. Her body responded to it like a flame to kindling. "Gregorio?" His name came out almost devoid of breath.

Suddenly she saw where this was going. She wasn't sure she could stop him from initiating it—she wasn't sure she wanted to stop him.

He pushed her backward step by step, until he was pressing her up against the wall behind them, the strategia game board long forgotten. This was not a game.

Fourteen

"Don't do this," she whispered.

"Do what? I won't hurt you, Evangeline. Nothing in the world could ever make me do anything to hurt you." The firelight lit half his face and left the other half in darkness. His breath was warm and sweet on her face, his calloused grip strong.

"I know," she breathed out in a sigh.

"I'm glad."

Gregorio's lips skimmed her cheek and her fingers curled into the fabric of his shirt. Her breathing hitched in her throat and her heart beat faster. Her body reacted, her sex growing warm and wet, her nipples going hard. She had strong feelings for Anatol and she wanted to be able to use them to push Gregorio away. Yet, there was a ragged emotional wound somewhere deep inside her that seemed to need what Gregorio was offering her.

His hands were rougher and stronger than Anatol's, and his touch made her shudder with desire. He took her hands and pinned them above her head. Her wrists were so thin and his hands were so big, he only needed one to immobilize her.

"Do you want me?" His low voice rumbled through him as he limned her jawline with his mouth. "Tell me to stop, Evangeline. Tell me to stop and I will."

She wished she could, but she yearned for his touch and for his kisses.

And so when he bunched her skirt up and slid his hand beneath the hem, she didn't stop him. He found the edge of her panties and pushed them to fall at her ankles. "Step out of them," he growled against her lips. "Spread your thighs. I want to touch you."

She did as he asked and his broad hand was on her, finding her wet and swollen before his first touch. He caught her dampness on his fingers and spread it over her clit, slipping back and forth over it until her hips bucked and she moaned low.

He groaned, too, closing his eyes for a moment as though touching her gave him great pleasure. "Do you like that?" he asked her in a low, husky voice.

She sunk her teeth into her lower lip and nodded her head. "More."

"More? Is this what you want?" He slid a finger deep inside her and thrust in and out. His fingers were large and when he used two within her, it made her gasp out loud. He fucked her with them, his hand pinning her wrists above her head and the action rocking her against the wall.

"Your cunt feels so sweet." He nipped her lower lip and then licked the slight wound he'd made. Slanting his mouth over hers, he kissed her, sliding his tongue deep into her mouth. He found her clit and rubbed it back and forth, his thumb nestling in her curls to press and rotate.

Her orgasm burst over her as delicious as a ripe berry in her mouth. She moaned and he caught it against his tongue, swallowing the sounds of her pleasure as she climaxed against his hand.

He released her wrists and tore the bodice of her beautiful dress, the one he'd bought for her, her breasts spilling free, the buttons popping off and hitting the floor. His mouth covered one nipple and then the other, nipping lightly, sucking and licking. Her nipples were hard, bright red, and tingling when he was done.

Gregorio unbuttoned his pants, sliding them down to his waist. Then he bunched her skirts up again and, parting her thighs further, hooked one knee over his hip and thrust the head of his cock inside her.

Her fingers gripped his shoulders and she gasped against his mouth. He was bigger than Anatol and Anatol was already large. But she was wet, dripping from her climax, and it eased his way. Inch by thick inch, he slid root-deep inside her.

Grasping her hips to keep her steady, he began to thrust in long, deep, driving strokes that made her bump the wall behind her. Pleasure blossomed over her body, growing and growing until it exploded over her in a sweet, all-consuming wave.

He cupped her buttocks and, grunting, thrusting harder and faster, extending her climax until she wanted to scream. His cock jumped deep within her and he groaned her name. Then he held her to him, kissing the top of her head as they came down from their sexual peak.

Both breathing heavily and sweating, they clung to each other.

"Evangeline," he breathed into the curve of her neck. His voice trembled with heavy emotion that she didn't need her magick to sense. He'd been deeply affected by this encounter and little of it had to do with reaching orgasm. Joining with her in a physical way was only a metaphor for what he really wanted from her—to join with her in love.

Shock stole her ability to respond. She'd known deep down that she'd never hated this man as much as she pretended. Lusted after him a little, yes, ever since the day in the alley. But this? She'd never expected to have sex with him tonight in his study.

And love? What he wanted from her was impossible. Couldn't he understand that?

Clinging to him, breathing heavily and sweating, she closed her eyes. Yet joining with him had been good. Almost as if it had calmed a part of her riotous soul, something she'd needed.

He cupped her face in his hands. Forcing her to look up at him, he searched her eyes. Seeing something there he liked, he relaxed, then leaned in and kissed her, his tongue easing deeply and tenderly between her lips to mate with hers, his cock inside her slowly going flaccid.

When he stepped away, he straightened her skirt and scooped her panties up from the floor.

She accepted them, staring down at the bit of silk in her hand. "I hardly know what to say, Gregorio."

"Say it won't be the last time I get to touch you." There was a note of desperation in his voice. "Say that the next time I can put you in my bed and take you slow. Say I'll be able to savor you. All night long, my body on yours."

She shivered and looked away, then busied herself with her bodice. He'd snapped off two buttons. Licking her lips, she turned from him. "I should let you sleep."

As she turned away, he caught her upper arm. She turned back to him and saw fear on his face. "Gregorio," she breathed and went back to him. Going up on her tiptoes, she kissed him. "You are a special, complicated man. I would like to know you more."

Then she backed away and left the room.

Anatol was in bed reading when she reached the bedroom. She'd hoped he'd be asleep. She wouldn't keep her unexpected liaison with Gregorio a secret, but she wanted to ease him into it, not shock him.

And even she, herself, was shocked.

But maybe Anatol wouldn't be. He had given her his permission, after all, to sleep with Gregorio before she'd even known she wanted to. That was Anatol. He saw into the truth of all things. It must be a heavy burden to bear, as heavy as the backlash of her own magick had been, she thought as she gazed at him. His long dark hair was unbound, falling over his shoulders. Sweet Joshui, he was beautiful.

He looked up at her from his book, gazes catching and holding for a moment, before she turned and began to get ready to bathe and then go to sleep. She cleared her throat, which seemed suddenly clogged with unnecessary guilt. "I expected to find you asleep."

"Come here, Evangeline." The sheets rustled and she heard him lay the book on the bedside table.

"I was going to take a bath and *then* come to bed."

"Come here." The words were laced with compulsion, a definite command. He already knew. He'd probably seen it all over her as soon as she'd walked into the room.

She hesitated a moment, then left her panties hanging over the edge of the drawer she'd pulled out. He watched her cross the room toward him, his keen eyes taking her in from head to foot. She reached the edge of the bed and looked down at him.

He slid his hand under her skirt and she flinched as his fingers traveled slowly up her inner thigh to her sex. He slid his fingers inside her and pulled them out wet. His eyes flicked to the bodice of her dress. "Buttons are missing. You and Gregorio were together."

"I'm sorry." The words came out in a sobbing rush. "I care for you, Anatol. I didn't mean to hurt you."

"You have no reason to feel sorry and you haven't hurt me." He paused. "Evangeline, I love you. I know that you need me. I can see that in you. I also know that I cannot claim you like something I bought in a store. You are trying to find your way in a brand-new world filled with feelings you've never experienced before. It would be wrong to tie your hands." He paused, searching her eyes. "Do you think I feel threatened by Gregorio?"

"Another man would feel threatened. Another man would call me a whore."

"But I'm me, not another man. I want you to know that I love you *no matter what*. Forever and always. I will be here for you until the day I die. Take off your dress and come to me. Now."

She flinched at the command in his voice, but her fingers found the remaining buttons of her bodice anyway. Undoing them, she let the dress drop to the floor and the chill air of the room bit into her skin and made her nipples hard.

"Straddle me."

"What—"

"Do it."

She climbed onto the bed and straddled him over the covers.

From the bedside drawer, he brought out the cylinder he'd used on her before. "Your body is ripe for sexual experimentation. Ready. Willing. Hell, Evangeline, it's exploding with eagerness for it. You're twenty-five years old, I was the first person you've ever had *real* sex with, and you've been having sex since you were eighteen, at least."

"Younger," she whispered.

He smiled. "I know. Remember, I've known you your whole life. I've been aware of you for as long as I can remember. I knew the very first day you lost your virginity and who you lost it to. I grieved it wasn't me."

"You did?"

"Gregorio was the second person who has ever made you come.

Your sex is still fresh from that orgasm. I'm going to make you come again. I like making you come. I like to watch you."

He slid the cylinder inside her. It was thick and ridged and spread her until she moaned. He held the end of it as she positioned herself on it, slowly stroking her clit with the thumb of his opposite hand. "Tell me how he took you, Evangeline. I want to hear it. Tell me how he made you feel."

"He—"

"No. Grab the headboard and ride the cylinder while you tell me."

She gripped the headboard and moved her hips. The object rubbed deep inside her, hitting places that felt so good she wanted to purr. Anatol kept stroking her clit as she rode it and soon pleasure was once again filling her up.

"Tell me," he commanded.

"He—oh, gods, it just happened." She panted the words, building up a steady rhythm on the object inside her. "We were talking and then he was there, pushing me up against the wall. He—pinned me there, touched my—" She broke off on a long moan, her head whipping back.

"He touched your what? Tell me."

"He stroked me between my thighs."

"Go on."

"He made me come with his fingers and the sound of his voice. He—he pinned my hands above my head so I couldn't get away."

"Did you want to get away?"

"No. I wanted him."

His thumb pressed and rotated on her swollen clit, sending ripples of pleasure through her. "Did you like being restrained?" His voice sounded as thick and breathy as hers.

"It was exciting."

"Why?"

Her teeth bit into her lower lip as she tried to examine the reason why she'd enjoyed it. "It took my responsibility away. It was as if I didn't have a choice in the matter, though I truly did. The conflict was out of my mind and I could enjoy it."

He hummed as though absorbing that. "Tell me about when he slid his cock inside this sweet, pretty cunt."

She moaned, the cylinder thrusting deep inside her with every roll of her hips. Anatol was controlling her orgasm, trying to get her through her story before she came. The pressure of his thumb on her clit would increase and decrease, the pace quickened and slowed. He kept her on the edge of an orgasm in that masterful way that only he could manage. She would come when he wanted her to come and not a moment before.

She licked her lips. "He was impatient, nearly tore his pants trying to get his cock free. Then he pushed me roughly up against the wall, hooked my thigh over his hip, thrust inside me, and fucked me there. Hard. Fast. Quick. It was almost guilty."

"Did you come again?"

"Yes, almost immediately. My orgasm was longer and harder with his cock inside me."

He rubbed her clit with just enough friction, just the right pressure. "Come for me now, Evangeline."

She did. Throwing her head back and arching her spine, her sex pulsed and rippled around the cylinder as she came. Anatol stroked her, riding her through it, lengthening it. It went on and on until she collapsed in a fatigued mess on the bed.

She lay, weak from the emotional turmoil of the night and her muscles limp from the climaxes she'd had. She felt the cylinder slip from her and a wet washcloth clean her up.

Anatol lay down beside her. "Sleep."

She reached for him. "No, Anatol. I won't be selfish that way. Come to me."

He kissed each eyelid in turn. "*Sleep*. I love you, Evangeline, more than you will ever understand."

"Good morning."

Evangeline averted her gaze from Gregorio's as soon as she walked into the dining room. Her heart hammered. She hadn't expected to see him this morning at all. "Why aren't you at the palace?" She poured herself a cup of coffee from the sideboard, took a piece of toast, and stood awkwardly.

Gregorio sat at the end of the table, a steaming cup of coffee in front of him and an oversized sheaf of papers at his elbow. "Please sit down, Evangeline. I won't bite you."

Yes, maybe not bite, per se . . . She could still remember the feel of him between her thighs and the press of his mouth on hers. It was not an unpleasant recollection. She sank down into one of the chairs farthest from him.

"The Council has declared today a holiday in honor of the revolution. Every year on this day, from now on, will be a day of rest to celebrate the independence of the masses."

"Ah." She looked down at her coffee. For her, this "holiday" would ever remain drenched in blood.

She changed the subject. "Well, I guess we'll be spending the day together considering Emily had to reschedule our sewing lesson."

"Yes, I ran into her in the foyer and she told me as much. I thought maybe you and Anatol would like to go with me to the Tinkers' Guild to see what they're working on now. Maybe we can even take a ride in a balloon, if that's what you'd like."

Her gaze lifted from her cup and her unease was suddenly forgotten. The Tinkers' Guild had been the organization that had published the book about the inventions that she'd loved so much. They were the ones who had created the stitching machine that

Emily was teaching her how to use. They had immediately taken over the building in Milzyr where the Edaeii family had locked up all the in-progress inventions they could find. "Yes! I would love to do that. I'm sure Anatol would like to go, too." It had been a very long time since she'd ventured any farther than the porch. It was time she left the house. She looked at the sheaf of papers near him. "What is that?"

He picked it up and she could see that it was covered with small black markings. "It's a newspaper."

"A newspaper?"

"It reports what's going on in the city of Milzyr every day." He held it out to her. "Come and take a look."

"I've never heard of such a thing." She rose, walked over, and took the paper into her hands. "It's not hand copied like a book?"

"No, it's ink, printed by a machine. It allows them to produce hundreds of copies."

"How do they get the print on there?" She scratched at it with her fingernail and it came away black. "Incredible."

"It's called a printing press. The Tinkers' Guild has all sorts of interesting inventions they've been introducing during the last month. Things the Edaeii suppressed for decades. We're entering a very exciting time."

"A printing press. How odd." She laid the paper down on the table, frowning. "Why would the Edaeii have wanted to suppress such a thing?"

"A printing press gives the people power, Evangeline. A daily newspaper, a way to disseminate information, gives the lower and middle classes more power than the Edaeii wanted them to have. It will make it easier to produce books, too." He grinned. "Subversive books like mine, for example. It would make them more affordable and far more widely read."

She still didn't want to believe that the Edaeii had done anything like that. "The middle class, maybe, but most of the lower class can't read. This newspaper is useless to them."

"No." He shook his head. "All it takes is for information to travel into the right channels. From there it spreads easily enough by mouth. Even now there are town criers stationed through the slums of Milzyr, yelling out the headlines for the benefit of all. The press is printing books now, too."

"Yours?"

"Yes."

"I haven't read your books yet." She looked away when she said it. She'd meant the words to sting, but she couldn't quite mean it. Not now.

"That's all right. I hope one day you will. I think you'll like them."

She wasn't so sure about that.

Anatol declined the trip to the Tinkers' Guild because he needed to break arrangements for the storefront rental. After admonishing Anatol to be careful on the streets by himself, she climbed into Gregorio's carriage. It was uncomfortable, as most of the day was destined to be without Anatol by her side.

The inside of the carriage smelled like Gregorio—tobacco and leather. She was probably the first female to enter his carriage in Joshui only knew how long. Maybe ever.

She'd worn one of the gorgeous gowns that Gregorio had had created for her. Made of peach and cream silk, it set off her complexion, hair, and eyes to perfection. The bodice was drawn tight, pushing her breasts up pleasingly at the top. The skirts were heavy and belled out wide in the latest fashion—a fashion, she supposed, that the middle class embraced now that there was no more royalty left.

Her hair was done up on the top of her head, leaving a few

tendrils to curl becomingly around her face. She wore a pair of white gloves and clutched a matching purse, but wore no jewelry—since she had none. That was fine. She'd been assured more than once that the length of her neck and the shape of her face were adornment enough. She hoped so, since she had no other valuables but her looks to fall back on these days.

She was trying very hard not to examine why she'd taken so much care with her appearance today.

Gregorio sat on the seat opposite her, his huge body taking up almost all the space in the small area. His gaze swept over her in clear male admiration, though with him it was always a touch more feral than with other men. Gregorio knew all there was to know about the world, it seemed, yet there was a brutishness to him that didn't fit with the bookishness and intelligence. He defied every stereotype Evangeline knew.

When Gregorio looked at her now, she could see—almost feel—him thinking about how her body had felt the night before when he'd taken her up against the wall. It was clear he was replaying the event in his mind and wondering how soon he could get this gown off her.

At least in this way Gregorio was the same as most other men. It was the only way.

"You are breathtaking," he murmured.

"Thank you. Your money did this, of course, and I appreciate it."

"I would have you no other way, Evangeline, but kept in the finery to which you are accustomed. I want the same for all the J'Edaeii. They deserve nothing less."

She almost called him on that statement, accusing him again of treating her like a kept woman: buying her clothes, feeding her—in exchange for sex. But she didn't actually believe he meant it that way. And she believed he meant what he said about the J'Edaeii.

That seemed to be Gregorio's way. Never in her life had she met a stronger idealist than him.

He rapped on the outside of the carriage and they set off with a lurch, the hooves of the horses clip-clopping on the cobblestone street.

She peered out the window at the passing shops. Only a small bit of snow still remained on the streets, mostly in the shadows where the sun didn't reach. Winter was very nearly over.

The world appeared back to normal after the time she'd spent behind Gregorio's walls after the incident with Anatol at Belai. People bustled here and there on the street—women dressed in folds of velvet and silk, belled skirts flouncing as they tugged children behind them, and men dressed in fine suits, hurrying wherever it was they were hurrying to. It was as if the nobles had never existed—never even mattered.

They passed Belai. The gates were thrown open and the flag of Milzyr waved at the entrance. The guillotine was gone. No trace of blood stained the steps. Nothing remained to mark the days of carnage. She understood that the governing council met there now, of which Gregorio was head.

"Have you seen any others?" Her voice held a note of wistfulness. The carriage rumbled past the sprawling palace lawns that were still being well cared for, as far as she could see.

"Any others?" He paused. "Do you mean the Edaeii?"

"The Edaeii, the nobles, and the Jeweled. Do you ever see any but me or Anatol?"

"There aren't many left in the city, though some nobles have remained to make a go of it here. The magicked have left or are in hiding. The Edaeii that survived have been exiled, so they had no choice but to leave. They've traveled to Arabelle and Garhe, mostly."

"Roane Edaeii?"

He inclined his head for a moment, then looked out the window.

"He was given the option to emigrate, but he chose to kill himself instead."

"Ah." She gazed back out the window. That wasn't surprising given the amount of pride Roane possessed. "Do you know any more about the magicked who have left the city or have gone into hiding?"

"Most of them have been reunited with their families. The new government is helping them resettle where they choose, those who have been brave enough to accept our help that is."

"The new government is doing that?"

He nodded. "The Council saw my reasoning that the J'Edaeii and the adepts were victims of the nobles just as much as the peasantry. They have been made to see that the Jeweled are very special, a unique part of our country's heritage, and they need to be protected and not slaughtered."

Victims? "They're not afraid of us?"

Gregorio stroked his chin. "There is fear, yes. Fear that the magicked are powerful beings, fear of the unknown. That's why, for now, the J'Edaeii who have survived are living in secret. Hopefully one day that will not be necessary."

"Anatol and I aren't displaying our magick on the street corners, but we're not living in secret either."

He leaned forward and his face took on a rigid expression. "Anyone who tried to harm either of you while under my protection would be asking for a lot of hurt."

She looked away, unwilling to admit that she liked Gregorio's protectiveness. "The J'Edaeii were not victims, Gregorio. Once an adept proved herself, she was given the world on a platter. Money. A good marriage. Palace life until the day she died. She became the most direct extension of royalty that was possible without pure blood. It was an honor to be J'Edaeii, not a burden." It felt strange to talk of the J'Edaeii in the past tense.

"I suppose it depends on your perspective. From my perspective, being forcibly taken from your family as a young child, imprisoned, worked to the bone to develop your magick, and then forced into a royal marriage like some stud or broodmare to take advantage of your magicked bloodline hardly seems like a good life to me, Evangeline."

"And I should have stayed in Cherkhasii, perhaps? Mucking out the pig stalls?"

"You would have had far more control over your life if you had."

She snorted. "You and Anatol would be in agreement on this. He thought of the J'Edaeii as lapdogs for the royals, performing tricks for table scraps."

"Not a bad analogy."

She rolled her eyes.

"Are you familiar with any sciences of the mind?"

She gave him a blank look.

"There is a man in the south, name of Enrich Gaustenburg. He is developing a theory of behavior for the condition of men. He believes there is such a malady of the mind that gives abductees sympathy for their abductors. It's a phenomenon that can be likened to a reorganization of the victim's thought processes. It happens over a long period of time, reconstructing the victim's reality to—"

She bristled, the heavy fabric of her skirts rustling. "And that's what you think happened to me?"

He shrugged. "Maybe."

"You think that I'm so weak-minded. So—"

He held up a hand. "Your eyes are flashing, and although you are particularly beautiful when angry, I don't want to make you that way. And I *don't* think you're weak-minded. On the contrary. It's not a question of weak-mindedness." The carriage lurched to a stop. "Luckily, we've arrived and I can cease enraging you."

He was amused. She could feel it coming off of him. She had a mind to pluck the emotion from him and toss it into the street at random, trading it for something else—*humility*, maybe—but she resisted. It was tempting to use her magick in such selfish ways, but it wasn't right.

Thunder crashed outside the carriage and made her jump. A soft pitter-patter of rain began. Gregorio glanced outside. "Cozy. It's a pity we can't stay inside and enjoy it a little."

She gazed outside at the darkening skies. The wind had begun to pick up. She forgot her anger in the face of the thunderstorm; she loved them—even when they came during such cold temperatures. "That will wash away the last of the snow for certain."

"Spring is on its way. The end of a long, hard winter and the rebirth of a new season."

"Feels like the rebirth of many things," she murmured.

"Hopefully good things."

She glanced at him. "I hope so, too, but then I have no choice but to go forward either way, do I? No sense in living in the past; the past is done with."

"And the future is full of possibility."

"Yes." Her stomach fluttered with fear. *And uncertainty. Risk.*

Fifteen

◆

The Tinkers' Guild was a large gray building on the edge of the city. The driver had deposited the carriage in a large, open area—now soaked with rain—in front of the double doors. The footman opened the door of the carriage as though it weren't raining cold, fat drops all down his face and soaking his clothes, and opened a rain parasol for her.

Securing her fur-lined cloak tight at the throat, she took the footman's hand and stepped down into the cobblestone area. The footman escorted her to the door with Gregorio following. They entered the building and Gregorio shook his head like a dog to get the rain off. Apparently he was too much of a man to use a rain parasol—she should have expected no less from him.

A tall, gaunt man with salt-and-pepper hair greeted them in the small office area that they'd entered. "Master Vikhin! It is a rare honor to have you visit us today," said the man, clasping Gregorio's hand.

"Master Roghman, thank you for having us," Gregorio answered.

"Ytoyi Roghman?" asked Evangeline. "The primary author of the book *The Theft of Invention*?"

"I am."

She reached out and clasped his hand in hers. "I enjoyed your book very much, Mr. Roghman! It's an honor to meet you!"

"Thank you!" Master Roghman gave her a dazzling smile. "But it's perhaps even more of an honor to have a former J'Edaeii with us! I have never had the pleasure of meeting anyone with the power of magick."

"Well . . . thank you," she responded, a little at a loss for words. She hadn't expected a reception like that at all.

Master Roghman turned and, linking his thin arm with hers, led her toward another pair of double doors, away from the office area. "Master Vikhin tells me you have the power to influence people's emotions. How incredible and rare! You know, you and I are not all that different."

She smiled at him. "How so, Master Roghman?"

"The tinkers also have a sort of magick, magick created through the use of science and invention. Yours is natural and ours is not, but incredible and rare they both are." Evangeline couldn't help but pick up on the excitement and enthusiasm of the Master Tinker. He clearly lived for the guild and his work here.

"I read in your book that the royalty didn't approve of these inventions."

Roghman tutted. "No, no, not at all. The Edaeii only approved of the natural sort of magick and they wanted it all in *their* bloodline. They felt very threatened by any sort of scientific invention that might diminish their grandeur. I never understood the reasoning since, to my mind, science is no match for real magick." He shook his head. "No. The things I'm about to show you today are indeed wondrous, but they're no match for you, Miss Bansdaughter."

He led her through the double doors and into a large, well lit warehouse. Gregorio followed behind. There were many different work areas set up as far as she could see. Some had objects covered with large tarps and others—mostly hunks of metal—had men hurrying around them while they tinkered with tools or scribbled notes on pads of paper.

Roghman stopped and threw an arm wide. "This is where the Tinkers' Guild does its work. The last few months have been very exciting. We have dusted off the inventions we had been forced to put aside and have been making great strides with them."

Gregorio walked up to stand near them. "I think Miss Bansdaughter might like to see the printing press."

"Oh! Of course. It's one of our most successful inventions so far. It has so much potential." He guided her forward. "It might put the scribes out of business, though." He winked at her.

Roghman chattered on about each of the twisted pieces of metal they passed. One was meant to help women with their washing, but was too huge and expensive to be practical and needed to be redesigned. Another was a contraption that was supposed to act like a mini steam transport, ferrying the occupant down the street on its own. It was ugly—all hard metal and sharp edges. She certainly couldn't imagine climbing into one. Evangeline didn't see the point when carriages and horses worked perfectly fine for such things.

There were half-designed machines that were meant to aid in preparing food, cutting grass, filtering the air, doing just about anything under the sun that a man or a woman needed to do. It was all quite mind-blowing. In all her years at Belai, Evangeline had never imagined such things, let alone known that someone had been trying to construct them all.

The printing press sat somewhere in the middle of the warehouse. "There it is," declared Roghman. "With the exception of the helium floating balloon and the steam transport, it's our finest invention yet. That one was our first prototype. We have constructed one other and given it over to the use of printing newspapers and books. More, of course, are in construction."

She inched closer to the thing. It was huge and oddly shaped. Like nearly everything in the warehouse it was also made of metal. Small letters and numbers lined a top plate, each apparently was able to be configured to print a certain word or sentence. She couldn't fathom how it worked. It was fantastical.

"It is! Oh, it is!" said Roghman, and Evangeline realized she must have spoken out loud.

Just then the contraption across the aisle caught her eyes. Half covered with a large tarp, multicolored swathes of fabric covered a large wooden frame. "What is that?"

"This?" Roghman flipped the tarp back, revealing what appeared to be a set of wings. In the center was a sort of small metal box attached to a set of suspenders.

She glanced at Roghman in surprise. "A machine to allow a man to fly like a bird?"

Roghman laughed. "We only wish. It doesn't work, I'm afraid. We're still trying to perfect this one. It's sent three men to the physician so far." He barked out a laugh.

"Speaking of flying. Would you like to take a ride in the helium float with me, Evangeline?" Gregorio touched her arm, the heat of his hand bleeding through the material of her dress and warming her skin.

She glanced up at him, smiling. "I would love nothing more to take a ride in the balloon, but it's raining, remember?"

"I think the rain has cleared up," answered Roghman. "I'll escort you to the back of the building. You are welcome to ride in the very first helium float the Tinkers' Guild ever made." He winked. "It's made only for two."

* * *

"Oh, it's so beautiful," Evangeline breathed.

The city of Milzyr stretched below the small balloon, looking like it was something made for dolls. Belai and its lawns stretched over there, gray and green and beautiful even from the air. Over there were the grimy slums of Cook Square. Over there was the merchants' circle, where Evangeline bought her gowns once upon a time. And there was the middle class area of town where Gregorio had his home. She wondered if Anatol was sitting outside on the porch watching the balloon in the sky right now. Around the edges of the city lay a patchwork quilt of greens and browns—farmers' fields, she supposed.

Suddenly it hit her how very far up in the sky they were. She grabbed Gregorio's sleeve. "Please tell me you know how to steer this thing."

He laughed—a deep, rich sound. "Don't worry. I helped finance this invention, helped to build it a little, myself. I'm a perfectly capable helium float pilot."

She relaxed and went back to marveling at the view. It was chilly up here. Despite her warm state of dress, icy fingers tugged at her wrap and whipped pink into her cheeks. She smiled, letting herself enjoy the experience for once—without second-guessing every aspect of it.

"You're so beautiful, Evangeline," Gregorio said in a throaty voice. His desire hit her full force, warming her.

She glanced at him. "Is that why you want me so much? Because you think I'm beautiful?"

"Partly." At least he was honest. "But there's more to you. You're very complex. You fascinate me. I find you intelligent and strong willed. Not many women are, you know."

She gave him a sharp look. "Not many women are intelligent?"

"No, strong willed. This world breeds all the backbone out of them. But you, growing up the way you did, it's made you strong. You challenge me and I find that most invigorating. I can have a conversation with you, an argument, even, and not necessarily know I'll come out the winner. I can play a game of strategia with you and not know whether or not I'll win."

"You like me because I argue well?"

He laughed. "Yes, I guess I do. I always know where I stand with you. You will never dissemble with me, never lie to me in order to get what you want."

She smiled a little, remembering her past, and looked at him. "I don't do that anymore, Gregorio. Once, I did. Once it was a life-style."

"And now you have a different lifestyle. I hope you will consider including me in it."

Her stomach did a little flip, not at the words he spoke, but the emotion behind them. Gregorio fancied himself falling in love with her. The lust she'd constantly felt from him was beginning to deepen into something else, something far more serious. In fact, it grew close to something like what Anatol felt for her, and she for him.

That confusing tangle of maybe-love.

She looked away, down over the city. That strong emotion he had for her scared her, but there was something that frightened her even worse . . . the emotion she was developing for him. For both Gregorio and Anatol. They were foreign feelings and risky. These emotions were a little like stepping out onto a thin wire in high winds with only these two men to hold on to her. If their hold slipped and she fell, she would be dashed on the pavement below—shattered.

"Evangeline?"

"I'm fine. Just enjoying the view." She glanced at him and found him staring at her.

"As am I." His voice was a low, hungry growl that heated her blood.

He reached out, caught her by the waist, and pulled her against him. His body was hard and warm. She wanted to back away, but she just couldn't make herself. His head dipped toward hers and his lips met her lips.

They clung together high over the city, mouths meshing and hearts almost touching.

"It was incredible!" Evangeline said as soon as she and Gregorio had cleared the doorway of the house.

Anatol's heart did a little flip as soon as he saw her. Her gray eyes shone and her cheeks and lips were rosy. For a moment he had a flash of acute jealousy that Gregorio could give her such happiness.

He walked over and touched her cheek. "You're freezing."

"It's a cold evening, but it's cozy and warm in here." While he helped her out of her wrap, she told him about all the inventions they'd seen and the ride in the helium float. "You should have come along, Anatol, you would have loved it."

Anatol met Gregorio's dark gaze. "Maybe next time." He was also slightly jealous that Gregorio had been able to spend the day with her. Spending the afternoon dealing with all the arrangements he'd made for the shop was no match for her presence.

Gregorio stepped forward and cupped Evangeline's cheek in his palm. "I enjoyed spending the day with you more than I can remember taking pleasure in anything for a long time."

Evangeline smiled up at him, her hand resting on Gregorio's sleeve. "It was an amazing day."

The flash of truth that swept through Anatol in that moment rocked him back on his heels. In that moment he saw straight through the illusion of pretense and proper behavior, through Evangeline's fear and Gregorio's yearning. Magick leapt unsummoned inside him.

Gregorio Vikhin wasn't just fodder for Evangeline's burgeoning and uneven emotions. He was no fling that she would soon forget. Gregorio was a man who had qualities that she needed for her well-being. Gregorio's presence in her life would be beneficial to her, as she would be beneficial to Gregorio.

An ember of love existed between them just as much as it existed between himself and Evangeline.

The wrap he'd taken from Evangeline's shoulders dropped to the floor.

"Anatol? Are you all right?"

He looked up at the sound of Evangeline's voice and forced his eyes to focus on her face. He couldn't answer her. He always saw into the truth of things to some extent, but this had been amazingly clear. Disappointment sparked in his belly and he drew a ragged breath. He'd hoped Evangeline would one day be his alone, but he saw now that was not to be.

If he was to have any kind of relationship with Evangeline, Gregorio would need to be a part of it.

"Anatol?" she repeated, taking a step toward him.

He swept the wrap up from the floor and moved to the rack by the door to hang it. "I'm fine. Just hungry, that's all."

Gregorio walked from the foyer into the small study. "I'll have the cook make something hot for us to drink. There's a fire in here, Evangeline. You should warm up a bit."

She followed him, gravitating toward the warmth, and sat down in the chair, still chattering on about all the inventions at the Tinkers' Guild, her eyes shining. He'd never seen her this excited—not even after she'd returned from a shopping trip when they'd lived at Belai. Clearly, Gregorio was good for her.

He sat down in a chair opposite her and waved away tea when

the cook offered it to him. Evangeline took a cup and wrapped her fingers around it, warming her cold hands. "So, what did you do all day?"

Missed you. He shrugged. "Read mostly. Sat outside. I need to get back to training. I'm recovered enough to take it back up now. If I don't I'll get soft as Czz'ar Ondriiko was."

"I'll go with you, if you like. I know a place where we can spar in the northern part of Milzyr." Gregorio leaned up against the mantel of the fireplace. "There's a club."

Anatol gritted his teeth. He fought the desire to lash out at Gregorio from a place of jealousy, but doing that would only cause him to lose Evangeline. He needed to come to terms with this truth. "All right. That sounds great."

"How are you going to find the time, Gregorio?" Evangeline asked. "You work so much."

Anatol watched Gregorio glance at her lingeringly while her head was down as she sipped her tea. "I have reason to take some time off."

Evangeline froze, blinked, and then took a quick sip of tea as if to cover her reaction to his words.

"Anyway," Gregorio continued, "the Council is going to have to start pulling its weight as a uniform body of governance. That won't start until I take a step back from it."

"Well, good. I think it's wonderful that you've decided to back away a little." Evangeline stood and set her empty cup on the table. "I think I'll go up and have a bath before dinner." She walked over and gave Gregorio a kiss on the cheek. Closing her eyes and touching his sleeve, she lingered. "Thank you for a most incredible day."

"It's only the first of many wonders I would like to show you, Evangeline."

She smiled in response. Then she turned from Gregorio, kissed Anatol on the cheek, and left the room.

Gregorio watched her leave the room. "She's wonderful. Like no other woman I've ever met."

"Or will meet. Evangeline is unique. I always knew she was, even at Belai, even when she was in the grip of her gift's backlash, with all those walls built up around her."

Gregorio turned. "But she needed those walls. I see fear in her now; she feels too much, too strongly. She doesn't know how to deal with it all. Those walls, no matter that they made her into a cold person who had no empathy for others, protected her. Now it's like—"

"Like she's walking around with her heart on the outside, just waiting for someone to stab it."

Gregorio turned back to the mantel and let out a breath. "Yes."

"Those walls were never any good for her. I hope they never come back. She needs to find a better way to deal with her gift." Anatol drew a breath. "I think I know how we can do that."

"We?"

"You have feelings for Evangeline." It wasn't a question since he already knew the answer.

Gregorio said nothing for a long moment, keeping his back turned to Anatol. "I've never felt this way about another person in my life." He sounded defeated. "You love her, too. I know I need to back away."

"No, you don't."

Gregorio turned to face him.

Anatol smiled. "I told you I see into the truth of people. You don't just want to *fuck her*. There's love there, too. You appreciate her, care about her, want to protect her. She needs all of that. She's like a dry sponge. Fill her up. And I will, too. We'll work together to make Evangeline bloom."

Gregorio shook his head. "If you love her, how can you want to share her?"

"It's *because* I love her that I'm *willing* to share her. She's too damaged for one man alone. She needs both of us to balance her. If she doesn't get that balance and stability, she'll run away from me. Be my partner, Gregorio."

Gregorio turned his back on him. "You're insane."

"Maybe." Anatol paused. "Think about it."

Gregorio turned to him, one hand resting on the mantel. "I don't need to think about it. I want her. I don't care about your reasons for wanting to share her." He rubbed his hand over his mouth, considering him. "But I don't understand your motivations. You could tell me to fuck off right now and I would. You'd have her to yourself."

Anatol paused, considering best how to explain things. "I will lose Evangeline eventually if I can't make her completely open up to love. I need your help to do that. If I want to keep her in my life, I need to add you to my life as well. I love Evangeline and I want what's best for her. What's best for her is you and me, *together*. The gift of my magick has shown me this is true."

"So you want us to enter into a three-way relationship—you, me, and Evangeline."

"Yes."

Gregorio's gaze flicked to him. "I'm not into men."

"I'm not either. I'm not proposing anything directly sexual between the two of us. I propose that she is the woman we both want and need, and we are the men she needs. I propose that our relationship holds her in the middle, that she is its focus."

"And you think she wants that, too?"

"I think she *needs* that. She needs us both. She just doesn't understand it yet. I'm not saying that it will be easy, not with a woman as hurt as Evangeline."

"You know her better than I do."

Anatol took a moment to answer. "Growing with up her, I

always knew there was a jewel beneath the ice. That ice has thawed and we're lucky enough to be in the presence of the sapphire."

"Sapphire? Is that what you see her as?"

"Deep blue, emotional, vibrant, beautiful. I think they chose well when they selected the sapphire to represent her jewel."

"She's a strong woman and kind."

"She wasn't always. Ah, well, she was always strong. The kindness is only a recent thing. She's becoming more the woman she would have been if she hadn't grown up at Belai."

Gregorio sighed, glancing into the fire. "Do you think she would like to meet her family? She seems unsure."

"I don't know. I think she wants to find them, but she's frightened she'll be rejected by them. I don't see a rational basis for that fear, but I understand it."

"I have access to the records at Belai. I think I could track down their location." Gregorio rubbed his chin. "Do you think I should?"

Anatol gritted his teeth for a moment. If Gregorio found her family, she might favor Gregorio over him. He gave his head a sharp shake. Damn it. *Jealousy.* If this was going to work he needed to defeat that emotion. He'd known it would be difficult. "Do it. She should at least be given the choice."

Gregorio said nothing for several moments. The clock in the room ticked off the seconds as the large man leaned on the mantel. "And in this new relationship, what about jealousy?"

Joshui, it was like Gregorio had magickal empathy of his own. "It will be present. We'll have to deal with it."

He nodded. "I have nothing to lose in trying, but everything to gain in succeeding."

Anatol nodded. "Good."

"Don't you think it's a little high-handed, deciding what's best for Evangeline without even asking her?"

Anatol shrugged. "It may be high-handed, but it's for the best. I can see truths that she can't. The danger is in making Evangeline realize this is for the best before she flees."

Gregorio raised his eyebrows. "Flees?"

"If we manage to draw Evangeline into a relationship with us, she will discover that she's deeply in love with both of us. It's going to frighten her."

"And you think she'll leave us then?"

"I hope not."

Gregorio let out a careful breath. "You just gave my fantasy to me on a platter and now you're taking it away."

"I see truth. I can't predict the future."

Gregorio looked at him, his gaze hard. "I want her."

"Then take her."

Evangeline reentered the study, seeing the two men staring at each other intently, as if they'd been discussing something of great importance. She immediately felt uncomfortable alone with the two of them—especially now that she'd had sex with Gregorio. She'd been with both of them. They both wanted her.

And she wanted both of them.

"What are you talking about?" she asked, forcing a smile.

"What else would we be talking about?" asked Anatol. "Or who else, I should say."

Her cheeks heated. She hesitated in the doorway and almost left the room. She had a good book resting on her bedside table. But that would be too much like running away and she wasn't doing that anymore.

She stepped into the room. "It's not polite to talk about people when they're not present," she tried to say lightly. Wrapping her silk bathrobe closer around her, she walked over to sit at the fire, comb in her hand.

"All right, then we can talk about you while you're here." Anatol's voice held a note of mischievousness. "Do you think she's beautiful, Gregorio?" He asked from his place at the couch, amber liquid in his glass swirling as he examined it.

The emotion in the room surged—lust, love. Mostly lust, coming from Gregorio. It made her knees go weak. She clutched the comb until it hurt her hand. It was a good thing she was sitting down.

"Of course I do." Gregorio's voice came out clipped and a little harsh. "She knows I do."

She gave Anatol a cold smile. "It's also not polite to talk about someone who is in the room as if they're *not* in the room."

"Play the game, my love. You know you want to." Anatol smiled down into his glass, but didn't look up at her. "Evangeline finds both of us attractive, don't you, Evangeline?"

She opened her mouth, then closed it. "I do. I fail to see the merit to this line of conversation."

"She has the most exquisite breasts; don't you think so, Gregorio? They're the perfect size and shape. A man could worship them for hours."

Gregorio glanced at her and she colored. "Given a chance, I might try," he answered with a twist to his lips.

"Anatol." She'd meant his name to come out as a warning, but her voice sounded shaky and a little excited instead.

"And her sex. It's the most gorgeous thing I've ever seen."

"I wouldn't know," answered Gregorio.

Anatol lifted his head. "You haven't seen it?"

Evangeline's mouth went dry. She knew what Anatol was doing and she wasn't sure she was ready for it. She wasn't sure she'd ever be ready for it. At Belai she'd slept with two men at once, two women—once two men and another woman. But this was different. Oh, so much different.

This time she wanted it. This time she would enjoy it. This time there was emotion in it. These men were special.

This time it would mean something.

Gregorio looked at her with such a massive amount of sexual hunger on his face that it made her stomach do a backflip. "I took her up against a wall, skirts raised. I fucked her cunt, but I never had an opportunity to see it."

Evangeline cleared her throat, half of her wanting to end the game and the other half wanting to see where it might go. Being with Anatol alone was mind-numbingly wonderful. Being with Gregorio had provided erotic delights she'd never before known. Both of them together would be an experience worthy of heaven. "I am, as you can both see, still very much in the room. Have you any awareness of your immediate surroundings?"

Anatol finally looked at her with lazy, heavy-lidded eyes. "Oh, I think we're both very aware of our immediate surroundings. We're both *very* aware of you right now, Evangeline. You are, by far, the most important person in this room to us both."

"What are you doing, Anatol?"

"I'm simply asking Gregorio if he would like to see your sex. Would you like to show it to him, Evangeline? It's a beautiful thing."

She glanced at Gregorio, who was watching her like a hawk, his dark eyes bright under his hooded gaze. She licked her lips and felt herself flush harder.

"What emotions do you feel from us right now?"

Her answer came quick, since she was being bombarded with them. "Lust. Hunger. Yearning." She paused, her breathing quickening. "Love."

The first three things she knew what to do with, but not the fourth.

Sixteen

When she didn't move, Anatol set his glass aside, rose, and walked over to her. Taking her hand, he helped her stand, then walked her over to a table. Sliding her robe off her shoulders, it dropped and pooled at her feet. He tilted her chin up to his face and kissed her long and tenderly. Then he slid the bodice of her nightgown down over her breasts. It gathered weight and fell into a puddle around her feet, leaving her in only her panties. Soon those were gone, too.

Now she was completely naked in a room with two fully clothed, very aroused men. Her body tingled, sparked. Two men who wanted her. Not just for her body, or for what she might be able to do for them at Court, or how she might look on their arm. They wanted her, the whole Evangeline.

Incredible flaws and all.

Anatol leaned in, nipped her lower lip and then laved the tiny hurt with his tongue. "Get onto the table and part your thighs."

Trembling with desire, she slid onto the table and spread her legs. The chill air kissed her sex, but Gregorio's gaze heated her.

He cleared his throat and fidgeted, almost like a schoolboy. It made a smile touch her lips. This was a large, imposing man, one of the most powerful in all the country—and she could make him nervous simply by spreading her thighs.

"She's beautiful everywhere," the powerful man said.

Anatol walked to her, pulling her up to the edge of the table, and stroked her clit. "Do you want Gregorio to touch you?" he asked near her lips.

She trembled. "More than anything. I want you both to touch me."

He smiled against her mouth and slid his hand down, stroking her until the breath caught in her throat and she creamed a little against his fingers. Then he turned and pulled Gregorio over, placing his broader hand between her thighs. She rubbed against him like a cat in heat. It was almost as if she couldn't help it.

Gregorio made a low, hungry sound in his throat.

Anatol backed away, taking a place near the fire. "I want to see Gregorio touch you the way he did the other night. You told me he made you come using his hand, Evangeline?"

Her gaze caught Gregorio's. She nodded.

Gregorio slid two of his broad fingers inside her up to his second knuckle. She closed her eyes and bit her lower lip at the sensation of her stretching muscles. In and out, she rocked on the table. She curled her fingers around the edge to keep herself steady.

When she opened her eyes, she saw Anatol watching them, his eyes dark with lust. Gregorio was watching her face as he thrust in and out of her. "You're so pretty." His voice came out thick with lust. "I love to watch your face when you're excited." He thumbed her clit over and over, pushing and rotating, pushing and rotating. The bit of flesh pulled from its hood and begged for attention, swollen and sensitive.

Her climax burst over her body like biting into a ripe berry. Toes curling, she arched her back and moaned as the pleasure rippled out through her sex and into the rest of her body. She held on to the table beneath her until her fingers were sore and white.

Then Gregorio knelt, putting his face against her sex.

The action was so unexpected that Evangeline gave out a little yelp that quickly turned into a moan. Gregorio found all her secret, sensitive places and lapped at them with an eager tongue. He found her clit and licked until it blossomed and grew large. She breathed heavily as his head moved between her thighs. Behind him, Anatol watched with dark eyes.

Gregorio's hands spread her at her inner thighs, keeping her in place as he licked and sucked her clit, rubbing it with his tongue and nibbling at it with his lips. She climaxed against his mouth, fingers trying to grip the table, back arching.

When it was over, he stepped aside, looking feral, like he had to have her now—how he'd looked the other night when he'd taken her against the wall.

"That was nice, but I want to see more between you and Gregorio." Anatol's voice sounded strained. His body appeared taut and lust poured from him.

She studied him, trying to understand his purpose. Was he trying to forge a link between her and Gregorio? Or was he legitimately excited by watching another man with her? Maybe it was a little of both, she decided.

"All right," she answered him in a shaky voice. She slid from the table on weakened knees, her sex still throbbing from her climax. She walked to the carpet in front of the hearth, the heat of the fire radiating out and licking her skin.

Anatol and Gregorio both stepped toward her, making her stomach muscles clench and her sex tingle with anticipation in equal amounts of apprehension and eagerness. Anatol took her hand, flipped it palm up and raised it to his lips, kissing the inside of her wrist. "Are you ready for both of us to touch you, Evangeline?"

"I-I don't know," she stammered. Her voice sounded breathless to her own ears.

Stepping up to her, his eyes dark with hunger, Gregorio took her other hand and kissed the inside of her other wrist. Pleasure skittered up her spine and made her shiver. "You have two men who want you very much. Once we get started, you'll know what to do." His voice was rough, such a contrast to Anatol's silkier tone.

She hoped she would. This wouldn't be the first time she'd been with two men at the same time, but this would be the first it had ever mattered. It made the entire experience feel like the first time.

Anatol's and Gregorio's hands were hot on her skin. She pulled away from them both and set her palm to each of their cheeks. Anatol was a little taller than Gregorio, she noted, but Gregorio was wider and bulkier. Both of these men were very different and very special. The one thing they both had in common was how safe they made her feel, how cherished and cared for. It was something she didn't deserve, yet she soaked it up like a dewdrop into parched earth.

"I want you both very much," she whispered.

Anatol's gaze met hers. "That's a good answer."

Anatol clasped her hand and led her out of the library, up the steps to the large room she'd been sharing with him since they'd arrived. The bed was big here, just big enough for three adults; it was a good choice.

She turned while Anatol closed the door. "Have either of you shared a woman with another man before?"

Gregorio walked over and hooked her hair behind her ear. He smiled. "Are you nervous?"

She licked her lips. "Yes."

He kissed her softly. "I have been with another man and a woman before, yes."

"So have I," answered Anatol. He'd taken a seat not far away. "I happen to know you've been with a healthy number of different sexual configurations, too, Evangeline. What makes this one different?"

Her gaze strayed to his while Gregorio threaded her hair through his fingers. He let it slip slowly through his fingers, staring at it like it was spun gold. She swallowed hard. "I'm not sure." Her voice trembled a little.

Gregorio cupped her cheek and leaned in, dragging his mouth over hers slowly. His mint-scented breath warmed her lips and the tip of his tongue stole out to trace the wake of his mouth's passage over hers. His kiss made her knees go weak and her head spin.

"I know what it is." Anatol spoke from across the room. "You do, too, Evangeline. You're just not ready to admit it out loud yet."

She gripped Gregorio's waist to steady herself while his hands slid down her back and cupped her rear. Her sex warmed and began to tingle in that telltale way, the same way it did any time he touched her. Her gaze skated to Anatol almost guiltily. He was the one who'd pushed for this, but she cared about him so much that doing this with Gregorio seemed wrong—even while Anatol was right there, encouraging it.

She was afraid she loved Anatol. Worse, there were glimpses of Gregorio that made her think she might easily fall in love with him, too. Two men. She wasn't sure she could handle two men in bed, let alone in love.

Anatol's eyes were dark with passion and some emotion she couldn't name. He sat back in his chair in a deceptively relaxed posture, though his shoulders were tight. He fastened his gaze on her and Gregorio. She could tell he was holding himself back from joining them, wanting to watch her with Gregorio.

Gregorio groaned in the back of his throat and kissed her deeper, his tongue sliding between her lips. She closed her eyes and suddenly her thoughts were on him alone. Anatol, and his murky motivations for this liaison, were momentarily wiped from her mind.

He pushed her back a step, then two, toward the bed. Her fingers found the buttons of his shirt and pants, undoing them as quickly as she could. She pushed the fabric down and away, finding bare skin, and smoothed her fingers over the warm, bunching muscle of his upper arms and chest, down the hard bumps of his abdomen. Finally her fingers curled over the long, strong jut of his hard cock. Now it was her turn to groan in the back of her throat. He was gorgeous.

Gregorio's hand dipped between her thighs and found her damp and warm, located her pouting clit and stroked it until she shuddered with pleasure. He bent his head and spoke near her ear, making her shiver. "I have wanted you ever since I first heard you maligning my work in the kitchen of the Temple of Dreams. I find you beautiful and desirable."

Anatol rose and walked toward them. His boots clicked on the polished wood floor with every step he took. He circled them with a predatory look in his eyes. Heat rolled off his body and his gaze was just as hot as it roved her body, catching at her breasts and the patch of hair between her legs.

"Gregorio, I'm going to love watching her face contort with the ecstasy of two men within her. I can't wait to hear her moan and whimper."

"Me, too," Gregorio growled against her mouth.

Anatol moved to her side, Gregorio making room for him. He bent down and laid a line of kisses along her shoulder, his arms coming around her waist to fight with Gregorio's for supremacy. Being bare and vulnerable between these two powerful men was arousing beyond belief. Her breathing came fast, her chest rising and falling. Her sex was plumped and ready, begging to be touched.

Anatol turned her toward him. Evangeline put her arms around his neck and let him pull her into an embrace. Gregorio's heat warmed her opposite side, his lips brushing down her shoulder and back. Anatol kissed her deeply, almost possessively, his tongue stroking against hers hard. At the same time his hand snaked between their bodies and pushed between her thighs. He found her clit and rubbed, making her moan. "Are you ready for us now?" he murmured into her mouth.

"Yes," she whispered. "Sweet Joshui, yes."

"Undress me," he ordered softly.

She licked her lips, her flesh pebbling in the cool air. Her fingers trembled as she undid the buttons of his shirt and pants, pushing away the offending fabric that kept his bare skin from hers. Behind her, Gregorio dragged his lips over her flesh, his hard, long cock occasionally jutting against her. He brushed her long hair to the side and grazed his teeth along the curve of her shoulder while she finished undressing Anatol. His hands and lips seemed to be awakening every last nerve in her body.

While Anatol pulled his shirt over his head, Gregorio slipped his hands around to her front to fondle her breasts, catching her nipples and rolling them between his thumb and forefingers until pleasure rippled through her and she moaned.

Then Anatol covered her front, his hands roaming her body restlessly. Suddenly she felt light-headed. Having four hands on her was exquisite—but only because it was *these* four hands.

Gregorio ran his palms down her sides in a gesture that almost made him seem like a man worshiping a beautiful statue. "Spread your thighs," he commanded in a low, needful voice.

She parted her legs and he slipped his fingers inside her from behind and thrust, making her gasp and hold on to Anatol as she soaked Gregorio's questing hand.

"She's very excited, Anatol," Gregorio murmured.

Anatol pushed her back toward the mattress. "Well, then, I'd say there's only one place to put her. In bed."

The men forced her sit down on the edge of the mattress, each of them on either side of her. She reached up and took both of them in hand, sliding her fingers over their cocks from base to tip.

Gregorio's cock was thicker than Anatol's, though Anatol's was longer. Both of them were the most beautiful of all men to her. She traced a thick vein from the crown of Gregorio's cock down the shaft, taking her time in experiencing the first good look she'd had of him naked. He tipped his head back as she explored him, a guttural sound of hunger coming from his throat. The fact that the touch of her hand could cause that reaction made delicious satisfaction shiver through her.

Leaning in, she slipped Gregorio's cock into her mouth, while stroking Anatol's shaft with her other hand. Gregorio's fingers fisted in her hair as she drew him in as far as she could. He shuddered against her, groaning, his gaze securely fastened on her lips and tongue moving over his shaft.

"Lay back." Anatol pushed her onto the mattress.

Gregorio came with her, kneeling on the bed beside her head. After a moment's interruption, she had Gregorio in her mouth once again, reveling in the sensation of his shaft sliding between her lips. He'd gone absolutely rock hard. She slid her hand around to cup his tight backside and he braced himself on the mattress, slowly thrusting into her mouth.

Anatol's warm hands spread her thighs, exposing her aching sex to the cool air of the room. He stroked her with fingers that knew how to touch her, coaxing her clit from its hood and exploring her entrance. Pleasure eased its way through her veins, growing hotter and hotter, until it began to eclipse her thought patterns with pure sexual need. She forgot to be nervous about joining with these two men at once and she dissolved into the act like a drop of water into the desert—complete immersion.

Anatol's warm breath breezed over her sex followed by the touch of his hot mouth. She jerked and moaned as his tongue found her clit and nuzzled against it in wet softness. One finger, then two, slipped into her entrance and thrust deeper, stretching her muscles deliciously. He pushed them in and out of her as she worked her mouth over Gregorio's shaft. She panted and moaned around his length, the sounds mingling with Gregorio's groans.

Anatol's mouth fastened around her clit, his lips sucking and his teeth rasping gently. She moved her body in ecstasy, moaning around Gregorio's shaft.

"*Enough!* I need to touch her." Gregorio pulled from her mouth and Anatol backed away, apparently willing to let Gregorio take the lead.

Gregorio scooped her into his arms and positioned her in the middle of the bed, pushing her thighs apart and staring down at her cunt that was still glistening wet from Anatol's mouth. His face appeared feral as he looked down at her, hands fisted, cock hard—like he was about to devour her. She was happy to let him.

Anatol lay nearby, watching them with solemn eyes. A flicker of worry penetrated her fog of lust and she wondered what he was thinking. Gregorio, too, hesitated.

Finally, Anatol spoke. "Take her. Don't hold back, Gregorio."

Apparently that had been what Gregorio had been waiting for. Permission, of sorts. He didn't need any more encouragement. He came down over her, his mouth on hers, hand between her thighs. She gasped and then let out a long moan as his fingers speared deep inside her, thrusting as hard and fast.

"You're so beautiful," Gregorio whispered against her lips the moment before his mouth came down on hers once more. His tongue forcibly parted her lips and brushed up against her tongue. This man never seemed to ask where sex was involved, he just took. It was arousing beyond belief.

His big calloused hand found her breast, toying with her nipple. Then he dropped his head to her other breast, sucking the opposite nipple between his lips and rasping it gently between his teeth. Her back arched with pleasure and she pushed her breasts farther against his hand and mouth.

Forcing her thighs apart, he positioned his cock to her entrance and pushed inside. Her fingers found the blankets to either side of her and she gripped as her muscles fought to adjust to his size. He sat up a little, hooking the backs of her knees over his thighs so he could look down at her.

Anatol moved in on one side, kissing her lips and stroking her breasts, while Gregorio pulled out of her and then pushed back in. She panted against Anatol's mouth as Gregorio set up a rhythm.

"Does it feel good?" Anatol asked, dropping his hand between her thighs. He stroked her clit as Gregorio thrust inside her. Evangeline suddenly felt delirious with pleasure.

Swallowing hard, she breathed, "Yes."

"Are you going to come?" He pressed down on her clit a little more, while Gregorio picked up the pace of his thrusts, harder and faster, rocking her on the mattress. The first telltale skitters of her climax hit her.

Of course Anatol knew she was ready to come; he was the one driving her toward it. She nodded, gripping the back of his neck and forcing his mouth down to hers. Her orgasm hit her extra hard, slamming into her body and washing through her in wave after wave of mind-numbing pleasure. Anatol kissed her deeply while she came, his tongue mating with hers.

The muscles of her sex pulsed and rippled around Gregorio's still thrusting length. Gregorio tipped his head back and groaned as his cock jumped deep inside her, releasing his seed. Her name tore from his throat in a guttural shout.

He collapsed to the mattress, panting, and pressed himself to her back, while Anatol snuggled against her front. Gregorio's lips skimmed the back of her shoulders and Anatol's fingers tangled in her hair as he kissed her over and over.

She rolled onto her back, wanting to give them both all the attention she could, but knowing that with two men concentrated only on her it was nearly impossible to do it. That was the reality of this situation.

Their hands roamed her body restlessly, as though drinking in sustenance from her skin. She explored them as well, her hands stroking Anatol's rock-hard shaft and Gregorio's partially flaccid one. They caressed her breasts, rubbed her nipples, and almost competed for time between her thighs, their hands bumping into each other.

It wasn't long until her body was ripe once again and she panted with arousal. Even her climax sensitive sex tingled with excitement. Gregorio had also had time to rest and she recognized the telltale signs of his mounting arousal.

And Anatol needed some attention.

Evangeline sat up on the mattress and, pushing her long hair away from her face, went down on her knees over Anatol and drew his cock into her mouth. She couldn't bear to leave him unsatisfied.

Positioning her rear toward Gregorio, she tilted her hips and showed him her well satisfied sex, glistening and swollen with excitement. It was an invitation she was sure he would accept.

Slipping her lips down Anatol's shaft, she brought him deep into her mouth, her tongue running over all the spots she knew were most sensitive. His fingers tangled in her hair and he moaned her name. From behind she heard the sound of Gregorio repositioning himself on the mattress and then he was behind her, his body heat warming her and his fingers slipping over her sex, readying her for his cock.

He pressed the head of his shaft into her and she tensed against the thickness. Inch by inch he pushed inside her. Finally he was root-deep inside her and thrusting long and hard. His thrusts knocked her into Anatol, so she used Gregorio's rhythm to help her set her tempo on Anatol's cock. Her fingers curled into Anatol's hips to give her balance. Anatol was suave in bed, but Gregorio was a brute—hard and rough.

Ah, this was better. Each of them giving pleasure to each other simultaneously. She opened her throat and took Anatol as deep as she could. Together the three of them moved like one animal, finding a rhythm that drove them all to a place of perfect, shared ecstasy.

Anatol slipped his hand down and stroked her clit—every one of Gregorio's thrusts brought her up hard against his hand. She exploded almost immediately in a climax that made her cry out around Anatol's cock. The muscles of her cunt released and contracted, milking Gregorio's shaft until he came, groaning, a second time.

Anatol went last, his body straining. He called her name and then shot down her throat, his fingers curling into the blankets on either side of him.

Gregorio pulled her down onto the mattress and cuddled her against him. Anatol joined her other side. The two men kissed her and she kissed them back, limbs and lips tangling.

Sated beyond belief and wondering what the next stage of this new arrangement would be, she drifted to sleep between two strong men who cared for her, feeling safer than she ever had in her life.

Amazingly. Unbelievably.

Irrevocably.

Sometime in the night, she woke to find Anatol sitting in the chair of the study, staring into the remnants of the fire. She moved Gregorio's arm that was draped over her waist and crawled over to Anatol, putting her head on his knee. Her body held a sweet ache from everything they'd done. Any time at Belai when she'd performed sexual gymnastics like that and had endured the consequences, she'd been annoyed. This time it was something she savored.

"Are you all right?" she asked.

His fingers stroked her hair. "I'm fine. I just couldn't sleep."

"I miss you."

He tipped her chin up. "I haven't gone anywhere."

She glanced over at Gregorio. "What now? This changes everything."

"For the better, I think. You need Gregorio, Evangeline. I saw the truth in that this evening. He's going to mean much to you in your future, as much as I will. Gregorio needs you, too."

"And you, do *you* need me, Anatol?"

His pupils focused on her face and his expression became fierce. "More than anything."

She rested her head on his knee for a long moment while he softly dragged his fingers through her hair. "Why is it that you don't think you're enough for me?"

The fingers stroking through her hair faltered for a moment. "It's not that I don't think I'm enough. I love you, Evangeline. I love you enough for two men, three men, an army."

She lifted her head. "So why? I'm not saying I don't have feelings for Gregorio, but I don't understand what it is that you think Gregorio has that I need."

Anatol's gaze skated to the bed, where Gregorio lay in the deep sleep of the sexually sated. "He's much different than me, wouldn't you say?"

"Like night to day."

"There's your answer."

"I don't understand."

He glanced at Gregorio's sleeping form once again. "What is it about him that you like?"

She rested her head on his knee again, articulating her thoughts.

"I enjoy his mind. We don't see eye to eye where politics are in-volved, but he's always well-reasoned and well-spoken. I love his cleverness and how odd it is that his body seems so much better suited to a thug than an intellectual. I love when he loses his pa-tience, which is often, how he pushes his hand through his hair the way he does." She laughed softly. "I even enjoy how easily he loses his temper, yet I know that I can trust him. As hard as I might push him, I know he'll never hurt me."

Anatol's fingers trembled on her head and she looked up at him again. "What's wrong?" she asked.

"You love him already. I can see it in your eyes when you talk about him."

She frowned. "And that bothers you?" He'd pushed for this.

He shook his head, then nodded. "A little. It's what I want be-cause it's the best thing for you, but I can't say I'm completely will-ing to give up any part of you to another man."

She shook her head. "You mystify me. I've never met anyone like you, Anatol. You're completely—"

"Stupid?" He smiled.

"Selfless."

He reached out and cupped her cheek. "Try to leave me and you'll find out how selfish I am, my love. You're mine. Now and for always."

"Yours and Gregorio's."

"Yes."

She laid her head back down on his knee and smiled. Maybe that wasn't the worst thing in the world.

Seventeen

The next day dawned bright and unseasonably warm. Looking out the window of the town house in the morning and into the bustling streets of the city, Evangeline could almost imagine that the revolution had never happened. Everyone had taken to the streets in the oddly fair spring weather. Women in well tailored dresses made their way to the hatmakers or the bakery. Men hurried down the streets on their way to work. Children ran up and down the cobblestone roads yelling to one another and laughing.

She let the gauzy curtain of the window fall back into place and looked over at Anatol, who was sipping a cup of coffee at the table. "Maybe we should bring lunch to Gregorio at Belai."

He set his cup down and looked up at her. "You want to go to Belai? Today? Do you think you're ready for that?"

"The times have changed. Seems silly to deny it. It's been close to four months since the executions and Belai is in the center of the city. I can't avoid it forever."

"So you miss Gregorio, then?"

She lifted her chin. "I'll admit to an ulterior motive, but it's not so I can see Gregorio. I'm curious about this Council for the People."

His eyebrows rose into his hairline. "Ah."

She walked toward him, dragging her finger over the smooth wood of a nearby table. The fine material of her gown rustled. "Like I said, times have changed."

"All right." He stood. "We can pack up some sandwiches and fruit and take it over to the palace. I'm sure it would be welcome. He works very long hours and rarely takes a lunch, as I understand it."

She nodded and smiled. "And it's a beautiful day."

Not long after, they'd packed up their food and were walking through the streets of Milzyr just like everyone else. Evangeline had to remind herself that she didn't have to duck her head or avoid anyone's gaze. The threat of being recognized as magicked and executed was over. Well, almost over, anyway. The threat of the Revolutionaries still lurked. But, for the most part, as long as they didn't flaunt their magick openly, they could live like normal citizens—whatever that meant.

Anatol caught her hand and brought it to his lips for a quick kiss. "Do you ever think of your parents?"

She almost missed a step at the abruptness of his question. "My-my parents?"

"Yes." He smiled. "You know, the people who gave you life."

"It's just that . . ." She sighed. "Yes, I do. Of course I do. I wonder about them now that I can feel again. I wonder if they're still living, if they miss me."

"Would you ever want to find them?"

She said nothing, only kept walking.

"Evangeline?"

She shook her head. "My answer depends on the day you ask me. Today my answer is no."

"Why not?"

"What if they never wanted me?"

He stopped and turned her toward him. People parted around them as they stood in the middle of the street. "I believe they wanted you."

Emotion rose up in her throat. She broke his steady gaze, turned, and began walking again. "From all accounts, they did. If it's not true, though, I don't know if I could handle the pain." Before he could say anything annoyingly insightful, she glanced at him. "What about you? Do you want to find your parents?"

He took her hand again. "Yes. They're not far from Milzyr. If I go, will you come with me?"

She squeezed his hand. "Of course."

They walked in silence down the streets of Milzyr, both of them enjoying the beauty of the day and marveling at how much had changed in the city since their flight from Belai on that cold winter's day. It seemed so long ago. The city seemed to have a lighter feel to it now that the commoners were under their own rule, or maybe it was the lightness in her own being that she was reflecting out into the world. She'd gone through hell since her ability to feel had flooded back into her. She'd thought that emotions would only ever bring her pain, but now she found they brought majesty, too, warmth to her soul, happiness, love, contentment—all very good reasons to live.

They turned down a corner and Evangeline braced herself for the sight of Belai rising at the end of the block, the midmorning sun glinting from behind the spiraling white and gold structure. She'd always thought Belai the most beautiful building in the city, a place of richness and culture. Now she knew that it was only the noble-blooded and the J'Edaeii who'd ever thought of it in those terms. For everyone else—the majority—it had been an uncaring place of oppression and torment.

The gates were open wide to receive visitors; not a guard was in sight. She supposed they weren't needed anymore. Everyone had what they wanted and there was no longer any reason to storm inside and start murdering people. She wondered if the commoners were bored now that the fun was over.

She averted her gaze from the palace steps, the one place she wasn't yet ready to confront. Anatol seemed to understand that, and he guided her away. Considering his own experience with those steps, she was sure he didn't want to travel up them either.

They entered through a side door that led into the main foyer of the palace. It still looked the same, she mused, yet it was so different. The high, arched ceiling was still painted with a fresco of the temptation of Joshui, in glittering golds, greens, and silvers. The walls were still a burnished gold and the floor still polished marble.

But all the rich furniture that had been present before was now gone. The paintings that had hung on the walls had been taken down. All of it looted, she was sure. The commoners had killed all the human beings in the palace that they could, yet the artwork and furniture she was sure they had treated with care since it was worth so much money.

That wasn't the most marked difference, however. The most marked difference was the silence and the immensity of the foyer when it wasn't filled with talking and laughing people. The palace seemed now devoid of energy and life—a cold, dead thing; a museum to the time when the royals ruled the country.

Cold fingers of dread crawled up her spine and she resisted the urge to turn and walk back out. Maybe coming here hadn't been such a good idea, after all. Maybe she wasn't ready.

"Blessed Joshui," Anatol breathed beside her, sounding just as amazed and as appalled.

"Can I help you?" said someone from the right, making Evangeline jump.

A tall black-haired man dressed in dark colors stood from where he'd been sitting near the wall. A guard? Both she and Anatol had been so busy staring at the changes in the foyer that they'd failed to notice him.

Anatol stepped toward the man. "We're looking for Gregorio Vikhin."

The man stiffened and shook his head. Before he opened his mouth to deny them—after all, Gregorio was now the most important man in Milzyr—Evangeline added, "Tell him that Anatol and Evangeline have brought him lunch." Anatol held up the small case of food they'd brought with them. "We live with Gregorio. He knows us quite well." *Intimately, in fact,* she managed not to add. *We're on the friendliest of terms that can be imagined.*

The man closed his mouth and nodded. "All right, come with me." He walked down the corridor and they followed. Her gut churned at having to view more of the palace in its stripped down, silent form.

She gripped Anatol's hand as they traveled up the main marble staircase that Evangeline had climbed every day from the time she'd been four. Yet she'd never been able to hear her footsteps echo on each step the way they did now. Anatol gripped her hand and she held on to it gratefully.

He led her to what had formerly been the throne room, the same place where she and Anatol had performed to become J'Edaeii not very long ago. She could faintly hear raised voices coming from beyond the sealed ornate double doors.

"Wait here," said the man. He disappeared within the chamber.

Evangeline wandered down the empty hallway, looking at the walls and wondering what had become of their things. Was some farmer's daughter now wearing her beautiful tailored gown to muck out the horse stalls? Evangeline tried to feel outrage, but found she couldn't summon it. That was a long time ago, another life, in which she'd been another person. That Evangeline was gone.

Maybe she never should have existed.

"Evangeline, Anatol."

She turned at the sound of Gregorio's surprised voice. He stood in front of the double doors, their guide now disappearing down the corridor the way they'd come.

His gaze was fixed on her. "It's so good to see you. A sight for sore eyes."

She smiled, blushing a little. Amazingly, he could still render her shy despite the intimate acts they'd shared. "I hope it's all right we came." She walked toward him. He looked very handsome in his dark suit, red cravat tied at his neck. She had a sudden urge to loosen it and press her mouth to the warm skin of his throat so she could feel his pulse against her lips and breathe in the scent of him. She gave him her hands, instead, and then went up on her tiptoes to buss his cheek.

"Of course. In fact, I'm very happy you came. Your faces are a pleasant sight on a tense day." Gregorio's eyes traveled to the case. "And you brought food."

"Are you hungry?" Anatol asked.

"I am." He pressed his lips together for a moment, as if in thought. "But first, would you like a tour?"

Evangeline looked at Anatol. That's what she'd wanted when they'd first come, but now she wasn't so sure. Anatol made the decision for her. "Yes, we would," he answered.

"This would be a great time for it." Gregorio looked a bit more relaxed. Apparently he must have been worried about their reaction to the changes in Belai. "The representatives are all arguing about setting proper protocol." He grinned. "The same thing they've been arguing about for the last two weeks. Visitors will interrupt their arguing and give them a chance to cool down a little."

"Representatives?" she asked. *Proper protocol?*

"Yes, representatives from every province in Rylisk have been selected. They are supposed to speak for their people, act as their voice and body in this new government. They represent their interests. Come with me. I'll explain things as we go." His voice and mannerisms had gone from exhausted to excited as soon as he'd started to explain the new system of governance. Clearly, he lived for this work.

He opened the double doors and ushered them through. Immediately a swell of angry voices hit them and then ebbed away as soon as they entered the large room. Instead of the graduated dais where Czz'ar Ondriiko, Czz'arina Prademia, and the rest of the Edaeii family had once sat, there were a series of long tables and chairs forming a *U* shape. The entire surface of the table was scattered with paper and pens. Old white men stood or lounged, appeared animated or bored—all of them gave them their attention when Evangeline and Anatol walked in with Gregorio.

"These are the representatives." Gregorio swept his arm to encompass the room. "It depends on the population of the given province how many representatives have been appointed, but it's about two for each one, on average."

"They're all men." Evangeline immediately thought of the late, great Prademia. She had been a woman, but a woman with a keen mind and a strong hand. "And none of them are a part of any ethnic or minority group. How can they be representative of their people?"

"Ah, Evangeline," Gregorio whispered near her ear, "how I want to kiss you right now for observing that. We are currently setting the proper protocol for upcoming elections. These men are only temporary selections. When the elections are held, I hope to see a more diverse crowd in this room."

Gregorio walked them toward the men, who had gone back to bickering among themselves, though on a less violent level. "Representatives of the Council for the People," said Gregorio in a raised voice. "I wish to introduce to you Anatol Nicolison and Evangeline

Bansdaughter, two people who occupied these halls for far longer than you have, though during a different time. They are both formerly J'Edaeii and I think we have a lot to learn from them."

She stiffened, and Anatol did beside her as well. Neither of them had expected Gregorio to tell the Council who they had been. After a moment of wanting to back away to protect herself, she lifted her chin and coolly gazed at the gaggle of wrinkled old white men in the room. She had magick and they didn't. It was something they'd never be able to take from her, even if they decided to lop off her head right now.

Gregorio wouldn't let them.

The reactions of the men were varied. Some glowered at her and Anatol, others beamed and looked interested, still others looked as if they were about to expire from boredom.

"They survived the revolution massacre and are now trying to create lives for themselves in this new world. I'm giving them a tour of the re-created Belai today and presenting them with an intimate look at the way the political system will function in the future."

One man tapped the bottom of his cane on the floor. "We are happy to have you here!" he declared, rising to his feet and clapping.

Several others followed his lead. Then more. Soon many of the representatives were on their feet, clapping for her and Anatol. Even the men who'd glowered at them were finally compelled to at least rise in their honor.

"Markoff Tolison," whispered Gregorio in her ear, his hand twined around her waist. "He's one of the representatives from Ameranzi Province and is one of my staunchest allies."

Befuddled at the standing ovation when she'd not even lifted a magickal finger, Evangeline took a step back. She sampled the emotional currents of the air and found them high with feelings of regret, anger, sympathy, and guilt.

She backed away another step, wanting to get away from it. Her feeling about this place, these people and their purposes, was yet undecided in her heart. The memory of the revolution and the beheadings were still clear in her mind. The last thing she wanted was to become a way to help these men assuage their guilt for what had happened.

Markoff seemed to realize that she was becoming overwhelmed. The smile fading on his handsome and distinguished face, he reached out a hand. "It's all right."

But it wasn't. She barely even knew it when she'd reached the hallway and stood beyond the double doors, breathing in as much of the empty, dead air as she could take in.

Anatol was right behind her with Gregorio on his heels. Gregorio touched the small of her back when she nearly hyperventilated. "Are you all right?"

She nodded, pressing a hand to her abdomen. Forcibly, she gained control of herself. "I'm fine, but maybe it was a mistake to come here. Too many emotions, too many memories."

Anatol drew her into his arms. "Gregorio, is there somewhere we can go to be alone?"

He nodded and led them down the corridor to another room. It had once been someone's apartment, but now it seemed to serve as Gregorio's office. Evangeline glanced around, taking in the sitting area with couches, chairs, and tables, as well as a large, polished wood desk scattered with papers. So this was where Gregorio spent so much of his time.

Anatol guided her to a chair and Gregorio poured her a glass of water from a pitcher, which she accepted from him gratefully.

"I apologize," said Gregorio, sitting down next to her. "I didn't mean to overwhelm you in there."

"No, it's not your fault. It's just that things have changed here so drastically. I thought I was ready to see it, but maybe I wasn't." She took a sip of water. "The guilt and anger coming off those men, that was what truly bothered me. I couldn't gate all of it and I had my own emotions to deal with." She smiled shakily. "I'm all right now."

Gregorio kissed her temple. "I hate that I must, but I need to get back to them. If I'm not there to watch them, they'll tear one another's throats out."

"It's all right," said Anatol, "I'll stay with her."

Gregorio nodded, hesitating a moment, then left the room.

Evangeline let out a long, slow breath and looked around at the room they were in. Once upon a time Czz'arina Prademia had held teas in this room. She recognized it now. Her face twisted in anguish.

"She's still alive."

She looked at him. "Czz'arina Prademia?"

"Yes. They were loathe to execute the females, so they waited. She was exiled when you intervened that day on my behalf and they ceased the beheadings for good."

She nodded, sipping her water. The Czz'arina was likely penniless and living in squalor, but at least she'd kept her head. That was more than most of the royals could say. She'd always respected Prademia. She'd been one of the few strong, intelligent women in Belai.

"I don't miss it here." Anatol glanced around at the room. "I don't mind the changes. I welcome them, in fact."

"Anatol, all the bloodshed—"

"Of course. That was tragic. But this place?" He motioned to the room with his hand. "This never felt like home to me."

She looked around at the elaborately painted ceiling, thick area rug, and the gold encrusted table and chairs. Home? She'd never really thought of Belai that way. Truly, the palace had never felt like home to her either. The room she'd shared with Anatol, *that* had felt like home—at least, eventually. Gregorio's town house felt like home. She surmised that home was where the people you cared about dwelled. She'd never cared about anyone but herself at Belai and so it had never felt like home.

Anatol stood and walked around the room, looking at the painted frescoes on the walls and ceiling. "This place will never be what it once was."

She blinked, remembering the falseness and the insecurity. She remembered the way people had used one another here and the sights and smells of the world outside the palace walls—the poverty of the general populace that she'd always ignored. She remembered how one was nothing here if one didn't have money. How she'd had to prostitute herself to position herself well in Court culture because of that.

"Maybe that's a good thing," she murmured, taking a sip of her water.

Anatol turned toward her. "Oh, yes, it is. Now this place is filled with possibility for a bright future for *everyone*. The road ahead may be bumpy and chaotic, occasionally bloody and unfair, but it's leading us to a place that's better than where we were."

He was right. Though the revolution had been tragic for some of them, though good people had died alongside those who weren't, and *none* of them had deserved such a violent end, it had ushered in what hopefully would be a shining time for Rylisk.

And Gregorio Vikhin was just the man to help lead it there.

Just then the door opened and Gregorio stepped back into the room. "I have an odd request for you, Evangeline. Markoff has led the others to consider an idea I never dreamed I would hear voiced in that room." The cuffs of his shirt were unbuttoned, as were the top few buttons of his shirt. His hair looked as if he'd pushed a hand through it in frustration a few times. All of it combined gave Evangeline the urge to muss his hair further, to continue to unbutton his shirt.

She sat up a little straighter in her chair, trying her best to push her suddenly lustful reaction away. Gregorio seemed flustered and uncertain, qualities he didn't often display.

He fidgeted, glancing away from her. "This is probably not the best time to request this, Evangeline, but they are asking if you'll sit in our meetings from time to time and help to direct the emotional currents in the room to a place where more work can be accomplished."

She set the glass of water down on the table and frowned up at him. "What? You're saying they actually *want* me to manipulate their emotions?"

He held up a hand. "No, not manipulate. They want you to act as a sort of peace-inducer. To engender calmness in them, since they fail to produce it themselves. We're not getting much accomplished with emotions running so high. But considering your recent reaction to merely being in the room—"

Anatol held up a hand. "Gregorio, I don't think—"

"I'll try," she answered quickly. "Although I'm not sure I can do what they're suggesting. There must be calm in the room already for me to draw from."

"Are you certain?"

She nodded. "If I can help to move things forward in Rylisk, I will. Even if it's something so small." She stood. "Shall I try now?"

Gregorio smiled at her and offered his arm. "You have no idea how much I want you right now." His voice came out a low, aroused growl.

She took his arm and Anatol fell into step beside her. The feeling was quite mutual.

Eighteen

The day was beautiful. It was one of those warm spring days that borders summer and it bathed Rylisk in a cheery, bright glow that chased away the last of the winter chill from Evangeline's body.

Her days were filled with work, either sitting in on meetings at Belai or finishing her dress designs. She'd taken to the stitching machine easily and often sat up into the late hours completing her gowns. Her next step was to find a shop that might take them on consignment, to see if they struck a chord with her intended market.

She had two of them wrapped in gown bags and draped over her arm as she made her way down to Madame Huey's shop. She pushed open the door one-handed and entered the small, fragrant store. During the first days of the revolution the glass windows and doors had been smashed, but by now they'd been repaired. In fact, the shop looked just as it did when Evangeline had lived at Belai and had scraped every coin together she could to come here to have clothing made.

Staring around her as though she'd suddenly taken a trip backward in time, she made her way to the counter.

"Miss Bansdaughter!" a woman squealed.

Evangeline turned to find Madame Huey moving her consider-
able bulk around the edge of the counter toward her. She embraced
her so tightly she crushed the gowns between them, then held her
at arm's length with an expression of awe on her face and looked
her up and down. "You survived!"

Evangeline smiled. "Yes, I made it through."

Madame Huey hugged her again. "I'm so happy to see you! So
many of you didn't, you know." She wiped away a smile and stared
at her with tremulous lips for a long moment, as though caught in
a memory.

She didn't quite know how to react. Madame Huey had never
been so friendly toward her before. Of course, much had happened
since then. Perhaps the times had changed Madame Huey as much
as they'd changed her.

"You look well," the madame said. "Healthier than you did
before. You've put on a little weight and your color is good. You
look . . . *happy*. You never looked happy before." She glanced down
at Evangeline's fine day gown, a gift, of course, from Gregorio.
"Looks as though times haven't been all that hard for you."

"I've been lucky. Much luckier than many of my peers."

Madame Huey patted her shoulder. "That's for certain." She
walked around the counter again. "Now what can I help you with?"

Evangeline laid her creations on the counter and unzipped them.
"I have recently begun to try my hand at dressmaking and wondered if you might consider taking these on consignment."

Immediately the madame went into business mode. Pursing her
lips, she unzipped the dresses the rest of the way and took them
from their protective coverings, hanging them from a nearby hook.

She stepped back from them both, putting a finger to her mouth. A frown of contemplation creased her fleshy face. Then she set to touching the dresses, testing their seams and buttons, the weight of the fabric.

Finally she turned back to Evangeline. "They're very beautiful, but they're also . . . unique. My customers will either love them or they'll hate them." She nodded and smiled. "I'm willing to try them out, however."

Evangeline let out the breath she'd been holding. "Thank you."

"It's my pleasure to help out one of the few Jeweled left in Milzyr. Now, would you like some tea while we discuss the terms?"

Evangeline stayed for tea and also remained to help Madame Huey in the shop for the afternoon, since she was badly understaffed. By the time she returned home, Gregorio was already home for dinner and the evening chill had begun to sap the promise of summer from the air.

She hung her wrap up near the door and entered the sitting room, where she could hear Anatol and Gregorio talking in their low, rumbling male tones. The fires in the hearths warmed the town house and the cook's efforts in the kitchen smelled delicious. *Ah, I'm home.* Comforting pleasure settled into her body, relaxing away all tension.

She went to Anatol and kissed him and then Gregorio. It was nice to have them both here and happy to see her. She wasn't sure how she'd gotten so lucky to have snagged both of them, but she wasn't going to complain about it.

She wasn't going to fight it anymore, either. What woman in her right mind would do such a thing?

Gregorio pulled her down into his lap. She went with a sigh and nuzzled into the crook of his neck, inhaling the scent of his skin. Anatol watched them with heat flaring in his eyes.

Occasionally she felt flashes of jealousy from Anatol, though they were quickly suppressed. They came from Gregorio as well, though he seemed to have his emotions under control a little better. Evangeline assumed it was because she'd been with Anatol first and because Anatol had loved her from afar for so long. Yet, most of the time Anatol seemed happy that she was with Gregorio and the jealousy was the infrequent interruption of that steady emotion. Mostly when Evangeline tasted his emotions Anatol felt calm, contented, and confident.

And, perhaps Anatol had been right; with both of them she *did* have what she needed.

Gregorio's strong arms came around her and held her close. He kissed the top of her head. "How did it go?"

"It went wonderfully. She remembered who I was and gave me a much warmer reception than I ever would have predicted. She's taking two of my gowns on consignment and has asked me to bring more by for her to look at."

"That's fantastic," said Anatol.

"I'm definitely pleased. It's yet another step toward carving a new life for myself post-revolution."

Now they had to get Anatol on track. He was still struggling despite his love for the new government of Rylisk. She looked up at Gregorio, who was studying Anatol fiercely. Was he thinking the same thing?

At dinner, over a baked chicken with peas and carrots, she discovered the answer to that question.

Gregorio raised his gaze to Anatol over the table. "I would appreciate your help at Belai, if you'd be willing."

Anatol looked up from his plate. "With what?"

"I could use a go-between, an emissary of sorts between the government and the magicked."

Anatol set his fork down and leaned back in his chair. "Yes, you will need a liaison, but why do you think I'm suitable?"

"Anatol, you're perfect. You're intelligent, magicked, devoted to the new order, and sensitive to your fellow former J'Edaeii. I couldn't think of a better, more qualified person to ask."

"I agree," said Evangeline.

Anatol looked at them both in turn, then leaned back in his chair. "Ah. I get it. You two think that I need a new occupation, especially since Evangeline seems to be finding her footing now."

"This is not charity. I do think that you need something to occupy your days, but that's not why I'm asking you. I'm not lying when I say I can't think of anyone more perfect than you to ask."

Evangeline took a sip of wine and then set her glass on the table. "I think you'd be wonderful. Gregorio, did I ever tell you about the day of the revolution?"

"No."

"I was so wrapped up in my little life that I had no idea what was happening. Then Anatol was there, rescuing me, dragging me out of Belai to safety. Even though the mob was ransacking the palace, he was behind the revolution from the first day, even when I was still in a shocked haze."

Gregorio had his heavy gaze leveled at Anatol. "I'm not surprised. That's why I think he's a good fit for this position. He is aligned with my vision for Rylisk and always has been."

Anatol sighed, then took a long drink, as though stalling in his reply. He set his glass down and sighed. "All right, I can try it. It won't be easy, seeing as most of the magicked have gone to ground, frightened for their lives. The government is going to have a hard time earning their trust. It would be better if it was someone they knew reaching out to them. Someone like me." He touched the back of his neck, where he was scarred from the violent removal of his jewel. "The fact that I was nearly beheaded by the mob, yet I'm still behind the new government, may hold some sway with them."

Gregorio smiled, raising his glass. "And those observations will be why you'll excel at this job. Perhaps now that Evangeline has begun to help me at the meetings with the province representatives, she might eventually help you."

Evangeline nodded. "I'd be happy to help draw the magicked back to Milzyr." She paused. "At least in a capacity where I'm not using my magick to impinge upon their free will."

A smile broke out over Anatol's face. "You've changed so much, Evangeline."

"For the better," she answered, taking a sip of wine. "Definitely for the better."

She woke to burning need in the dead of night. Opening her eyes blearily, she saw someone had pushed her nightgown up to her waist and her thighs were spread wide. She moaned at the pleasure coursing through her. She was hot and wet, like someone had been teasing her while she slept.

Gregorio loomed over her in the half light of the room, his hand stroking her clit softly and slowly in the quiet of the night, arousing her straight out of her dreams. Her breath hitched at the look of feral hunger on his face. On her other side, Anatol slept.

"Gregorio, what are you doing?" Her breath came out, as it so often did these days, breathy with arousal.

He speared a finger inside her, drew it back out, and added a second, drawing a low moan from her. "I wanted to see if I could make you orgasm in your sleep."

Her hips rolled as she met the thrust of his hand. "You almost did," she whispered. "I'm close."

He stroked her clit with his thumb, nestling it down in her curls and applying just the right amount of pressure. "I love to watch you orgasm. Come for me."

She shattered, a moan of pleasure ripping from her throat as it crashed over her. Before the tail end of it was gone, Gregorio was between her thighs, sliding his cock inside her. She lifted her hips, welcoming him into her body. He seated himself deep inside her and her teeth sank into her lower lip as the muscles of her sex stretched pleasurably to accommodate him.

His hand skated down over her hips to the back of her knee and lifted her leg as he pulled out and thrust back in, setting up a slow and steady rhythm.

Anatol woke and watched Gregorio take her for a couple of minutes before he reached out and stroked her clit. Evangeline shuddered. Anatol always knew exactly how to touch her there, either withholding her climax or bringing it forcefully. Now he withheld it, letting it build, making her mindless with need and passion. Then he yanked her nightgown up farther and leaned forward, sucking one of her nipples into his hot mouth and flicking the hard peak with his tongue.

Gregorio and Evangeline came at the same time, her back arching and her cry splitting the quiet air of the room while Gregorio groaned, releasing his seed deep within her.

Breathing heavily, Gregorio collapsed to her side, holding her close against him and nuzzling her hair. Anatol fit himself against her other side and she reached down, catching his shaft in her hand and stroking him until he groaned. This was one of the tricky things about being in a relationship with two men, making sure neither of them felt left out.

"Now we're all awake," she murmured, kissing Anatol.

He pushed her to her back and slanted his mouth across hers hungrily. He pulled away after he'd kissed her breathless. "I won't be able to sleep after waking up to that."

She grinned at him. "Me neither."

"And I can't think of a reason why we should," said Gregorio. He met Anatol's eyes over her head for a meaningful moment.

"What are you two not saying?" she asked.

Gregorio was already out of bed and going through a drawer in a nearby dresser. He came back and sat on the edge of the bed. "Come here, Evangeline."

She eyed him curiously in the flickering half light of the dying fire in the hearth. He had a few objects in his hand, but she couldn't tell what they were. "For what?"

He smiled. "Don't you trust me?"

"Of course I do."

He inclined his head. "Then take off your nightgown and come over here."

She pulled her nightgown over her head and let it fall forgotten to the mattress, anticipating a long night of eroticism with Anatol and Gregorio. She scooted over the bed toward him and he pulled her facedown into his lap. Yelping in surprise, she opened her mouth to ask what he was doing, but he slid his hand down over the curve of her buttocks and then in between her legs, making the question dry up on her tongue.

He toyed with her rear entrance, making delicious shivers run through her. "Have you ever taken a man here?"

"Several times. Men are oddly fascinated with the act, I've found." Her breathing quickened as his hand stroked down between her thighs, rubbing her clit.

"So you've never enjoyed it?"

Anatol moved to lay on his side by her head. "Of course she hasn't, Gregorio. Until she could feel emotion, she never enjoyed any sex act."

Gregorio stroked her climax-sensitive clit straight into bliss. "Ah, well, I think she'll like this new experience, then. Don't you, Anatol?"

"What are you doing?" she asked thickly.

"He's preparing you," Anatol answered. "You can't take both of us at the same time without a little practice first."

"Both of you . . . at the same time. *Oh.*" A shiver of unease went through her. Though she didn't want to deny them anything they wanted, her history with this particular act was an especially bad one. It had hurt every time.

The sound of a bottle opening caught her ear. "You must be stretched a little. Neither myself nor Anatol are small men."

"Stretched? I never had to be stretched before."

"No?" asked Gregorio. "And how did you like taking a man in your rear, then?"

"It was awful, painful. I endured it badly."

"Ah, yes. So you see you need to be prepared. This will be cold." Gregorio smeared something on her nether area and she jolted in his lap. "Sorry. It will soon be forgotten."

He eased the tip of an object inside her and her body tensed. Sweet pleasure with the slightest edge of discomfort to make it more poignant eased through her body. Her breath hitched in her throat.

"Good?" Gregorio asked.

"Odd, confusing." He eased the object in another inch and she could feel it was graduated in width, stretching her wider as it went. She moaned. "It's good."

"I thought so." Gregorio's lust-husky voice held a note of satisfaction.

He stroked her clit, keeping her right on the edge of a climax, as he worked the object in and out of her, pushing it farther within until she was squirming on his lap in a hot mess of need. Pairing pleasure with an edge of pain so sharp she barely felt it.

"*Please,*" she cried. Arousal held her body in tight grip and she needed to be released.

Anatol watched Gregorio thrusting the object into her rear with eyes dark with desire. One of his big hands stroked his rigid cock from base to tip, making her crazy at the sight.

"Gregorio," she implored, "please."

"Yes, my sweet. It's almost time." Gregorio pulled the object from her body and Evangeline pushed him back onto the bed, desperate to have him inside her.

She crawled up his body and lowered herself down onto his hard cock, sinking him deep within her cunt. She flipped her hair back from her face, arching her spine and moaning as she rose up and sank back down on him, riding him.

Then Anatol was behind her, pushing her forward to lay on Gregorio. His cock was slicked with some kind of lubricant and the crown breached her nether entrance easily. Her breath hissed out and her fingers clenched the sheets. Inch by inch he speared into her, filling her up.

Soon the three of them were joined in the most intimate way imaginable, Evangeline between the two men. She panted, her thought processes sluggish at best from the massive physical experience they were giving her. Both her entrances filled and stretched beyond belief, the sensations seemed to mesh and merge, weave and blend.

All of it was pleasure.

Then the men began to move. Soon they found a rhythm that connected all three of their bodies in concert. The sound of their breath and the slide of skin-on-skin was soon all that could be heard. Gregorio yanked her head down to his and speared his tongue deep into her mouth. The sensations seemed to blend seamlessly; she wasn't sure where Anatol began and Gregorio ended.

Their cocks thrust in and out, building ecstasy inside her until she couldn't think or form words. All the pleasure centers of her body were stimulated and she held perfectly still, letting the bliss wash over and through her. Giving her men sexual ecstasy as they gave it back to her.

Her climax built to an incredible level and exploded. Evangeline cried out when she came in the most powerful climax of her life, the pleasure pouring through her like a heavy wave that made her knees weak and made her vision grow dark for a moment. Her eyes filled with tears and her hands found Gregorio, her fingers twisting his hair.

Her orgasm triggered Gregorio's and then Anatol's. The men groaned, their cocks jumping deep within her body as they spilled their seed.

Exhausted, they fell into the middle of the bed and curled up with one another, limbs intertwined. Evangeline's breath came fast and her heart pounded. She had no words to describe the experience of having both these men she cared so much about making love to her at the same time.

Tears pricked her eyes and Anatol wiped them away when they fell, while Gregorio nuzzled her hair and neck. They finally fell asleep wrapped around one another, Evangeline nestled safely in the middle.

"It's beautiful here." Evangeline stared down into the tree-lined, cobblestone streets of Arentz, the capital of Ameranzi Province.

"Yes." Anatol came to stand beside her at the window of the hotel where they were staying. "I don't remember it, of course. They took me when I was four years old."

She glanced at him. His brows were drawn up and the lines around his mouth seemed abnormally deep. "Are you sure you want to do this?"

He took a moment to answer. "If I don't do it, I'll always wonder." He paused. "Yes, I want this."

She looked back down at the street. Anatol was much braver than she was. She still wasn't sure if she wanted to track down her birth family yet, the way Anatol had done. By this time tomorrow they would be at his family's hat shop, a store that was only a few streets away from the hotel. Arentz wasn't very far from Milzyr, but even leaving early in the morning they'd arrived in Arentz too late to visit today. The shop was already closed.

"I'm just sorry that Gregorio couldn't be here," Anatol murmured.

Evangeline tasted his emotions and found calm. That meant he was likely speaking the truth. He and Gregorio had developed a deep friendship over the last few weeks and the flashes of jealousy she got from him—from both of them—had waned considerably. She thought that was partly because she never missed an opportunity to show Anatol or Gregorio that each one of them was special to her.

She turned to face him, winding her arms around his waist and burying her face in the crook of his neck. "I'm sorry he's not here, too."

Anatol grunted his agreement. His arms came around her and held her close. For a moment the only sound was the fire crackling in the hearth and the thump of Anatol's heart. She closed her eyes and enjoyed the moment.

"Of course, there is a part of me that's happy I get some alone time with you." Anatol's voice rumbled out of him.

She lifted her head and smiled at him. He hooked her hair behind her ear. "Hmmm, yes, and alone time we have since it's only twilight and we have to wait until morning to see your family." She affected an innocent expression. "Whatever shall we do with all that time alone?"

Anatol let out a low chuckle, drew down the blind, and led her to the bed. "I can think of a few things."

"You can?" she continued with her mock innocence. "Will you . . . *show* me?"

He growled and pulled her against him, covering her mouth with his while he worked at getting her out of her clothes. Moments later they collapsed naked onto the bed, laughing.

Anatol rolled her onto her back and stared down at her. "I love you, Evangeline."

Her smile faded as she looked up at him. The words were there, right there in her throat. *I love you, too.* All she had to do was give them a little air and they'd be free. And yet that old fear still lurked. The shadow of that deep, unending well of grief deep inside her. Of memories just out of reach. They made her too afraid to admit she loved him. So afraid that if she made that kind of commitment and then she lost him, she would fall into that well and be lost forever.

"It's all right." Anatol kissed her. "You don't have to say it. I can see it. You show me you love me every day."

He slipped his hand down to her breast and toyed with her nipple until her breathing hitched. She found his cock and stroked it from base to tip until a shudder of pleasure escaped him.

"Are you sure you won't be bored with just one of us here to pleasure you?" Anatol growled as he dropped his hand between her thighs and found her warm and willing.

She sighed as his hand stroked her, tasting his emotions. *Curiosity. Unease.*

Rolling him onto his back, she mounted him, his cock sliding deep. Arching her spine and letting her hair cascade down her back, she closed her eyes and moaned as he filled her. His hands roved her outthrust breasts, teasing and tweaking her nipples. "Oh, Anatol," she sighed. "No, not bored. Never with you."

Satisfaction infused his emotions, followed quickly by complete and total lust.

Her hips rolling, she rode him, his cock sliding in and out of her and sending waves of pleasure through her. He found her clit and stroked it with his thumb until she was a quivering mess of need.

Suddenly he flipped her to her back. Anatol rolled her to her stomach and she pushed up onto her knees, offering her backside to him. He was on her in an instant, his chest warming her back and his cock tunneling hard and fast into her cunt.

Her fingers found and gripped the blankets as he took her aggressively. His hand snaked around her front, stroking her clit and the sensitive folds of her sex around her filled entrance until she spasmed in climax on the bed beneath him.

When her climax ebbed, he withdrew and flipped her to her back, lifting her knees to spread her wide and entering her once again. His mouth came down on hers as he hilted inside her and her fingers tangled in his hair. Mouths meshing, they moved together.

She proceeded to show him she was not bored until well into the morning hours.

The next morning dawned unseasonably warm. Hands linked and dressed in their finest, they traveled to Anatol's parents' hat shop several streets over. When they neared it, Anatol paused on the street, staring through the plate glass window at the stout woman taking inventory behind a long counter.

Evangeline squeezed his hand. "Is that your mother?"

He nodded. "I think so."

She smiled. "I can sense her emotions. She feels like a very biddable woman, compassionate and caring."

"I can't see any truth by just looking at her."

"Maybe it's because you're too close to this emotionally. You feel twisted up inside."

He swallowed. "I am."

After a moment, he seemed to shake off a little of his worry and walked to the door. The little bell attached to the top tinkled brightly as they entered.

The smiling woman turned with a hatbox in her hands. "Can I help you—*oh!*" The hatbox tumbled to the floor.

Anatol knelt to pick it up at the same time his flustered mother did. His mother suddenly burst into tears and embraced him, fair tackling him to the floor of the shop. "Anatol, we thought you'd been killed during the revolution! We thought we'd never see you again!" She dissolved into noisy tears, rocking Anatol back and forth as though he were just a toddler again.

Anatol enveloped his mother in a tentative embrace at first. Then his emotion seemed to break and he embraced his mother with everything he had, burying his face in her hair.

Tears pricked Evangeline's eyes at the sight. She stood watching the scene with a hand pressed to her lips to keep from crying.

"Emelda, *what* is going on out here?" A man that looked like a much older version of Anatol came out from behind the counter. "Blessed Joshui," he breathed, seeing his wife on the floor. "*What are you doing?*"

"It's Anatol, Nicoli," she cried. "He's come home. *Finally.*"

Nicoli went red, then purple. Not with anger, but with the effort it took him not to burst into tears. Evangeline felt his emotions go from disbelief to wistful joy in under ten seconds. "Anatol?"

Anatol and his mother separated and pushed to their feet. Anatol stepped toward his father, offering his hand. Nicoli took his hand and pulled him into an embrace, finally breaking down into tears. "Son, we feared you'd never return to us. We didn't want them to take you. You have to know that. We never wanted it. We tried to visit, but—"

"I know." Anatol patted his elderly father's back. "I know, Papa. I'm here now, though, and we can make up for lost time."

But Evangeline could feel the swirl of Anatol's mixed emotions and part of him was enraged right now, enraged that he'd missed knowing his family. No matter how calm he sounded, he was livid that he'd missed out on all this time with them.

Anatol stood back and swept his hand out to encompass Evangeline. "This is my friend, Evangeline. My very good friend." He paused. "My love."

"Oh!" Emelda immediately gave her a warm hug. "It's wonderful to meet you."

Nicoli wiped away a tear. "Our son comes home and he brings a woman with him." He chuckled. "Maybe we'll get those grandchildren yet, Emelda?" He gave Anatol a wink.

Anatol met Evangeline's eyes and gave her a little smile.

Then Nicoli turned and walked to the back of the shop. "Well, come on up to the apartment. We've got lots to talk about."

Emelda flipped the sign on the door of the shop to closed, then took Anatol's hand. "Come on home, son."

Evangeline followed behind. Would her reunion with her parents be this heartwarming?

It almost made her want to find out.

Nineteen

Gregorio walked into the room with a sheaf of papers in his hand. As it did frequently these days, her stomach tightened in his presence. It wasn't an unpleasant sensation. On the contrary, it was a feeling of anticipation. Anticipation of hearing his voice, feeling the warmth of his body, sharing her thoughts with him and enjoying the singular scent of him—musk, wood smoke, and man.

It absolutely frightened her to death.

She'd already had a powerful desire to be with Anatol and now she felt the same connection to Gregorio. It was an emotional dependence she didn't want but was powerless to stop from evolving. Every time that strange tendril of feeling curled itself around her and became stronger, it made her want to run away.

Anatol had known this would happen and he was convinced it was a good thing, *what she needed*. But she wasn't so sure Anatol could see the truth in everything. The closer she got to Gregorio and Anatol, the more unease and fear filled her.

That couldn't be what she needed, could it? That couldn't be that elusive thing called love?

Yet the unease and fear mixed with all sorts of pleasurable feelings, too. Caring. Stability. Happiness. Excitement. Anticipation. It was another example of the confusing sea of emotion she was now drowning in. Perhaps love was all these feelings combined, perhaps not. She had no way to measure.

Sitting on the couch with her legs curled under her, she took a bite of the fruit she was eating and watched him carefully. Gregorio had barely glanced at her since entering the room. He looked at the papers in his hand.

"Why so serious, Gregorio?" she asked with a smile, trying to pretend she wasn't so disturbed by his presence in the room or by how much she wanted to walk over and kiss him.

He sat down in a chair and looked up at her. "I've found your family, Evangeline."

"What?" she breathed.

He pulled out a chair beside him. She dropped the rest of her fruit onto a plate, walked over, and sank into it. "When you first came to live here, I went to the records kept at Belai and I found the names of your mother and father. I discovered their last known address and then hired someone to track them down."

"Oh, my sweet Joshui." She put a hand to her mouth. "They're still living?"

"They own a farm in Cherkhasii. The same one you were born on. They haven't budged an inch."

"They're still . . . pig farmers?"

"Dairy, actually." He wrinkled his brow. "To my knowledge they never farmed pigs. They own the biggest dairy farm in the province. Who told you they were pig farmers?"

"The housemother at Belai."

"Hmmm. Well, she was misinformed. You have a younger sister named Arabella. She's getting married in the spring."

Evangeline blinked, trying to comprehend it all. She went silent for several moments, studying a little mark on the table in front of her. "I think I remember my mother a little. Maybe."

"You showed your talent from birth, Evangeline. Your parents tried to keep it a secret. They didn't want you taken from them. Someone in their village discovered your magickal proclivities and turned in the information of your whereabouts for money. Your parents fought the guards when they came to remove you. Your father sustained an injury that, according to my information, gives him a limp to this day." Gregorio reached out and tipped her chin up, forcing her to look at him. "They love you."

"Loved me, maybe." She moved her head and looked down again. "It's been so long."

"They love you still. How could they not? I propose a trip to Cherkhasii. The three of us. Anatol has found his family and now it's your turn."

She looked up at that. "You? All the way to Cherkhasii? How can you take time away from your work here for that? It's a long trip."

"I have business there. In the coming year I have to visit with almost every province in Rylisk to help bring their new governments into alignment with the central government here in Milzyr. Cherkhasii is on that list. We can leave as early as two days from now. I have a very comfortable carriage for the long ride into the country. What do you think?"

She rubbed at the mark on the table with her thumb. "I don't know." Things had turned out well for Anatol, and all indications seemed to point toward a happy ending for her, too. Yet something was telling her not to go.

"I strongly urge you to do this. You'll have no regrets if you do.

Later in your life, when your parents are gone, you won't wish that you'd traveled out to see them. You won't always wonder what would have happened if you had."

She sighed. "If you and Anatol come with me, then yes. Let's go."

"Of course. We'll be right at your side the whole time." He pulled her across the distance that separated them, putting her in his lap. She turned and placed her hands on his shoulders and ducked her head, giving him a light kiss on the mouth.

He made a hungry sound in the back of his throat. "You taste like strawberries." He threaded his hand in the hair at her nape and crushed her mouth to his, skating his tongue between her lips to mate it with her tongue. Her body quickened for him almost immediately, her sex growing warm and wanting.

"Where is Anatol?" he murmured against her mouth.

"Due back soon."

"You're all mine then for a little while."

She moved so that she was straddling his lap. His thick, hard cock pressed up against her. "Do you want me to be all yours, Gregorio?" She worked at unbuttoning his shirt and pushed it off his shoulders.

He nipped her lower lip. "Not all the time. I like to watch you with him. I like to watch how your body moves when you make love to him. I like to watch the pleasure that he gives you show on your face."

She smiled. "I think you just like to watch."

His finger worked the buttons on the bodice of her dress, opening it enough to bare her breasts. His gaze ate in the sight of them. "Both Anatol and I enjoy it. That's one reason why the three of us is working." His hand eased under skirt, found her silk panties, and yanked. "Off."

She smiled. "You're the more demanding one of the two."

"Do you mind it much?"

She slipped her panties off and straddled him again. Her fingers found the button and zipper of his pants and undid them, freeing his cock. "You know I don't."

He pulled her dress over her head and she sank down on his shaft, feeling him slide deep within her. Her teeth sank into her bottom lip and she tipped her head back on a groan. Gregorio closed his eyes and groaned, too.

She unbuttoned his shirt, exposing his chest and running her palms over his smooth, warm skin. Then she lifted up and sank back down on him, drawing ragged sighs from both of them. She moved slow, wanting to feel every vein and bump of his magnificent cock deep inside her and also wanting to tease him like he teased her so often.

He reached up and cupped her cheek. "I saw you with Anatol like this once, on the porch when I came home from lunch."

"You did?" She remembered back. "Ah, yes. That explains why you were so flustered that day."

He cupped her breasts as she rode him, gently pinching her nipples with his index finger and thumb until she gasped in pleasure. "You are the most beautiful woman I've ever seen, Evangeline." His voice shook with emotion.

Love. Overwhelmingly, it hit her, breaking through all her shields.

She leaned forward and kissed him as she moved up and down, taking him as deep into her body as she could. "You are also beautiful to my eyes," she murmured against his mouth. "And to my heart."

He slid his hand between them, finding her clit. She moved a little faster and soon all their words were gone, washed away in the ecstasy of joining their bodies. He pressed and rotated his thumb on her clit, driving her closer to orgasm. Soon she was reduced to just pants and moans, leveraging herself on his body and driving his cock deep inside with every downward thrust.

Her climax hit her suddenly. She threw her head back on a long moan, the muscles of her sex pulsing and releasing around his shaft. Gregorio held her to him, kissing her breasts, as he expended himself with a long groan.

She slumped over him when the waves of her orgasm finally ebbed away. He pulled her into a strong embrace and kissed her throat and face. Finally, when they could both move, he lifted her off his lap, wrapped her in a blanket, and they settled down in front of the fire.

Leaning her head on his shoulder, she sighed. Being with him was something she could get used to. He had his arms around her and she snuggled into his chest.

"I'll have the carriage readied for the journey."

She nodded, though a thin, curling thread of fear wove its way through her stomach. "All right." She couldn't help the quaver in her voice.

He held her tighter, dropping a kiss on the top of her head. "It will be fine."

The carriage came to a stop outside the steam transport station. The footman helped Evangeline out and the men followed. She stood, gaping at the transport with one hand on her hat as steam billowed around her dark red skirt. It stretched almost as far as she could see, the long length dotted with boarding passengers and transport employees.

Gregorio led them forward, the footman following with their bags. Evangeline and Anatol followed, watching Gregorio hand over three long slips of paper to a uniformed transport employee.

She nodded at the employee, whose eyes were wide as he accepted the tickets. Clearly he recognized Gregorio. Therefore, he must also know who she and Anatol were. He'd probably never seen a Jeweled in his life. At least he didn't look as if he wanted to murder them. That was a nice change of pace.

She walked up the few steps and into a long, narrow room lined with seats—some occupied and some not. The passengers seemed to be mostly middle and upper class.

She glanced back at Gregorio. "I don't see very many poor people riding the transport. How effective was the revolution at bringing true equality, I wonder?"

"Well, Evangeline," he answered with an arch of one brow. "The poor people may not be riding the transport yet, but they're no longer starving, either. First step in achieving equality, don't kill off over half your own people."

As usual Gregorio had an answer for everything.

He guided her forward. "We have a private car."

She gave him an arch look.

"Everyone knows who we are. We wouldn't have any peace if we rode in the general compartment," he explained. "In addition, you and Anatol might be put in danger. Not everyone likes the fact the magicked are walking around free."

The compartment was about the size of eight seats, with four places to sit and a narrow bed. Evangeline knew they'd be traveling all day into the night before they reached the far-off province of Cherkhasii, so she was grateful for the space. She went to stand by the window that faced away from the transport station and stared out at the field on the other side, a knot in her stomach. Soon she would be reunited with her family.

What if they didn't want to see her? What if they didn't want . . . her?

Anatol cupped her shoulders, his heat warming her back. "It

will be all right, Evangeline. No matter what happens, Gregorio and I will be there for you. Always."

She closed her eyes. Who in her life had ever been there for her always? *No one.* So how could she believe that he and Gregorio would always be there? Still, it was a nice lie; one she needed to believe right now. She covered his hand with hers. "Thank you."

Eventually she went to sit on one of the chairs, Anatol on one side and Gregorio on the other. Having them with her was a comfort with which she didn't want to become too at ease.

In so many ways she felt like a small child crossing a ravine on a tightrope. How could she know where to step? How could she know what emotions to trust? What emotions would betray her? She'd never in her life had anyone to trust and now these two men swore she could trust them.

It seemed too good to be true, and she had no experience with *good* at all.

They reached Malbask, the capital city of Cherkhasii, by midnight. Fatigued by the constant rumbling of the transport—yet oddly still invigorated by the experience of seeing Rylisk through the large window of their compartment—Evangeline followed the men out of the station to Gregorio's carriage, which would take them to a hotel. He had stored it on the train for the long trip to Malbask. It would take them the rest of the way to her parents' farm, about a five hour ride from the city.

The streets of the small city of Malbask were utterly silent this late at night, all the shutters of the houses and shops shut tight against the dark. It was as if the revolution had never touched this place, but as they rolled past the former province ambassador's mansion, she saw the evidence that it had. The great house sat desolate on the top of the hill, its windows and porches smashed, rotten food smearing its once regal brick walls. At least the house was still standing; she was certain its former occupants were not.

The hotel was a narrow building, fitted between a cookshop and a dressmaker. It wasn't up to the standards of Belai, of course, but it was several steps above the hovel she'd stayed in with Anatol.

A tall, gaunt man with almost no hair helped Gregorio and Anatol get their bags upstairs. The three of them were sharing a room. The hotel owner didn't even raise an eyebrow, though such three-way relationships were not as common in the rural parts of the provinces as they were in the cities.

After the man set a fire in the hearth and Gregorio tipped him, he left the room with a merry good night, even though it was closer to morning.

Evangeline stifled a yawn and began to take off her clothes. Sleep on the transport had been difficult for several reasons—not the least of which was her growing anxiousness about tomorrow morning. She wondered how many other Jeweled were going through this same thing—finding their long-lost families and hoping against all hope that they weren't rejected by them.

She turned and looked at the bed. Gregorio had collapsed in a chair by the fire and Anatol stood at the window, looking out at the black. A light rain had begun to fall against the glass. She walked toward him. "I don't know if I'll be able to sleep tonight. My stomach is in a knot."

Gregorio stood and walked to her. "We can leave if you want, Evangeline. If you don't think you're ready to do this. We'll just call it a jaunt to the countryside on the steam transport as a vacation and have done with it. Go home."

"But don't you want to meet them, Evangeline?" asked Anatol. "You've come this far and it's been so long."

"I'm afraid." She pressed her lips together. "What if they don't want me?"

Gregorio tipped her chin up. "Who in their right mind wouldn't want you?"

Her lower lip trembled and she steeled herself. "With the return of my emotions comes the possibility I could be hurt so badly I would never recover. It makes me want to draw in on myself, make a little hard shell all around me."

"That's the nature of emotion," said Anatol. "Sometimes it's sweet. Sometimes it hurts. It's always a gamble. As we grow up, it's a thing we all learn to deal with. You're just learning how to deal with it a little later than others." Anatol paused. "I think you should stay, Evangeline, and face whatever may come tomorrow. We'll be there for you."

Yes, so he kept saying. She knew he meant it, but the world worked in a different way. Much harsher than that.

Not telling him what she really thought, she smiled at him and looked out the window. The rain was coming down heavier now, making thick rivulets down the pane of glass. It was a good thing they'd arrived at the hotel when they did. "I'll stay," she said finally. "I need the answers to many questions; questions I never knew I wanted to ask before the revolution. I want to know what happened when I was a child and whether or not they truly cared for me."

"And no matter what happens tomorrow," said Gregorio, who had come to stand beside her, "we do care about you."

"With all our hearts," said Anatol.

Anatol pulled her against his chest and she snuggled into his strength and heat, watching the rain come down while the fire crackled and snapped in the hearth behind them.

Gregorio sat in the chair near the sputtering fire in the early hours of the morning, while Anatol and Evangeline lay tangled together on the big bed. Evangeline had finally fallen asleep laying in between

them, though it had taken her a long time to free herself of the
anxiousness of her thought patterns.

He couldn't sleep at all, worrying about tomorrow on Evangeline's behalf. She seemed so fragile. Any rejection she received now
would be devastating to her. Everything that Gregorio had read
about her family pointed to a situation like Anatol's, but they
wouldn't know for certain until tomorrow. He was nervous because
she was nervous.

Anatol tightened his grip around Evangeline's waist and nuzzled
his nose into her hair. Evangeline and Anatol had a bond that he
would never share. The experience of being taken from their families at such a young age and being raised at Belai had given them a
special link. Gregorio had grown up in a warm household, raised
with love and caring.

His family was very proud of him. He'd grown up in a hard-
scrabble part of Milzyr, in the shadow of Belai. His family had been
poor, yet noble-blooded, giving them a highborn surname. What his
family had lacked in wealth they'd made up for with strong, solid
minds. His father had always encouraged Gregorio and his sister
to get a good education, and any extra money they'd been able to
raise had gone toward this purpose.

His sister had received a good education just as he had, something poorer families normally didn't provide for their female children. Their father and mother had always encouraged them to
think for themselves, to challenge authority, and to always believe
that their lives could be better through hard work.

Most importantly, their parents had taught him and his sister to
dream.

Thanks to his father, Gregorio had been able to go on to the
university. He'd gone on to teach, at least until the royals had
caught wind of his democratic leanings and fired him. After that
he'd written books, handed out leaflets.

Started a revolution.

He passed a hand over his face. His father was so proud of him—executions and all.

His mother was gone now, from a sickness that had taken her a few winters back. She'd never lived to see the revolution he'd helped to incite, but she would have been proud, too. His sister, Sophia, was married to a scholar who enjoyed her outspoken and educated nature.

In many ways, Evangeline reminded him of his sister. Evangeline was very intelligent—if not educated, though she seemed keen to learn—and very outspoken. He'd known only a few women in his life who would tell him exactly where he stood instead of mincing words and prancing around the truth in order to try and please him. That was one of the reasons he was so attracted to her and had been from the first.

Evangeline woke a little and poked her head up, eyes drowsy and hair lusciously tousled from their hands. "Gregorio, come back to bed."

He went to her, snuggling in against her other side. Her body was warm, soft, and sleepy. She molded to him so sweetly.

"I wanted to tell you," she whispered, "I'm reading your books."

"You are?" He kissed her temple. "I thought you said you never would."

She smiled. "Things change."

"And what do you think of them?"

Her smile widened in a teasing way. "I'll get back to you on that."

"I'm sure we'll have plenty to discuss when you're through," he replied wryly.

"Oh, you can be sure."

Then she settled against his chest, her ear near his heart, and closed her eyes. He curled his body protectively around hers and drifted off to sleep.

Twenty

The hired carriage let them out at the end of a long, dusty road lined with painted wooden fences. Cows grazed in the pastures stretching to either side.

Evangeline had chosen a dark green velvet dress that buttoned well above the swell of her breasts. She wore a pair of sturdy black button-up boots—happily, since it looked like they were going to be walking quite a ways. An emerald that had been a gift from Gregorio nestled in the hollow of her throat, just above the first button of her dress. For a moment she stared up the road at the buildings she could see in the distance and trembled. Then Anatol took her hand and they started to walk, Gregorio on her other side, and she relaxed a little.

As they approached the first of the dairy barns, she could see scurrying milkmaids wearing aprons and carrying pails. All of them had strange looks to give them, but said nothing as the three of them made their way up the lane toward the main house in the early afternoon sunlight, following the neat, even white fencing. She wondered if they were all hired hands, or if one of them was Arabella, her supposed younger sister?

The house was a large brick affair with porches all around the outside. It was nothing like she'd ever imagined. Throughout her years at Belai, when she'd even bothered to think of her family, she'd imagined pigs and squalor—but warmth and love as well, though that was something she never would have admitted out loud.

In actuality, there was no squalor at all. This seemed like a well-run farm, and a profitable one at that. And there wasn't a pig in sight.

As they walked toward the front porch of the house, she tried to imagine growing up here. Would she have been happy? Would she be, even now, hurrying around with those milkmaids in the barn, trying to get all the cows milked before twilight?

An older man came out of the house before they'd even stepped onto the stairs. He was tall, sunshiny in color—just like Evangeline—and reed thin. He walked with a limp.

Evangeline's breath seized in her throat and she went still, staring up at him.

"Can I help you?" the man—her father, she was sure—asked with a scowl on his face. "Got no milk to sell to travelers. It's all promised to businesses in Malbask."

Evangeline tried to speak, but emotion stopped up all her words in her throat.

Anatol spoke for her. "Are you Ban Donnelson?"

"I am." He smacked his lips together, examining them up and down. "Who wants to know?"

She steeled herself and forced the words out of her mouth. "My name is Evangeline Bansdaughter." She meant to introduce Gregorio and Anatol, too, but she found she suddenly couldn't speak again. Her throat was too tight.

"Bansdaughter?" He squinted down at her. "Evangeline?" Realization overcame his face. "*You*," he breathed.

"*Evangeline.*" Anatol's voice held a hint of warning, but she ignored him.

She nodded, licked her lips, and started walking up the stairs toward him. This was her *father*. Her mind whirled.

He held up a hand. "Don't you come any closer. Not a step closer to me, do you hear?"

She stopped on the stairs, confused. He sounded frightened. His emotions *felt* frightened, too. They broke through her excitement as if she'd been pelted with ice cubes.

Anatol started up the steps after her. "Evangeline, come back down here."

Just then a woman came out of the door behind him and went still, staring at her. When Evangeline had seen her father, she'd assumed instantly that's where she'd gotten her appearance, but she'd been wrong. This woman, her mother, most assuredly, was the parent from whom she'd received her looks. Evangeline was her spitting image.

"Oh, sweet Joshui," her mother breathed. "How can it be?"

Evangeline took another step up the stairs, a flash of a memory whizzing through her mind—playing on a rug with wooden blocks while her mother bustled in the kitchen making dinner. Being held in her mother's arms when she'd been sick as a child, feeling warm and safe and cared for. These were memories triggered by seeing her face.

Suddenly Evangeline's arms ached to embrace her mother, to make up for all the lost years. In that moment she hated Belai, hated being Jeweled, hated even her magickal gift. If given the choice to go back in time, she would have traded all of it for a chance to grow up here, on a cow farm in Cherkhasii, with a father, a mother, and a baby sister named Arabella.

She ached for that loss. Her chest went tight and her eyes became moist.

She had a mother.

A warm, light feeling of love and joy filled her heart and she took the stairs more quickly. "Mother?" she breathed. "Is it really you?"

"Evangeline," said Gregorio behind her. He sounded worried. Why was he worried? This was the best day of her life. She'd found her family!

"I told you. No closer!" her father yelled as she reached the top of the stairs.

Her steps faltered and her smile faded. The warm, joyous sensation in her chest turned leaden. Neither of these people looked happy to see her. Her father looked angry and her mother cowered near the door, her eyes wide and her mouth agape—with fear. Her own joy had blocked her ability to clearly sense their emotions, just as Anatol had been unable to see any truths while looking at his mother through the hatshop window.

She aggressively reached out with her magick and felt the same emotions she saw on their faces—dread, shock, and anger. No happiness. No love here. They were not happy to see her.

"Why?" Evangeline stopped at the top of the steps. "I don't understand." She took another step closer and her father rushed forward with a bellow, his face twisted with panic and hatred.

Oh, please, sweet Joshui, make me a stone.

"Stay away! You're no daughter of ours!" His hands made contact with her shoulders, pushing her away.

Evangeline took a step back on the steps, her gaze flying to her mother and then to her father a scant second before her boot slipped on the top step and she tumbled down. Pain exploded in her head as it cracked against the stairs. She rolled to the base, hitting her knees, hips, and elbows as she went.

Everything went black and then Anatol was looming over her,

saying her name. His mouth formed the words, *Evangeline, are you all right?* But she couldn't hear anything. She lay stunned for a moment, then sat up, shaking her head and assessing her injuries. Nothing broken, though her head throbbed.

Oh, please, sweet Joshui, make me a stone. She remembered making a similar plea when she'd been brought to Belai as a child.

Joshui had granted her wish. Her emotions were numb—her old walls back up and firmly in place. She felt almost *nothing.* Hardly any emotion from herself or from others.

Oh, it was good.

Sounds began to filter into her awareness once more. Anatol fussed over her, asking if she was all right. Gregorio was shouting on the porch—angry, bitter words were being yelled back and forth between him and her father.

Feeling disconnected, the way she used to feel, she looked up at the men on the porch. Gregorio had her father up against the wall of the house, gripping his shirt and shaking him while he bellowed into his face. Her mother had apparently retreated into the house.

Wincing from the pain in her head and body, she stood with Anatol's help. "Gregorio," she said softly, cradling her sore arm. She was going to have a bad bruise on her elbow. He didn't hear her. *"Gregorio!"*

Gregorio stopped, stared her father down for a long, dangerous moment in which she wasn't sure what he'd do. Violence seemed to emanate from his body. Then he turned toward her.

"It's all right, Gregorio. Let's just go."

"It's not all right, Evangeline. *It's not.*" Gregorio's hands were clenched at his sides.

But it was all right. She couldn't feel a thing and it was wonderful. She was a stone, just as she'd asked Joshui. "No, really. It's all right." She turned and began to limp her way back down the road.

"You never come back here, do you hear me?" her father yelled after her retreating form. "We cut off your tainted branch of the family tree as soon as we could! You've been dead to us since you were four!"

Evangeline didn't turn around. She made no indication she'd even heard him. More shouting met her ears, a thump, a muffled sound, and then silence.

Gregorio and Anatol caught up to her near the dairy barns.

"Are you all right?" Gregorio growled, looking over his shoulder.

"I don't think I broke anything, but I have a headache. I'm probably bruised."

He whirled her to face him. "I can tell you're all right physically. I didn't mean that."

She blinked. "I'm fine. I prayed to Joshui to give me my walls back and He did. I feel nothing but a headache and some aches in my arms and legs, really." She pulled away from him and began walking again.

For several moments she traveled down the road alone, then the men fell into step beside her. They walked in silence. This time when they passed the dairy barns, the milkmaids didn't just cast the occasional curious glance their way. This time they stopped and stared.

One blond woman wearing a more fashionable blue dress stood out from the rest. Evangeline gave her a critical head-to-toe sweep as the woman wavered in an indecisive manner for several moments, then suddenly bolted toward them. "Wait!" she yelled, her long, fair hair streaming behind her.

Feeling deliciously numb, she turned to face the woman who was most assuredly Arabella Bansdaughter.

"Are you my sister?" the woman asked, coming to a stop. She was out of breath.

"I'm Evangeline. I'm apparently your sister, yes." She blinked. "In blood, at least."

"Evangeline?" She stared for a moment, her hands twisting near her abdomen. "They never told me your name."

That cut through her emotionless cocoon and made Evangeline flinch.

Anatol made a noise next to her and Arabella's gaze flew to him. "I'm sorry. Forgive me." She pressed a hand to her mouth for a moment. "They would never speak of you. I found out by accident. When I asked they said you'd been born deformed and they'd been forced to give you away. When I pressed they called you mentally damaged." Arabella studied her for a moment. "They said you stole their emotions." Her voice was almost a breathless whisper. "When you were a baby. That you sucked their joy and happiness right out of them. They said you caused emotional chaos."

She flinched again, but Joshui had been good to her. Her walls were still mostly intact.

"I do steal emotion," Evangeline answered. "I steal it, twist it, and trade it. It's the nature of my magick. It's why the Edaeii prized me above all others." She raised a brow. The last part went unspoken—*over you.* "That's why the Edaeii wanted me to marry into their family, to bring back the magick to their bloodline."

"Are you doing it . . . now?" she whispered, her eyes wide and a trembling smile of excitement on her lips. "Are you manipulating my emotions?"

"You are a complete moron, aren't you?" Anatol exploded. "This isn't a sideshow act. Get away from her!" Anatol pulled her away from Arabella, who had taken several steps back in the face of his rage.

"Wait!" Arabella called. "Don't go yet."

Evangeline turned and looked at her with numb eyes. "I'm sorry I never knew you, Arabella."

Arabella's lip quivered. "I am, too."

In the distance she heard Arabella's father—for he was no father of Evangeline's—bellowing for Arabella to get back, get away. Even through her walls and even at such a great distance, Evangeline could feel the love and concern he had for Arabella. There was none of that for Evangeline, only fear, sadness, and shame. He was worried that she would do something with her magick to harm his daughter.

Arabella took one last lingering look at Evangeline and then walked toward her father.

Gregorio took Evangeline's hand, and together he and Anatol led her down the road.

When they were ten steps from the waiting carriage, the walls that had so protected her shattered like they'd been hit with cannonballs. Her knees went weak and she stumbled on the gravel road, going down on her knees. Bowing her head, she covered her face with her hands and sobbed. Viscous black grief covered her, making her muscles weak and wracking her body with uncontrollable tears. She'd dipped into that well so far down inside her.

Now she was drowning in it.

She couldn't remember the last time she'd cried this hard. Had she ever cried like this? Maybe when she'd been four and taken to Belai. She might have cried then, but she didn't remember. It was strange to feel the tears in her eyes, on her cheeks. Odd to have these uncontainable sobs shaking her body like a dog with its favorite toy.

Anatol and Gregorio came down beside her, their heat radiating out and warming her.

"They sold me, didn't they?" she asked into her hands. "Once they found out about the magick, they became frightened of me and they wanted to get rid of me, so they sold me to Belai." She shook her head. "My father didn't get that limp trying to defend me. It was all a lie."

Gregorio rubbed her back. "I don't know. Maybe . . ."

She looked at him. "It was a *lie*."

She'd heard of it happening, of course. The royals had offered substantial sums for families to turn over their magicked children if the line of magick was rare enough. Since she was the only of her kind that she knew about, she supposed she'd qualified. She wondered how much they'd gotten for her. Did they owe the obvious success of their farming operation to her sale?

Gregorio rubbed his chin and glanced away like he was looking for a palatable answer to drop from the clouds. "Maybe someone in the string of record keepers had half a heart. Maybe they tried to give you something to hold on to for later. Maybe, yes, it was a well meaning lie." He stopped and stared at the carriage for several moments. "But you're right; your father got that limp from somewhere else."

"He's not my father," she growled, pushing up. "I have no father, no mother."

Anatol tried to help her and she was grateful for it, but she pushed past him anyway. This only affirmed what she'd always known while she'd been growing up; you always had to stand on your own feet. You could never count on anyone being there for you. She'd almost forgotten that over the past few months, but now she remembered.

Twenty-one

✦

Back at the hotel, Anatol rubbed the washcloth over her back and asked her if she was all right for the hundredth time.

"I'm fine, Anatol, really." She was lying for his sake. They were both trying so hard to make her feel better.

Smiling, she nuzzled his wet palm. Both the men had been pampering her since they'd reached the carriage. Once back in the room, they'd cleaned and dressed her hurts, called a doctor to examine her head, and then ushered her into a nice warm bath. "I'm still glad I came. At least now I know."

"Now you know, yes, but that means you lose the comfort of the fantasy."

"Anatol, you and your *truth* are not helping," Gregorio gritted out where he sat by the fire.

"It's all right, Gregorio," Evangeline answered. "Anatol can't help pointing out the truth any more than I can help feeling it. He's right. The fantasy is gone. That's both a good thing and a bad thing."

Gregorio came over to stand near the tub. Whereas Anatol could easily discuss his feelings, Gregorio often had difficulties. Evangeline could tell he was struggling with it now. After watching Anatol wash her back for a moment, he knelt beside the tub and looked into her eyes. "I wish I could take it away or make it different. You didn't deserve that."

She reached out and touched his face with damp fingers. "Thank you, Gregorio." Although she wasn't really sure what she did or didn't deserve.

"We love you very much," he finished, emotion clouding his eyes.

Ah, sweet Joshui, they were both the best of men. In all her life, any woman's life, could she have found better men than these? And most women, even if they were lucky to find a good man at all, never got *two*. Maybe the universe was making up for the lack of love she'd had growing up.

Because, oh, she did love them.

She cupped his cheek and stared into his beautiful dark eyes. "I don't know why you love me, Gregorio. I don't understand how I got so lucky to have you both or what it is you see in me." He started to interrupt her, but she put her fingers over his lips and shook her head. "And I love you back." Her eyes pricked with tears as she admitted it out loud for the first time. "More than anyone in the world, I love you both."

Gregorio leaned forward and pressed his mouth to hers. It was a deep and loving kiss, filled with the sentiment that she saw so clearly in his eyes and heard in his voice. A tear squeezed out and rolled down her cheek as she clung to him, getting his clothing wet, though he seemed not to care. He pulled her out of the bathtub and up against him. Soaking the front of his clothing, she held on to him tightly, her eyes closed.

Anatol came up on her other side and she launched herself into his arms. "I love you," she whispered near his ear.

His arms came around her. "I know. I always knew you did. Still, say it again."

"*I love you.*" Her voice broke on the words.

He let out a deep sigh, his body relaxing.

After a moment, Anatol pulled her toward the bed. She laid down and closed her eyes, exhaustion taking over.

The rustle of clothing being removed met her ears and soon both men were bracketing her, their heat keeping her warm and their presence making her feel safe.

If only it could always be this way. If only she could trust them when they told her it would last.

Their hands and mouths began to move over her flesh. Her body began to sing to life again, tingling with the awareness of her men. Clearly, they were going to do their best to make her forget the events of the day. She was more than happy to let them try. At least for a little while.

If anything had been shown to her today, it was something she'd always known. Love didn't last and it was never unconditional. Anatol and Gregorio might love her now, but that could change in a moment. They could discover something about her that they didn't like, or she could do something wrong. Then they would reject her and her heart would break so badly she'd never heal.

She couldn't allow that to happen.

But as Gregorio covered her body with his and Anatol parted her thighs with a sure hand, she pushed that thought away to deal with later. Tonight she would take what these men offered her.

Take it and drown in it.

Gregorio's mouth covered her nipple and sucked it to a sensitive, reddened peak, then moved to the other breast, while Anatol found her clit with his tongue.

She jerked, moaning, losing herself in the feel of them. Two mouths on her flesh, four hands. Her fingers twined in Gregorio's hair as they pushed her into a state of incoherence. Anatol tongued her clit into swollen need, then stroked it with the pad of his finger. She shuddered, nearly coming.

She pushed up, rolling Anatol to his back on the mattress and straddling him. The head of his cock sank easily into her damp sex and she bit her lower lip, taking him deep inside her.

A ragged moan escaped his lips and his hands came up to cup and play with her breasts while Gregorio sought the bottle of lubricant and coated his fingers in it. She rode Anatol slowly, teasingly, while Gregorio speared inside her nether hole, up to the second knuckle.

She moaned and bucked on Anatol, all the nerves in that not often touched area of her body springing to delicious life. The sensation of having both her orifices stimulated at the same time was an indescribable, overwhelming thing. Pure pleasure.

Gregorio played until she was stretched and ready to take him. Then he coated his cock in the lubricant, straddled Anatol's legs, and guided his cock into her rear.

She lowered her chest to Anatol's, waiting for Gregorio to hilt inside her. As he worked his shaft in slowly, inch by slow inch, Anatol kissed her roughly, eating at her lips and spearing his tongue into her mouth while he ever so leisurely rocked his cock back and forth deep inside her cunt.

When she was filled with both of them, they began to thrust. Pleasure took her over, chased everything else away. They found a rhythm, all of them moving as one being, straining toward release and immersed in the act of giving and receiving pleasure.

Evangeline's body tensed and her orgasm slammed into her. It was always more intense with both of them together. She cried out, her body spasming in intense pleasure. The sound and sight of her climax triggered first Anatol's and then Gregorio's.

They collapsed to the bed, spent, sweaty, and satisfied.

* * *

They stayed in Malbask for nearly a week longer. A week that originally she had planned to spend with her family while Gregorio and Anatol did the work they needed to do in Cherkhasii Province. Instead, she spent it with Anatol, cautiously approaching the known magicked in the area and coaxing them to trust the new government.

Many doors were slammed in their faces. Anatol's new job would not be an easy one, but he knew that. By the week's end they'd made a little progress, but time and multiple trips to the province would be necessary to make any true headway.

Evangeline managed to take a positive step forward in the city, ironically enough, by securing a dressmaker there who loved the collection of designs she'd brought and wanted to stock them in her store.

After Gregorio and Anatol had done all they could do, they boarded the train once again and undertook the long journey back to Milzyr.

She was happy to be leaving Malbask. This city would always be a place of grief for her. She hoped any business dealings she would have in the future could be accomplished through wire communication and long-distance delivery.

On the way back she stared out the window at the passing scenery and didn't say much, though she caught the occasional looks of concern that Gregorio and Anatol shared. She'd done all she could to insulate them from her emotional turmoil. They didn't deserve to suffer it. It was hers and hers alone. She could wish all day that the situation might be different, but wishing to change a truth was like blowing a feather at a boulder.

"Evangeline?"

She turned her head to find both of her beautiful, perfect, strong, loving men looking at her. *Would that she could keep them forever.* She smiled. "I'm fine." Then she turned back to looking out the window.

"You're not fine, Evangeline." Anatol's voice sounded hard. "Have you forgotten the flip side of my gift? I can see your lies very well."

She sighed and looked into her lap. "Nothing lasts. Nothing is forever." She paused and swallowed hard. "If my parents didn't want me, how can I believe that anyone else will want me? The pain—" she broke off. "It's like nothing I've ever felt before. It's physical as well as emotional. I'm afraid that if I lose you two that it would kill me."

"You're not going to lose us." Anatol came to sit beside her, drawing her into his arms and burying his nose in her hair as if she were going bolt away and leave him forever. "You will never lose us, Evangeline."

Gregorio came down on his knees in front of her. "You are ours, Evangeline. Do you hear me?" Gregorio's rough voice rasped over her and made her shiver. "The only way you'll lose us is if you leave us. And you can't leave us. Not now. Not ever. We belong together— the three of us. We'll make it work."

She shook her head and tried to speak, but found she had no words.

Anatol let Gregorio haul her down into his lap. He sat on the floor of the car cradling her.

"You don't understand." A tear dripped off her cheek. "Not even I understand. You scare me, both of you. All I've ever had in my life was myself to rely on. Now you're here, *two* of you, and—"

"But that's a good thing, Evangeline. Why should that scare you? Yes, we're here for you. Yes, we'll support you. We love you."

Her fingers tightened in Gregorio's shirt and she gritted her teeth for a moment. "And I'm in love with you, too, you and Anatol, both. What if I completely lose myself in you, invest all this emotion in you, and you leave me? What if you fall out of love with me, but I stay in love with you? What if—"

He pressed his lips to hers to stop the rest of her words. "That won't happen, Evangeline, because we're both already invested completely in you. We belong to one another now. If one of us hurts, the others hurt. We're connected."

She sagged against him, wanting to bathe in that sentiment.

"What-ifs will kill you, my darling," he murmured against her mouth. "Just let go of those and trust your emotions."

"But that's the thing, Gregorio. Emotion is new for me. It's hard for me to trust it."

He took her hand and placed it on his chest. "Then trust me. Trust Anatol."

She closed her eyes and melted against him. She wished she could.

It wasn't enough.

They took the steam transport back to the city in almost near silence, the weight of her grief holding all of them down. Anatol might have been able to see the truth of things, but that didn't mean that she couldn't, too. Right now she could see into the truth of this situation quite well—crystal clear. She didn't like what she saw, but there was nothing she could do about it.

Love wasn't enough.

It couldn't protect her against what had happened back on her family's farm. In fact, it made it worse. Love crushed when it was rejected. Hope pierced more surely than a sword when it was disappointed. She couldn't withstand anything like what she'd endured on the steps of that farmhouse again. Not from Anatol and Gregorio.

And it was inevitable, wasn't it?

She hadn't been enough for her parents. So she couldn't be enough for Anatol and Gregorio. Not for forever. Eventually, as she grew more and more attached and dependent on them, they would grow further apart from her. Eventually she would be on her knees somewhere alone, suffering the gut-wrenching pangs of rejection and love lost, only ten times worse than what she'd experienced at her parents' hands.

If she didn't get out now, before she slipped even further in love with them both, that would be her fate.

Every moment she spent with them, she slipped further.

They made it back to Gregorio's house shrouded in a sense of sorrowfulness so thick that most people instinctively got out of their way on the street. As the moon shone overhead, they entered the town house and were greeted by a welcome late dinner of lamb and steamed vegetables. The servants had affected a feel of cozy joy in the house, something she couldn't share in. Not tonight.

After dinner Evangeline opted to sleep in a guest room alone, complaining of a bad headache. She exchanged lingering kisses with her beautiful men and then entered her room for the night, closing the door behind her.

As soon as the door closed and she was alone, she leaned up against the back of it and closed her eyes, feeling the grief of what she was about to do. She couldn't stay here with them. She couldn't risk another tearing injury to her soul when they rejected her. They deserved better than her. They deserved a woman who could love them with all she was, without pain and confusion, and without reservation. She was not that woman. That meant she had to get out of here while she could—it was better for all of them.

She waited until she was sure that the men had gone to sleep in their respective rooms and the town house was quiet with the heaviness of rest after a long, exhausting journey. Then she packed a bag with only the clothing items she'd had when she'd come here and she stepped out into the hallway.

Every step she took down the gorgeous runner rug of the corridor, every move she made as she traveled down the stairs to the front door, she did with total in-the-moment consciousness, wanting to absorb this place into herself and keep it with her for the lonely nights ahead when she would remember this time and think about could-have-beens. Could-have-beens were so much better than reality.

She had only one place to go.

Twenty-two

A s she neared the Temple of Dreams she thought of how she'd told Anatol she wouldn't abandon him. That had been when they'd been destitute, though. Anatol would be fine without her now. He had a job with the government and a bright future, one without her in it. He could find a woman worthy of him and she could avoid having her heart shredded.

The lights of the Temple of Dreams were all ablaze on the otherwise dark street. Low music could be heard as she turned from the sidewalk onto the path leading up to the door. Voices, male and female, droned from inside, punctuated by laughter and the clinking of glasses. A party every night; that's what life at the Temple of Dreams would be like. Her heart was heavy; that's not what she wanted tonight. Now she craved shelter, a dark, quiet corner where she could grieve her losses in private.

Her knock on the front door revealed Dora's smiling, round face. Her expression went blank for a moment, then registered recognition. "Are you here to see Lilya?"

Evangeline forced a smile. "If she's not busy."

"I think she is." Dora ushered her inside. "But I can put you in a waiting room and she'll come to you when she can."

"All right." She walked into the cheery, posh interior with her bag in hand. She hoped Lilya would let her stay here tonight; otherwise she wasn't sure where she'd go. Luckily, though, she felt strong enough to manage any challenge that came her way. Being pushed out of Belai and being forced to stand on her own two feet had done her good in many ways.

All the people in the thronged sitting room paused to look at her. Evangeline's cheeks heated as her gaze flitted to all their faces, half looking for anyone she knew.

"There's a pretty one," said one man to another. "With any luck she works here, too."

Evangeline let her gaze linger on the speaker, a tall, not unhandsome man in his mid-thirties. If she worked here, this was the type of man she'd have to entertain. Could she do it? Could she really allow another man to touch her after Anatol and Gregorio? She imagined the stranger's hands on her, his mouth kissing her.

No.

The answer was no. She was done with men forevermore if they weren't Anatol or Gregorio.

Dora stepped into her line of sight. "Come this way."

Grasping her bag firmly, she turned and followed Dora up a flight of stairs and into a small room that held a couch, two chairs, and a table with a small clock.

Dora moved toward the door. "You can stay here to wait for Lilya. Would you like anything to drink?"

Evangeline shook her head. "Thank you."

Dora closed the door behind her, leaving Evangeline alone with the ticking clock. She set her bag down beside a chair and sank onto the couch. She was exhausted from the trip back from Cherkhasii and her bones melted like butter against the softness. *Tick, tick, tick* went the clock as she waited. Her eyelids grew heavier and heavier until she could no longer keep them open.

The next thing she knew, Lilya was gently shaking her awake. "Evangeline?"

Her eyelids opened to find Lilya's frowning face an inch from hers. "Are you all right? What's happened?"

Evangeline pushed up and looked at the clock. She'd slept for an entire hour and she hadn't even been aware she'd drifted off. "Everything's all right, Lilya. I'm sorry to disturb you so late."

"You're not disturbing me at all." Lilya sank down onto the couch beside her. Evangeline noticed for the first time she was wearing a long, silk bathrobe embroidered with roses and her feet were bare. "And I know perfectly well that everything is not all right, or you'd be at home right now with your two men."

Evangeline looked away, biting her lip at the sudden sting of tears.

"Evangeline." Lilya put a hand on her arm. "What is it?"

"That's just it. They're not *my men*, Lilya. How could they be? They're far too good for someone like me." Someone whose own parents had rejected her.

"What do you mean? They love you. I would give anything to be loved by such men, Evangeline. You're very lucky."

She made a scoffing sound. "I can't comprehend for a moment why they love me, Lilya. It's like some magick spell that's been worked on them. One day that spell will be broken. They'll stop loving me. And then I will also be broken." She shook her head. "I'm coming to love them too much. I can't go through it again. The pain's too deep."

Lilya said nothing for a moment. "I'm afraid I don't understand."

Evangeline turned and looked at her. "I left them. I left for good and forever before something awful could happen. You don't need to understand it, Lilya, you just need to be my friend."

Lilya's brows were drawn up above her pretty dark eyes. "I am your friend. You know that."

"I'm glad because you're the only one I have." Evangeline smiled at her sadly.

Lilya studied her for several long moments, chewing her bottom lip. "Have you come because you want to work here? Evangeline, I don't think that's a good idea. You're in love, and women in love . . . they don't do well here at the Temple of Dreams."

"You're right." She clasped Lilya's hands in hers. "I could never give my body to any other man, not after Anatol and Gregorio. I just need a place to stay for a little while, until I get on my feet. I have my dressmaking business. I'll be able to provide quite well for myself."

Lilya blinked. "This is a mistake. Evangeline, they love you! Don't run away! Don't let your fear rule you! This is a bad decision and—"

"It's *my* decision, Lilya. I know better what lies between myself, Anatol, and Gregorio than you do." She paused, searching Lilya's eyes. "Please. Let me stay here, just for a while."

Lilya hooked a tendril of her hair behind her ear, her eyes glittering with tears. "Oh, Evangeline, you're so lost and alone in this new life, aren't you? Now you're afraid of being even more lost and alone. Afraid of risking yourself in love."

"With Anatol and Gregorio, I risk losing myself completely. I risk giving over everything I am and trusting them not to squeeze me to a bloody pulp. If they ever rejected me, I would be hurt so badly, lost so completely, that I would not survive." She studied Lilya, thinking of the trip to see her parents, thinking of the crushing pain of her disappointment. "I don't trust them not to reject me—"

"Because you don't think you're worthy of them," Lilya finished for her with a sad little smile.

"Of course I'm not," Evangeline answered on a breathless whisper.

Lily bowed her head and shook it, allowing a teardrop to fall into her lap. "I don't agree with you. I think you're making a mistake."

"Lilya—"

She looked up, tears rolling down her cheeks. "But I understand. All right, of course you can stay here. Let's put you in a room and let you sleep tonight. We can talk more in the morning, all right?"

Evangeline slumped against the couch in relief. She was so tired and overwrought. All she wanted was to sleep. "Thank you."

Lilya touched her face. "You are a very good friend to me. Of course I'll do all I can to help you."

Evangeline grasped her hands. "One last thing, Lilya, I beg you to not send for Anatol and Gregorio."

She blinked. "But they'll come anyway. As soon as they realize you're gone, they'll come here. They'll know immediately where you are."

"Then deny them entrance. I cannot see them. I *won't* see them. If I do all my resolve will vanish and I'll be right back where I started with them—in grave danger. Please."

Lilya said nothing for several heartbeats, then she nodded slowly. "All right. I'll see you're not disturbed. At the very least, I can see that you need some time on your own to think."

"Oh, Lilya," she cupped her cheek in her palm, "this isn't a question of a few days alone to help myself think. I'm not going back to them. Not ever."

Anatol knew she was gone as soon as he woke. The house felt cold of her riotous emotion, empty of her confused fire. He rubbed a hand over his face, fighting the grief of her loss and the pain it caused him to speculate why she thought she needed to run from them. Forcing himself to remain calm, he got up and dressed, then went to the room where she'd wanted to sleep alone.

Opening the door, he found Gregorio standing at the edge of the carefully made bed holding the nightgown he'd purchased for her last week. Anatol went to stand next to him, tamping down the flare of jealousy at the realization that Gregorio had tried to come to Evangeline early that morning for some alone time with her.

Well, there was nothing to be jealous about now. She was gone.

Gregorio fisted his hand in the material of the nightgown. "I told you we were pushing her too hard."

"If we were going to lose her, we would have lost her anyway. She's running scared because of what happened on the farm."

"I want to go back and strangle that man with my bare hands." Gregorio's voice was a low growl.

"You're not the only one, but taking our revenge on him won't do Evangeline any good." He paused and smiled slightly. "Though it would be satisfying."

"Where do you think she went?"

"There's only one possible place and you know it. Unless she left the city completely, but I don't think she did that."

Gregorio gave him a sharp look. "How do you know?"

He shrugged a shoulder. "I know her."

"The Temple of Dreams," he growled and dropped the nightgown to the bed. "The thought of a man other than you touching her makes me want to tear someone's head off."

"I don't think she'll be able to do that. Not now. She's different now, changed. She might think she can take that life up, that it's safe, something she knows, but she won't be able to allow another person to touch her that way. Not after us."

"You sound pretty confident about that."

"I am."

"I hope you're right."

"Me, too, because even though I might hide it well, I'd want to rip off heads, too."

"I'm not letting her go, Anatol. How about you?" Gregorio started toward the door.

Anatol followed. "I've never have any intention of letting her go. Never will."

Evangeline sat on the end of her bed with a long, gauzy pink gown that Lilya had given to her clutched in her hands and held to her bosom. She closed her eyes as voices emanated from the hallway beyond; Anatol and Gregorio asking to see her and Lilya telling them they couldn't. Anatol spoke in his normal, low, level voice, full of reason and control. Whereas Gregorio, balanced on the edge of his bad temper, sounded ready to lose hold of his emotions.

She was riled by their presence and their voices. All she wanted was to run to them and never leave them, to give over every part of her secret self, sacrifice herself on the altar of love, and let come what may.

But then she remembered the farm, the stairs, the way her father had pushed her away, the fear and hatred in her mother's eyes, and the way her emotions had shut down. She couldn't do that again. So she closed her eyes, clutched the gown to her, and held on until they left, fighting the urge to go to them.

Lilya opened the door and Evangeline finally relaxed.

"They love you very much." Lilya walked to her. "I would give anything to be loved that way by men as good as they are."

She said nothing in response, only looked at the floor. Lilya didn't understand, but she was a good friend to respect her wishes even so. Finally she looked up at her. "I know they're the best of men. It's what makes the risk even greater."

"What will you do now?"

"Find a place to live, continue with my designs. I think I can make a living with the dressmaking. Eventually I'll be all right."

Lilya shook her head and smiled sadly. "No, you won't. You'll never be all right again."

"Evangeline!"

She closed her eyes. It was Gregorio in the street outside her window, bellowing her name. His emotion hit her right in the stomach. It was so strong that she sensed it without even trying; instead of reaching for it, it reached for her.

Despair.

"Evangeline!" This time it was Anatol. His emotions nearly brought her to her knees. Rejection. Disbelief. Misery. "Don't do this," he yelled. "Remember what Gregorio said on the train. The only way you'll ever lose us is by leaving us."

She put a hand to her solar plexus and closed her eyes. Her instinct was to block their painful onslaught with magick, but how could she? She'd caused their emotional agony; it was only right she suffer it with them.

Lilya walked to the window to look down at them. "Don't do this, Evangeline."

"I have to do this now to avoid worse pain later."

Lilya stared into the street at the men who still called for her. "How could this be any worse?" she whispered. "They love you."

"And I love them."

"Then go! Go to them, Evangeline! Stop this and accept what they have to give you."

Evangeline squeezed her eyes shut against the seductiveness of Lilya's suggestion. Anatol's and Gregorio's emotion pounded at her. She bolted from the bed, needing to get away—out of the room, maybe out of the house.

"Yes, go to them!" Lilya called after her, misinterpreting her action. Evangeline didn't correct her; she just needed to get away from Anatol's and Gregorio's heartbreak for a little while so she could think.

She burst into the corridor and made her way toward the stairs.

Dora blocked her path. "Anatol and Gregorio are inside. Are you going to them?" She held a hand to her heart. "That was so romantic."

"No." She grasped Dora's hands. "Where are they? I can't see them right now. I—I need to—"

Dora squeezed her hands. "It's all right. They're in the foyer. Go downstairs, take a left, and go past the kitchen. You'll find solitude in the lavender room."

"Thank you." She raced past Dora and traveled down the stairs to the lavender room.

Tears marked her face. She couldn't stand knowing they were feeling so much pain over losing her. This was for the best, but it was the hardest thing she'd ever done.

Bursting into the lavender room, she skidded to a halt. There were two men in there. She frowned at them, confused. "Who are you?"

"Evangeline Bansdaughter?" asked the dark-haired one.

"Yes."

An unseen person behind her slipped a burlap sack over her head.

Twenty-three

◆

Anatol gave the Temple of Dreams a wide berth on his way to and from Belai every day, directing his carriage to go several streets around the building. Normally he'd go directly past it twice a day. He and Gregorio had not given up on Evangeline and they never would; they were simply giving her a few days to realize she'd made a mistake and come back to them.

But it had been three days. Evangeline had not returned.

A cold little voice he tried never to listen to whispered that maybe she didn't think she'd made a mistake and that maybe she would never return. That voice also whispered that perhaps Evangeline had already left the city.

Maybe she was lost to them forever.

That's why he never went past the temple. He was certain that little voice would scream at him as soon as he saw the building. If that happened, he would surely stop the carriage and run inside yelling for Evangeline. If he had to endure any more days of her absence and this maddening silence, that was exactly what he was going to do.

Gregorio seemed to be handling her abandonment of them even worse. He hardly said a word, sulking and storming around the house and Belai like a wounded bear in bad temper. He'd sent his cook and cleaning woman away so no one but Anatol would be witness to his grief. They were eating takeout from the cookshops every night and the house was a mess. Most people had learned to stay out of his way. Gregorio was heartbroken and that pain manifested as anger. Anatol was heartbroken, too, but he understood Evangeline better than Gregorio did.

She was terrified of being abandoned again, so she'd done it first.

But surely the ties of love they shared were strong enough to see them through this. She couldn't mean it. She'd remember she loved them, that they loved her, and she'd return. Wouldn't she?

Damn that little voice.

The carriage came to a stop and Anatol pushed the curtain aside to verify that they'd arrived at the cookshop. He pushed the door open and entered the shop, barely even noticing the patrons or the delicious smell of food wafting around him. He headed straight for a waitress to put in an order. Then, like every evening, he'd return to the carriage to wait for them to prepare it and box it up for the ride home.

"Anatol?"

He turned to see Lilya smiling at him. It was a courtesy he couldn't return. It still hurt him that Lilya had turned them away that night. "Hello, Lilya." He continued past her toward the waitress.

"Anatol? Is something wrong?" she asked behind him.

How could she even ask him that? Gritting his teeth, he turned. "Just about everything at the moment, yes."

Her smooth brow crinkled. "Did Evangeline leave you again?"

"Again?" He took a step toward her, his anger rising. Gregorio wasn't the only one on the edge of his temper these days. "What do you mean, *again*? She left us once and that was enough."

"I'm confused, Anatol. Why are you speaking to me this way?"

He forced himself to take a breath and speak in a measured tone. They were drawing attention in the cookshop with their conversation. "Because you wouldn't let us see Evangeline the night we came for her. If you had allowed us in perhaps things might have turned out differently. Maybe she would have come back to us." He paused and swallowed hard, glancing away. "How is she?" Joshui, he feared her answer would be that she'd left for another province.

"How is she? Anatol, I have no idea what you're talking about! She left the Temple of Dreams when you and Gregorio called for her out on the street. She felt your heartbreak with her magick and it broke through to her. She realized the mistake she was making, and she practically ran me over to get to you. I haven't seen or heard from her since."

Anatol went silent for several long moments, processing what she'd said. He could detect no lie in Lilya through his magick—she believed everything she said was true.

He pushed a hand through his hair. Evangeline had wanted to come to them? Then why hadn't they ever seen her come out into the street? "She never made it." His voice sounded as hollow and cold as he suddenly felt. "We haven't seen her since the night she left."

Lilya went pale. She grabbed him by his upper arm and pulled him out of the shop. It was a good thing; he wasn't sure he could move on his own. She rounded on him as soon as they were out onto the street. It was early evening and there was a chill bite to the air, he noted numbly. "Then where is she?"

"I don't know." He shook his head, contemplating what he didn't want to contemplate. "Maybe it was just an act. Maybe she only said she was going to meet us, but in fact she was running away from all of us. Maybe—"

"*No.*" Lilya shook her head. "It couldn't be that." Lilya turned and began to pace. "She raced out of the room and met someone in the hall. They spoke and I heard Evangeline say *thank you* as she hurried away."

"To whom was she speaking? What did she say?"

Lilya stopped and looked at him. "I couldn't hear their conversation, only the louder thank you. I think it was Dora in the hall, but I can't be certain."

His shocked numbness eclipsed into icy purpose. If Evangeline was missing, they were going to find her. He grabbed her arm and hauled her toward his carriage. "Come on."

"Where are we going?"

"We'll stop and get Gregorio, then we're headed to the Temple of Dreams to talk to Dora and anyone else who remembers seeing her that night."

It was perhaps a mistake picking up Gregorio before they went to the Temple of Dreams because finding out Evangeline was missing threw him into a rage.

"Which one is Dora?" Gregorio growled as soon as they'd cleared the threshold.

Lilya halted in the foyer with a hand on her hip. "I'm not going to tell you until you calm down, Gregorio."

He paused in his restless, predatory examination of the sitting room and everyone in it to look at her. "I'm calm."

Anatol didn't need his gift to see that was a lie. His hands and jaw were both clenched. He also knew it was a lie because Anatol felt the same way; he was just better able to control it.

Lilya sighed. "Come with me."

They followed her up a flight of stairs and into a large room decorated with a couch and a couple of comfortable-looking chairs. "Wait here and I'll bring her in." She wagged a finger in Gregorio's face. *"Be nice."*

Lilya left and he and Gregorio shared a look of anger borne from a sense of helplessness. Then Gregorio began to pace while Anatol watched him.

Dora came in a few minutes later. She was a tall, thin woman with long black hair and very white skin. Her dark blue eyes regarded them with suspicion. "Lilya said you wanted to talk to me?" She closed the door behind her.

Gregorio made a move as though to jump on her, but Anatol swiftly stepped in front of him. "Were you here the night Evangeline Bansdaughter came to see Lilya? She was distraught, wanting to stay here for a while."

"Yes. I'm the one who answered the door when she arrived. I summoned Lilya for her."

Gregorio muscled his way past him. "Did you see her as she was leaving the Temple of Dreams? In the hallway? She's been missing since that time. Lilya said Evangeline met someone in the hallway on her way out."

Dora went silent for a moment. "Yes, I think I do remember that."

"What did you two discuss before she left?" asked Anatol.

She glanced away from them, licking her lips, as though thinking back—or stalling for time. She shouldn't have had to think that hard, it hadn't been that long ago. "Let's see . . . I asked where she was going in such a hurry and she told me she needed to get away, go somewhere quiet. She didn't want to see either of you."

Anatol's jaw locked. Lilya had said Evangeline had hurried out of the room to meet them in the street. He could detect no lie in either woman's story. Who was right? He looked at Gregorio. Pain was evident on his craggy features.

"I haven't seen her since," finished Dora.

"Neither have we," growled Gregorio.

"She was very upset. She ran out the back door of the house and down the street."

Anatol flinched. His magick gave him a flash through the illusion Dora presented. She hadn't been lying about Evangeline saying she'd needed time alone. Lilya was wrong; Evangeline hadn't been running out to meet them in the street—she'd been running to flee the onslaught of emotion. That was Anatol's best guess anyway.

The part where he'd glimpsed the lie had been when Dora had said Evangeline had run out the back door and down the street. *That* was a lie and he saw it clear as day.

The room went silent. Finally Anatol cleared his throat. "Thank you, Dora, You can leave now."

Dora smiled at them and left the room, closing the door behind her.

Gregorio hit a nearby wall open-handed. "That was a waste of time. She told us nothing of value."

Anatol stared at the closed door. Gregorio was wrong. Dora had been very helpful. "She's lying."

"What?" Gregorio turned toward him. "Lying? How do you know?"

Anatol gave him a look.

"Right. Lying." Gregorio rubbed his hand over his mouth. "All right, we need to question everyone in the house about that night. What they saw. The people who came in and left. Everything." His expression turned savage. "And I want to talk to Dora again."

And this time Anatol would let him do it without intervening. They wouldn't do that right away, however. First they needed to arm themselves with as much information as they could glean from the rest of the staff. That meant they needed to talk to everyone individually.

"I'll get Lilya." Anatol headed for the door.

It took them until the early morning hours to gather the information they needed. Men often came in and out of the Temple of Dreams, of course, but there had been an above average number of them on the night in question. That was remarked upon by several of the people who worked there.

In addition one of the cooks had told them she'd seen Evangeline entering one of the rooms off the kitchen. The cook said she'd seemed like she was desperate and in a hurry. The door had closed after she'd entered and the cook hadn't seen anything else.

Gregorio closed the door behind the last employee they could interview. "Time to talk to Dora again."

They brought her back in and this time Anatol stood back.

At first she played innocent, but Gregorio threatened her quite convincingly. Anatol imagined the whole house could hear the shouting. A scant hour locked in the room with them and the woman was crying. Anatol did not pity her.

"The Revolutionaries took her," Dora sobbed into her hands.

The room went silent. It was Anatol's worst fear made real.

Gregorio grabbed Dora roughly by the upper arm and muscled her toward the door. "You're under arrest for conspiring with a terrorist organization," he growled. "You're lucky if you ever see the light of day again."

Anatol watched them leave, Dora trying to pull away, screaming and crying. He was sure that Gregorio wasn't done with her yet. They needed to know more. Where they'd taken Evangeline. What they planned to do with her.

The Revolutionaries. *Sweet Joshui.* He hadn't been this scared since his head had hit the chopping block on the steps of Belai.

Twenty-four

✦

Evangeline's eyes opened to slits. Slowly becoming aware, she noted how cold she was. The iciness of the concrete floor beneath her seeped through her clothing and bit into her skin. Directly across from her stood a wooden table and two rickety-looking wooden chairs. The walls of the room appeared to be thin wood as well. The ceiling of the room had been discolored in several places from leaks.

She pushed up slowly, touching her aching head. Her mouth tasted as though it had been stuffed with fabric and her eyes were sticky from watering—crying?—while she'd had them closed.

Flashes of memory returned to her. Entering the room at the Temple of Dreams with her chest bursting with despair, needing to find a quiet place where she could parse her feelings and think about what she'd done. The strange men. Confusion.

Then the hood.

It had frightened her into complete immobility for a heartbeat and then she'd driven herself out of the shock and fought. But three men on one blinded woman hadn't been good odds. She didn't re-member much after that, though she did recall that the fabric of the sack had been slightly damp and had smelled sweet. Perhaps they'd drugged her?

Oh, Joshui, *Dora*. She'd been the one to lead her into the trap. Had she been a sympathizer to the Revolutionaries? Had Dora called her friends when she'd shown up that night to the Temple of Dreams? It was beginning to seem that way.

After the burlap sack she remembered waking for short periods of time, drowsily consuming food and water, taking care of all the necessary things it took to stay alive. The faces of her captors swam in her mind's eyes. Harsh faces. Harsher hands. In those brief pe-riods when she'd been aware she had been so confused by the drugs they'd given her that she hadn't even fought.

The drugs had finally worn off. *Now* she wanted to fight.

She pushed to her feet, her unwashed hair hanging into her face. Reaching out with her magick, she tried to sense emotion in her surroundings. Emotion meant her captors were nearby. Imme-diately she picked up one person just outside the door. She had a guard.

Turning in a circle, she glanced around the room for something she could use as a weapon. The only things in the small room were the table and chairs. There were no windows and no doors other than the guarded one. She considered the chairs. She couldn't break any of the legs off because that would make enough noise to rouse suspicion. Hefting the chair and using it to bludgeon her captors was also not an option simply because she lacked the strength. The conditions of her captivity had left her legs and arms shaky, her mouth parched, and her stomach gnawing on itself.

Her only hope was to find a way to run.

Just then the doorknob turned. Her body on alert, she watched as the door slowly whined opened, revealing a shadow on the floor.

Then a large, dark-haired woman stepped through. "Ah, you're awake. Been wondering when the drugs would wear off."

Evangeline tasted the woman's emotions and found not anger or hatred, but a mild dislike and a sense of duty. She licked her dry lips, examining the stout woman from head to toe. In her weakened condition she didn't think she could fight her. "Who are you?"

The woman smiled, revealing one missing tooth in front. "Who are we? You haven't figured that out already?"

"The Revolutionaries."

She nodded. "I'm sorry, girl, no offense against you, but you people can't be allowed to run around free. Vikhin, great man that he is, has a soft spot for the magicked, but he fails to see the larger picture. We are striving for true equality, and as long as there are people out there who have abilities that go beyond the ordinary, true equality cannot be achieved."

Evangeline took a step backward, away from the woman. Again, there was no outward hatred, just a matter-of-factness. "We didn't ask to be born with these abilities. It's Joshui's will that makes us so." Invoking Joshui's name was deliberate. An appeal to her religious side wouldn't hurt.

"Joshui created the magicked to test the rest of us. The magicked are an abomination to be rid of. Joshui will bless us for recognizing the blight and correcting it."

Or maybe mentioning Joshui wasn't such a good idea. Nausea roiled in her stomach at the woman's rationalization.

"What do you plan to do with me?" she asked, taking another step backward. It was an involuntary action. It wasn't as though she had anywhere to go.

The woman just gave her a look that said *you already know* and smiled sadly. "Sorry, child."

She swallowed hard. "Then why am I still alive?"

"We're waiting for the boss. He wants to talk to you."

Delightful. "I'm the lover of Gregorio Vikhin. Don't you care that this will hurt him?" *Was* the lover, but she didn't need to know that.

"We know that Vikhin has taken up with you and one other. This was a mistake on his part and many of his people are not happy with him for it. We intend to take care of the other magicked who lives with him, too. The opportunity to take you simply fell into our laps like a gem from the sky."

Cold fear washed through her. "*You leave Anatol alone!*" she yelled.

The woman laughed. "Or you'll do what? Don't worry. We're very humane in our disposal methods."

She swayed on her feet. *Humane in our disposal methods.* As if they were diseased cattle that needed to be slaughtered. She had to get out of here. To save her own life, to be sure, but also to warn and protect Anatol. She needed to find a way out of this room, first of all. Into the air and open sunlight. She wasn't well enough to fight, but she might be well enough to run.

"I need to go to the bathroom." She glanced toward the door. "Before you humanely slaughter me, do you think I might be allowed to relieve my bladder?"

That earned her a cold little smile and a flash of annoyance. Evangeline was pleased to feel an emotion from the woman that wasn't borne from a sense of doing a good deed. "Certainly." She paused. "But I hope you understand that since you're not groggy from the drugs anymore that I'll have to tie your hands."

Her hopes sunk. Tied hands wouldn't help her keep her balance if she had the opportunity to run. At least it wouldn't be her feet. Evangeline gave her a smile of cold, haughty hatred—the muscles of her mouth remembered how to do it well. "Do what you feel you need to do."

The woman produced a length of rope from the pocket of her

dress and came toward her. Evangeline watched every move the woman made, wondering if she could dart around her and out the door. She couldn't sense any more emotion nearby, but that didn't mean there weren't more guards outside the building, beyond her ability to sense. She needed to go along with this and get a better idea of what she would find before she took such a big risk.

The woman knotted the rope tightly around Evangeline's wrists, making her wince and her fingers begin to immediately go numb. Then she pushed her forward. Evangeline stumbled on purpose and then shuffled her feet slowly out the door. It was better that the woman think her more affected by the drugs than she actually was—it was better to be underestimated in this situation.

The room beyond was also mostly bare and completely empty of people. A moment of disorientation hit her when she looked out the window. The sky was that hazy gray that might be early morning or could be twilight—Evangeline had no idea which.

The chill outside air forced her already cold body into a bout of wracking shivers, also not an advantage for her plans to escape. Two men sat outside on a couple of fallen logs talking to each other in low, rumbling tones. They both broke off when she came out and hot anger hit her in a wave that almost drove the cold from her bones. Evangeline returned their looks of cool hatred with practiced indifference.

"Need some help with her, Vita?" one of the men called, eying Evangeline from head to toe. She prayed that Vita wouldn't say yes.

"I have her," Vita called back and Evangeline let out a careful breath.

The men's eyes followed them into the nearby woods. Vita directed her a short ways into the foliage and then directed her behind a tree. "There's your bathroom. Hope you don't mind if I don't give you any privacy."

Evangeline glanced around for something she could use to help her escape and then spied a heavy branch in the deadfall. "How am I supposed to lower my panties or squat with my hands tied this way?" she asked, raising her arms to demonstrate. "I'll have no balance."

"Do whatever you need to do." Vita shrugged. "It's not my concern if you pee on yourself."

Great.

Evangeline glared at her, then made a show of reaching out to the tree trunk in front of her to steady herself. When she got down low enough, she grabbed the branch and brought it up hard and fast, right into Vita's face. It was a good shot—right in the eye.

Vita screamed in pain and began to sob, holding her hands to her face.

Evangeline didn't waste any time, knowing Vita's cries would bring the hateful men. She plunged through the undergrowth and ran, dodging trees and leaping over clumps of deadfall and rotting logs. Branches caught at her skirt and clawed her cheeks. Her hands and abused physical condition hindered her, but her body had not forgotten her years of training. The dancing she'd done at Belai helped her now—to move fast, to move well, to keep her balance and not slip in the slick leaves.

Yet behind her she could hear the men shouting, branches breaking under their boots. They were following her trail easily and they were gaining on her. She forced herself to move faster, her breath huffing out white in the chilly air of what she had determined was early morning. Her legs muscles protested every movement, wanting non-drugged rest, wanting water, wanting the sustenance she'd had so little of for whatever amount of time she'd spent drowsing in and out of consciousness.

"There!" one of the men yelled. "Right there!"

Ah, Joshui, they were close. All the hope she had died with a quiet gasp in her chest. Still her legs churned as fast as they could go. She held her bound hands in front of her and moved them as required to best keep her balance as she fled.

A log rose up in front of her and she jumped it. On the other side was a bog. Her feet sank into the muck and she slipped, falling backward and narrowly missing hitting her head on the log. Footfalls approached and she scrambled to get back onto her feet. As long as they didn't have her, she would try and get away.

"There you are, you bitch," growled one of the men, coming around a tree about five feet away from her.

She turned and pushed to her feet, lurching out of the mud, but the other man was there. He grabbed her by the upper arm and hauled her out of the bog, making her stumble. She jerked her arm away from him, but he only held on tighter.

"Hey, girl," he growled, "I admire your spirit, but it's not going to get you anywhere." He smiled into her face, though it didn't reach his cold eyes. Hatred rolled like a poison out of him and into her. "The boss is here and he'll have you put down right away for doing this."

So if she had "behaved" they would have let her live a few more hours before ridding the world of her pestilence? She could be glad she'd *mis*behaved in that case.

"I bet Vita wants a word with her first," said the other man picking his way around the bog toward him.

Evangeline was too exerted and heartbroken to say anything in response. She glared at them, her breathing heavy and her body shaking from the cold and the wet. The man holding her arm yanked her forward and she had no choice but to follow.

Her steps heavy, they made their way back to the house.

Anatol and Gregorio.

They were her biggest regrets. That evening would be the last memory they had of her. They would never hear how sorry she was she'd hurt them. Mostly likely they would think she'd just run away and never returned.

Ah, Joshui, what had she done?

Yearning for them filled her, made her knees go weak. *Love.* Love was everything. She'd had it—truly, deeply, completely. And not only once, but twice over.

And she'd thrown it away because she was *scared*.

Tears pricked her eyes, but she swallowed them back. Crying in front of these men would only make them revel in her misery and she didn't need that.

She'd made a horrible mistake and she would never be able to set it right.

As they approached the house she picked up on the pain and rage of Vita. She'd hurt her badly with the branch. They came through the tree line and Evangeline saw her sitting on the ground by the house with another woman who glared at Evangeline as they passed. Blood streamed down Vita's face, but it was hard to feel regret when she'd inflicted the injury while fleeing for her life.

Besides the two men who guarded her, Vita, and the other woman, Evangeline sensed another's emotion. Contentment. A sense of satisfaction. Righteousness. This person had no guilt. No anger, either. Like Vita, he or she believed this was the right thing to do. Perhaps he or she even believed, like Vita, that it was Joshui's will.

The sound of twigs breaking under a person's tread came from around the side of the house.

The men stopped and she was forced to halt also. "Boss is here," murmured the one on her left. "You're dead now, girl."

Numbly she glanced at him. She already knew that.

Their boss turned the corner and shock broke through her frozen grief. "Markoff," she breathed. Disappointment hollowed her stomach. "How could you do this?"

Markoff came to a stop and smiled at her. "I truly am sorry, Evangeline. It's nothing personal. I actually even like you." He paused. "But this is the only way to make sure Vikhin's vision is truly realized. Don't you see?"

"Considering that you're about to kill me, no, I don't see."

He gazed up and down her body. "You're lovely even now, after a week of abuse and a dunk in a bog. I can see why Gregorio has been so affected by your absence. I almost feel sorry for him. Especially since he thinks you've run away from him. But, of course, he was terribly ill-advised in falling in love with a magicked. He should have known better." Markoff *tsk tsk*ed. "Oh, I see that stricken look on your face. Don't worry, darling, he'll get over you eventually."

"What should we do with her?" asked the thug on her right.

Markoff studied her critically for a long moment while she shivered. "Normally I would interview her, but—"

"Interview me?" she asked.

"Gather all the information about you that I can. About your magick. About your friends. That's why we've been keeping you alive for the last week. I do the interviewing and I couldn't get here until now."

"Ah. Interviewing. But you actually mean *interrogate* me for information."

He smiled. It was maddening how nothing seemed to sway his temper. This man was in complete, icy control. She had nothing to work with here, no emotions to trade to help her gain the upper hand. "Yes, you could put it that way. However, considering how much trouble you've been . . ." He glanced at Vita. "And considering the fact you seem to be a bit more dangerous than you appear, I believe we'll kill you now." He glanced at the two men in turn, giving them each a little nod.

She should have been expecting it, but the words still made the blood drain from her face and the strength go out of her limbs. She didn't want to die. Not like this. Not after having made the worst mistake of her life. Not after leaving the men she loved in such pain.

She would give anything to tell Anatol and Gregorio how she felt and to apologize to them. If she could do that, she would be able to die in peace.

But she would like better to spend the rest of her life with them.

"Oh, child, surely you must have known you've been living on borrowed time since the storming of Belai."

"Actually, I'd hoped I'd have more time than this." She swallowed hard.

Markoff smiled apologetically and shrugged. A rush of anger hit her and all she wanted in the world—other than to be with Anatol and Gregorio—was to lunge forward and strangle this man.

Instead the thugs jerked her to the side, around Markoff, and began dragging her to the other side of the house.

"Good-bye, my dear," called Markoff as she rounded the corner. "Be confident that your demise is for the best. For Rylisk and for Gregorio."

What she saw on the other side of the house made her stomach drop into a cold hell. The setup was simple, but chilling. A pillow on the muddy ground. A stump to the side and a little behind it. A shiny, sharp axe suitable for removing heads.

The dry grass in the area in front of the pillow had been stained dark brown with blood.

Her stomach roiled at the sight. "Why a pillow?" she asked, her voice shaking. "Do you really care how comfortable your victims are right before you take an axe to the back of their necks?"

"It's not our idea," growled the man on her left. "The boss thinks it's more humane."

The other man pushed her toward the pillow. "Kneel."

She stared down at the filthy red cushion. How many others of her kind had knelt here? Died here? These people were systematically killing all the magick in the world.

Time crawled to a near standstill as she stood there. Suddenly every sound near her registered—the few birds in the trees, Vita's low sobbing, the murmuring of others who milled around the small house. These would be the last moments of her life. She'd wanted to spend them with Anatol and Gregorio when she was old and gray, having enjoyed a long life with them.

She would never have children. Her chest clenched. She would have liked to have children . . .

She squeezed her eyes shut against the rising tang of regret at the back of her throat. She would give anything to go back in time, make a different decision. Lilya had been right, she'd been a slave to her fears.

Now, finally, Evangeline had clarity.

No one could know the future. She couldn't be totally sure that one day she wouldn't be rejected by Anatol and Gregorio. Words and feelings given today could change tomorrow. But she couldn't run from their love based on that possibility. Their love was worth the risk. She couldn't flee her *tomorrows*. She had to live *today*.

Of course, today would be the day she died.

Oddly empty of fear, she opened her eyes and stared at the stump.

"Kneel!" one of the men barked at her.

When she didn't immediately drop to her knees, he pushed her. One kneecap hit the pillow and the other the half-frozen muddy ground, making her wince. The pain hardly mattered since it was only a drop compared to the intense—but brief—agony to come.

The two men positioned themselves behind her and she heard one of them close his hand around the handle of the axe. With a grunt, he pulled it free from the stump.

She twisted her bound hands, hearing the rope creak. A curious numb disconnection stole over her. A tear rolled down her cheek, but she didn't feel inclined to beg for her life or try to run. She would have thought that in this situation anyone would do that. That no one would be able to look death in the face and not cower.

Yet, here she was. Perhaps it was Joshui enfolding her in his warm embrace, helping her to accept this as her end.

The cold edge of the axe touched her neck.

Her executioner drew the axe back, steadied his boots on the ground for balance.

Twenty-five

She closed her eyes, her face wrinkling with mingled grief and fear.

"What? What is go—whoa!"

The axe clunked to the ground. Men and women screamed and yelled. Boots pounded on the ground. Something growled.

Evangeline opened her eyes to chaos. Out of nowhere a huge brown bear rushed past her. She blinked, not fully comprehending. Then her limbs unfroze and her will to survive took over.

Wide-eyed, she struggled to her feet and carefully walked backward, keeping her eye on the house. The bear had disappeared around the front. She could tell because of all the bloodcurdling growling. It actually sounded as though there were more than one bear, but how could that be? Bears didn't run in packs.

No matter. She glanced at the woods. Maybe this was her chance to get away.

Strong arms came around her and she yelped with surprise and began to struggle.

"It's me!" Gregorio yelled.

She turned to see Gregorio's beloved face. She let out a sob and threw herself against him. "I'm so sorry," she cried into the curve of his neck. His arms came around her and her knees went weak from relief that he was here. "I'm so sorry," she breathed. "I made a horrible mistake and ran from you out of fear. I love you and Anatol so much. I never wanted to hurt you. I never—"

He held her away from him a little and cupped her face in his hands. "We know that, Evangeline. It's all right. Let's get you out of here and then we can talk." He began to unknot the rope around her wrists.

She nodded. "Where's Anatol?"

"He's throwing the illusion of those bears. We brought a whole contingent of armed guards with us. The bears are herding the Revolutionaries right to them. They'll be arrested soon."

She slumped against him in relief. Now she and Anatol were even. She'd used her magick to save his head and now he'd used his magick to save hers.

Gregorio finally freed her hands and crushed her to him, kissing the top of her head. Heavy, warm emotion rolled out of him and covered her over like a blanket. *Love and gratefulness.* "We were almost too late." He shuddered.

"But you weren't," she murmured against his shoulder.

In the distance the growling ceased and the yelling grew louder. The soldiers were here.

"Evangeline!"

She turned to be immediately embraced by Anatol. He spun her around in the air, holding her tight. She wrapped her arms around him and held on. This time she would never let him go.

He collapsed to the ground, holding her in his lap and rocking her back and forth. "I thought you were gone forever," he sighed into her hair. "I never thought I'd be able to hold you again."

Tears ran down her face. "I thought the same thing." She lifted her head. "I'm so sorry I left you and Gregorio that night. I can't regret it any more than I do. I never meant to hurt you. I love you both so much. I was stupid and I was—"

"Shhh." He smiled and smoothed her hair behind her ear. "You were frightened. We both know you love us, and we always believed you would come to your senses."

"How did you find me?"

Gregorio came to kneel beside them. "For several days we didn't know that you'd been taken. Then Anatol ran into Lilya and we discovered you were missing. A little investigation led us back to the Temple of Dreams."

She felt her expression go dark. "And Dora."

Gregorio nodded. "I arrested her and managed to get some information out of her that led us here." He swallowed hard. "Any delays and we would have been too late."

"Where are we?"

"Illyana Province."

She blanched. No wonder it was so cold. They'd taken her all the way to the northern edge of Rylisk.

"But we're going home now," Gregorio finished. "Our home. The three of us. *Forever*."

Twenty-six

A week after her ordeal and Evangeline was finally beginning to feel a little like her regular self . . . only better. Oddly, her emotions had seemed to settle into a more manageable ebb and flow. It was almost as if being terrified and grieved nearly out of her mind had jerked her emotions into alignment.

Whatever had happened, it was an improvement.

Even the weather matched her mood. The day was warm enough to leave the house without a wrap, and all the doors and windows of the town house were thrown wide open.

She walked into the kitchen where Anatol and Gregorio were talking with the cook. Gregorio handed her a cup of tea while she went to the open doors that led out to the porch and leaned against the doorjamb, breathing in the clean, warm air and closing her eyes for a moment.

She could feel safe now, as could Anatol and the rest of the magicked. Most of the Revolutionaries had been arrested, including the head of the beast, Markoff. Gregorio was going particularly hard on him because of his immense betrayal.

Of course there were still other magick haters out there, other people who would attempt to target those who were different from them. That would never end, not completely. Still, Anatol and Gregorio were doing a good job of drawing the magicked out, binding them together, and making them stronger. Evangeline was optimistic that even though hatred and bigotry would never be completely eradicated, at least some of the ignorance about the magicked could be vanquished through their efforts.

They were good men doing the best of work. She would never leave them again and she felt confident they would never leave her, either. Their love was way too strong. Instead she had thrown her heart wide open to them. Given all she was to them. Invested herself completely in them.

She was theirs, wholly and without reservation.

And they were hers.

Anatol, with his quiet strength and his uncanny ability to look into the hearts of those around him. Gregorio, with his intelligence, fierce protectiveness, and his gentleness that was so at odds with his gruff appearance. She couldn't ask for two better men.

Anatol came to lean against the opposite doorjamb, looking up into the blue sky. "I think we should get a cat."

Gregorio gave a bark of laughter as he walked past them both to settle in one of the chairs on the porch. "A cat? Where did that suggestion come from?"

Instead of answering, Anatol looked over at her. "What do you think, Evangeline? Should we get a cat?"

She smiled and looked down into her half full teacup. "I've always wanted a cat."

"I thought so," answered Anatol with a secret little smile playing around his mouth.

She sighed, giving in. Sometimes Anatol's ability to read her was eerie. "And I've been thinking about other things I might want in this lifetime." She paused. "With you both."

Gregorio turned in his seat to look at her.

Evangeline stepped onto the porch and sat down in the chair opposite him. She held his gaze, since Anatol already knew what she was going to say and this would come as a shock to Gregorio. Her stomach tightened a little at the prospect that Gregorio might not want what she and Anatol wanted.

"It would be a very large thing, larger than a cat. Actually, it would be a small thing . . . at least at first." She smiled and then grimaced. This wasn't going the way she'd planned it in her head. Nervousness was making her babble.

Gregorio frowned at her. "What are you talking about, Evangeline?"

She glanced at Anatol. No help there. He just grinned at her. She directed her gaze back to Gregorio. "What I'm saying is . . . what I mean to say is . . . that . . ." She paused, and then blurted it out, "I want children. With you and with Anatol."

Gregorio sat up in his chair, as though alarmed.

She held up a hand. "Not right away. I mean, we can take this slowly. Whenever you and Anatol are ready. I'm willing to—*ah!*"

Gregorio had lunged at her, enveloping her in his arms. He knelt on the floor of the porch in front of her and cupped her cheeks in his hands. "I have always wanted children, Evangeline. *Always.*"

Anatol came to sit next to her. "You already know that I want this, too."

She smiled, covering Gregorio's hands with her own and closing her eyes, bathing in the moment. "It will be complicated. We'll have a lot to talk about, since there will be two men involved and we won't know who the biological father is."

"Maybe not at first." Anatol grinned. "But once the child hits adolescence and starts planning a revolution, we might have a clue that Gregorio is the father."

"And if the boy or girl is peering into our souls at age seven and ferreting out truths we don't want to face, he or she is probably Anatol's biological offspring," offered Gregorio.

"Either way," Anatol broke in, "we'll *both* be fathers to the child. The biological parentage will matter little."

Evangeline's smile grew larger. It felt as though sunlight had entered her chest—light, bright, beautiful. "And either way, chances are good that the child will be magicked."

Gregorio stroked her cheek. "I wouldn't have it any other way."

Anatol wound his arm around her waist. "So, when should we start trying to make a child?"

Gregorio grinned. "There's no time like the present."

"See?" Anatol answered. "We're already in accord."

Evangeline allowed herself to be pulled into the embrace—both of them—of the two men she loved most in the world.